Praise for Too ...

"Phelps is the Harlan Coben ..."

—Allison Brennan, *New Yor...*
of *Fear No Evil*

Praise for Kill for Me

"Phelps gets into the blood and guts of the story."

—Gregg Olsen, *New York Times* best-selling author

"Phelps infuses his investigative journalism with plenty of energized descriptions . . . interesting . . . [an] enormous effort."

—*Publishers Weekly*

Praise for Death Trap

"A chilling tale . . . a compelling journey . . . Fair warning: for three days I did little else but read this book."

—Harry N. MacLean, *New York Times* best-selling author

Praise for I'll Be Watching You

"Phelps has an unrelenting sense for detail that affirms his place, book by book, as one of our most engaging crime journalists."

—Dr. Katherine Ramsland, author of *The Human Predator*

Praise for If Looks Could Kill

"M. William Phelps, one of America's finest true-crime writers, has written a compelling and gripping book."

—Vincent Bugliosi, author of *Helter Skelter* and
Reclaiming History

"Starts quickly and doesn't slow down. . . . Phelps consistently ratchets up the dramatic tension. . . . Readers will feel the effects of Phelps' skill from beginning to end."

—Stephen Singular, author of *Unholy Messenger:*
The Life and Crimes of the BTK Serial Killer

"This gripping true story reads like a well-plotted crime novel and proves that truth is not only stranger, but more shocking, than fiction. Riveting."

—Allison Brennan, *New York Times* best-selling author
of *Fear No Evil*

"M. William Phelps is the rising star of the nonfiction crime genre, and his true tales of murderers and mayhem are scary-as-hell thrill rides into the dark heart of the inhuman condition."

—Douglas Clegg, author of *The Lady of Serpents*

Praise for *Lethal Guardian*

"An intense roller-coaster of a crime story . . . complex, with twists and turns worthy of any great detective mystery, and yet so well-laid out, so crisply written with such detail to character and place that it reads like a novel."

—Steve Jackson, *New York Times* best-selling author of *No Stone Unturned*

Praise for *Perfect Poison*

"A stunner from beginning to end . . . Phelps shockingly reveals that unimaginable evil sometimes comes in pretty packages."

—Gregg Olsen, *New York Times* best-selling author

"True crime at its best—compelling, gripping, an edge-of-the-seat thriller."

—Harvey Rachlin, author of *The Making of a Detective*

"A compelling account of terror."

—Lowell Cauffiel, best-selling author of *House of Secrets*

"A blood-curdling page turner and a meticulously researched study of the inner recesses of the mind of a psychopathic narcissist."

—Sam Vaknin, author of *Malignant Self Love—Narcissism Revisited*

Other books by M. William Phelps

Other books by M. William Phelps

TOO YOUNG TO KILL

M. WILLIAM PHELPS

PINNACLE BOOKS
Kensington Publishing Corp.
http://www.kensingtonbooks.com

PINNACLE BOOKS are published by

Kensington Publishing Corp.
119 West 40th Street
New York, NY 10018

All Kensington titles, imprints, and distributed lines are available at special quantity discounts for bulk purchases for sales promotions, premiums, fund-raising, and educational or institutional use. Special book excerpts or customized printings can also be created to fit specific needs. For details, write or phone the office of the Kensington Special Sales Manager: Kensington Publishing Corp., 119 West 40th Street, New York, NY 10018. Attn: Special Sales Department. Phone: 1-800-221-2647.

Pinnacle and the P logo Reg. U.S. Pat. & TM Off.

ISBN-13: 978-0-7860-2485-8
ISBN-10: 0-7860-2485-2

First printing: August 2011

10 9 8 7 6 5 4 3 2

Printed in the United States of America

For Matty,
Work hard.
Realize your dreams.

CONTENTS

AUTHOR'S NOTE

Writing about teen violence is not something you do with a light heart. The brutality involved in this particular case was something I had never considered to be any more encompassing or taxing on the soul than the other murder books I've written. Yet, there is an implausible layer of malevolence involved in this story (surprisingly transparent if you do not know where to look), an innocence all kids possess that was egregiously neglected. This is, perhaps, an all too predictable and familiar American story; and yet the audacity and total lack of respect for human life still nagged at me from the beginning.

Part of my struggle was wrestling with the notion that *children* could commit such horrific, evil acts, and hate one another as much as this case proved. Another was coming to grips with how a sixteen-year-old boy could use a household saw to dismember one of his peers into seven pieces. Then, when asked why he did it, give such a nonplussed, casual, and cold answer, as he did. This boy cut up a girl with a miter saw that his grandfather likely had used to build toys and a tree house for him, and he didn't think anything more of his behavior than the idea he was helping a few friends get away with murder.

Makes you wonder how high the bar has been set within our culture today.

In *Base Instincts: What Makes Killers Kill?* (an important book by Dr. Jonathan H. Pincus, chief of neurology at the Department of Veterans Affairs Medical Center in Washington, D.C.), Pincus claims there's an "interaction of childhood abuse with neurological disturbances and psychiatric illnesses" in some people, which is directly related to an explanation of the murders these same individuals later commit. Pincus lays out his theory clearly, telling us that the "abuse" a person suffers in childhood "generates the violent urge."

This comment is easy enough to understand: we are *taught* to use violence as a means to an end.

Yet, it's the "neurological and psychiatric diseases of the brain"—I like the use of the word "diseases" here—that ultimately "damage the capacity" for a preordained violent person (a tendency, per se) to "check that urge."

Keep Pincus's theory in mind as you read this book; and when you're finished, come back here and read it again. You'll realize what I mean.

There is another component figuring prominently in this tragedy: the inner world of a wayward, aimless, depressed, and sometimes violent, group of people who paint their faces, wear symbols of violence, and call themselves "Juggalos" (known formerly as Insane Clown Posse, or ICP, Kids). The Juggalo culture played a role in both the life and death of the victim in this book. Insane Clown Posse, the self-proclaimed "horror rap" group that inspired the Juggalo army to form in the late 1990s, continues to write and record songs that incite violence, oversexualize kids, and preach drug use and death, among other disturbing things, to put it mildly. These songs are as graphic and violent as anything I've ever heard; many of the songs exploit women as objects and disrespect a woman's place in society as an equal (something I have no tolerance for and denounce vehemently).

In exchange for me being allowed access into this world, I was asked to change names, which I did. I chose to change the names of several others due to the information that that person provided, either through a personal interview with me or law enforcement, information of which is revealing, shocking, and rather alarming. I am indebted to those who came forward and helped me understand the true nature of today's teen culture, at least as it pertains to this story.

* * *

During the late winter of 2010, the tragic story of fifteen-year-old Phoebe Prince's suicide became fodder for prime-time cable TV shows (Nancy Grace, Larry King et al.), talk radio, and the tabloids. Phoebe, whose photo graced the cover of *People* magazine, was the "new girl" at her high school in South Hadley, Massachusetts. She had moved to western Massachusetts from Ireland. She was allegedly driven to suicide by the bullying she endured at school and electronically. Nine of her peers were indicted. The case is still pending as I write this. Reports claim a group of students at South Hadley High School knocked books out of Phoebe's hands on a daily basis. Flung things at her at random. Scratched her face out of photographs around school grounds. And sent threatening text messages to her cell phone. All this, mind you, beyond spreading vicious and humiliating rumors about her on the Internet and at school.

"The investigation revealed relentless activity directed toward Phoebe designed to humiliate her and to make it impossible for her to remain at school," District Attorney Elizabeth Scheibel told the media after announcing the indictments of Phoebe's classmates. "The bullying, for her, became intolerable."

Phoebe was routinely called an "Irish slut" and "whore" in person, on Twitter, Craigslist, Facebook, and other social networks.

The harassment was consistent, unremitting, and cruel.

The case exploded while I was working on this story of Adrianne Reynolds's murder, the sixteen-year-old student at the center of this book who was, like Phoebe, tormented to the point of death. The difference for Adrianne, however, was that, unlike Phoebe, she was brutally murdered and dismembered.

The similarities in these cases are instantly recognizable, but so are the differences. Murder is a selfish act driven by love, revenge, or money, with various additional motivations branching off from there. As it is with kids murdering their peers, there's an emerging dynamic playing out in every case I have researched: almost an elemental instinct inside these kids continually pushing them to take things to the next level, with no cognizant indication here that they care about the ramifications of their actions. Some kids today are essentially living on the adrenaline rush of fear and violence, as if both have become drugs, giving them highs they cannot get anywhere else. These kids know what they are doing. They understand the consequences of their behavior. They know that this type of conduct can lead to death and torment, emotional or psychical, for their victims, and years behind bars for them. But something inside encourages them to keep pushing forward; and keep taking things to another level. Adrianne Reynolds's murder, maybe more than any of the other cases I have covered in my books, is one of those—like Phoebe Prince's suicide—stories that, when you look at all the evidence in its entirety, you scratch your head and ask yourself, *Why did this have to happen?* I don't buy the argument of snap judgment and anger boiling over and erupting into violent rage. There's another element at work here—one that I set out to explore in depth in this book.

I had several courageous sources come forward and tell me their stories; likewise, I had over two thousand pages of police reports, search warrants, witness statements, interviews, letters, journal entries, and other documents (many of which the media has never seen), including psychology reports, to sift through for information. The paper trail for this case is well documented—and that doesn't include two trials, several additional court appearances by the perpetrators, and the dozens of hours of interviews I conducted myself.

—M. William Phelps
Vernon, CT
March 2011

"Dimiter was haunted all his life . . . by The Problem of Evil. 'A heart-stabbing mystery,' he called it. But came to believe there was a mystery much deeper that he spoke of as the 'mystery of goodness.'"

——William Peter Blatty, *Dimiter*

PART I

JUGGALO HOMIES

1

Joanne "Jo" Reynolds pulled into her driveway on Seventh Street in East Moline, Illinois, near 4:00 P.M., on January 21, 2005. As she did every early evening after arriving home from her shift at the local Hy-Vee supermarket, Joanne checked the mail, then headed into the house. Inside, she tossed her keys on the kitchen counter, started down the hallway toward the bathroom to freshen up. Joanne's husband, Tony, had just gotten home himself. The Reynoldses had their slice of the good life here in the Quad Cities (QC). Located in the Mid-Mississippi Valley, the towns of Moline, East Moline, and Rock Island, Illinois, along with Bettendorf and Davenport, Iowa, house some four hundred thousand residents making up the QC, with an imaginary state line running through the Mississippi River, splitting the east and west sides of the quad in half.

We're talking Middle America here. Small-town USA. John Deere's world headquarters is located in Moline.

Pure Americana.

Tony and Jo were high-school friends who had lost

touch for twenty years and met again later in life. Theirs was a rough road to love. Tony had done some time in prison, been married once. Joanne was divorced, too. Her two adult boys—twins—lived with her and Tony, along with their wives, a baby, and Tony's adopted daughter, Adrianne. No, not the perfect, textbook family unit, scripted on the pages of some sappy, glossy magazine, but they loved one another and, for the most part, got along. When the statistics said it shouldn't, the blended Reynolds family, like so many in America today, worked.

From the late-afternoon twilight, as the sun did its downward, lazy dance over Mark Twain's Mississippi, which is located approximately three miles north of Jo and Tony's modest ranch-style home, Jo had been thinking about Adrianne, Tony's sixteen-year-old daughter. "Lil' Bit" was what they called Adrianne. "Texas," too. Or "Tex." Adrianne was the pride and joy of Tony Reynolds's eye, a man whom Adrianne had called "Dad" all her life. Adrianne had moved in with Tony and Jo in November 2004. This was after a spell of living in the Reynoldses' East Moline home a year prior. That first time Adrianne had gone to live with Jo and Tony did not go so well. Adrianne and Jo disagreed. Fought like cats. Stopped talking for days at a clip. Tony was constantly stressed, he said. Always caught in the middle of some drama between his wife and daughter. A truck driver, Tony was always on the road, leaving Jo to deal with the bulk of Adrianne's teen angst.

"I want her out," Jo had said, probably more times than she wanted to recall, this back when Adrianne had lived in the house that first time. She later admitted she was scared for her two boys. Adrianne had made an accusation against her stepfather back in Texas, recanted, then made the accusation again. Jo was concerned she might do the same to one of her boys. She wanted no part of Adrianne's dysfunction.

But ever since Adrianne had been back, she and Jo, although not skipping stones together, taking sunset walks along the Mississippi, had reached an impasse. Perhaps it was a tough decision, but they were getting along. In fact, Jo and Adrianne had a scheduled session with a therapist on that Friday night, January 21, a follow-up to a session the previous Friday, which, according to Jo, "went very well."

In truth, they had reconciled. They were on the path of healing a broken relationship.

And Tony, of course, was all for it.

When Jo walked past Adrianne's room on her way to the bathroom, she noticed Adrianne's work garments all laid out.

Odd, Jo thought, stopping, staring. *She should be at work.*

So Jo took a quick peek around the house. Nothing had been touched. She had asked Adrianne to empty the dishwasher and do a few additional chores. Adrianne had always done what she was told to, as far as her chores were concerned.

Where is she?

Jo quickly succumbed to the opposite of one of those feelings you get when, after walking into your house, you just know—that feeling of violation—someone has been inside while you were gone. It was different for Jo, because she felt *no one* had been home all day long.

Which was strange. Adrianne got out of school at noon. She was generally home every day, all afternoon.

"Tony?" Jo yelled. Tony was glad to be home— a Friday night, nonetheless—from his truck-driving shift. Ten hours on the road wreaked havoc on the guy's back. Tony needed some rest.

"Yeah?" Tony answered.

Jo knew Adrianne had to work that night. "I woke her up this morning," she told Tony. "She told me she had to be in at five."

"Ain't dat right," Tony said in his heavy Southern drawl.

They both peered into Adrianne's room. There, on the floor, was Adrianne's work uniform. The room was a mess—as most teenagers feel that cleaning is one of those "things" that can wait until later on in life.

"Yeah, she said five." Jo was certain.

"She done went to work *without* her uniform?" Tony asked, more to himself than Jo. He looked at his watch. It was close to five. Adrianne should have been home to get dressed and head out to work.

Jo spotted Adrianne's work shoes on the floor. She'd never go to work without them. Moreover, Adrianne Reynolds was not a teen who blew off her shift. She loved the job at Checkers, a nearby fast-food joint. It was easy. Very little stress. Plus, it put a little pocket money in her purse. Adrianne was in a GED program at the Black Hawk College Outreach Center, nearby on the Avenue of the Cities. High school had been something Adrianne, to put it mildly, despised. So much so, she had not accumulated any credits to graduate—heading toward the end of her sophomore year—and would need to step it up in order to get her GED. The outreach program fit Adrianne's school work ethic, her attitude toward education in general. No homework. Everything you did, you completed at school. You got out near lunchtime. This allowed a "people person," like Adrianne, plenty of the day left for socializing, something the young girl had put at the top of her "to do" list every day.

"Adrianne," an old friend said, "wanted to be liked. She loved to have friends."

An understatement.

Slightly concerned about Adrianne's work uniform still at home, Jo called a few family members and friends, while Tony went about his daily routine, undeterred by Adrianne's sudden disappearance. Who knew—maybe she had *two* uniforms? Perhaps she didn't have to work, after all. She could have blown it off to meet up with friends.

A thousand and one possibilities.

"I was not the least bit worried," Tony later said. "Not then."

Adrianne had been making lots of friends since moving into town. She was always hanging out with someone. One of her favorite places these days was the teen center at the YMCA. And, of course, the local mall.

Ten minutes went by. Jo made several additional calls.

"No one's heard from her," Jo told Tony. She said it, but didn't like the feeling of those words coming out of her mouth. Something was wrong. Jo could sense it.

Gut instinct.

"Let's take a ride to Checkers," Tony suggested.

2

Jo and Tony didn't say much to each other as they made their way to Checkers. The restaurant was just a short ride from their home. Adrianne had started working at Checkers only a few weeks back. She had never voiced any concerns about a problem at work, nor had Adrianne *not* come home from school. Still, Tony and Jo had an initial, nagging feeling that Adrianne had taken off. Run away. The rigors of teen life—that constant battle to find the right group of friends, how to fit in, to do or not do those drugs put in front of you, take a swig of that bottle, keeping everyone at home happy and content—had worn on Adrianne in the past. Jo and Tony were under the impression that Adrianne's time of rebellion and contempt had come and gone— but maybe not. Perhaps she had packed it in. Teens can be so unpredictable. Maybe Tex decided to blow off work and go party with friends.

Unanswered questions were all Jo and Tony had to go on at this point.

"We were getting scared," Jo said.

Sometime after five o'clock, Tony pulled into the

Checkers parking lot. Got out. Ran into the restaurant, Jo following behind. And found Adrianne's boss.

"No, we haven't heard from her," he said after Tony explained what was going on. "We were expecting her at five."

Jo and Tony looked at each other.

"Her check is still here, in fact," Adrianne's boss said.

Those words hit like a punch. Tony knew how kids thought. He had owned a bar once. Ran in that living-life-in-the-fast-lane crowd of druggies and drinkers. All of it was behind Tony these days, but he never forgot where he came from.

What kid would take off without her paycheck? Tony told himself, standing inside Checkers.

Something wasn't right.

Jo calmed Tony, while at the same time trying to convince herself. "Everything's goin' to be okay, babe. You'll see."

They took off home. Anxiety pumping through their veins, those unanswered questions tugged: Why would Adrianne run away? Where was she?

As Tony drove, Jo thought about the past few weeks at the house, and all that stress between her and Adrianne. The tension had been taut, sure. But now they were getting along. Moving forward.

"We'll find her, Tony, don't worry," Jo told her husband.

Two weeks before Adrianne went missing, Jo and Adrianne had had a nasty argument. Jo was home. Adrianne walked into the house. She had a Band-Aid on her right eye, up near the brow.

"What happened to your eye?" Jo asked, mildly concerned, knowing what was going on.

Adrianne didn't hesitate: "Oh, that. I was at work and cut my eye on something."

"Oh, okay . . . ," Jo said, playing along, not wanting to cause any more conflict than necessary. She'd fill Tony in when he got home and let him handle it.

But before walking away from Adrianne, Jo said, "Let me see it." She said she wanted to make sure "the cut" was okay.

Adrianne jerked backward, away from her stepmom. "No," she said, holding the Band-Aid. "I'm fine. I'm fine, Jo. Really."

"Let me see it," Jo insisted, looking more closely at the eye.

"I'm okay, really. I am."

Sizing Adrianne up, Jo realized she had gone out and done exactly what Jo and Tony had told her *not* to do: had gotten her eyebrow pierced. Jo and Tony didn't want Adrianne showing up at home one day with a face full of metal, silver BBs under her lip, barbell through her tongue, silver rings in her nose and eyebrows, same as those friends of hers she was hanging around with lately. Jo, Tony, and others called the group "Goth." But the correct term was "Juggalo," a cluster of disobedient, directionless teens and twenty-somethings, some of whom went to Adrianne's school. They liked to paint their faces with black-and-white greasepaint makeup and listen to groups signed to Psychopathic Records, namely Insane Clown Posse (ICP), a "horror rap," anti-establishment, two-man band that dressed up like killer clowns and recorded songs with such titles as "Murder Rap," "Birthday Bitches," "Hell's Forecast," "Dead Pumpkins," "Graveyard," "I Didn't Mean to Kill Him," "Witching Hour," and so forth. Supposedly, ICP had coined the term Juggalo during a concert one night when one of the band's two rapper frontmen addressed the crowd as Juggalos, a mutant pairing of the words juggle (i.e., a clown) and gigolo, a male prostitute. The lyrics to ICP songs—same as with other groups signed to their record label—are vile, sexist, violent, profane, vulgar, and nasty. Many of the band's songs promote murder and torture, blood and guts.

Dangerous stuff. If you happen to have a fragile psyche to begin with, this music and culture can be a catalyst for any number of self-destructive and aggressive behaviors.

Adrianne wasn't a Juggalo (or, rather, a Juggalette), but she was certainly interested in running with the crowd. There was a house many of them hung around at in Rock Island, a skip from East Moline. Adrianne had spent her fair share of time at the house partying, fooling around with some of the guys, just hangin' out. And there was plenty of other stuff she did that Jo and Tony hadn't a clue about. This piercing on her eyebrow, Jo knew, was the beginning. She didn't like the road Adrianne was heading down.

Adrianne and Jo commenced a catfight. They yelled and screamed at each other. F-bombs here. "You bitch" there. And all those nasty, hurtful turns of phrase some hurdle at each other when embroiled in a heated argument.

"Whatever," Jo finally said, fed up, walking away from her stepdaughter.

"Yeah, *whatever*!" Adrianne sassed back. Adrianne was never one to back down from anything. She spoke her peace—even when she knew it better to keep her tongue tied. Part of being a sixteen-year-old who knows everything, perhaps.

When Tony got home, Jo pulled him aside and

explained what had gone down earlier. As Adrianne listened with her ear up to the door, Jo told Tony how unhappy she was about being betrayed by Adrianne, and would surely not accept Adrianne yelling at her, obscenities aside. The situation was turning into what had occurred the last time Adrianne had stayed with them, when all Jo and Adrianne did was fight. Jo didn't want that. She loved Adrianne. She wanted what was best for the girl. She was dealing with it. Jo knew Tony wanted his daughter with them. They were probably the last chance Adrianne had left. She had met with so much disappointment and trouble back in Texas.

Tony came storming out of the room and cornered Adrianne. "Let me see your eye," he said, playing along with the ruse. "How did you do it? How'd you get hurt at work?" ("I don't talk," Tony said later, "I act. I have no patience for bullshit.")

Adrianne said she opened a cupboard and a bunch of boxes and food items came raining down on her and cut her eye open. It was no big deal, really.

Tony walked out of the room. What a joke. She was lying to their faces.

Sometime later, while Adrianne was in her room, she screamed loud enough so Tony and Jo could hear her: "That bitch doesn't think I heard her telling on me! What a bitch she is! Fucking bitch!"

This was out of the norm for Adrianne. She wasn't one to disrespect Jo so profanely.

Jo barged into Adrianne's room. "This is *my* house," she snapped, pointing around, while Adrianne went on and on about how Jo had ratted her out to her father.

There had been a trust between them that Adrianne felt Jo had broken. There was nothing, Adrianne and

Tony had always told Adrianne, she could ever tell them that would make them stop loving her. Anything could be worked out. Just be honest. And here she was lying.

One step forward, two steps back.

"If I want to *tell* my husband what you're doing," Jo screamed back at the teen, "that's my *damn* business. You got that!"

Adrianne didn't say a word. She stood, staring contemptuously at Jo, all up in her face.

"We had told her from day one," Jo said later, "that what we say goes. Period. No discussion."

Adrianne had agreed to live by that rule.

After everyone had a chance to calm down, Adrianne realized she was wrong to disobey them. She came forward, admitted to the piercing, and said she was sorry. It was tough out there in Teenville, USA. Peer pressure sucked. As a kid, you felt like you had to keep up with the Joneses, too. You'd be ridiculed and cast out if you didn't go along. Couldn't they see both sides?

Tony understood this, but his contention had always been: "Find new friends, then."

Jo and Tony wanted to know how sincere the apology was, so Jo recommended family counseling. Perhaps she and Adrianne needed to sit down with a therapist and talk things through. Any problem could be worked out. Adrianne knew she had a good life with her father and Jo—the best she'd ever had, possibly. She came from an unstable life back in Texas, mostly by her own doing, but an unhinged environment, nonetheless.

With Jo and Tony, Adrianne could depend on stability and restraint. Discipline. Rules. As much as she balked at being told what to do, like any kid trying to figure life out, Adrianne Reynolds knew deep down her dad and stepmom understood what was best for her.

Tony and Jo weren't even making Adrianne complete four years of traditional high school. She was getting her GED. She was working. She was allowed to have friends. My goodness, her curfew was ten o'clock on weeknights and midnight on weekends. What more could a teenager with Adrianne's background and history of trouble ask for?

Adrianne looked at Jo. "Yeah," she said. "Let's do that."

Jo said she'd make an appointment.

It was a major step in a direction Tony was glad to see her take it.

3

When Jo and Tony returned home from Checkers, Jo went back to working the phone lines. In this situation, when parents can feel helpless, not to mention guilty, you do what you can to keep yourself occupied and focused on locating your child. It wasn't quite the heart-pounding moment of turning around in the supermarket and realizing your toddler was gone. After all, it was only six o'clock in the evening. Adrianne hadn't come home. Was the situation truly that dire? She was a teen. She had a history of running away and drug use. There was no reason to panic. Not yet, anyway.

Still, that sour pang in the gut, that internal alarm system, is something most parents have a hard time dismissing. Every emotion is rattled. Tony and Jo were doing their best to hold it together and believe—*hope*—that all would be well in due time.

"Hey," Jo said to Jo's best friend, reaching her by phone, "you heard from Adrianne?"

"No."

"Yeah, we can't find her. Was wondering if you've seen her."

"I haven't. Sorry, Jo."

Tony was beginning to climb the walls a little as the evening wore on. Every car that drove by the house was enough to draw him to the window to push the curtain aside.

Adrianne?

Nope.

Jo suggested they go through Adrianne's room and look for phone numbers of her friends. Maybe some-one had seen her. Or knew where she had run off to.

It wasn't easy, but they found a notebook with several numbers in it.

Brad Tobias (pseudonym) was a kid from school whom Adrianne had dated for a short time. He was probably as good a source as any to begin with.

Jo dialed the number as Tony paced. Each ring seemed to take forever.

"Hey," Jo said when Tobias answered, "glad I caught you."

She explained what was going on. Jo didn't sound nervous or scared, maybe not even worried. She made it appear as though she needed to get ahold of Adri-anne for some reason.

"I saw Adrianne leave school with Sarah."

"Sarah? Ah . . . Sarah."

Sarah Kolb, a tomboyish-looking sixteen-year-old stu-dent at Black Hawk Outreach, was one of the girls Adri-anne had met this second time while living with Tony and Jo. Sarah was openly bisexual, but much more in-terested in females than males. She had a boyfriend, but it was no secret Sarah preferred girls. At any given time, Sarah presented herself with a different look. One day her hair was hay blond. The next, black as oil. She wore baggy black clothes. She had a face full of piercings that would send a metal detector into a frenzy. And she boasted a rep for being a tough little girl— "little" being an accurate description of her five-four, 110-pound figure. Adrianne hadn't mentioned Sarah much around the house, only because she knew that Tony (more than Jo) would not approve of her hanging with Sarah and a group of Juggalos that Sarah favored. But Adrianne and Sarah had quite the history behind them in just the short time Adrianne had been back in the QC. There was even the chance they might have been lovers at one point.

"What time?" Jo asked Brad.

"Noon, as usual."

After a brief chat, Jo and Brad hung up. Jo went and sat down. Thinking things through, she wondered if Adrianne and Sarah had made up. There had been some trouble between the two girls over the past few weeks. Adrianne had mentioned the spat in short bursts of conversation. Girl stuff, Jo presumed. Territorial things from Sarah's side of the argument. Adrianne was a tough chick; she was not afraid of Sarah in any way. Violence was not something Jo and Tony preached, but Adrianne, they both agreed, had every right to protect herself. And Adrianne had no qualms about raising her fists if she believed the situation warranted an ass kicking.

Sarah, however, was the same with regard to fighting, maybe even a bit more aggressive and violent than Adrianne.

So here you had two powerful and colorful personalities butting heads.

Sparks.

"She was not at all worried about Sarah," Tony said, with Jo agreeing.

What Tony and Jo didn't know, however, was that

Sarah had wanted to date Adrianne. "She's hot," Sarah said the first time she laid eyes on Adrianne. "Whoa!"

Adrianne, herself playing both sides of the field and experimenting with same-sex relationships, had been trying to get with Sarah since that first day they met in November 2004. They had exchanged a few romantic notes. Adrianne had indicated that she might fall for Sarah. Perhaps they had hooked up and went somewhere together, out of cell phone range.

Or maybe out of state.

Jo and Tony didn't have a phone number for Sarah.

Tony said, "Me and Joshua (Jo's son from a previous marriage) are heading over to Cory's house to see if he knows anything."

"Okay," Jo said. "I'll stay here and work the phones."

Cory "Cor" Gregory was a seventeen-year-old Adrianne had been hanging around with since being back in town, more so over the past few weeks. Cory was a full-fledged Juggalo. A pudgy kid at five feet eight inches, near two hundred pounds, Cory kept his short-cropped curly hair (like spring coils) hanging over his face. He dressed in the same baggy black clothes and chains as Sarah did. He had that punk attitude about him that was clear in the way he walked, talked, acted. Adrianne was somewhat interested in Cory, who, on the other hand, was infatuated and—according to many in the group—obsessed with Sarah Kolb.

"Cory was Sarah's dog on a leash," said a Juggalo from that crowd. "Her puppy."

On his right leg, Cory had a tattoo of a devil, a sign of perhaps what he felt like inside. Cory was experiencing that you-don't-understand-me torment that many teens go through. His parents were divorced. Cory lived with his dad. He was heavily involved with drugs—"Anything he could get his hands on," said one friend—and drinking as if prohibition was going into effect at any moment. But there was also an indication that Cory was into violence of a different sort: blood and guts, the gory-movie type.

Sarah knew Cory was totally into her and would do anything she asked. She knew his feelings for her bordered on mania, and she used that to her advantage. Adrianne was in the middle, working both ends of the relationship between Cory and Sarah, feeling out where she fit in.

Regardless of the social dynamics involved inside the group, they were a tight bunch. That much Tony and Jo knew. Cory would know where Sarah was—and maybe even where Adrianne had run off to.

Tony said he knew where Cory Gregory lived.

Cory's dad answered the door. "Come on in." He seemed helpful and concerned for Tony and Adrianne. Bert Gregory wanted to help.

"I'm lookin' for Adrianne," Tony pleaded. He had a distant gaze about him that only another father could relate to. Tony wasn't broken yet, but he was clearly getting more worried and scared for Adrianne as the night wore on.

"I think they had a fight," Bert Gregory told Tony, according to what Tony later recalled. "Sarah and Adrianne, I mean. Cory said something about dropping Adrianne off at the McDonald's by your house." The fast-food restaurant was a few blocks away from Jo and Tony's place. The idea behind the statement being that Adrianne didn't want anyone at the house to see her get out of Sarah's car. She knew her dad didn't want her hanging around with Cory and Sarah.

"No kiddin'?"

Bert explained that he didn't know where Cory was right at the moment, but Cory had been home earlier and explained what had happened. He seemed upset about it. Apparently, Sarah and Adrianne had gotten into a fight, a nasty argument that turned into a shoving match, but that was all Bert knew.

Tony asked for Cory's cell number. Bert handed it over, wished them good luck. Then Tony and Jo's son took off.

Back at home, Tony told Jo, "Let's go. . . . We'll see if we can't find Sarah's house." He gave Cory's phone number to Jo. "Call him on the way."

They took off, driving around the town of Milan, about twenty minutes southwest of East Moline. Making matters worse, freezing rain had started as they left. Milan is on the outskirts of the Quad City International Airport (QCIA). It has a small-town charm and quaint atmosphere. Sarah lived in town with her mom and stepfather. Jo thought she knew the type of vehicle Sarah drove: an old beat-up red Geo Prizm. Not knowing exactly where Sarah's house was located, if they couldn't spot the car, Tony and Jo were hoping to find someone who could lead them in the direction of Sarah's house. Or get ahold of Cory on the phone along the way and have him explain where Sarah lived.

But no one was around, and Cory wasn't answering his cell phone.

As they headed back home, it was near eight o'clock, dark, and snowing like the dickens. The temperature had dropped from the mid-thirties into the low twenties. Tony was concerned that his baby girl was out in the night roaming around by herself, cold and wet, feeling lost and possibly ashamed of something she had done, not wanting to face up to it back at home. Driving, he watched as the snow spiraled in swirls through the bright beams of the headlights.

Where is she?

He and Jo looked at each other. Without saying anything, they knew what the other was thinking.

"There ain't nuttin' we can't fix," Tony had told his daughter once.

He was hoping Adrianne was playing that same tape over in her confused head at that very moment.

Turning the corner near the street they lived on, Tony thought, *Maybe she'll be home when we pull in.*

4

Jill Hiers (pseudonym) dated one of Cory Gregory's best friends. Nathan "Nate" Gaudet also knew Sarah fairly well, but he and Cory had known each other for years, going back to grammar school. Nate was an average-sized boy, with tightly cropped dark black hair, chiseled (gaunt) facial features, and a penchant to roll with the crowd he tore it up with, whichever way they went. He liked playing paintball, smoking cigarettes, drinking booze, and doing drugs. When everyone headed out to a concert, Nate was right there—painting his face with black-and-white makeup, like the rest of them, dyeing his hair, wearing the same baggy black clothes and black gloves, with the fingertips cut out, and showing off all those face, eye, and ear piercings.

Nate was at Cory's house that night, January 21, 2005, when Jill Hiers arrived. Sarah was there, too, Jill noticed after walking in. Cory and Sarah had shown up not long after Tony and his stepson had stopped by and talked with Bert Gregory.

"What's up?" Jill said.

Everyone nodded.

Cory and Sarah said people were calling them. Adrianne was missing.

"What—missing?" Jill didn't really know Adrianne that well, only through Sarah, Cory, and Nate.

At some point, a neighbor of Cory's, Katie Singleton (pseudonym), came by. Katie bore a striking resemblance to Adrianne.

Right away, Sarah called Katie a "scabey," a derogatory term, meaning that she was a whore or slut, and liked to sleep around. But Jill was certain that Sarah meant it as a slight to Adrianne, because they looked so much alike.

Sarah told Katie that she and Cory were the last ones to see Adrianne. "We dropped her off at McDonald's," Sarah said of Adrianne, "and I don't know where she went after that."

"Really," Katie said.

"Ah, Adrianne runs away all the time," Sarah added, laughing.

Katie left. Jill watched as Cory, Nate, and Sarah broke out some cocaine Nate had on him, packed a few bowls full of marijuana, and, forgetting about Adrianne and her whereabouts, got to work getting high.

5

The time had come, Jo and Tony felt, to call the East Moline Police Department (EMPD). They didn't want to do it, but Adrianne was nowhere to be found. It was going to be a long night for the two of them if Adrianne wasn't home, sleeping in her bed.

"We'll send someone right out," an officer told Jo.

Sometime later, Officer Josh Allen showed up at the house.

"It's my daughter," Tony said. "She's been missing since twelve thirty today." Tony explained where Adrianne went to school.

Allen took notes and wrote down a description of Adrianne. Then, offering some comfort, he said, "She's probably a runaway. We'll find her, Mr. Reynolds."

Tony and Jo gave the officer a few names of friends of Adrianne's, saying, "It's very odd for her to run away. She's lived here since November. She doesn't know many people." Tony mentioned Adrianne was supposed to be at work at 5:00 P.M., but never showed up.

"She call?"

"No."

Jo and Tony considered they had better give the officer a bit of information about Adrianne that not too many people knew—something the police should be made aware of if they were going to be any help. It might answer a few questions as to what could be going on here.

"What is it?" Allen asked Tony.

"Um," Jo said, "Adrianne's a cutter."

"She's got some scars on her wrists from a few previous suicide attempts," Tony added.

The latest episode had occurred two weeks prior to Adrianne's disappearance, when Jo noticed Adrianne had cuts (this time) on her wrists. It was the day after she and Jo had gotten into that spat over the piercing. But they came to find out, it wasn't necessarily the argument they had that had sent Adrianne into a cutting fit the following day at school.

Instead, it was Sarah Kolb.

Jo was called out to the school to come and pick up Adrianne. When she arrived, the psychologist explained that the school was recommending Adrianne be taken to the Robert Young Center (RYC) immediately. The center, a crisis intervention facility that primarily treats psychiatric disorders—from alcoholism to drug addiction to schizophrenia, bipolar disorder, depression, and everything in between—is located in Rock Island. The school wanted Adrianne to enter into a program there, even if it was outpatient. She was struggling in school—not only to fit in (whatever that meant), but with her studies and social network as well. The school Adrianne attended took those kids who had dropped out of public schools and failed to meet the standards and grades. Socializing and behavior were another thing. Essentially, many of the kids Adrianne went to school with had gotten into trouble at some point along their educational path. This GED program was, you could say, a last chance for many of them, Adrianne included.

Jo told the school psychologist that she had a psychiatrist of her own, and she and Adrianne were planning to go see the doctor together.

After leaving school, an uncomfortable silence fell between stepmother and stepdaughter inside the car. Jo asked Adrianne if she wanted to talk about what was going on and what had sparked this latest cutting incident. Someone at school had seen Adrianne's wrists. This was an odd place to cut yourself—even for a cutter like Adrianne, who, when she became angry and upset, took a razor or sharp object and cut her arms and/or thighs. Not deep. Just enough to draw some blood and release the pain. Cutting was liberating. Sort of like turning on a pressure valve and letting out an excessive buildup of emotion. As profoundly shocking and unstable as it seemed, and in no way a proper response to dealing with life's pain, it helped the cutter cope.

Experts claim that self-mutilation and self-harm are not suicidal acts, but rooted in self-abuse psychology. The numbers are staggering: somewhere near 2 million people—mostly teens—are said to self-mutilate. Cutting incidents, like the one Adrianne had, usually occur after an overwhelming or distressing incident. It is, experts claim, the direct result of "not having learned how to identify or express difficult feelings in a healthy way." The theory is that by "deliberately" harming yourself, exposing that pain in a public way, as opposed to internally (hiding it), your "injuries will be seen," which would, effectively, help them heal. It also helps the cutter, by showing this "physical evidence," or public manifestation of their emotional pain, prove that the pain is "real." They see it in the injury, which continually reminds them of that.[1]

Validation.

I hurt; therefore, I am.

Jo had not seen the cutting on Adrianne's wrists and asked her about it as they made their way home.

At first, Adrianne didn't seem too interested in sharing what was going on. Then, out of nowhere, she said, "Sarah told me to kill myself."

"What?" Jo asked, shocked.

"Sarah. She told me to kill myself. So I tried."

According to Jo, they had no idea how long Adrianne had been cutting, but, she added, "Adrianne was cutting herself long before she got here to East Moline." According to a Q&A from a psychology report dated October 13, 2003, which Adrianne filled out, she said she had been smoking marijuana since the age of nine and had graduated to snorting cocaine and smoking crystal meth by twelve years old.

---

[1]From HelpGuide.org, a nonprofit online resource that helps people "understand, prevent, and resolve life's challenges." If you need more information about this all-too-common problem of self-mutilation many teens suffer from (and are very good at hiding), or you suspect a loved one might be cutting, please visit HelpGuide.org at: http://www.helpguide.org/mental/self_injury.htm, or call a professional who can help.

In between, Adrianne said, she used everything from booze (almost daily) to Xanax, and something she referred to as "footballs," speed, uppers, and other drugs. She had given it all up at fifteen, but found no other outlet to express those feelings of never being good enough and never being loved. That was when she began to cut. Evaluating Adrianne in the same report, her doctor wrote she was *very impulsive, cannot focus . . . [feels] extremely depressed [and] suicidal. She admits to running away from home several times.*

This was revealing info. But the shocker in the report was: *She reports to trying to kill herself twenty to thirty times . . . taking overdoses, trying to hang herself, trying to cut herself, jumping off a bridge, etc.* Adrianne even said she had "auditory and visual hallucinations" at times. *She hears her deceased maternal uncle talking to her, she sees him, she sees people, she hears voices in clear consciousness.*

Jo didn't take Adrianne directly home. She drove to her girlfriend's house so she and Adrianne could have some privacy and, as Jo put it, "Talk it out." This was a personal issue, Jo felt, between her and Adrianne. Adrianne needed to know she could trust Jo.

When they sat down inside Jo's girlfriend's house, Adrianne showed Jo her wrists. They weren't badly cut, Jo said later. It was clear Adrianne had no intention of killing herself with these particular wounds. Still, what in the world was happening here? Jo wondered if Adrianne hated her home life all that much. Where was all this self-hatred rooted? Were things at school *that* bad?

"What's going on?" Jo asked. Adrianne knew the talk was going to stay between them. This time, Jo wasn't going to be running home to tell Tony what was up. Girl to girl. Jo wanted to help. She promised confidentiality.

Adrianne didn't cry. She was depressed, sure. But, at the same time, Adrianne could be tough as Teflon. "They—mostly Sarah—were telling me to commit suicide."

"But why, Adrianne?"

She shrugged.

"Come on . . ." Jo wanted her to open up. *Talk to me. Tell me what is really happening.*

"I slept with a few boys," Adrianne admitted.

"Okay," Jo responded. *So what?*

Adrianne said the group of kids she hung with at school were calling her "whore" and "slut" because she'd had sex with two different boys in a short period of time. She said Sarah had told her that the only way to get rid of all the pain—and effectively redeem herself—was to take her own life. Sarah thought Adrianne was weak emotionally. She could dictate Adrianne's life for her, and she'd listen. Sarah had some sort of strange control over a few of the other kids in the group, and she assumed Adrianne was going to be as easily influenced.

But Adrianne—good, bad, or indifferent—was her own person. She was smarter than that. She didn't want to die. No one who tries to commit suicide twenty to thirty times without success wants to leave this earth; they want help. Adrianne wanted the kids to stop calling her names. She wanted their respect—their friendship—not ridicule and harassment. All the bullying was getting to her. She was desperately trying to find her place in that crowd. Hell, she was trying to find her place anywhere. She had no interest in being a Juggalette, but she wanted to be part of the group, nonetheless. Part of sleeping with the two boys was Adrianne's way of saying, *I want you to like me.*

"I don't feel right in any place, being away from my

mother," Adrianne told her therapist in 2003, "and it bothers me."

In another section of that same Q&A, Adrianne seemed to think she had a problem with sex—as in, she felt she could not control herself or abstain.

Jo had been hard on Adrianne ever since she'd been back living with them this second time.

"I didn't want you here," Jo admitted to Adrianne that day as they sat and talked. "I really didn't. Now I do. I am *so* sorry I felt that way. Let's go to that counseling session together. I want to make things right between us."

Adrianne didn't need problems at home on top of the problems she had at school.

"Yes, let's do it," Adrianne said again.

Jo said they would go that night.

Upon returning to the station house, EMPD Officer Allen called Sarah Kolb. A woman answered and told the cop to hold on. As soon as they started asking around, looking for Adrianne, the EMPD had heard that the last two people with Adrianne were Sarah Kolb and Cory Gregory.

"Is this Sarah?" Officer Allen asked after a young female voice got on the line.

"Yes."

After a few introductory words, Allen said, "Are you friends with Adrianne Reynolds?"

"To be honest, no!"

"Okay, but you had contact with her earlier today?"

"Yes, I did," Sarah said.

"When was that?"

"Oh, in between twelve thirty and one." Sarah sounded

calm. Maybe even a bit concerned for someone she had no trouble saying was as a *former* friend.

"Were you and Cory Gregory giving her a ride somewhere?"

"Yes, sir." Sarah told Officer Allen that Adrianne did not want to be dropped off at home. So they let her out at the McDonald's near her house. "Because," Sarah added, "she said that she didn't want her parents to see that she was in the car with a boy. And before, when I had hung out with her one time, she told her parents that Cory was my brother, and he's not."

"Okay . . . ," Allen said, beckoning Sarah to continue.

"So I dropped her off at McDonald's, which is, like, you know, right across the street from her house."

"Right."

"And that was the last time I saw her."

At one point, Sarah said Adrianne was wearing an "orange hoodie and blue jeans," when she and Cory last saw her. Sarah gave Allen a few names of friends who might have seen Adrianne *after* they dropped her off. People the cops should be checking in with to see if Adrianne was with them.

"You haven't heard from her since then?"

"No, I haven't," Sarah said before suggesting Adrianne had probably run away. "If you *do* hear anything," Sarah added before they hung up, "I would appreciate it if you would call me and let me know."

6

As the nine o'clock hour came to pass on Friday night, January 21, 2005, the light snow that had started to fall earlier began to come down more steadily. Standing in his living room, looking out onto Seventh Street, watching the snowflakes collect on the grass, Tony Reynolds shook his head and wondered about his daughter. She was just a tiny thing: five feet four inches, 107 pounds. Her brown hair matched the color of her eyes. Tony kept seeing Adrianne's smile. Hearing her voice. Seeing her walk through the front door into the living room.

"It's okay," Jo told him, walking up and consoling her husband. "We'll find her, Tony."

During that counseling session, which took place the Friday before Adrianne disappeared, Jo and Adrianne had had a breakthrough. Through tears and honesty, Adrianne admitted, being the intelligent young person (maybe beyond her years) she was, that by her "defying" Tony and Jo, she had been wrong. There was no room in their lives for insubordination, disobedience, and immature behavior, Jo contended. Adrianne was smarter than that. More grown-up. Jo and Tony had not asked for a lot from Adrianne, and she finally seemed to realize this. During the session Adrianne was asked how the problems she had been causing in school and at home affected her life.

"I cannot be trusted," she answered. It was a terse, direct response, which told the counselor that Adrianne understood the ramifications of her behavior.

A major step forward.

Later, during the same session, Adrianne added that she had done "nothing" to resolve those problems and wanted more than anything "to be able to tell the truth . . . and to know that I have earned back [that trust] I have broken."

"I brought all of this on myself," Adrianne said, taking full responsibility for her life.

She was on her way toward healing.

Jo couldn't believe what she was hearing, but then again, she knew Adrianne was a smart kid, with a big heart, who just needed to understand and feel that she was being loved.

By the end of the session, they had made plans to go back in two weeks.

But Adrianne was nowhere to be found, and the time for the second session had come and gone.

Shortly after the nine o'clock hour, Jo found Sarah Kolb's phone number and called her.

"Hey," Jo said, explaining who she was, "have you seen Adrianne? We can't find her." Jo sounded more worried than scared. More concerned than snappy.

Flies with honey . . . and that whole thing.

There was concern and sincerity in Sarah's voice, Jo recalled. Sarah said she wanted to help. She had seen Adrianne earlier that day and dropped her off, just as Cory had explained to his dad, at the McDonald's. But she had no idea where she went after that.

"I dropped her off at the McDonald's," Sarah explained, "because she didn't want you guys to know that there were boys in the car."

"What happened? When?"

"Oh, there was an argument in the car . . . ," Sarah offered, but didn't say between whom. Jo assumed it was between Sarah and Adrianne; she had been given some of the details from Adrianne about her on-again, off-again relationship/friendship with Sarah. "Adrianne wanted to go home. She told me McDonald's because of the boys in the car, and she didn't want to get into trouble."

Jo thought this was odd for Adrianne to be concerned about someone being home at noon.

Tony and I are both at work then. . . .

Not a chance of anyone being around.

Why would she care about that?

On the other hand, Adrianne felt Jo and Tony were always on her back, asking her who she was "running around with." They would certainly have a few questions about Cory Gregory being in the car with Adrianne. Tony didn't like him, the way he dressed, his attitude, or that look in his eye. Tony knew the type of people Cory hung around with and judged them. Tony wanted and encouraged Adrianne to do better. Cory looked like trouble.

"That's it?" Jo asked Sarah. Now that she thought about it, perhaps Adrianne was worried a neighbor would see Sarah and Cory drop her off and then blab to Tony.

"Yeah, I haven't seen or heard from her since then."

"Call me if you do, okay?"

"Sure," Sarah said.

* * *

On a questionnaire Adrianne answered during a return trip to the psychologist back in 2003, she said she had no religion. Her hobbies, she listed, were singing, drawing, and dance. She said growing up was "hard," the drugs she watched people do around her, she claimed, made life "hard." She said the two things she liked best about school were "friends and lunch." She listed the two most important people in her life as a "deceased uncle" and "two friends, also deceased." She claimed to be only ten years old when she started dating, and fourteen when she lost her virginity. One of the questions Adrianne was asked on that day seemed to draw the most jarring answer.

What do you read?
Murder.

Sleep was not going to come with smiling sheep jumping through their dreams, singing "Kumbaya," offering Tony and Jo beautiful thoughts on this night. Tony's daughter was out there . . . somewhere.

In trouble.

He could feel it in his bones.

Yet, Tony and Jo needed to try to find some rest if they were going to be any good to Adrianne.

Jo and Tony's bedroom was in the basement of their ranch-style home. Adrianne's room was directly above them on ground level. Jo's twins, Joshua and Justin, also had rooms on the same floor as Adrianne.

Before heading downstairs to bed, Jo and Tony discussed what they should do.

Tony had an idea. They'd done it before.

He and Jo placed several empty cans on the top of Adrianne's door, so if she tried to sneak in during the middle of the night, the cans would fall, make a racket on the floor, and wake them up below.

A booby trap.

If nothing else, it helped them to cope. Gave them hope. Maybe a false sense that Adrianne was out and about, perhaps drunk, high, or finding trouble with a boy, and she would be coming home eventually when the bender was over.

Optimism. In this situation, you grasp on to any thread you can.

"Typical of Adrianne," Jo remarked later, "because she loved to talk so much, we *honestly* believed at that time that she had maybe gone over a friend's house, got to talking, and lost track of time."

Tossing and turning, every time a car drove by the house and the headlights bounced off the top of the wall in Tony's bedroom, or an engine roared, maybe footsteps outside, he opened his eyes and looked up. A few times, he even got out of bed as a shadow passed by the head-level basement windows, because he thought someone was walking into the house.

Adrianne?

Nope, just the trees blowing in the wind. Kids out on the street messing around.

Nestled back in bed, Tony considered tomorrow to be another day. If she didn't come home tonight, they'd find her in the morning. It was a good bet Adrianne hightailed it back to Texas, and her mother was covering for her, allowing Tony time to blow off some steam. Adrianne was probably fed up with all those kids at school she called friends and decided she was better off in Texas.

This thought, if nothing else, was enough to cradle Tony to sleep.

7

Early the next morning, Saturday, January 22, Jo and Tony got up, had their morning coffee, showered, and hit the road. It was slow going, because the overnight snow had turned back into freezing drizzle, which put a slippery glaze over everything.

There had been no word from Adrianne throughout the night.

Something was wrong. Tony knew it.

They drove out to Port Byron, a twenty-minute ride northeast, snaking along the bank of the Mississippi. Adrianne had a friend there. She had sometimes gone over to his house to hang out.

"Nope. Haven't seen her," her friend said.

They drove over to the Black Hawk College Outreach Center, Adrianne's high school. Parked. Got out. Began searching around the premises, like detectives.

"We were actually looking through the bushes at this point," Jo recalled. "We knew there was a fight in the car"—something Sarah Kolb had told them the previous night—"and now our imaginations got the best of us and we were searching on our hands and knees through the bushes."

Looking for what?

"Adrianne's body," Jo said.

Anxiety now dictated their actions. So many different scenarios ran through their minds. Tony and Jo had a hard time keeping reality on track. They allowed their emotions to control their thoughts and what they did. There had been no indication that Adrianne was in trouble, other than her not calling and not coming home. Yet, they expected the worst.

Then they didn't.

That roller-coaster ride had begun: one minute, things were fine and they presumed Adrianne was going to be home when they pulled in the driveway. The next, they were burying her, writing a eulogy.

"Adrianne," Jo said, "had never gone twenty-four hours without contacting us."

They were closing in on that hour.

With no luck at the school, they drove home. Throughout this time, Tony and Jo had called the EMPD to see if the cops had uncovered any news of Adrianne's whereabouts.

The EMPD said they did not have any new leads, but they were working on the case.

Jo called Sarah Kolb again to see if Sarah had heard from Adrianne throughout the night. If she was in trouble, Adrianne would likely call her friends first. She did not have a cell phone—so Jo and Tony could not track her down that way.

"No, I have not heard from her." Jo could tell Sarah was with someone. She heard voices in the background.

"Here," Sarah said, "talk to Cory. He might know what's going on."

Jo waited.

"Yup?" Cory Gregory said.

"Have you seen or heard from Adrianne? We're really worried about her."

Cory had a noticeable Midwestern drawl, with a heavy Southern effect. A cocky attitude.

"We done let her off at McDonald's," Cory said. Then explained why, giving Jo the same answer Sarah had already given them.

Jo and Tony did not know Cory that well, other than what Adrianne had said about him. They had seen him one time, and he was sitting inside a car. They had heard about Cory enough from Adrianne, but even Adrianne was guarded regarding what she shared. No doubt she wanted to protect his image because she wanted to hang around Cory without Jo and Tony worrying about her. There was something between Cory and Adrianne—that much was no secret. The one time Jo and Tony had seen Cory, Sarah had shown up at the house to pick up Adrianne for a party. It was the previous year, 2004, a few weeks before Christmas.

"Who's that?" Tony asked about the boy sitting in Sarah's car.

"Sarah's brother," Adrianne lied.

"Yeah," Sarah added, backing her up. Cory gave the old man a wave and smile.

"It's Sarah's brother. He's cool, Dad. Don't worry."

Yes, she said those often regrettable two words mothers and fathers hear repeatedly: "Don't worry."

Everything is going to be just fine.

Except it wasn't.

Adrianne was missing. And Sarah and Cory, supposedly the last two people to have seen her, had not heard from Adrianne, so they claimed, and had no idea where she might have run off to. It was as if Adrianne Reynolds, a sixteen-year-old girl who never had direction in life, to begin with, had turned into dust and had blown away with the wind.

8

Fox Pointe Apartments on Seventh Street in East Moline, a two-lane road with a snow-covered grass divider between, was a place Tony and Jo knew Adrianne had hung out at, once in a while. Near Wiman Park, Fox Pointe was not one of those places Tony would have chosen for his baby girl to be running off to, if it was up to him. But what was a father to do? Adrianne was going to go where she wanted. As much as he would have liked to do it, Tony couldn't lock his little girl up in the house. She was sixteen going on thirty. Giving her that freedom and space to be her own person, to come and go as she pleased (with restrictions), even though she had messed up in the past, was something Tony had wrestled with, but decided Adrianne needed it. After all, he and Jo wanted Adrianne to understand that they trusted her to make the right choices.

Jo and Tony drove to Fox Pointe. Trolling slowly through the parking lot, Jo looking at cars, Tony staring toward the front doors of the apartments, they hoped to recognize a car or maybe even bump into one of those boys Adrianne was coming to visit. They didn't know why Adrianne came here. All she had said was that she had "friends at Fox Pointe." Tony, more than Jo, knew what her "friends" looked like, who they were by face, but not name.

After a careful drive through the parking lot, once again they met a dead end.

From there, they drove to the EMPD. Tony wanted to pass on to the cops a few names and addresses and see what was going on, if they had uncovered anything new.

"We wanted to give them the Fox Pointe address, mainly," Jo said. "Maybe they could find out more than we did."

A strange thing happened as Tony and Jo stood inside the EMPD. On the desk of the officer they were giving the Fox Pointe address to were several photos of those "friends" Adrianne had visited at Fox Pointe. Tony recognized them.

Jo felt Tony bump her with an elbow; then he nodded in the direction of the photos.

"Is this the people who live there?" the cop asked.

"Yeah," Tony said.

Come to find out, these were friends of Sarah Kolb's. She had introduced them to Adrianne.

More Juggalos.

The cops said they were looking into it. And it appeared they had a bead on someone. There was nothing Tony and Jo could do standing inside the police station, asking questions the police could not answer.

Go home. Wait for her to call. Continue to contact Adrianne's friends. Let us do our jobs, they were told.

She's going to turn up somewhere, Tony told himself as he and Jo left the station house.

Soon.

* * *

Leaving the EMPD, Tony and Jo took the same route they had the previous night, going back out to Port Byron to see Adrianne's friend.

He wasn't home.

Next, they trekked back to the school to conduct a more thorough search of the grounds.

Déjà vu.

"Let's try McDonald's," Jo suggested. They hadn't been there.

The snow continued to fall as the wipers on Tony's vehicle knocked back and forth against the sides of the windshield; fear and worry swelled inside the car like a stink.

Silence became the enemy.

"I am going to beat her ass when I find her!" Tony said to Jo at one point.

"No, you're not. You better not."

It turned into an argument.

At McDonald's, they found nothing. Not one sign of Adrianne. They showed photos of Adrianne to patrons and employees. No one seemed to recognize her. Or could think of anything they had seen out of the ordinary recently.

They were back at square one.

The sad and sobering statistics regarding runaways and missing children in the United States suggest a bit of confusion and misinterpretation on the public's part—that is, if crime television, the media in general, and the Internet are the places you get your data. Watching television, one might think that child abductions happen every hour of the day. And yet, breaking the data down, according to the Department of Justice (DOJ), the truth of the matter doesn't quite add up to the frenzy of fear and worry we have shown in recent years. One in seven kids between the ages of ten and eighteen will run away from home at some point in his or her life. Shockingly, there are 1 to 3 million runaway/homeless kids living on the streets in the United States. Of these children, 797,500 (younger than eighteen) were reported missing in a one-year period of time, which equates to an average of 2,185 children being reported missing each day.

That's a lot of kids—no matter how you add it up.

Yet most of these children have left home by their own accord.

Now, here is where the statistics get interesting. Of those nearly 800,000 reported missing kids, 203,900—a little over a quarter—are said to have been victims of family abductions; 58,200 of those are victims of non-family abductions (meaning neighbors, friends, acquaintances, strangers). But here's the shocker: 115 children are victims of what the Department of Justice refers to as "stereotypical" kidnappings, a snatch and grab by *someone the child does not know or someone of slight acquaintance, who holds the child overnight, transports the child fifty miles or more, kills the child, demands ransom, or intends to keep the child permanently,* the DOJ reports state.

In other words, that pedophile in the park, the one all parents fear will snatch their kid out of thin air and do God knows what to him or her, is a rare culprit.

So, based solely on the numbers, there was a good chance Jo and Tony should have considered that Adrianne—had she been abducted—would have been taken by someone she knew. Or, as the data seemed to bear out, it was a good bet that Adrianne had left home on her own accord.

By late afternoon, Saturday, January 22, 2005, Jo and Tony hit the local airwaves pleading for Adrianne's return.

"We seriously thought—and firmly believed at that moment—she was hiding out at a friend's house," Jo said.

Family and friends printed flyers. Adrianne's photo—her sad brown eyes, a stray bang floating down off to the right side of her blemish-free face, her long, bulky signature earrings easily noticeable—was positioned front and center, the largest item on the flyer. Jo and Tony, along with Justin and Joshua, their spouses, Brooke and Kristen, Adrianne's friends from the YMCA and neighborhood, along with cousins and other relatives, tacked flyers up wherever they could, passed hundreds of them out to passing motorists, and hoped for the best. One important location was on the drive-through window of the Checkers restaurant where Adrianne had worked. Tony had never thought he'd see the day, but there was his Lil' Bit's photo, the word "missing" scrawled in large font across the top, a description of her below, posted on the window where she worked.

Adrianne Reynolds was now one of those numbers—every parent's nightmare.

Jo's niece was also deeply affected. She drew a photo of herself staring at a telephone pole with one of those missing person flyers tacked at eye level, an arrow pointing to the child and the rock she stood on to step up and look at the flyer. It was more of a note to Adrianne, written by the innocent mind of a seven-year-old. *I miss you*, it said. *I miss you very much.* She pleaded for Adrianne to *come back home . . .*

For we all miss you.

The late edition of the local paper on Saturday night printed a brief article that would run again in the morning. It displayed the same photo under the banner headline: SEARCH FOR MISSING E.M. GIRL EXPANDS.

Looking at that, Tony felt his heart race. The situation was becoming more unwelcoming as each hour passed.

For the first time, a description of Adrianne was published. But it wasn't the publication of her features that led police to believe they were dealing with a runaway— it was a line in the article that suggested Adrianne had taken off. The second-to-last paragraph, after describing what Adrianne might be wearing, said: *She may have been carrying a backpack.*

This one implication, allegedly given to the newspaper by a source inside the police department, suggested to law enforcement that Adrianne was a runaway. Why else would she be carrying a backpack?

To Tony and Jo, however, that nagging feeling, turning more dire in the pit of their stomachs, was becoming a thing of its own, too strong not to notice. The more time that went by without a call or indication from Adrianne that she was okay, Tony felt, the better the chances were that Adrianne had met up with trouble. And if there was one thing about Adrianne, it was that trouble for her could include any number of things— all of which spelled disaster.

9

Adrianne's sometimes friend Sarah Kolb was at work on Saturday afternoon, ushering at the Showcase Cinemas just across the Mississippi River, in Davenport, Iowa, when Jill Hiers drove boyfriend Nate Gaudet, Cory Gregory, and Sean McKittrick—Sarah's "boyfriend" when she swung the pendulum toward the male persuasion—to a local Best Buy store to look around. It seemed they were all waiting for Sarah—their archetypal leader—to get out of work.

As they walked into the store, under the blue-and-yellow Best Buy logo, Cory caught Jill off guard when he whispered in her ear, "I'm going to prison. . . . The cops won't stop calling me. They are going to just come and get me." Then he laughed. "They won't stop calling me about Adrianne." This was in response to the breaking news that Adrianne was considered officially a missing person. Police had called Cory's house looking for her after hearing he was one of the last two people to see her.

"What are you talkin' about, Cory?" Jill asked.

He put on a mock sad face: "Will you come visit me?"

"Is it your fault that Adrianne is missing, Cory?" Jill asked. What in the world was Cory implying with this conversation? Jill knew Cory was off-the-wall and said some crazy stuff, but was he just toying with her?

"No, [Jill]! But let's keep it quiet."

Jill shot Cory a look of confusion and decided to heed his direction not to talk about it again, at least for the time being.

At the Davenport, Iowa, Showcase Cinemas, Sarah clocked in for her 3:00 to 10:00 P.M. shift. Primarily, after punching in, Sarah spent as much time as she could hiding out and talking on her cell phone. At one point late into the evening, Sarah was talking to a coworker friend of hers, when another employee, a girl she knew from school, walked by and overheard part of the conversation.

"Yeah," Sarah bragged. "I beat her ass. Broke out four of her teeth."

Sarah was always talking about how tough she was, how big and badass she could be whenever she wanted. This time, she'd had a brawl, it appeared, with another girl, and was playing up the idea of how badly she'd whooped the girl's butt.

"Why did you get into the fight?" the employee asked. "What happened?"

"Bitch was dipping in my Kool-Aid—and she knew the fucking flavor!" Sarah said.

"No kidding?"

"I have her blood and one tooth in my car," Sarah said, never mentioning who she was talking about. Everyone knew it was Adrianne, however. "You know how I can get rid of the blood?" Sarah asked them.

"Doesn't matter," said another kid, who had walked up and stepped into the conversation. "Ever see that *CSI* show? The cops will find it, even if you get rid of it."

"What happened?" someone else asked. A little crowd was gathering.

Sarah enjoyed all the attention. It not only fed a low self-esteem problem she contended with, but made her feel as if she was fulfilling that role of leader she saw herself in.

"After beating her ass," Sarah continued, "I dropped the bitch off at McDonald's and left."

A friend of Sarah's had gone to the movies that night with his brother. They ran into Sarah on the way out. It was near the end of Sarah's shift.

"Hey," he said, walking over.

"I told Adrianne not to hang with us anymore," Sarah said for no apparent reason, after catching up with the kid. He was from that group that Sarah, Cory, Nate, Sean, and the others hung around.

"You did?" he asked. They all knew Sarah and Adrianne hadn't been getting along for more than a month now, and Sarah was pissed off more recently because she believed Adrianne had made a play for Sarah's place in the gang. Not to mention several other things Sarah didn't have time to talk about at the moment.

"Yeah . . . I got into a fight with her today in the car and it went into the McDonald's parking lot. I just left the bitch there."

"Later," the kid said.

Sarah went back to work.

10

Saturday evening turned solemn inside the Reynolds household, now considered to be ground zero, a residence full of people wanting to help any way they could. It was funny how when you needed people most, they came, Tony thought, standing around, looking at everyone, wondering where his Lil' Bit had run off to. Inside, a fire burned, tearing Tony apart. He was unable to help Adrianne, perhaps when she needed him the most. Here was a big powerful guy like Tony taken down to his knees, wondering what had happened to his only child.

Helpless—the worst feeling in the world for a parent.

There was a negative undertone to all this public attention being focused on Adrianne's disappearance. But what could he do? As a father, he had to involve the press. The worst part of it stemmed from the same dynamic playing out during any number of high-profile missing person cases that CNN and the other networks jumped on as soon as the first whiff of fresh blood emerged. The problem was that as the community rallied, friends and neighbors got together to help and posters went up, the news coverage picked up pace, and the missing child might decide to go deeper underground, for fear of now being the cause of such a massive manhunt. Publicity could work against a family in a situation like that.

Definitely a God-fearing man, Tony could only hope and pray that this turned out to be the case; that Adrianne, scared and not wanting to cause any more trouble for her family, didn't want to come out of hiding.

Jo had gone into work on Saturday. She was a basket case, and they sent her home.

"It was beginning to look like Adrianne was gone," Jo recalled.

Puff!

No one could deny that feeling of absence. Adrianne was all about being the center of attention and making her presence known, wherever she was or whatever room she entered. Part of what she had wanted out of the therapy, Adrianne had told her doctor, was to learn "how to talk less." Her life revolved around friends. The fact that no one had seen her since school on Friday was beginning to concern Tony and Jo more than an itchy feeling of her being a runaway.

Just a week or so before she went missing, Adrianne had asked her father and Jo if she could spend the night at Sarah Kolb's house. Adrianne said she wanted to go to a party with Sarah and then crash at Sarah's after the party. She didn't want to come home late and wake everyone up. It would be a lot easier to stay at Sarah's.

Tony said, "Sure. Go ahead."

Jo wasn't that naïve. She piped in, "Oh no, she's not!"

Jo explained: "We didn't know Sarah's parents. It wasn't that we didn't *trust* Adrianne." That was something

Adrianne never really *got.* "But we never met Sarah's parents. How would we know if Sarah was in the house at midnight?"

Or at all, in fact.

Tony agreed. He went and told Adrianne that she was to come home after the party, adding, "And make sure you're home by midnight."

"Okay," Adrianne said. Since being back in Illinois this second time, Adrianne knew better than to give Tony any lip. She understood that when Tony spoke, that was the final word. She was on borrowed time here, anyway, so why make matters worse?

On the night of the party, Adrianne went out—and returned home by midnight.

Staring out the window, thinking about that conversation, Tony quivered. That feeling was back, tugging at him. The silence . . . it was so unlike Adrianne.

Where in the heck is she?

During that Saturday afternoon, the EMPD had made contact with Sarah Kolb for what was the second time since Adrianne had gone missing, this after hearing from several people they had interviewed that Sarah was bragging about a fight she'd had with Adrianne earlier in the day on Friday. None of this information, however, was ever relayed to Jo and Tony. It wasn't the right time. Cops don't fill the family in on every single detail of an ongoing investigation. They like to keep their cards close. Just in case, of course, someone in the family is involved.

"I'm calling because of Adrianne Reynolds," the cop

explained to Sarah. "She's been missing and could be a runaway. Do you know where she is, Miss Kolb?"

The EMPD was looking to resolve this case. It was dragging on. Was Adrianne a runway or not? The best place to uncover that fact was with her friends. Her closest allies. If no one else, Adrianne's friends would know where she had run off to.

"I dropped her off at McDonald's on the Avenue of the Cities," Sarah offered. "I wish I knew more because now *I'm* concerned."

"Contact us if you find anything out," the cop told Sarah.

"I will. You do the same."

Sarah was inside a friend's van outside Showcase Cinemas after her shift ended, when she once again brought up that fight she said she'd had with Adrianne on Friday. Sarah said that a guy Adrianne knew was supposed to drive Adrianne home from school, but that he never showed up for class. So the chore fell on Sarah.

She laughed. "Fucking Jiffy!"

"Jiffy" was one of those terms Sarah used for a girl who, she later said, "spreads her legs easy, like peanut butter." Sarah hated the idea that Adrianne slept around. Sarah despised easy girls, who she believed disrespected the female culture in general.

"What happened?" the girl in the van asked.

"Ah, she said something that upset me and it started a fight in my car. . . . She punched me. I punched her. Broke four of her teeth. I was choking her and then she started choking on her own teeth!" Sarah stopped then, she explained. "She spit her damn teeth out at Cory. He was in the car, too. There was blood all over my car, on my clothes. On Cory, too."

"Did she go inside [the restaurant] for help?"
"We made up. I dropped her off at McDonald's."

At some point on Saturday night, after Sarah got home from work, the EMPD made contact with her again. They had spoken to Cory Gregory earlier in the day, the cop said, and there were some differences—slight as they were—in the stories Sarah and Cory had told police. The EMPD needed to clear things up.

Were Sarah and Cory covering for Adrianne? Making up a story so Adrianne could run off without being chased?

It was after 10:00 P.M. when Officer Kevin N. Johnson called Sarah on her cell phone. Johnson wanted a complete description of the events that Friday—exactly what happened, when, where. He needed to fill out a report, get Sarah Kolb on record with her version of the story from the time they left school until she dropped Adrianne off at McDonald's.

"Okay," Sarah explained without hesitating, taking a breath, as if to say, *Here we go again.* "I was driving to the Taco Bell in Moline. Sean [McKittrick], Cory, and Adrianne were in the car. I wanted one of those half-pound things at the Taco Bell . . . you know. I started arguing with Adrianne. She had told me that she was falling for Cory and that she had never met anyone like him."

"Okay. Continue."

"I mean, she barely even *knew* him. Cory wasn't interested in her."

"What was *he* saying?"

"He wasn't saying anything. I made a reference that she was sleeping around with a lot of guys. . . . She called *me* a whore! I punched her. She punched me back."

"What about Sean?"

"Sean got out of the car and started walking back toward Black Hawk Outreach in East Moline. Adrianne and I continued arguing. At some point, I told her I was taking her home."

Sarah went on to explain how she and Adrianne "made up on the way" to McDonald's, a location where Adrianne had insisted she be dropped off. "She said something about her dad seeing Cory in the car and being upset that she was with a boy."

"So what did you do?"

"I dropped her off in the front parking lot of McDonald's and drove around to the drive-through. When we left the drive-through, we did not see Adrianne again."

"We spoke to Cory," Officer Johnson explained. "Why wouldn't he tell us why you two were arguing? Or say anything about you two punching each other?"

Sarah went quiet for a beat. Then: "I asked him to lie about it, since Adrianne is missing." Sarah said she didn't want any trouble. She and Adrianne fighting; Adrianne turning up missing; she and Cory dropping her off; the last two people to see her. . . . Two and two made four. Sarah didn't want to be blamed for something she didn't do. "I didn't want anybody to know I was fighting with her just before she came up missing, you know."

"Tell me about Adrianne—what she was like?"

Sarah had no trouble answering this question. "I'd estimate that she has slept with, oh, maybe about fifty guys in the time she moved back up here to East Moline. She constantly writes me notes about how bad her life is and everything she does. I was there one night when she took off and had sex with a guy."

"You remember his name?"

"No. *Adrianne* didn't even know his name. She's disturbed and unstable. I know she went over to [a friend's house] with Cory one day and she asked them about a threesome, but Cory wasn't interested."

Johnson said the EMPD would be back in touch.

11

On Sunday morning, Jo got up and went to work. What good was she at home, wandering around, numb as an infected wound, wondering what was going to happen next? Work would keep her mind off what was looking to be the inevitable: Wherever Adrianne had run off to, or whatever had happened, she wasn't coming back. There had not been one word from Adrianne or the police throughout the night.

Early morning, Tony pulled into the parking lot of the Hy-Vee where Jo worked and ran inside. He seemed desperate to find his wife. Frazzled. In a hurry.

Watching him walk toward her, Jo considered Tony had some news.

"What is it?" Jo asked when Tony came up on her.

"I'm worried," Tony said. Jo could see it written all over his face. Tony had a melancholic twist about him she had not seen before. He looked beaten, as if tossing in the towel. "I don't know what to do, Jo."

Tears.

The guy was lost.

Jo started crying. "Tony . . ."

Adrianne didn't have a cell phone; she talked too much, Tony said, and "she knew that she could never afford the bill." Now Tony was wishing he'd paid for the damn thing himself. It seemed so long ago, the last time he saw Adrianne. It was Thursday night, January 20, near bedtime. Adrianne was in her room. Tony opened the door like a proud father checking on his child. Peeked his head in. "Just wanted to say g'night, Lil' Bit. I love you." He walked over, gave his daughter a peck on the cheek.

"I love you, too, Dad," Adrianne said.

Adrianne never got her driver's license. She hardly knew her way around town, better yet the area.

Tony had never caught Adrianne drinking or using drugs. "Look," he said, "she was no saint. But then again, she was different than any other sixteen-year-old."

All of these feelings and thoughts, as they began to flood Tony, were both cumbersome and comforting, an off mixture of emotion. Anxiety pumped through Tony like a drug, leading him to believe that if Adrianne was out there, in trouble, she would have found a way to reach out to someone.

She would have called by now.

Jo decided to stay at work. Tony said he was going to drive around and see what he could find. There was no way he could sit home. It was close to two full days that Adrianne had been gone. Any anger Tony had when he first learned Adrianne had failed to come home, figuring she was out running around, had been replaced by fear, dread, worry. The quote Tony gave the newspapers that Sunday put it all into context: "I was mad, but now I'm scared."

Every car he passed, Tony looked inside.

Adrianne?

He was desperate. He hung more flyers. He called family, friends, numbers he pulled from Adrianne's address book.

Again and again, no one had seen or heard from Adrianne Reynolds.

12

Nate Gaudet slept late on Sunday, emerging from his room inside his grandmother's house between 10:30 and 10:45 A.M. Nate was a handful. Drugs. Drinking. Loud music. Strange friends coming and going. He sometimes wore a weird set of contact lenses that made his eyes look like that of a reptilian monster in a sci-fi film. Unbeknownst to his grandparents, Nate Gaudet was out of control.

To his grandmother's surprise, Nate opened the door of his room and walked out wearing a black trench coat, same as one of those boys from Columbine. The old woman did not like the way Nate was dressed.

It scared her.

At almost the same time that Nate came out of his room, a "red car," his grandmother later reported, pulled into the driveway.

Sarah—the only friend of Nate's who drove a red car.

"Your friends are here," his grandmother said.

Nate's grandmother watched from behind a curtain as Nate sat inside the car for "a couple of minutes." There were two other males, the grandmother thought, sitting inside the car. One she knew to be Cory Gregory, she recalled to police.

They talked back and forth for a short time.

When Nate got out of the car, he walked back into the house, went down into the basement for a few moments, moved some things around, then went back out the door and got into the red car again.

A short moment later, the car pulled out of the driveway and drove away.

Nate's grandmother called Nate's mother. "He left with two other boys," she said. It was easy enough to mistake Sarah Kolb for a boy. Many had done it.

"And? . . ."

"He was dressed in all black—pants, shirt, and a black beanie hat."

Nate looked like a Black Panther. Ready to riot.

The other strange thing about Nate was that he was wearing contact lenses: black "with a white conclave or a X" for the irises.

Scary stuff.

"He's still upset over a fight with [Jill] last night," the grandmother concluded. She was worried about Nate and what he was up to. He and his girlfriend had gotten into it loudly the previous night. Nate was prone to depression. Things set him off.

"I'll call him," Nate's mother said. "Try not to worry."

An hour later, Nate's mother reached her son on his cell phone. There was loud music playing in the background. She could hardly hear him.

"What are you doing? What is going on with you?"

Nate sounded upbeat. "We're watching a music DVD at Cory's house." He never said who else was with him.

"Where are you going after you watch the DVD?"

That music was blaring now. What an annoyance.

"Probably go to the movies," Nate said.

"Nate, are you going to be returning to your grand-mother's tonight? She's worried about you."

"Yes . . . yes."

"Are you mad at them (his grandparents), Nate?" If anyone knew, Nate's mother understood that he had a bad temper and it could get out of hand at times. "You need to control your temper better."

They hung up.

Sarah Kolb had to work Sunday afternoon into the evening. She and a coworker were cleaning the bath-rooms when Sarah, looking at herself in the mirror, said, "Someone called me 'pizza face' the other day." She smiled at herself and looked at the skin on her cheeks and forehead, from side to side.

The coworker walked over and stared at Sarah. She noticed red blemishes all over Sarah's face.

"It's not acne," Sarah said, moving closer to the mirror. "They're scratches."

The conversation ended there. Sarah never said how she got the scratches. Both girls went back to work.

Later that evening, Sarah and the same coworker went on break together. Sarah told the same story of going to Taco Bell with Adrianne, "the Mexican" (Sean McKittrick), as Sarah called him, and Cory, and how she and Adrianne got into a fight. And she knocked her teeth out, then dropped her off at McDonald's.

"What was the fight about?" the girl asked.

Sarah thought about it. "She was dipping in my Kool-Aid. . . ."

"Adrianne will be at school tomorrow," the coworker prophesized. She was certain of it.

Sarah didn't respond.

Outside a while later, Sarah was smoking a cigarette by the Dumpster with another coworker. She talked about Adrianne and the fact that she was missing.

"Do the cops think you whacked her?" the coworker asked. It was Sarah's tone, the way she described all the calls from the cops and how she was the last one to be with Adrianne.

Sarah shrugged. "I guess so."

In the past, this same coworker later explained, Sarah had been open about her sexuality. One day, Sarah had said that "she had been with Adrianne" sexually, but Adrianne had "slept around too much" and Sarah became uninterested.

"Plus, she was with a guy I know—*and* she gave me chlamydia!" Sarah said. "I had to let her go after that. I didn't want any part of that shit. I got more class than that."

13

Sunday evening began on a low note for Jo and Tony Reynolds—as if things could get any worse. Tony called down to Texas to see if Adrianne's mother had heard from her. Tony and Carolyn Franco, Adrianne's biological mother, had been in close contact throughout the ordeal, but Tony was beginning to think that maybe Adrianne and her mom had gotten together and pulled one over on him—even though the scenario didn't make much sense. Custody of Adrianne was never an issue in Tony's life, for him or for Carolyn.

"They . . . handed sole custody over to us," Tony said; though Carolyn later disagreed with Tony's explanation.

The EMPD had checked with the local airlines, bus depots, trains, and any other way Adrianne could have skipped town via public transportation.

They found nothing.

The idea that Adrianne was hiding in Texas with Carolyn was ridiculous, Tony realized after thinking about it. He and Carolyn did not always see everything under the same light, but they got along enough to understand that doing something like this was equal to torture.

No way.

Tony had no other choice but to get up and go to work on Monday morning, January 24. He couldn't give up. He needed that sense of normalcy in his life. If something happened, or Adrianne came home, Jo would call him.

Jo had other plans, however. She became more worried that Adrianne was in big trouble and unable to call or contact anyone.

"I was frantic. I just wanted to know that she was okay."

Uneasy to the point where Jo picked up the Yellow Pages, riffled through while licking her fingertips, and, in desperation, called a psychic.

She asked the man to come over to the house. Jo had gone paranormal in the past. She called a psychic long ago and the woman, Jo claimed, had been spot-on with several of her "visions" (if you'll allow that term).

"I *was* desperate."

There was a knock not long after Jo made the call. She got up and opened the creaky door.

On her front steps stood an old, frail man, Jo recalled. "Creepy and short." He had a scraggly, unkempt beard, a reserved look in his eyes. It was as if he knew something but didn't want to divulge the information just yet.

Jo invited him in.

"Can I go into her room?" the self-proclaimed psychic said without much small talk.

Jo led the way.

The old man took off his fedora, held it in his hands, stared around the room, then walked slowly toward Adrianne's bed. There was some indication that he was

familiar with the case from reading about it in the newspapers and seeing some of the television coverage.

He gestured toward the bed, motioning that he
wanted to sit down. Was it okay?

"Go ahead," Jo offered, thinking, *What am I doing? . . .
If Tony only knew.* She had never told her husband.

"Can I have something of hers?" the man asked in a
gentle voice. "Something personal and dear to her heart."

That was easy for Jo. One of Adrianne's favorite
things was her stuffed teddy bear. It was a shade of red,
almost rust colored, black eyes, a pink bow around its
neck, a half-moon black button nose. Adrianne adored
the furry creature and rarely ever slept without it.

Jo picked up the bear, stared at it, a twist of pain in
her gut, then handed it off.

The guy closed his eyes, massaged the teddy bear
some, and seemed to be meditating, or, as he put it,
calling upon his "gift."

After a few moments, he said, "She's alive."

Then he opened his eyes. Stood.

Jo nearly broke down. It was like being underwater
longer than your lungs could take, then coming up for
that first burst of air.

Relief.

"I'm getting that she's in somebody's basement," the
man said.

"Oh my," Jo responded. A smile. Then a quick flush
of anguish and respite. "Thank you. Thank you."

The man walked out of the room. That was all he
had. He grabbed his jacket and hat, and headed for
the door.

"How much do I owe you?" Jo asked as the psychic

stepped over the threshold and onto the porch. He had never told Jo what he was going to charge.

"Don't worry about it. No charge."

And then he was gone.

Jo wanted to call Adrianne's mother in Texas. She ran to the phone after the psychic drove away.

She explained to Carolyn what had just occurred inside the house, adding that the way the psychic had phrased his "visions" indicated that Adrianne was hiding out in someone's basement. She wasn't being held against her will. She was scared. Yes. She'd done something wrong. She didn't want to come home.

Adrianne's biological mother was speechless.

While Tony was driving on that Monday, he said he looked into every vehicle he passed. There were times when he was four hours away from home, but he still wanted to know that his angel wasn't inside one of those cars he'd passed. It made for an excruciatingly painful, long day. He'd stop and call Jo periodically: "You hear anything?"

"No. Sorry, honey."

There was another part of this drama playing out almost nine hundred miles south of East Moline, in Gregg County, Texas, where Adrianne had lived for most of her life with her biological mother and, at times, a stepfather.

Prosecutors in Gregg County, hearing now for the first time that Adrianne Reynolds, a juvenile they knew quite well, was missing, *instantly wondered,* said an article written by Barb Ickes, a *Quad-City Times* reporter, *if the teen's parents in Longview, Texas, were somehow involved* in her disappearance.

From all reports, it appeared there was a lot about Adrianne's life back home in Texas that Jo and Tony Reynolds had never heard about.

14

Adrianne was born in El Dorado, Arkansas, an industrial town mainly run by oil companies, in the deep south-central part of the state, nearly on the Louisiana border. It was 1988, the year George H. W. Bush was elected, taking over the Oval Office from Conservative superhero Ronald Reagan, and also a year that brought the opening of the Berlin Wall's west end that November. Tony Reynolds was living in El Dorado. He had met the woman who would become Adrianne's grandmother, Beverly, and they hit it off. At the time, Beverly had a teenage daughter, Carolyn, who was pregnant (with Adrianne). Tony didn't have kids. They all lived together in the same house. After Adrianne was born, just a few weeks after Carolyn's sixteenth birthday, Tony and his wife welcomed the baby into the home.

Soon it was decided that Tony and Beverly would adopt Adrianne from Carolyn, who was admittedly too young to take care of the child herself. Tony and Beverly were in their late twenties, ready to be parents, anyway.

When Adrianne was two months old, Carolyn signed

over parental rights to Beverly and Tony, who was now Adrianne's legal father.

"We all got along pretty good," Tony said. "Eventually Carolyn met some guy, moved out, and went on with her life. Adrianne stayed with us. Bev and I done raised her from that point on."

According to Carolyn, giving up Adrianne wasn't something she did willingly, or as simply as Tony had explained it later.

"I had wanted to live out on my own," Carolyn later told me. "It was supposed to be a temporary thing— that they (Tony and Beverly) were going to keep Adrianne until I could get on my feet. And things got kind of hard. They got attached. And didn't want to let her go. But the adoption was done because Adrianne's [biological] dad was trying to fight me for custody . . . and we were worried he would get custody."

Tony turned thirty that October. He had just purchased his first house. He was manager of a tire company, a job he'd had for over a decade. He had a child. Things were going all right. Tony and Beverly enjoyed Adrianne. Life was not perfect, but it was getting better every day.

As time went on, however, problems between Tony and Beverly started. Then verbal fighting became the norm. Like many households, the center of their arguments was about finances. Tony felt Beverly wasn't managing the family money the way he wanted. One day, he told Bev, "Look, if I cannot trust you with my money, I sure as heck can't trust you with anything else!"

The disagreements between them continued, and silence replaced the trust a marriage needs to survive. "We parted ways," Tony recalled. "She went hers. I done went mine."

Beverly took Adrianne. (If you're keeping score, this would be the second time Adrianne had had her young life racked by separation—and the kid was just about old enough to start talking.)

In the divorce decree, Tony was obligated to pay child support. Adrianne was three years old. It was 1992.

"Bev and I remained good friends, as far as being exes an' all," Tony explained. "I could still go over and see Adrianne anytime I wanted. In fact, I helped them get the house they moved into [there in El Dorado]. I never wanted to be mean."

In 1995, shortly before Adrianne turned six, as she was getting ready to start school, Beverly took Adrianne and Carolyn and moved to Longview, Texas. Longview was a haul from Arkansas. For Tony, it was approximately a three-hour ride, or 160 miles due southwest. Beverly had family in Texas, where she was born and raised. Beverly's parents, on the other hand, were still living in El Dorado. So Tony understood he would see Adrianne quite a bit as Bev and Adrianne returned to visit family and friends.

"They made trips back to El Dorado pretty regular," Tony recalled, "and I made trips down to Texas."

Adrianne's biological mother, Carolyn, eventually met a man, got married, had another child, and "got her life back on track while they was in Texas," Tony recalled.

Now she wanted Adrianne back.

"Me and my ex," Tony said, "talked about it. Then decided, you know what, that might be the best thing for Adrianne."

As Adrianne entered her formative years, Carolyn divorced her husband. This was the third blow to Adrianne's view of what a healthy family unit should be. The idea of family life—up until this period, hard-wired into Adrianne's fragile psyche—was that every couple of years you moved or someone left the home. It must have been devastating on her young mind. It seemed Adrianne's idea of a family was constantly changing.

And it would get worse.

The only man she had ever called "Dad" soon disappeared from Adrianne's life. Tony had stayed in Arkansas. He started running a bar. With that came a different mix of people Tony became involved with and hung around.

"I got busted for selling crystal meth," Tony admitted, "and I went to prison. . . ."

From prison, at different times, Tony called Texas. "They all said Adrianne was doing fine."

Probably more for Tony's sake. The guy was in prison. Did he need to know that his daughter was getting into trouble? And Adrianne was getting seriously into drugs, alcohol, and boys about now.

Tony had learned his lesson in prison, he said, and made a plan to go straight when he was paroled. But things seemed helpless and hopeless there for a while—biding his time, day in, day out, climbing the concrete walls, staring at that shiny barbed wire that was keeping him from the outside world.

How the hell did I get myself into this?

Time, of course, does not wait for anyone.

Tony got out of prison, got his life on track. Yet, somewhere along the way, Adrianne's life spiraled out of control.

"Whenever they [Adrianne and her mother] had a problem," Tony said, "they called on me."

He didn't mind. Tony was that type of good-natured soul; he would give you the shirt off his back if he believed in his heart it was going to help. On the other hand, if he thought it would hurt, no matter how bad he wanted to, Tony pulled back.

Tony never heard—perhaps until it was too late—that Adrianne was having a difficult time with life in Texas as she grew out of her grammar school years and into a teen.

Carolyn soon married a man, David Franco. Now there was another stepparent in Adrianne's life, a fourth try at realizing every kid's dream of the perfect family. Carolyn later admitted that she and David worked "long hours" and were hardly ever home. There were extended periods of time when Adrianne was left home alone, unsupervised.

"Then all I heard about was Adrianne beginning to mess around with boys," Tony recalled. "Adrianne was never much into the drug or drinking thing." At least, that's what Tony believed, he said. Adrianne's psychology reports from this period prove differently: she was enmeshed in a life of alcohol, hard drug use, and promiscuous sex.

By this time, Tony had married Jo. She and Tony had been high-school sweethearts. After getting out of prison and putting his life together, Tony moved back to East Moline, Illinois, where he had grown up. Tony had graduated from high school in 1977, joined the army, and, as he put it, "I done stayed gone from Illinois for a good twenty years.

"Things happen for a reason," Tony recalled, looking back.

Two weeks after he got out of prison, Tony went to visit an old boss.

"Some girl has been calling here, looking for you," Tony's old boss said.

"No kidding." Tony had no idea who it might be.

"She left her name and number."

Tony looked at the piece of paper.

Jo.

"I had not spoken to her since 1977," Tony said. "We talked for like a month on the phone. I told her I done just gotten out of prison and I ain't got nothing. She says, 'I want you to come up here [her home]. I love ya—and always have. I want to help you start your life over.'"

Lots of people, Tony said, "they go to prison and they done keep messin' up. It done learnt me my lesson, let me tell you that."

Carolyn said later that during this period—those crucial years when Adrianne drifted off into a life of self-medicating—Tony never called for his daughter, sent a card, or reached out. Carolyn didn't frame this accusation with anger or judgment; she simply said that—for whatever reason—Tony lost touch with his daughter.

Word came back from Texas to Tony and Jo (after Tony reconnected), as Adrianne hit her prime teen years, that she hated—utterly despised—going to school. For some reason, Adrianne had developed a profound detestation for anything having to do with school; she did everything she could to get out of it.

But then something else happened. Adrianne's behavior went from out of control to borderline psychotic and criminal. More than just skipping school, she began acting out. Part of it centered around her voracious appetite for sex.

The questions became: Why? Where was this behavior rooted?

"In my opinion," Tony said, ". . . she had accused her stepfather there of sexual assault, and I could tell

Adrianne wanted to get away from there because of that."

Adrianne's stepfather was soon indicted by a grand jury, and he was formally charged with sexual assault and indecency with a child.

"I believed her one hundred percent," Gregg County prosecutor Stacey Brownlee told reporter Barb Ickes years later. "I never doubted her story for one second."

The accusations by Adrianne opened up an investigation into what was going on inside Adrianne's home, which led to additional allegations of neglect and abuse. Terry Roach, a sergeant with the White Oak, Texas, Police Department (WOPD) handling the case, found many problems with the way in which Adrianne was being raised. For one, Carolyn Franco had been indicted on charges of threatening to burn down the house of a woman in Texas, charges that stemmed from the sexual molestation allegations Adrianne had made against her stepfather. The woman Carolyn threatened had supposedly tape-recorded Carolyn in the act.

"There's just so much hatred on those tapes," Prosecutor Brownlee told Ickes. "You listen to it for a while and you just want to throw up."

The one thing that wasn't on the tapes, according to Carolyn, was that spurious threat Carolyn had allegedly made of burning down the woman's house.

So the charges were dropped.

"You have to understand Adrianne at this time," Carolyn later told me. "She's lying about everything. She called the state and told them I was beating on her. Then turned around and admitted she had lied because she was mad at me. The night before she had [said she was sexually abused], she had gotten into trouble. There was a birthday party she was supposed to be going to. She got a little smart mouth with me, and David (Franco) told her she was grounded and she couldn't go. She got really angry at him, screaming, yelling, and really belligerent, and turned around the next day and told this (sexual assault) story. She had a history of making things up when she was mad at people."

But it was the detail in the accusations themselves that made many believe Adrianne.

"I didn't automatically *not* believe her," Carolyn added. "I was in shock. When they told me what the accusations was, I totally fell out. I could not even put my mind around it. She and [David] had always been real close. He had always . . . Well, he had grown up without a dad, and he knew how she felt. You have to understand. When my mom and Tony split up, and Tony went to prison, he stayed in contact with Adrianne. He said he was going to live closer to Adrianne when he was paroled. But when he got out, that was the last time we heard from him. . . . He never called her. He never sent a birthday card. When things started to happen with Adrianne, we had to find Tony on the Internet."

With her life heading in a complete downward spiral in Texas, near the fall of 2003, it was decided that Adrianne should move to East Moline and live with her father and his new wife for a while. Jo took the call from Carolyn.

"Adrianne's been taken out of our home," Carolyn explained. "Could you two take her?"

The state had stepped in and was ready to take Adrianne away from Carolyn for good.

Not thrilled about the idea of having Adrianne come to live in Illinois with them, Jo said she'd talk to Tony about it.

The next day, Jo called the Department of Family

Services in Texas to inquire about Adrianne. They told Jo that Adrianne had made a sexual molestation accusation against her stepfather, and said Carolyn had "threatened to kill her [Adrianne]." So the state had stepped in and had taken Adrianne out of the home and placed her in foster care while the investigation was going on.

That night, Jo talked it over with Tony.

"I don't want Adrianne here," Jo said. There had been an indication that Adrianne had lied about "the whole thing," Jo explained. "I had two grown boys living at home and going to college. Tony was still on parole. What if she accused one of my boys of something? If she accused them, I would have left Tony. It would have destroyed my marriage."

Tony was firm, though. "I adopted Adrianne. I *have* to take her."

Jo relented.

Maybe Tony and Jo, in offering Adrianne a stable environment, could straighten her out. It was late 2003. Adrianne had just turned fourteen. Jo had planned a trip to Little Rock, Arkansas, to visit Tony's sisters. She called and told Carolyn she'd meet up with her and Adrianne there.

It was a quiet ride back to Illinois. Yet, Adrianne was holding on to some rather shocking news.

"I think I'm pregnant," Adrianne said when she arrived.

Tony had been in the hospital on the night Adrianne was born. She was such a tiny baby, purple, red, shiny, and underweight. Tony had dubbed her Lil' Bit that night. How time could change your life. Here was his precious Lil' Bit, showing up with her bags, a trail of sexual abuse, drinking, drugging, and more problems at home than most kids endured in a lifetime, telling the only man she knew as a father that she was pregnant. Such a damn vicious circle, an unbroken cycle: Adrianne's mother had Adrianne when she was sixteen. Now Adrianne, just shy of that same age, was apparently following in her biological mother's footsteps.

As it was, Tony had not seen Adrianne for several years. Now this.

Thanks a lot, Tony thought, adding, *They send me this fourteen-year-old pregnant girl. Unbelievable.*

15

After she got settled in East Moline, Adrianne went for a checkup.

Turned out she wasn't pregnant, after all.

"Thank God," Tony said. One less thing to deal with.

Still, he called Adrianne's mother.

"Why in the heck don't you have this kid on birth control?"

It was clear that although she was not going to have a baby, Adrianne was having casual sex whenever she felt like it.

"I can't make her do nothing," Carolyn told Tony.

"Well, shoot, I can."

Tony went to Adrianne. "You've got two choices. You can go on the shot, I ain't gonna remind you to take a pill every day. Or you can stay home." Tony meant in the house. All the time. Adrianne, in refusing birth control, would confine herself to the four walls of Tony and Jo's ranch. She would not be able to go out.

At all.

What a choice.

"She didn't argue none," Tony recalled. "And that

was the end of that 'I think I'm pregnant' problem, you know."

Meanwhile, Jo stood behind the scenes, scared Adrianne might one day accuse one of her twins of the same thing that she had alleged against her stepfather back in Texas. As Jo saw it, Adrianne was volatile. Unpredictable and on the edge, always, of being one step away from making that major mistake in her life no one could fix.

Eggshells.

Broken glass.

Jo wanted no part of it.

Tony and Jo enrolled Adrianne at Glenview Middle School.

"Adrianne hated homework," Jo explained. "We went to her first parent/teacher conference and found out she was getting straight zeroes. She wasn't doing her homework. So we bought her an assignment book and her teachers wrote out her homework."

Every night was a battle. Tony and Jo made Adrianne sit down and do her homework in front of them. Adrianne had to read a certain amount of pages per night in this one particular book. There was a night when Jo took out the book and placed it on the counter. Tony, the strict disciplinarian who cut no corners when speaking to his daughter, said, "Read!"

"I don't want to do my fucking homework," Adrianne shot back.

A fight between the two brazen personalities—dad and daughter—broke out. Soon Adrianne and Tony were in each other's faces.

Jo was able to restrain Adrianne on her bed, telling Tony, "Get out of here. . . . Just stop yelling at her."

Chaos.

Exactly what Jo was afraid of.

Looking back on it all, Jo recalled, "I wanted Adrianne to go home so bad. I would try thinking of all kinds of ways to get her to go back."

Things got a bit better, however, before they got a whole bunch worse.

By May, and into June 2004, Jo and Tony, working with Adrianne, were able to get her grades up to D's.

There was one afternoon when Jo went to the school to check on Adrianne's progress. She and Adrianne met inside the principal's office.

"Her math grade is a D," the principal said.

Adrianne and Jo looked at each other. Hugged. Jumped up and down.

Not long after, Adrianne graduated middle school.

Still, with all the growth she had made, Adrianne had a strong desire to go back to Texas. She came out one day and said, "I want to go home. I miss my friends." There was pain in her voice—certainly for the loss of those friendships in Texas that meant something to her—but also for facing the feeling of not being wanted. Adrianne had been shuffled around all her life, from one parent to the next, then into foster care. It's safe to say that she had an internal alarm system, one that picked up on Jo not entirely wanting her there. She could sense Jo's trepidation and resentment and wanted no part of it.

Tony called Carolyn.

"Adrianne don't like it here. We're sending her back."

Carolyn said, "Yes. Absolutely."

Adrianne went back to Texas.

"She was so confused by her family," Prosecutor Brownlee later told Barb Ickes, talking about Adrianne's life in Texas. "They were putting so much pressure on her."

Adrianne walked back into her life in Texas and recanted her story of the sexual abuse allegations. She said it never happened, that she made it all up.

Despite Adrianne having pulled back on the allegations against her stepfather, Brownlee pursued the case, anyway. Her problem, though, was that without a witness, she had no case. After moving back home, Adrianne took it a step further and wrote a letter to the judge overseeing the case, part of which read: *I have told an outrageous story that is not true. I didn't think it would go this far.*

The charges against her stepfather were dismissed.

This time, Adrianne stayed in Texas for about four months before things took a turn. Near October 2004, Carolyn called Tony. Adrianne had turned sixteen on September 12.

"I'm having problems with her again. She's talkin' 'bout running away and stuff. She said something about wanting to go live with a friend of hers."

That wasn't the half of it. Adrianne had driven her bike in the pouring rain a distance of nearly thirty miles to a boyfriend's house, just so she could "get away from her mother," the boy's mother later said. Adrianne wanted to move in with the boy's family. She was also best friends with his sister.

This wasn't the only family she had expressed a desire to live with, near this period.

Again, no one wanted Adrianne.

It is clear from the reports Adrianne's psychiatrist generated during these months that Carolyn and Adrianne had a love-hate relationship they both thrived on and needed. There was codependency on both their parts. When Adrianne was with her mother, there always came a time when she wanted nothing more than to leave. When she was away from Carolyn, Adrianne craved that internal motherly affection only Carolyn could give to her.

Tony rolled his eyes as Carolyn explained the latest dilemma. *Here we go again. . . .*

Finally, after some conversation, Tony said, "Let me call her, Carolyn, and see what's up."

Adrianne sounded confused, frustrated, and fed up with life in general when Tony got her on the phone. Tony put on his stern father's voice. "Hey, listen, you can't just go stay with a friend of yours. You're only sixteen! You can't just go and do that."

Part of what drove Adrianne's desire to go live with anyone that would take her in, according to friends in Texas, was that Carolyn demanded she go back to live with Tony and Joanne. And Adrianne didn't want to. She couldn't stand to be away from her life in Texas.

But Adrianne never argued with Tony, he said. "She always showed me that respect. I told her it just wasn't right for her to be goin' an' piling up in somebody else's house." As he spoke to Adrianne, it sounded to Tony that she was not getting along with Carolyn. "How 'bout you done come back up here to Illinois?" Tony asked. "I am not going to let you go live in no streets." He pictured Adrianne hopping from friend to friend, staying a few days here, a few there. In that world, her life would fall apart quickly. There was a sense that she would be pregnant and on state assistance inside a few years.

Adrianne thought about it. How could she deny her father's advice?

"Okay," she said. "I'll do that."

Was Adrianne serious, or was she telling her father what he wanted to hear?

A few days after Adrianne and Tony spoke, as plans were made for Adrianne to move back north to East Moline, Carolyn called.

"You can send her that plane ticket," Carolyn said, "but Adrianne said that if you make her come back up there, she's gonna get off the plane in Atlanta"—where she was scheduled to make a connecting flight—"and no one will ever see her again."

"I understand," Tony said. "You just put her on the plane."

Tony knew Adrianne. He had no worries whatsoever that she was going to show up in East Moline. "She was just telling Carolyn that," Tony recalled. "It was a game she played."

Just to be certain, however, Tony phoned his daughter.

"Hey there, you listen to me. I am going to send you a plane ticket. You had better be honest with me. Are you comin' all the way here?"

"Yeah."

"That's all I need to know, Adrianne."

A couple of days after that telephone conversation, Adrianne arrived in East Moline, Illinois, on schedule, for a second time in a little over a year.

It was the fall of 2004. She was sixteen. Within three months, Adrianne Reynolds would turn up missing.

16

Sarah Kolb's mother called the EMPD at some point during the first four days of Adrianne's disappearance. Kathryn "Kathy" Klauer knew the cops had been asking her daughter questions, and Sarah had been the last person, along with Cory Gregory, to be with Adrianne.

Kathryn told police she had some information to share.

She didn't say from whom, but the information she had been given was that Adrianne "was supposedly going to babysit . . . sometime this past week[end]."

Which, by itself, didn't seem so suspicious.

"But what was odd," Kathryn Klauer relayed to cops, "was that the male [she was doing the babysitting job for] is twenty-six years old. . . ."

Ten years Adrianne's senior. Enough to worry any parent.

Cops already had heard that Adrianne had a "crush" on this same guy, with whom she worked at Checkers.

Could they have run away together?

The EMPD called the AirTran airways at Quad City International Airport. Adrianne had flown AirTran in the past. They wanted to see if that guy (or Adrianne) had taken a flight via AirTran at any time recently.

"Last time she flew with us," a ticket manager said, "was in the fall of 2003. She flew from Dallas to Moline."

After calling additional airlines, it was clear that if Adrianne had flown out of the QC alone or with the guy at Checkers she'd had a crush on, she had not left from Quad City International Airport.

Another lead.

Another dead end.

17

The EMPD located three boys Adrianne had had close contact with over the past month. The idea was that any one of them could have helped her run away. Without money, a change of clothes, or a ride, Adrianne would have needed help. As much as Tony and Jo didn't want to think she had taken off, there was still the possibility that Adrianne had disappeared because that was what she wanted to do.

"I have not seen or heard from her," said one male student, a kid from school Adrianne hung around with frequently.

"Harboring a runaway," the cop warned, "is a crime."

The boy said he understood.

Another friend said he had not seen or spoken to Adrianne in two weeks, adding, "She does like to fool around, though. Party a lot. Use drugs."

"That all?"

"She has problems with depression."

Finally they got ahold of that twenty-six-year-old guy Adrianne had worked with at Checkers—the man she supposedly had a crush on.

"Sure," he said, "she was supposed to babysit for my kids." He explained that Adrianne was scheduled to watch the kids on that Saturday, the day after she went missing. "I have not seen or heard from her lately, however."

And so whatever stone the EMPD turned over, it appeared another obstacle or unanswered question rose from out of the dirt. As much as the EMPD was in need of leads, however, and still asking questions of many people, a blurry picture of what had happened to Adrianne Reynolds was slowly coming into focus.

Late Sunday evening, January 23, 2004, Nate Gaudet called Jill Hiers.

"Pick me up," Nate said to his girlfriend. "I'm at Cory's."

Jill said she couldn't.

During several phone calls, Nate pleaded, "I need a ride!"

He sounded desperate.

Jill got a feeling something was up.

After she pulled up to Cory's house, Jill watched Nate walk out. He was wearing that trench coat and carrying a black-and-red book bag. He looked withdrawn. Out of it. Depressed. Solemn.

In another world.

Nate placed the book bag in the backseat and told Jill to drive.

"Take me to my grandmother's house," Nate explained on the way. Nate's grandparents' house was out in the country. He lived there, when he wasn't staying at the party house in Rock Island.

When they got to the house, Nate told Jill to wait

downstairs in the kitchen for him after they walked in. He needed to do something in the basement.

"I'll be right back."

Nate grabbed the book bag and headed toward the house.

Jill followed.

When they arrived at the back door, Nate let Jill enter first.

Inside, Nate headed down into the basement, reminding Jill one more time to wait.

Inside the kitchen, just off to the left of the back door, Nate's mother and grandmother sat at the kitchen table with Nate's ten-year-old sister and played Scrabble.

Jill walked over.

When Nate returned, he stood next to his girlfriend.

"You two want to play?" Nate's mother asked them.

"No," they both said.

"I hate those things," Nate's mother said, pointing out Nate's strange and scary contact lenses.

Jill said, "I know—me, too."

Nate took off into his room without saying anything more.

Jill leaned down and whispered into Nate's mother's ear: "He's high."

Then she walked into Nate's bedroom.

What in the heck was going on with Nate all of a sudden? Jill wondered. What was he up to? He had been acting strange all weekend, Jill noticed. They had been fighting more than usual.

Nate was on the bed. He appeared to be crying, Jill realized.

"What the fuck is going on?" she asked.

Nate wouldn't say.

"He just became very emotional," Jill later told police.

The EMPD called Carolyn Franco, down in Texas, on Monday morning. They wanted to know if she had any news to share, or if she could shed some light on the situation.

"I haven't seen or heard from her," Carolyn said. "Something must have happened to Adrianne. . . ."

"What would make you say that?"

Carolyn reiterated what Tony had been saying all along: Adrianne had never picked up her paycheck. She had no clothing with her. She would have never left home without a change of clothes. And certainly not without her paycheck. Adrianne knew the value of money on the streets.

"Anything else?"

"Adrianne had a drug/alcohol problem when she was twelve," Carolyn said. "She was unhappy in Illinois. That I know."

What Tony and Jo were not being told—as Monday evening, January 24, 2005, fell over the Quad Cities— was that as much as the EMPD had kept quiet about what they were doing behind the scenes, they were working diligently and, together with the Illinois State Police (ISP), had started to make some progress.

What was shaping up, however, was not the news Tony had wanted to hear.

Jo called one of the officers she had been in contact with throughout the weekend. "Can you tell us *anything*?"

"Yeah, we're trying to get a search warrant for Sarah

Kolb's car, but the state's attorney's office won't give it to us."

What? A search warrant for Sarah's . . . ?

This sent the butterflies in Jo's stomach into a frenzy. *Why a search warrant? What are they looking for?*

"Why?" Jo pressed.

"Well, we know there was a fight in Sarah's car." According to Jo, the cop explained that they had interviewed Sean McKittrick, who had claimed to be Sarah's boyfriend. He also said he was in the car with Adrianne, Sarah, and Cory Gregory on that early afternoon when Adrianne disappeared. Sean had reported that when Sarah and Adrianne started yelling back and forth and fighting, he got out of the car, slammed the door, and walked back to school.

They had interviewed every McDonald's employee working on that Friday afternoon, and not one person had reported seeing Adrianne or Sarah's red car. Not that any of them would recall such a thing all that easily, suffice it to say, as busy as McDonald's was on any given day. But if Adrianne had had her teeth knocked out and was bleeding, as Sarah herself had proclaimed, the theory was that she would have gone into the restaurant to clean up before walking home. Or risk waltzing into her house with blood all over her face and several teeth missing.

Tony had also heard—which he had passed along to the EMPD earlier—that Sarah and Cory had devised some "plan on being nice to Adrianne to get her into Sarah's car." The EMPD, in turn, had located the source of the information and interviewed the girl.

Turned out she was a neighbor of Cory's who sometimes hung around with the Juggalo crowd. She told police that Sean McKittrick had knocked on her door late Friday afternoon, January 21, and asked to come in. He appeared upset and pissed off. He explained how he had jumped out of Sarah's car in a huff at the local Taco Bell because Sarah and Adrianne were fighting, and he kept telling them to stop, but neither would listen.

"Sean told me," the source further explained to police, "that Sarah and Cory tricked Adrianne into getting into Sarah's car with them. They took her to the Taco Bell . . . [and] they argued . . . and Sarah grabbed Adrianne by the hair. Sean said he told her to stop it, but Sarah told him to get out if he didn't like it. He called Sarah from my house to ask her if everything was okay. Sarah told him she and Adrianne had made up."

A detective found Sean. Spoke to him. He backed up what this new source claimed. Without being given any details, Sean told the same story, in fact.

That night, just to be sure, the EMPD gave Sean a polygraph.

Confusing matters, however, he failed part of it.

The EMPD knew something was up—the Taco Bell/ McDonald's story was not adding up. Investigators had a feeling Sarah was lying about a few things, which prompted the question: why would Sarah Kolb lie if she *didn't* have anything to hide?

On that afternoon, the EMPD was able to get Sarah, with her mother, to come into the EMPD station house for an interview. But there was someone else with them, a man whose presence put another spin on the investigation. Sarah Kolb was now lawyered up. His name, Bob Rillie.

Why did Sarah Kolb need a lawyer?

"We agree to this interview," Rillie said, eyeing both investigators, "only if no questions are asked about the fight—or a direct question asking if Sarah killed Adrianne."

The detectives running the interview looked at each other.

A video camera recorded the interview. Sarah sat and told the same story she had over the past few days, adding how she knew a girl who worked at McDonald's and was there that day, and had also "possibly seen Adrianne enter the restaurant."

"Was Adrianne in good physical condition when she left your vehicle?"

"Yes," Sarah said.

"Would you consent to a polygraph?"

Sarah and her mother waited a beat.

Then they shook their heads.

"No," Sarah and her mother said at the same time.

18

Jo and Tony had no choice but to go to bed on Monday night without knowing where Adrianne was, or what might have happened to her.

"At this point, we're back to thinking she's a runaway," Jo explained.

The Natalee Holloway syndrome: She's alive. She's dead.

Alive.

Dead.

Adrianne's parents had no idea how they were feeling anymore because they were numb. Each hour that passed brought with it another theory or thought. An impulse. An *aha* moment. Then more questions. Confusion. Finally . . . pain.

It was maddening.

On Tuesday morning, a day anyone connected to the case would not soon forget, Tony got up and went to work. Jo had Tuesdays off, as a normal course of her workweek.

Not long after Tony left, the EMPD called the house.

"Can you bring your computer down here?" an investigator asked Jo.

Now they were getting somewhere. There was obviously a break.

Jo got that sick feeling back in her stomach as the investigator explained how they needed to go through the computer and find out if there was any communication between Adrianne and Sarah at all over the past week, month, or before Christmas the previous year.

Jo packaged the computer and drove it down to the police station. She and Tony had been "very strict" with Adrianne regarding use of the computer. "I didn't allow her on the computer unless I was home."

Adrianne herself talked about this to her psychologist, saying she was watched so closely on the family PC, it got to the point where it wasn't worth using it anymore. That said, however, as any parent knows, unless you stand over the shoulder of your child and watch every mouse click and tap of the keyboard, you could be standing in the same room while she "chats" with someone you don't want her to be.

Sarah Kolb, though, was not on that list of people Tony and Jo did not want Adrianne communicating with via the computer.

"I didn't allow her in the chat rooms," Jo recalled.

While she was down at the EMPD, Jo found out that the ISP had been called into the investigation on a more hands-on basis. This, of course, worried her. Things were damn serious if the state police were involved.

"Can [the state police] go out and search Adrianne's room?" a cop asked Jo. Two ISP detectives were ready to drive out to the house right away.

Jo said, "Yes, of course." She had that *what's going on?* look about her face.

"Ma'am, we're looking for any connection or communication between Adrianne and Sarah."

Jo understood, but she wondered why.

"We want you to know that Sarah and Cory are refusing to take a polygraph test."

The EMPD had reached out to Cory and asked him the same set of questions as they had Sarah—and they got, basically, the same answers.

A lump developed in Jo's throat. *What is going on here?* One of the questions that kept popping up in Jo's mind as she heard that lie detector tests were being offered and refused became: *Why aren't they asking me and Tony to take a test? My boys? Neighbors? Known pedophiles?*

Must mean they know something they're not telling.

Jo got herself together and called Tony, but she gave him only certain details. Why worry the guy when he was two hundred miles from home. It would only cause unneeded stress.

Smart move.

With information coming in gradually, Jo felt Adrianne might not be coming home. Such a seesaw of emotions. Such a litany of situations to consider.

Alive. Dead.

To Jo, it still didn't feel as if Adrianne was *not* ever going to come home. It was just that she was, well, gone. Like they had dropped her off at the airport and she had gotten on a plane and traveled. But had not reached her destination yet.

Limbo.

This was the beginning of that "closure" everyone involved in these types of situations will eventually talk about.

Answers become imperative to one's sanity. Without them, a parent is left in a state of perpetual grief and mourning. It's like leaving a movie ten minutes before it's over: You will wonder. You will ask yourself questions. You ultimately will write your own ending.

The two detectives doing most of the footwork, Sergeants Timothy "Tim" Steines and Mike Britt, went over to interview Cory Gregory's neighbor Clair O'Brien (pseudonym) on January 25, 2005, at 11:34 A.M. They figured Clair knew a lot more about the case than they had thought previously.

While they were driving up to Clair's house, who came walking out the door?

None other than Cory Gregory himself.

He was carrying a CD.

"Cory," one of the cops said, nodding. "How are you?"

Cory appeared very nervous at the sight of both detectives as they greeted him, a report detailed.

As Cory walked home, the detectives found Clair and she let them into her home. As they got settled inside the house, Clair's doorbell rang.

Was it Cory?

Clair said, "Yeah?"

"Are they cops, [Clair]?"

"Yes."

Cory didn't say anything more. He turned and walked back toward his house.

Clair recalled exactly what she had told the other cops the previous night, adding that Sean McKittrick "had lived with Cory and was basically a homeless kid otherwise."

Which begged the question: was Sean more involved than he had let on?

One of the things Sean had told Clair, which she explained in great detail to Steines and Britt, was that Sarah had become upset at Adrianne because she found out that Cory and Adrianne were "passing love notes." Another piece of information Clair relayed—that had not been known until then—was that Cory's father, Bert Gregory, had advised Cory not to have any additional contact with Sarah.

They asked about Cory and what he was doing at her house before they arrived.

"Strange," Clair said. "He came over here to use my phone to call Sarah. Then he took it and went upstairs to talk privately."

"Why is that odd?"

"He's never done it before. They've never hid their conversations from me. I tried to ask him about what happened Friday . . . but he only told me the same story."

The fight . . . McDonald's . . . the last time they saw Adrianne.

Near lunchtime, ISP special agent Chad Brodersen, along with Special Agent Chris Endress, caught up with Brian Engle, Sarah Kolb's grandfather, at the Treasure Hunt Antique Shop in Aledo, Illinois. Aledo is about an hour south of East Moline on Route 67. It's a quiet ride through the country: farms, dirt roads, roadside diners, and vegetable stands. That sort of thing.

Brian and his wife, Mary, owned a farm with some land in the same general region, and Sarah, along with her mother, made the drive out to visit them from time to time. In fact, Brian Engle said, Sarah was out at the farm on Friday night, January 21. But not with her mother. This time, she was with Cory Gregory, he said. But that was not the first time Brian had seen his granddaughter that day.

It was somewhere between 4:50 and 5:00 P.M., Brian recalled, when he first ran into Sarah.

"She was driving her red Geo Prizm." Brian spotted Sarah at the intersection of Millersburg Road and Route 17. He was heading to his farm; Sarah was driving in the opposite direction, toward Aledo.

"I just assumed she must have been coming from my house," he said, "after visiting with her grandmother." (The Engle house and farm are not on the same property.)

It was Mary's birthday. Why wouldn't her granddaughter be out there saying hello?

"Did you see her anywhere else on that night?" one of the agents asked.

Brian hesitated, a report of the conversation noted, as if he didn't want to answer the question.

"What is it?" the agent asked.

Brian looked down at the ground. Then: "I saw her parked on the back side of the farm, later on that night."

"Explain. . . ."

Brian said it was strange because a person had to leave the road to get out to that section of the farm where he saw Sarah's car. Off-road driving in a Geo Prizm was not recommended by the manufacturer—that's for sure.

"Would you know of any legitimate reason why Sarah would be driving her car off the road onto the back of the farm?" one of the agents asked.

"I do not know what she was doing out there," Brian answered.

"Could we have your consent to search the farm?" Brodersen asked. The implication was implicit in the agent's tone: they could do this easily, without any trouble, or go through a judge.

But a search was going to be conducted, one way or another.

"I have a nephew . . . who is a former police officer," Brian said. "He checked out that area already."

"We're talking about a detailed search, Mr. Engle, of the *entire* property."

"I have over one hundred sixty acres, sir. It would be impossible for you to conduct a detailed search alone."

"We could bring whatever resources were necessary, Mr. Engle. We need your permission first, however."

Brian thought about it. He wasn't thrilled with the idea of allowing the Illinois State Police to go through his entire farm, acre by acre, but he said he'd sign the waiver.

Special Agent Brodersen explained that they'd be heading out there at once. It would help if Engle followed.

Brian Engle said he'd meet them. He had a few more things he wanted to share, now that he had thought about it, regarding what had happened that night.

19

Jo was at home on Monday afternoon. Alone. Waiting for any news that might come in. She had Adrianne's favorite teddy bear braced against her chest, hugging it tightly, as the ISP searched Adrianne's room behind her. It was clear they knew a hell of a lot more than they were sharing.

Jo was cool with that. A tragedy coming in little by little was okay.

Good news all at once; bad news in spurts.

It helped numb the pain.

Cushion the blow.

Cops don't drop painful bombshells on family members as a case is unfolding, even if they know the ultimate outcome. Police give them time to take things in, bits and pieces, gradually.

After a time, the detectives searching Adrianne's room came out with several items. Papers, mainly. Notes. Letters. Address book.

One of the cops sat down next to Jo. He must have picked up on what she was going through, how she was feeling.

Was there any other way to put this?

"Listen," he said as Jo stared at him, "sometimes . . . you know, sometimes they don't come home alive."

Jo was floored by this comment. What was he trying to say? *Spit it out, man. Tell me.*

"Yeah . . . I guess" was all Jo could manage. She wanted to run, she said. Scream. Curl up in a ball. Roll away.

"We're hoping to have this case wrapped up real soon."

Jo shook her head and looked at both detectives.

One of them said, "Somebody's likely going to be going to prison for a long time."

"Is someone hiding her out?" Jo still wasn't sold on the idea that Adrianne was dead. "Could they go to prison for a long time for that?"

"Sure, they could." There wasn't much left to say. "We'll be in touch soon, okay, Mrs. Reynolds," one of the detectives said as they left.

Still believing Adrianne was alive and hiding out somewhere, Jo called Adrianne's work and told her boss, "If someone comes down there to pick her check up, do not give it to them. Call the police."

"Will do."

Somewhat panicked, not knowing what to think, Jo called the EMPD and told the officer in charge, "If you find Adrianne's body, *please* don't call Tony. Allow him to come home first." She didn't want Tony to have to drive all the way home from his shift with the burden of death on his shoulders.

This damn roller-coaster ride. Jo hated it. Wished it would stop.

Tony made it home a few hours later. They sat together and waited—hoping like heck Adrianne was going to call and say she had run away. Or maybe she'd even walk through the door. It's a funny thing how hope has a way of always hovering there in the background, even when one's gut says it's over. It was hope keeping Tony in check, stopping him from driving over to Sarah's or Cory's and grabbing those kids by the neck and shaking them until they coughed up where the hell his daughter was being hidden. Hope kept Tony from a breakdown. Hope stopped Tony from driving down to the EMPD and demanding to know what the hell was going on. It was there in that possibility—small as it was—that Adrianne could walk through the door and Tony could erupt into *Where the* hell *have you been?*

Hope, indeed, is what keeps most people from acting irrationally at times when the situation calls for it.

Hope keeps emotions teetering on the balance between sanity and insanity.

Hope allows people to go forward in the face of tragedy.

Jo called some friends and family and explained the latest developments.

Tony said he was driving down to those apartments nearby to have a look around again.

"Someone's got her! I know it."

It was all he could do not to knock on every single door.

20

Special Agent Chad Brodersen was escorted around Brian and Mary Engle's farm by Brian Engle and a family member who had shown up at the family's antique shop while Brian was answering questions. It was late afternoon now, January 25, Tuesday, the sun tucking itself behind the countryside, an orange ball of fuzzy fire getting ready to disappear for another night.

Agent Brodersen wanted to begin the search at the spot where Brian had seen Sarah. There would be a team of investigators and crime scene techs coming out to the farm, but for now, Brodersen, Brian, and Brian's nephew were the only ones out there.

The area of Brodersen's focus was secluded, about a half mile off the main drag (135th Street), set atop a steep grade near a couple of abandoned vehicles. What farm worth its salt doesn't harbor the rusted carcasses of a couple of old cars and trucks perched up on cinder blocks, weeds growing crazily around, the windows smashed out, varmints of every type living inside.

Around where Brodersen and the Engles walked,

there were several brush piles *concealed within several acres of thick timbers,* Brodersen's report noted.

This was the sticks, as they say back East. Acres upon acres of what some call "God's country."

Woods surrounded by flatland.

By now, Brian Engle had told Special Agent Brodersen that Sarah was with Cory Gregory on that night he saw her car on the farm.

Interesting.

As they walked, Brodersen asked Brian, "Do you think maybe Sarah and Cory were 'parking' out here?" He meant like on lovers' lane, getting their groove on.

Brian Engle quickly shook his head no. "Not a chance."

"Why not?"

"They're both gay!"

"Okay."

"They were probably smoking."

"This is quite a distance from the road and your farmhouse to sneak a smoke."

It was near 4:00 P.M. by the time Brodersen was told that the Mercer County Sheriff's Office (MCSO), along with other agents from the ISP, were going to be part of the search. The troops were on their way.

As Brodersen and Brian walked, Brodersen asked Brian to go through one more time how he saw Sarah and Cory, using the landscape they were standing on as a model to explain that night.

Brian talked about how he was feeding his cattle near 7:00 P.M. when he noticed a car parked across the field.

He pointed.

Then, he explained, he got into his pickup, shut off the lights, and began driving toward the car.

"When I got to it, I saw this small red car speed off with its lights out. I followed the car north on 135th Street and was able to copy the license plate number."

He went back to feeding the cattle, telling himself that he'd call the police if he found anything missing or any part of the farm vandalized.

After feeding his cows, Brian returned home to find the same red car parked in his driveway. The license plate matched his notes.

Sarah!

Brian got out of his truck and tossed his hat on the seat. He walked inside the farmhouse.

Cory and Sarah were sitting there.

As soon as Brian opened the door, Sarah said, "Grandpa, you scared the hell out of me!"

"Why did you run off?"

"I was scared," Sarah said.

"I wrote your plate down and gave it to the cops."

Grandpa Engle was playing a game with his grand-daughter. He had never done that.

Cory looked at Sarah, and Sarah at Cory. "Her mouth dropped," Brian said later.

He then left the room.

"This was the first time," Brian told Brodersen, "that I ever recall Sarah coming out here to visit us *without* her mother."

As they waited for the other investigators, Brodersen and Brian continued talking about Sarah and the past weekend. Brian explained that his wife, Mary, had told him she thought Sarah was "the last person to be seen with the missing girl," Adrianne something. In almost the same breath, Mary had said, "Brian, Sarah is in trouble."

Brian said he had become concerned, after adding up all of the circumstances, and then went to check on his safe, where he kept his guns. He noticed the dial had been turned, but that no one had gotten inside.

"She's made a lot of positive changes in the last three months," Brian Engle said of his granddaughter. "Sarah had removed all of her body jewelry, colored her hair back to its natural color, and she even started bathing again. She's always been weird."

As the interview concluded, the search team arrived.

21

Somehow, perhaps by God's grace, or maybe pure emotional exhaustion, Jo and Tony managed to go downstairs, crawl into bed, and fall asleep on the night of January 25, 2005. They didn't know it, of course, but that search out at the Engle farm had yielded some answers—and more questions—into the investigation surrounding Adrianne's disappearance.

At 2:00 A.M., now January 26, the Wednesday after Adrianne vanished, Jo rustled around in bed, trying to find a few winks. Tony was sound asleep next to her. Then Jo thought she heard the telephone upstairs in the kitchen ringing.

So she got up to make sure.

And as she did, there was that sinking, sick feeling: nobody calls in the middle of the night with good news.

Yet, in this case, it just might be that Adrianne was ready to come home.

Jo put on her bathrobe and hurried upstairs.

Maybe they found her.

"Hey . . . we're at your front door."

It was the police. They were calling from a cell phone

outside on the front stoop, a little over twenty yards from where Jo was standing, holding the phone, inside her kitchen.

Jo hung up. She stood for a moment in the kitchen, taking in the silence of the night. Bracing herself, she headed for the front door.

22

There is no silver lining in the news that a child has been found murdered. There is no way to sugarcoat what are the most disturbing and painful words a parent will ever hear. There is no way to prepare for the unbelievable truth that a sixteen-year-old child, a precious little *girl* who never seemed to find a home, will not walk through the door again. Her family will never hear her voice. See her smile. Watch the rise and fall of her chest, listening to that cute nose whistle, as she sleeps.

A cop can only hope to catch the monsters responsible and bring *that* news to the family, too, at some point, but not right now.

After Jo opened the door, she stared at the two detectives standing before her. There was a gaze of despair and dread on their faces.

Right then, Jo knew Adrianne was gone. Nobody had to tell her. It was in the stillness of the early-morning hour.

She felt sick to her stomach.

"Is everyone here?" one of the detectives asked. "Are your sons home?"

There was a glimmer of hope there for a brief moment.

What, are they now going to accuse my sons of doing something to Adrianne?

"I wanted to run . . . ," Jo recalled. "Just run as far away as I could get."

Hug herself. Crawl into a corner. Hide from the world.

Tony was downstairs, still sleeping. He had no idea what was going on.

"Come in," Jo said. She started to shake. "Yes . . . yes . . . everyone is here. What's going on?"

Heading toward the back door of the Reynolds home, a breezeway led outside. Jo brought them into that area of the house.

"Tony's still downstairs sleeping," Jo said as they entered the small foyer. Then she stepped out of the enclosure and yelled, "Tony! Tony! Tony!" Her voice cracking, a pain, buried deep, emerging. "The police are here, Tony. Oh, my goodness."

Tony came running up the stairs in his shorts. Sleep crust still in his eyes.

"What—what is it?"

Tony was told to sit down.

"And as the detective was saying the words—that they had found Adrianne—I am telling myself that this really isn't happening," Jo recalled.

"In a park . . . ," the cop said, his best game face on.

Tony broke down. Bawled. Dropped his head into his hands.

Which kept Jo busy. She was determined to calm Tony down. Comfort him.

I cannot believe this. . . . This cannot be true.

"What happened? What happened?" Tony said out loud.

"Look, we found her body in a park and we arrested a girl."

Sarah.

"We don't want you to try to take the law into your own hands. We're going to see that justice is done."

Tony collected himself, best he could. A thousand questions, like inaudible whispers in his head, taking the place of any serenity he had left.

Jo called her brother.

A police chaplain arrived.

The detectives left the house. They had work to do. There was a bit of information they had not shared with Jo and Tony at this time, for whatever reason. It was the manner in which Adrianne had been murdered, and, more gruesomely, what her killer (or killers, they didn't say) had done to her *after* she had died.

She had been found in a park, the cops had said.

Not a farm. But a park.

How in the hell did Adrianne end up in a park?

At eleven o'clock that same morning, law enforcement held a press conference. Jo and Tony watched from their living room. It would be nice to get a few details about what had happened to Tony's baby girl. Thus far, the cops had been tight-lipped.

Friends, family, and even strangers stopped by the house to offer support. Jo and Tony had not slept all night. They were tired, upset, in a state of shock.

Definitely not prepared to hear what was coming next.

Carolyn Franco, Adrianne's biological mother, had made the trip up from Texas and was at the house, too.

It was the headline that startled them.

When the announcer said it, it was as if it didn't register.

According to what the news conference reported, Adrianne's murder was a buildup, beginning back during those three-plus months between the time Adrianne arrived in East Moline from Texas for the second time and the day she went missing. During this brief period, the complete story of how she had turned up dead, and—as that headline had so soberly broadcast—was *dismembered* into pieces and left in that park and another part of the state, unfolded in a way that is maybe all too common these days. A tragedy began for Adrianne Reynolds on the day she first walked into Black Hawk Outreach and met up with a group of kids with whom she never truly fit in.

PART II

"LIKE SLAUGHTERING SHEEP"

23

When Sarah Kolb was a freshman at Rock Island High School in 2002, she dated a junior, Danielle Mayor (pseudonym). The relationship was a bit rocky and tenuous because Danielle's mother did not like Sarah and did not want her daughter hanging with her, much less dating.

Sarah's reaction to Danielle after being confronted with this news said a lot about where her life was headed: "I cannot hang out with someone who can't stand up for themselves."

Before they broke up, while standing in the parking lot of the school one afternoon, Sarah talked about one of her favorite subjects.

Death.

"I wonder," Sarah said, according to what Danielle later told police, "what it would be like to murder someone, cut them up, bury their body in a park—and get away with it!"

Danielle didn't know how to react to such a statement. She was "freaked out," a report of the conversation explained, and probably glad to have Sarah out of her life not long after.

Asked to describe Sarah, Danielle gave cops one word: "Angry."

Sarah could snap at the simplest suggestion or comment. In 2003, a friend e-mailed Sarah and asked if she was "having sex" with another girl at school. Sarah was openly bisexual by then; there was no question about her sexuality or who she dated.

Sarah wrote back, threatening the girl, saying: You have it coming, bitch. . . . [I am going to] fucking cut your throat.

A short time later, another girl texted Sarah and asked the same question about the same girl, who was now in college and much older than the fifteen-year-old Sarah.

Sarah sent a message back, warning: I'm gonna climb in your window, slit your throat, and cut you to pieces.

When Sarah saw the same girl at school a day later, she grabbed her by the arm in the hallway. "Bitch, I'm going to kill you!"

Asked later about these incidents, the girl said, "Sarah had a split personality. . . . One minute, she could be normal. Furious the next."

Melissa Duggan (pseudonym) dated Sarah for a time during an early stretch of 2004. Sarah was impulsive when it came to reacting to what people said to her, Melissa later said.

"She could be verbally mean." Of course, it generally came on after Sarah didn't get her way. There was one night when Sarah told Melissa, "I want to marry you."

Melissa didn't know how to respond.

"I hate you. . . . I'll kill you," Sarah snapped after not getting the answer she desired.

Melissa's mother had cancer. "I hope you get cancer and die with your mother," Sarah said another time.

Then she apologized.

Then she said something else offensive and mean-spirited.

Back and forth. That was Sarah.

Alive. Dead.

According to a former coworker, Sarah had a fascination with dead bodies. There was one day when, while at work, Sarah went on about how being around the dead did not bother her. She had been desensitized to death.

"Why?" asked her coworker. How could Sarah know what it was like to be near a dead person?

"I saw [a relative] hang himself," Sarah explained.

As Sarah met and started hanging with the Juggalo crowd, she found a way to channel all of this bottled-up negative energy, which was perhaps one reason why she felt so at home inside the Juggalo world of darkness, blood and guts, and filthy, vile music. Sarah's mother had once filed a runaway report with the Milan Police Department (MPD), fearing that Sarah had taken off. When she went missing, Sarah could often be located in a park somewhere close by, hanging out, or walking in the woods. This was a time when Sarah had both her nostrils pierced with loop earrings, her hair dyed a dark ink black. She liked to wear bandanas around her head then, and also long trench coats she had decorated (or defiled, depending on who was asked).

Another popular Juggalo location Sarah gravitated toward with the QC Juggalo crowd was the Singing Bird Lodge, a center where families and park dwellers had cookouts and get-togethers, located inside the Black

Hawk Forest Nature Preserve in South Rock Island Township, just outside Rock Island. Police reports from the summer of 2004, not long after Sarah met and attached herself to Cory Gregory, described several instances where *20 to 30 JUVS in their teens . . . all dressed in black and [with] their faces painted* were reportedly causing problems inside the park and near the shelter. Most of the time, they were throwing rocks, screaming, and acting crazy, as kids, in groups, sometimes do. But there were other times when park patrons reported sightings of kids in large numbers surfing on the hoods of cars driving through the park's grassy areas and cars driving in circles in the grass, tearing up the park's lawn. Sometimes the kids were caught walking around the park in packs: *hitting garbage cans with bats and setting them on fire,* said one report.

There was also a group of Juggalos prone to hassling people in local parks, walking around and scaring those hanging out with their families, minding their own business. One of the last times Sarah was involved, a group of "JUVS," dressed down in baggy clothing and black-and-white face paint, stood around a large bonfire, tossing gasoline on the fire and kicking over garbage cans.

And yet even within this setting, which seemed to offer Sarah a way to vent her frustration and introverted feelings of rage, Sarah sought another outlet.

Near this time, not a week after she met Adrianne, Sarah turned to a friend one night while hanging out and expressed how much she liked Adrianne. She could see herself dating her, Sarah said. There was chemistry there between them. Sarah could feel it.

"I'm thinking of getting her name tattooed on my upper arm, near the shoulder," Sarah explained, pointing to the spot.

24

Beyond her explosive temper, Sarah Kolb also exhibited an almost cruel, evil, and domineering disposition that would emerge from time to time. In her writings and behavior as the fall of 2004 came, Sarah articulated a deep hatred for anyone she saw as a threat, adversary, rival, or beneath her on the food chain. At the same rate, though, Sarah was also very much afraid of sharing her innermost feelings—unless it involved her berating someone—with friends, family, or in a group setting. Her journal writing, however, was another story; this simple exercise that millions of kids do every day in school gave Sarah the opportunity to talk about who she was and what she truly thought of people.

Journaling in general, Sarah noted, was not for the person writing the journal (as in its therapeutic value); it was for "other people," she believed. As much as we all want to convince ourselves we're writing our deepest thoughts in some sort of cathartic Freudian analysis, what we're doing is revealing, Sarah pointed out quite astutely, *secrets [we] don't want to tell but . . . want everyone to know.*

Sarah felt the only "safe place" for a person's thoughts was inside his or her head. On October 6, 2004, about six weeks before she met Adrianne Reynolds, Sarah wrote that she was afraid people were taking her journal and reading it when she wasn't around. This—added to a growing list of additional anxieties she was experiencing at the time—bothered Sarah Kolb.

She wrote how she considered the Internet to be *the CB radio of the 90s,* while calling the home PC *the trailor* [sic] *park of the soul,* a *dangerous tool* when *in the hands of idiots.*

At times Sarah displayed her paranoia, noting at the end of the same entry that *self-imposed fascism* [would] *destroy man* because he would ultimately convince *himself he doesn't have to think anymore.*

A day after she wrote that rather critical entry, Sarah was back to being angry at the world, wondering if the people around her had been replaced by a group of imbeciles who had been beamed into her life only to irritate her. She felt everyone was driving her crazy. In response to those who were getting in her face and giving her problems, Sarah waxed violently about *slaughter[ing] them like fucking sheep.* She wanted to be left alone when angry. Why couldn't people stay out of her face? Not speak to her. Not touch her. Not look at her. Breathe on her. Smile at her. Even think about her. She was becoming frustrated because people were asking why she was so pissed off all the time. And all they were doing was shortening the wick burning inside her. She was desperate for some sort of relief from the agony of her mind.

Why?

So I don't hurt people, or myself. . . .

* * *

As Sarah was dealing with the torment inside her own head, Adrianne had just turned sixteen on September 12, 2004. She was still in Texas going through another dark period of her life, depressed and ready to pack it in. As an exercise, Adrianne sketched out her feelings one day. She was tired of the people in her life letting her down.

Why don't they care? she asked. *I'm tired of all this. I'm ready to sleep—sleep it all away.*

Adrianne hated ignorant people, yet made no mention specifically as to whom she was referring. She was "grieving for darkness." She was "tired" and in "pain." She wrote she *hoped for the best* but *longed for the worst.*

Part of Adrianne enjoyed the process of expressing her feelings on the page in the form of poetry and lyric writing. Yet, there was a certain tint of gloom—and certainly emotional pain—in everything she wrote. *I'm broken* was a familiar phrase Adrianne leaned on. *I don't feel right* was another. She missed people immensely, likely because her life had been, up to then, a series of people (whom she loved) being taken away from her, and she being taken away from those same people. This hole in her heart was replaced by the transparent pull of promiscuous sex. Adrianne filled the void with the love that anyone offered, in any form: whether it was genuine or a one-night promise in order to get her into bed, Adrianne thought it would help her feel better about her life and herself.

Near the middle of October, Adrianne penned a poem that was, sadly, a harbinger of what was to come:

Knocking at death's door,
Entering through hell's gates,
Better do something now,
Before it's too late.

Adrianne had a clever way of expressing her feelings: might be a sentence or two, a doodle, or three pages of scattered sentences with no literal meaning or connection. They all tell us something about the person behind the pen. In one, she wrote: *You said you couldn't stand to see my heart broken. . . . So when you broke it, did you close your eyes?* Another read, *Breaking my heart . . . ripping my soul.* Most of this centered around the boys who were bedding (and then letting) her down. Adrianne wanted love—and everything that came with it: commitment, respect, friendship, peace. All things, according to her own hand, she had never experienced.

Heading into Black Hawk Outreach that fall, meeting Sarah for the first time, Adrianne soon felt as though she might have just found what she had been looking for all along—that one person who understood how she felt, might one day love her unconditionally, and not let her down.

25

Sarah Kolb viewed any attention taken away from her as a personal attack and blow to her ego. Her girlfriend had just broken it off and was now seeing someone else, a rival Sarah viewed, in her words, as "my replacement." It was that insecurity and low self-esteem directing how Sarah felt, how she thought, with whom she socialized on a particular day, and on whom she would take out her repressed feelings of contentiousness. In Sarah's skewed view of her life, her girlfriend had left her because Sarah was worthless. Not because there was no love or she had no feelings for Sarah. This was just another in a series of bad things Sarah saw happening in her life, all of which she viewed as entirely her own fault. Sarah saw herself as worthless.

By October 18, 2004, Sarah had been put on a new set of medications to manage her feelings of suicide and fury. She was, truly, out of control. Her high-school life, for no apparent reason, had been consumed up to this point by chronic drug use, abusive lesbian relationships, aggressive and near-violent sex with males—"She liked to bite my neck while we had sex," said one male, "until it was bruised"—booze, cutting herself, fighting, and more anger than her delicate emotional state could handle. Still, all that being said, the medication they were now trying on Sarah had turned her into a "zombie," she described.

"I feel weird."

The drugs made her lazy and lethargic, as though she could sleep for "three . . . days." She questioned that maybe she *should* sleep more. Or, in a burst of inspiration and clarity, simply solve her *problems and move on with my life,* she wrote.

In one brief journal entry, Sarah talked about how her previous girlfriend had just up and decided one day to break up with her. She asked herself why she even bothered to care so much. She wondered what "happy" actually was and how she wasn't accomplishing anything in life. She had no job and no friends. What she had was *a shitty car with shitty grades.* All of it, she wrote, was an obvious indication of her life in general, which she referred to as *shitty shit.*

On October 20, Sarah was feeling a bit better about herself. It was her baby sister's one month birthday—something she took a bit of pride in, now being a big sister. Yet, as soon as she seemed to teeter on the verge of happiness, clinging to a modicum of light, Sarah was back in the darkness, chastising and blaming herself for the breakup with her last girlfriend, whom she could not seem to let go of. The breakup, she concluded, was the impetus for her being in such a traumatic psychotic state and on the periphery of suicide. She said she wanted to find her ex-girlfriend, run up, and kiss her. But she realized that if she did that, the girl would probably slap her across the face. Sarah mentioned how she couldn't seem to get over this particular girl, as though the former lover had some sort of magnetic pull on her emotions Sarah couldn't break free from. It was strange, too, Sarah thought. The girl wasn't pretty. On top of that, she had bad breath and was a drunk, not to mention she nagged Sarah about everything. On the other hand, Sarah thought, she did *make me laugh* and *feel good about myself.*

This was the type of lifestyle that mainly drove (or fed) Sarah's anger: any self-esteem she acquired from another human being became like a drug; she craved attention and love as much as Adrianne Reynolds did. Yet, the moment it was taken away from her, Sarah went into withdrawal, so to speak, and dealt with it vis-à-vis that internal, explosive rage that exposed itself every once in a while.

Two weeks later, as Adrianne was making preparations to move back to East Moline, Sarah was dreading the time she had spent at Black Hawk. She had been a student there since December 9, 2003. It was the beginning of November 2004, a dreary month of cold rain and sharply falling temperatures. A few days before, Sarah mentioned how she had gone out for Halloween and got blasted drunk on Bacardi Hurricane, Skyy Blue (vodka), Smirnoff Twisted (a hard tea), Bud Light, and Captain Morgan. What a mixture! It must have been some night with all those different liquors and—at the least—some morning after. Sarah was "cold and tired" as she wrote—and no wonder. She was missing her gal pal again and still having trouble getting over the demise of the relationship. The failure of the love was all her fault, she told herself again and again. She had cursed the relationship and scared her girl away, she now had herself convinced. Her "broken heart" was only half of what troubled her—because she also believed

she had a "broken spirit," before asking herself if she
would ever be totally over this chick, all coupled with a
constant feeling of being "alone and empty."

A day later, Sarah was preparing to celebrate Cory
Gregory's birthday, but she didn't know what to get
him. Sarah's mother had said she was going out to get
Cory a present, but didn't mention what. This thought—
that her mother was spending money on one of her
friends—sent Sarah down that slippery slope that was
her self-esteem once again, crying out for a hand to
hold. She was discouraged because she couldn't pay her
mother back right away for all the money she had spent
on her and now a gift for Cory. This made Sarah's soul
recoil; she spiraled down into another level of darkness.
Sarah pleaded with herself not to quit her job, which
was something she generally did the moment somebody pissed her off, she wrote, or she didn't get what
she wanted. She hoped she could get a raise "or employee of the month." Not for herself. But because she
wanted to make her mother proud. She said she loved
her mom, and needed to "do good" because that was
one way she could at least prove to her mother that she
cared about her.

Here was a girl dying a slow death on the inside, fill-
ing the void with abusive relationships, drugs, booze,
and rage.

An emotional jack-in-the-box.

Seven days later, November 9, Sarah was again looking to lie down somewhere and sleep her life away. She
penned the word "sleep" in her journal sixteen times in
a row, only to interrupt the repetitiveness by saying how
irritated she was by *these fucking niggers* who were *singing,
actually rapping*. She hated these kids. The music. And
found it all annoying.

After the bitchy rant about the music, Sarah went back to repeating the word "sleep," ending the half-page entry on an entirely different subject: *I hate my job.*

As the Thanksgiving break neared, Cory Gregory had not yet shown up at Black Hawk. He was supposed to start attending classes months ago. But on November 22, Sarah noted, Cory—that "stupid fuck"—finally walked into the school as a student.

Cory's teacher later told police that on this day, Cory "was very quiet and sat alone. He isolated himself from the other students. He wore dark clothing, but no jewelry or piercings."

Sarah said she hoped Cory failed his test on that first day. She did not want him in her class, she said. *I'll snap!* she wrote. She felt so strongly about this, she claimed she would drop out of school before sitting in the same class as Cory.

To his face, however, Sarah was one of the best friends Cory thought he ever had. He and Sarah became inseparable.

A day later, November 23, Adrianne Reynolds was on the scene, combing the halls and classrooms of Black Hawk Outreach, looking to hook up with a new set of friends. She dropped by Sarah's desk soon after beginning classes, flipped open Sarah's journal, and left this girl, whom she found attractive and interesting, her phone number and an introductory note:

> *Hey, girl, what's up? Not shit here. Just chillin. We need to hang out one of these days and get drunk over the weekend. . . . But you should call me sometime. . . . Love ya!*

Sarah Kolb had a new friend. A girl she found appetizingly striking and new to the neighborhood.

Fresh meat.

Just maybe everything Sarah had been waiting for.

Still, Sarah played hard to get.

Sara [sic] hasn't said anything to me at all: a hi, or anything like that, Adrianne wrote in a notebook she passed back and forth between her and the other students in her class.

The boy she wrote to suggested Sarah might be shy.

She don't seem like the shy type, Adrianne responded.

Her friend wrote back that Sarah *sayz she's 17* but looked more *like 15.*

If Sarah likes me, Adrianne wrote, having been told that Sarah was bisexual and on the prowl, hoping to hook up with her, *then she needs to start talking to me because I already made the first move. . . .*

By the end of November, Sarah was over her girlfriend and trying to get with another girl in school, who seemed to be nothing more than a pain in her ass.

I really don't think about [my old girlfriend] anymore . . . , Sarah wrote.

But this new friend couldn't understand that and apparently didn't believe her. The journal entry made two things clear about Sarah's life: One, she seemed to always find a group of people to hang around with who seemed to thrive on a daily dose of drama and chaos. Two, as much as she said she hated these same types of people, Sarah kept going back to them.

In response to Adrianne, Sarah wrote a letter Adrianne received the following Monday. In it, Sarah asked Adrianne about her weekend, saying hers was "okay, I guess." She shared her work schedule and said she was hard to get ahold of on the telephone, but encouraged

Adrianne to keep trying, because she would always return her call. She offered to do something with Adrianne that coming weekend, adding how she wanted to get to know Adrianne better by talking a little more. By the end of the note, Sarah apologized for not saying much during hallway breaks, concluding that the reason was—just as Adrianne's friend had predicted—her shyness.

Some days later, in her journal, Sarah talked about maybe getting "in the hot tub" with her new friend (not Adrianne), but decided against it because she had to leave the house sooner than she had anticipated (she chickened out).

She had just gotten her left eyebrow and tongue pierced, she wrote.

A day after, she talked of a dream she had about this new girl she was pursuing. *It was so real. . . .* Now she couldn't stop thinking about this girl and *had* to have her. From one obsession to the next. Sarah wanted to walk up to the girl in the hallway and plant one on her. *I want her to let me love her,* Sarah wrote. Yet, she convinced herself by the end of the journal entry that it was not going to happen because the girl had just turned eighteen, and no eighteen-year-old, Sarah surmised, wanted anything to do with a sixteen-year-old whacked-out freak of nature. With all that said, she decided she *had to let her go.* She couldn't do *it* anymore."

For Sarah, she had made up her mind: no more pretending to be someone else—which was right where Adrianne fell into Sarah's new view of herself.

She wrote Adrianne a two-page letter asking all sorts of personal questions that might be asked on a first date: Where you from? What's your favorite this and that?

From there, she went on to tell Adrianne about herself.

"Sarah Boo" was one of her nicknames. Her favorite color was purple. She loved Chinese food and "Sketti-O's and pizza w/beer." Metal was the music Sarah adored: Coal Chamber and Otep were the two hard-core metal bands on the top of her list. She called herself "very open-minded" and "love[d] cheese," ending, *Please write back.*

Not long after, Sarah invited Adrianne on a date. She said she had an eighteen-year-old friend who was dating a fourteen-year-old girl (who basically lived at his apartment); and his roommate, a nineteen-year-old, was dating a fifteen-year-old. The apartment was near Adrianne's house. Sarah said she was planning on going over there to hang out: *We're prolly just gonna Drink a little and watch movies. . . .* It was a Friday night, Sarah explained, her only day off all weekend, and she really wanted Adrianne to go with her.

26

The music was concert loud, thumping through the walls, blaring underneath the door. It was a week after Thanksgiving. Adrianne was at home in her room, singing along to "A Moment Like This" by Kelly Clarkson, her favorite tune to mimic these days. She had sung it at a talent show. Now she was planning to audition for America's most fashionable popularity contest, *American Idol.*

When Adrianne was alone, singing, those in the house "couldn't tell if it was her or the radio," Jo recalled. "Her dream was to make it on *American Idol.*"

Singing along to Kelly Clarkson's megahit, driving the house crazy, was probably the best practice for Adrianne. Millions of kids dream of auditioning but don't even come close to obtaining that yellow—"I'm going to Hollywood"—ticket, but Adrianne, her family claimed, had a serious shot at making it on the show. She was gifted. A video of Adrianne trying out for a talent show backs up this claim.

Funny, how when those familiar sounds are no longer ringing throughout the household, the silence is more piercing. More deafening and cumbersome. Those around her would have given their lives to hear Adrianne sing one more song.

"Amazing Grace" was another one of Adrianne's songs of choice when she wanted to belt something out without musical accompaniment. It was, in a peculiar way, a strange selection for the child, considering Adrianne had lost her faith before her death.

"I've given up on God," she told Jo.

"Why?"

"Look at my life."

Adrianne didn't think a compassionate God would allow her to live the way she had been for the past sixteen years. She didn't see the value in believing that it was human behavior saddling her. She could, if she chose to, view each day anew and start over.

"Adrianne had been passed around a lot," one family member said. "From place to place. Home to home."

"When she first moved in with us," Jo remembered, a modicum of pain and remorse in her voice, "I was doing everything I could to get her to go back to Texas. And after she went missing, well, I would have given up everything I own and have to have her back—only if God would just allow Tony to have her back."

As much as she fought with Jo and Tony, Adrianne knew when she had messed up. In a letter she wrote to Tony, she said, *I know I've said it a million times, but this time I mean it. I'm sorry for saying I hate you. . . . I just get angry when you get angry with me, and that's my fault.* She went on to add that whether she liked it or not, *from now on I am going to complete my homework.* Further along, she promised not to curse or yell in the house anymore.

I love you and I hope you love me too! the letter concluded.

From the view of her family, Adrianne wasn't different

from many kids her own age. Struggling to break through that teen angst and attitude she often had, her bright smile shined. She had a Texan's heart, through and through, tough as a longhorn steer, but when it came to academics, she was uninterested. Adrianne had dreams and goals, like any other kid. She talked about being a fashion designer and backed it up with sketches and doodling: trendy hats, necklaces, shoes, shirts, pants. She had a knack for designing clothes and accessories with a retro 1920s feel, but a style still grounded in today's more contemporary and casual fashions. If she worked at it, Adrianne could have had a future in design.

When she lived with Tony and Jo during 2003 (into the winter and spring of 2004), Adrianne went to a public school. Twice, she got kicked out. Both times for fighting.

"She was tough," Tony remembered. "She wasn't gonna take any shit from no one."

Because she had such an obvious Texas accent (an unmistakable, deep Southwestern *y'all* type of drawl was more like it), Adrianne got picked on. More sincerely, kids called her Tex or Texas, but there were those who mocked her tongue. It was hard for Adrianne to find her place then; she wasn't going to back down from being called names. Bullying often led to fisticuffs.

Jo was generally the one to fetch Adrianne at school after the fights. She even defended Adrianne to school officials once, saying that the girls had jumped Adrianne and she had a right to defend herself.

Looking back, Jo admitted that she had never said those indelible words—"I love you"—to Adrianne, which is something Jo regrets. Yet, by Jo's actions as a stepparent, it was obvious that she showed Adrianne love in taking care of her and giving her a home. Even by disciplining her. Telling her what to do. Not allowing Adrianne to treat her like she was a peer. Jo might have seemed like the clichéd wicked stepmom Disney portrays, with warts and all. However, in her own way, Jo was loving Adrianne, and Adrianne was accepting that love by fighting her. Any kid will rebel against discipline if he or she has never been subjected to it. Yet, all kids *crave* obedience or order. They view it as a sign of love. Studies claim that the more time you spend with a child, the less discipline you'll need to expose her to. Jo, Tony, and Adrianne were somewhere in between all of this, trying to work it out—rather, trying to figure out how to make it work for them.

"We really had to keep on Adrianne's back about school," Jo added. "She hated it. I mean it—she *hated* school."

As an over-the-road truck driver, a job that took him away for ten, sometimes fifteen hours per day, and put him three or four hours away from home at any time, Tony wasn't around much. So it was left up to Jo to hold down the fort. She didn't mind. She was there to help Adrianne, but she would not allow Adrianne to be rude, insubordinate, or step on anyone. She wanted Adrianne's respect. And, quite honestly, she deserved it.

There were times, few as they had been, when Jo and Adrianne had bonded like mother and daughter, a place they were heading toward more frequently at the time of Adrianne's murder. One day, they were driving to the school to go see a teacher. A car full of boys drove by.

"Oh, he's so hot," Adrianne remarked.

Jo would find a not-so-hot man in another car and say, "He's hot!"

Then they'd laugh.

Leaving the school that day, when they got back into the car, Jo turned to Adrianne and said, "You can get into trouble anytime you want."

"What?" Adrianne asked, confused.

"That teacher of yours is *hot*!"

They had a moment. Together. Jo explained that fighting was no way to respond to bullying or insults by the other kids. There were other—adult—ways to deal with it. Adrianne understood, but anger, festering inside her for all the things she felt had been done to her, was dominant. She needed help.

There were other times when Adrianne talked about joining the marines and leaving everyone, busting out on her own in the military. Then, almost in the same breath, she'd mention a boy back in Texas she loved and planned to marry one day. So, like any child trying to find his or her place in the world, Adrianne Reynolds was confused.

According to how Jo and Tony saw the situation, part of Adrianne's deep scorn for education was born from not being pushed to succeed. After Adrianne gave up on eighth grade back in Texas, Jo said, she went to work for someone in the family "running a hot dog stand." The family told the school system, Jo added, that they were homeschooling Adrianne at the time.

But they weren't, Tony said. They were working together.

Carolyn Franco disagreed with this.

"She *did* work with me at the business," Carolyn told me, "but we were trying to do homeschooling. The problem was financially, homeschooling cost so much, so I was doing my best to keep her up. I had only pulled her out of school at that point because she was refusing to go."

Carolyn said her goal was to save the $500 she claimed it cost to enroll her in homeschooling, but while she was saving the money, there was no way she could leave Adrianne alone at home, so Carolyn ended up bringing Adrianne to work with her.

"It wasn't a matter of her working in the family business," Carolyn said. "It was a matter of, if she wasn't going to go to school, she wasn't just going to sit around the house and watch TV and sleep half the day."

No one seemed to mind that Adrianne didn't have an eighth-grade education. This was one of the reasons, when Adrianne moved back into her father's house and began to get comfortable at Black Hawk Outreach as winter 2004 to 2005 settled on the QC, she had no credits for high school, both Tony and Jo thought.

Adrianne had never gone.

Sixteen and no credits. They had no choice but to enroll Adrianne in that Black Hawk GED program and hope she could squeak out the equivalent of a high-school diploma.

27

The Black Hawk College Outreach Center program for high-school students in East Moline was the perfect fit for Adrianne's sluggish and hostile attitude toward obtaining an education. Jo's niece had gone through the same program. It seemed to be designed for Adrianne's caliber of study: she could go in the morning and be home by early afternoon—which, in and of itself, proved to be an incentive for Adrianne to get out of bed every day.

According to Black Hawk's website, students must be at least sixteen years old and no longer enrolled in a high school in order to qualify for its GED program. Black Hawk made *agreements with the six public high schools in the Rock Island Educational Service Region,* essentially allowing *students to earn diplomas from their home schools by completing requirements at an Optional Education site.*

For those first few weeks she was enrolled during the early winter of 2004, Adrianne acclimated herself to an environment of kids whom she could relate to on many different levels: broken homes, troublemakers, drug users, boozers, you name it. Society's broken, beaten, failed. Not that every kid from Black Hawk fell under this wide and dysfunctional umbrella, or the school catered to what might be seen as a "misfit" generation of children; but a good portion of Black Hawk's enrollment at the time Adrianne went there included kids using their final educational lifeline. Black Hawk was a teen's last shot. Fail here and a student was out of options.

The photo Tony and Jo had given to the press and police after Adrianne went missing, which became the image of Adrianne everyone in town recognized, was not, according to some of the kids she attended Black Hawk with, an honest depiction of Adrianne. The photo captured Adrianne sporting a semi-bob hairdo, like Victoria Beckham. In the photo, Adrianne had that signature lock of hair protruding over the right side of her face, the rest of her dark brown mane pulled back tightly, exposing her pierced ears. Her lips were bright red; her brown eyes wide and engaging. She came across innocent and sincere, and there's no doubt her character and comportment could be described by both those adjectives. But more than that, Adrianne had a childish look in her eyes. She embodied the spirit of the generation she came from; there was a certain honesty radiating from her in that photo—a genuineness that spoke to the nature of her failings and desire to make a better life for herself.

Adrianne was not a quitter. She didn't generally give up on things. She wanted to succeed, but life had not always cooperated.

Still, this photo, said a former classmate, was not the Adrianne Reynolds he met at Black Hawk when she first walked through those doors. And for many of those who hung around with Adrianne at school and out in the social world of being a teenager, she was a different person from the naïve young girl with the loud and sometimes nasty mouth she displayed at home. It's clear Adrianne lived two separate lives. This is not to say that she deliberately changed who she was when in either environment. It meant that like most kids Adrianne's age, she acted differently depending on who she was with, perhaps without realizing it herself. And this was never more evident than after she met and started hanging around with Sarah, Cory, and that core group of QC Juggalos.

Brad Tobias went to school at Black Hawk and openly admitted, "I was a pothead and smoked with Sarah [Kolb] and them."

Sarah, Cory, and those they ran with perceived themselves as being part of the Juggalo crowd. Brad, on the other hand, did not.

"Oh, *hell* no," he remarked later. "Not me."

Brad tagged along with Cory, Sarah, and the others once in a while, because they liked to smoke weed. Sarah, he added, was "cool to hang out with then." To Brad, Sarah seemed to be "just another girl." She had her differences. Indeed, they all did. But there was nothing easily recognizable in her social personality to make Brad feel uneasy, uncomfortable, or particularly anxious around her. She was just one more kid who had rebelled against a system she felt was out to destroy her chances in life.

Sarah made no qualms about telling people she liked being with guys *and* girls. Beyond that, and the way she dressed, the only other obvious characteristic Sarah displayed within her peer group was that she wanted people to know she was tough.

"She really thought she had balls," said a former friend.

For reasons no one seemed to know, Sarah was afflicted with a repressed rage that showed its face in the crowd every so often—sometimes for no apparent reason other than she just lost control of her emotions. This image of who Sarah was meshed with the Juggalo way of life she fell into. The Juggalo insignia was found on everything from T-shirts to jewelry, from websites to decals and posters, from tattoos to the Psychopathic Records label. It depicts the shadow image of a guy with a clown Afro running, and what appears to be a meat cleaver in his hand (sometimes a chain saw). The icon screams violence. Certain groups of Juggalos like to paint their faces with black-and-white "killer clown" makeup and carry hatchets and knives and skulls as props, presumably for effect. That Juggalo insignia of the running, meat cleaver–yielding madman in the Afro is often drenched in, and dripping, blood. To say the least, it all promotes aggression. Doesn't mean Juggalos run around killing people and look to perpetuate violence; what it *does* say, however, is that there is a desire there to wade in the waters of the darker side of life. An indication that they want to be separated from the world they live in. If Quentin Tarantino had a fan club following him around, dedicated to celebrating the blood and violence depicted in many of his movies, Juggalos would fit that bill. Insane Clown Posse, the popular Detroit band (which dresses in full face paint— think Ronald McDonald meets KISS, with a little Rob Zombie and Slipknot tossed in for effect), coined the Juggalo term. They claim their music is in a category of its own—the genre is horror rap.

Blood. Guts. Violence. Hard rock. Some rapping.

The songs these kids listen to have lyrics that speak to a rebellious crowd of teenagers and twenty-somethings who seem to have little direction and choose to assuage their aggression and to speak socially through the way they dress and the music they listen to. Juggalos, it should be noted, are no more prone to committing crimes or perpetrating violence in numbers than other violent sects found in communities throughout the nation. They are a generally calm people, looking to make a statement about the way they view (and value) life. And this was the bait Cory and Sarah, along with the group of friends they hung around with, became attracted to. They felt comfortable within this environment. They had finally found a place to fit in.

Especially Sarah.

"Sarah could be a real bitch, like hard-core," said a friend.

In that environment of Juggalos, that crazy, bitchy attitude Sarah embodied served her well. She could be who she felt she was, and no one said anything.

There was one day when a group of them stood around in a circle playing hacky sack outside on the grounds of Black Hawk. Hacky sack is a game whereupon you kick a small beanbag ball (a little smaller than a tennis ball) back and forth, trying not to let it hit the ground. Kids like to play this game at concerts, in parks, standing around convenience stores, on the corner, and in between classes at school.

When break was over, the kids stopped the game and went back to class.

Sarah thought she had the hacky sack, but when she realized she didn't, "she started freakin' out," said a student inside the classroom.

Actually, Sarah Kolb lost it.

She snapped.

A full-fledged panic attack set in.

For a few minutes, absolute terror, as though she had lost a family heirloom or her wallet, settled on Sarah. She was stricken with a terrible bout of anxiety. She rummaged through her desk, hurriedly looking for the hacky sack.

She couldn't find it.

The kid who had the ball on him said, "Hey, Sarah, I have it." He sort of rubbed it in her face, taunting and teasing Sarah a little bit, allowing her to freak out and go crazy looking for it, while knowing what she was frantically searching for. He had let her stew.

Sarah didn't like this. She turned red. Then she hit the kid holding the hacky sack in the face with a punch, storming out of the classroom in a rage.

All over a hacky sack ball.

"She had a short fuse," said a friend, "that could go off at any time."

This anecdote explained, in a subtle way, that you had better not mess with Sarah's possessions. Her "things" were important to her. She was territorial.

And this, Adrianne Reynolds was about to find out, included her friends—girlfriends, particularly.

28

Brad Tobias met Cory Gregory at Black Hawk. Cory hung around with Sarah Kolb. The way Brad viewed that relationship, "Cory was just another guy obsessed with a chick."

Everyone seemed to see Cory in this way.

Sarah and Cory were best friends. At least in terms of how the relationship progressed. Cory was smitten. Totally taken in by whatever aura Sarah had.

"Man, and I have no idea why," said a kid from that group of friends. "Have you ever *seen* Sarah? I mean, why was Cory so into her?"

Cory had wanted to date Sarah for the longest time—ever since he met her. Their friendship began when they ran into each other in town one day. They were both sophomores in high school then, going through the same problems, embodying the same defiant natures. They believed society had perpetrated difficulties and barriers against them, which no one else seemed to understand. Cory was going to a public school, but Sarah soon convinced him to transfer to Black Hawk and leave the alternative school connected to Moline High School, which he was registered at.

"He seemed to be doing okay there," his mother, Teresa Gregory, later told me.

Cory came home one afternoon and told his father, Bert Gregory, whom he lived with, "I transferred schools."

Not that he *wanted* to transfer, or was asking his dad for his permission, but that he had already gone and done it.

"What?" Teresa asked when she heard.

"We accepted it," his mother later remarked. "It was better than him dropping out."

Just before Cory turned seventeen, in the fall of 2004, he told his mother he had decided to join the military. Teresa thought it was a good direction for her boy, who, same as many kids his age, did not seem to have any direction whatsoever.

After going down and talking to the recruiter, Cory came back with, he claimed, disappointing news. He said he was told that he had to get his GED (or have a high-school diploma) before the military would take him.

"Too bad they changed that policy," Teresa Gregory said later. Their lives would have likely been a whole lot different if Cory had joined the military.

This is simply not true. Either Cory lied to his mother, or he never bothered to check with the military, because the army, for one, will allow an enlistee to join while still in high school. (A recruit can even go to boot camp between his or her junior and senior years.) And there is no regulation stopping someone from applying to the army with a GED.

Cory continued hanging (and now doing other things) with Sarah Kolb, who was no doubt influencing his life and decisions, if not telling him what to do and when to do it.

"I met Sarah at the mall," Cory said during an interview with NBC, "and then we ended up going and smoking weed behind [a department store]."

Weed and booze—both became Cory's greatest loves, besides, that is, Sarah Kolb, whom he was now seeing every day. Cory wanted to sleep with Sarah something bad, friends said. Sarah knew this, of course, and used it to keep him on a leash. In this early stage of the relationship, she never came out and said no to Cory, but then she didn't say yes, either. Cory was always left to feel as though he was in the middle, and had a shot with Sarah.

"In the back of his mind somewhere," Teresa Gregory said, "Cory always believed there was a chance for the two of them—that if he just *hung* in there long enough, best friends would become lovers."

"He was always trying to get with her and she wouldn't have anything of it," Brad Tobias explained. "She used him for whatever she wanted to use him for. If she wanted to use him as a ride somewhere, she used him as a ride. If she wanted to use him as someone to cry on, she used him for that. If she wanted him to beat up someone, she had Cory beat someone up."

As they became closer, the relationship with Sarah defined who Cory became. Some said he liked the idea that she was "in control" of his life and told him what to do. He needed that sort of direction. Cory had come from a broken home in which his mother had left the household. That's a very important factor in how his life was shaping up with Sarah, who quite possibly picked up on this lack of femininity in Cory's everyday life and filled that role, knowingly or not.

At times, Cory wrote Sarah letters, telling her exactly how he felt. In one, he said he loved her: *I have since I first laid eyes on you.* Sarah was all he ever thought about. She was the only person, Cory wrote, *I [feel] I [can] speak my emotions [to]. . . .* He concluded by saying he would be there for Sarah in the same way, no matter what it was she needed.

That last line spoke to the manipulative temperament brewing inside of Sarah, giving her a considerable amount of power over Cory. Something she learned to coddle and experiment with—a switch she could turn on and off whenever she wanted.

Sarah liked the idea of being in charge—the leader of the pack. And this was how the relationship between her and Cory progressed. Every day Sarah began to feel more in control over Cory Gregory.

But then, Adrianne Reynolds walked onto the scene, nudging her way into Cory and Sarah's lives.

Which changed everything.

29

Cory Gregory never had a reputation for being a tough kid. Those at Black Hawk who knew of him saw Cory as another Juggalo who liked to do drugs, drink booze, smoke cigarettes, stick to Sarah Kolb like pants, and follow the crowd with whom he ran—whatever it was they decided to do on any given day.

"If Cory was ever to try to step up on you," a former Black Hawk student recalled, "you would just have to say 'shut up,' and get up in his face, and he would back *right* down."

And yet, others said Cory had a mean streak you didn't want to mess with. A temper that, same as Sarah's, erupted at any given moment for no apparent reason.

Nate Gaudet and Cory were tight. They went back five years, to grammar school. But that anger inside Cory exposed itself inside the dynamic of their friendship every so often. There was one day when Cory and Nate were driving around the QC. Cory sat in the front. Nate drove. There was another kid, a Juggalo, in the backseat. There wasn't much talk going on inside the car. Music played. They smoked cigarettes.

Suddenly, out of nowhere, Cory punched Nate on the side of the head as Nate drove. No love taps here; these were hard shots to the face and head that rattled Nate's cage damn good.

"What the *fuck*?" Nate said.

Cory laughed.

"Come on, man. What'd you hit me for?"

Cory replied with a straight face. "I done felt like it, that's all." He laughed then and raised his fist, without hitting Nate, kind of taunting him.

"That's how Cory was sometimes," said a source. "He would snap. He gave Nate a few bumps on the face that day. Nate never said or did nothing about it. And we're talking these two were 'supposedly' best friends."

Then there was the pot-smoking side of Cory. He loved to get high, as often as he could. And what would he talk about afterward, with the mellow buzz of the weed fueling an inherent desire he harbored for freaking people out?

"How he wanted to set up a chain on girls with a bunch of kids and fuck them," said a friend. "Nate Gaudet was into this, too."

Cory and Nate often talked about what they called "tag teaming" girls. And the most shocking part about this, perhaps, was that they rarely had a hard time finding a girl to take part. In fact, there was a time in the basement of Nate's when twenty or so kids got together and listened to music, drank, and got high. Nate and Cory and a few others set up a train on a girl and video-taped it.

Nate's father found the tape after kicking the kids out of his house.

"You'd be surprised at how many of the girls we knew were open to it," said a source.

One more sign that this group was out of control.

Nate, Sarah, Cory, and several others hung around what was a genuine party house located outside Moline in Rock Island. Nate met Sarah through Cory. For just about a two-year period leading up to January 2005, Nate, Sarah, and Cory spent most of their time together.

"Nate seemed like a normal kid," said a former classmate. "He was another one of those adolescent kids that was trying to be what he *wasn't*."

Maybe they all were.

Sarah, Adrianne, and Cory fell into that same clique. They fit themselves into a group of Juggalos more than the group fit into who they were. Juggalos not only dress a certain way, but true Juggalos speak their own language and drink a beverage called Faygo, an inexpensive soft drink. Being a Juggalo wasn't the same as belonging to the 4-H club or Boy Scouts—it was a way of life.

A religion.

Juggalos will say they are misunderstood. That society doesn't quite "get" who they are, or what they represent. According to some, however, the attitude many in the East Moline sect of the group (aptly called the QC Juggalos) routinely displayed was "I'm better than you, *so shut the F up* and stay out of my way."

Badass people haters. Counterculture wags.

"Social rejects," one Juggalo from the area explained to me. "We do not like society," he added. "Society judges us. We hate people. Society is nothing but a bunch of ignorance. Everyday people are just ignorant. They choose not to open their eyes to the things that are happening right in front of them. . . . They want to blame everything negative that happens with kids on music. I'm sorry, but if you are that fucking stupid that you'd listen to a song and that makes you kill someone, you're a problem to begin with. Would you blame country music for a redneck guy who goes out and drives his truck drunk? Or beats his wife? Course not. You're not going to blame that on the country music. But if a kid does it, you're going to say it was the music he listens to that made him do it."

Hanging out together as a group, Juggalos found solace in one another. Camaraderie. A common understanding. A bond. It was a brotherhood, a place wherein everyone agreed that society didn't know jack shit about who they were or what they felt.

The connection between the QC Juggalos, it is safe to say, was also fueled by the drugs they used.

"God yes," said that same QC Juggalo.

Their everyday lives were centered on drugs.

When one looks deeper into the Juggalo group Sarah and Cory were now a part of, however, a skinhead-like undertone emerges. For example, Sarah kept a club in her car, half of an old broom handle, duct-taped on one end. She had a name for it: the "nigger stick." And there's no hiding the fact that although Juggalo sects have been popping up all over the country, a majority of the groups are from the Midwest and the South; and more and more, these groups have been associated with violence against African Americans and other nonwhite groups. In Seattle, for instance, seven people were arrested in 2009. They ranged in age from fourteen to twenty-nine. They had been charged, according to a *Seattle Times* article, with attacking a group of park dwellers. The victims explained in police reports that the gang *carried machetes, beat and robbed people and threatened decapitation.* Two kids from the group admitted *they were Juggalos,* the *Times* reported, and *that Juggalos have become increasingly ganglike.*

In another example reported by the *Times,* an eighteen-year-old Juggalo entered a known Massachusetts gay bar yielding *a hatchet and gun and assaulted three patrons.* The kid ran off to *Arkansas,* the report said, *where he killed a female companion and a police officer before police shot him dead.*

On his website, the kid had posted a simple—but telling—message: **Are you a Juggalo?**

30

Brad Tobias had moved to the QC from Texas not long before the 2004 Black Hawk Outreach semester began. When he heard Adrianne was from a town in Texas not far away from where he had been born and raised, Brad wanted to meet her.

"When I first met Adrianne, I found her to be giddy," Brad recalled. "Bubbly. Friendly."

They were interested in each other from the start. As if in junior high again, Adrianne wrote their names all over her notebooks, with hearts and *XOXOXO* around the names.

But as Brad got to know Adrianne more personally, he began to see that she was trying to be somebody she was not. Adrianne was never one to spike her hair, he said, or wear black clothes and dark makeup, Goth-like. Yet, when she started to hang out with, and grow affection for, Sarah, Brad said, "Adrianne changed." Now she wanted to be a Juggalette, same as Sarah. But only because she believed it allowed her to fit in with Sarah and that group of people Sarah ran with, including Cory and Nate.

"What Adrianne was," Brad remembered, "was a goody-good girl."

Adrianne was bisexual, Brad said. "She told me. We discussed it."

And now Adrianne wanted to date Sarah.

Brad was curious. Adrianne was talking about Sarah one afternoon: Sarah this. Sarah that. All things Sarah.

Adrianne was infatuated with Sarah and her lifestyle, and she wanted in on it.

"What is the interest in Sarah?" Tobias asked Adrianne. He and Adrianne were dating by then, but they had an open relationship, one could say. It was the first week of December 2004.

Adrianne shrugged. Smiled. "I think Sarah's cute."

"How?" Brad wondered, a laugh in his voice. He was shocked by the comment. He found nothing about Sarah "cute." Sarah was an angry girl, more Joan Jett than Jordin Sparks. Rough around the edges. Even dirty and crude. There were times when she didn't bathe regularly. What was so darn attractive about any of that? Brad wanted to know.

Adrianne saw something different in Sarah, she explained.

"She's popular," Adrianne said.

And there it was: the true attraction Adrianne had for Sarah in this courting stage of their relationship. Adrianne wanted to be popular. Same as Sarah. She wanted the kids to notice her. Same as they did Sarah. She felt that if she hung around with Sarah, that mystery surrounding the girl with a face full of piercings and badass attitude would rub off on her.

Sarah was one of only a few Juggalettes in that Black Hawk sect of the group—and Adrianne was now desperately seeking to be the next.

"Adrianne was all about making friends," Brad observed. "If Adrianne could have made everyone her friend, that would have made her the happiest, the best day of her life."

Adrianne reached out to Sarah during the latter part of that first week in December. She wrote a note to Sarah and placed it on her desk. Adrianne wanted Sarah to understand a few things about where she was coming from. The letter was neatly written in Adrianne's near-perfect penmanship—an important point to note, because Adrianne apologized to Sarah in the letter for her "sloppy handwriting."

Next to Sarah's name, Adrianne drew a heart, half colored it in:

Hey babe, what are you doing? Nothing too much here except lying in bed being very bored.

All of the periods and dots above the *i*'s were hearts.

They had apparently made plans to go out, but Adrianne wanted to know if Sarah had decided what they were going to do. Adrianne said she had to work from either "eleven to two, or eleven to three." She asked Sarah if she *just wanted to stay here (Adrianne's house) and sleep until I get off work, or if you are wanting to spend the night with me.*

Adrianne went on to warn Sarah that it would *be a few days before I could actually probably stay with you because I have to get on this birth control shot because my parents know how much I love kids and how bad I want them and they don't want me to get pregnant.*

Adrianne had been on birth control. There's no obvious explanation as to why she felt the need to mention this, other than to test Sarah and see how she would react to the statement. It turned out to be a mistake on Adrianne's part. She was telling Sarah that she was having sex with boys, which Sarah did not appreciate. Sarah demanded monogamous relationships, with boys or girls.

Near the end of the letter, Adrianne said she was bisexual and hoped Sarah didn't have a problem with it. If Sarah was "straight lesbian," Adrianne made a point, it didn't matter to her.

It appears that Adrianne never heard back from Sarah.

Hey sweetheart, Adrianne wrote a few days later, *do you like me at all? If so, in what way?*

Adrianne needed to know if she and Sarah were becoming lovers, friends, or enemies: *I really like you, as in I'd like to go out with you. But do you like me enough that if we went out that you'd respect me enough to know that I'm not going to sleep with you right away?*

In an attempt to find out if all the rumors she had heard about Sarah being a troublemaker with a cold heart were true, Adrianne asked Sarah straight out: *You wouldn't do anything to put me in danger, would you?*

Sarah had visited Adrianne at her East Moline house a few days before Adrianne wrote this latest letter. Adrianne explained that her brother (Jo's son) thought Sarah was trying to come across as tough. He didn't like it.

My brother thought you were trying to act hard, Adrianne wrote, *so you could . . . do me a favor of just relaxing.*

Then came more rules for the relationship. Adrianne wanted Sarah to dress nicely the next time she came over to her house: *And do something with your hair before you come and meet my dad. . . . DON'T WEAR BAGGY CLOTHES. PLEASE.*

These letters are extraordinary if we note the timing.

Adrianne was as confused as she was desperately reaching out a hand to a torn and tattered, angry Sarah Kolb. On that same day Adrianne had written to Sarah, she had also written a letter to a boy back home, telling him to relay a message to another boy:

I miss him and still love him with all my heart.

31

In the beginning, Adrianne Reynolds wanted nothing more than for Sarah Kolb to like her. She did what she could to get Sarah to understand that she wasn't trying to be phony, and she yearned for nothing more than to be a part of Sarah's life.

Sarah was leery, however.

Adrianne pushed the idea of a romance. And at first, Sarah seemed to be genuinely interested in dating her.

"I first saw her outside on one of our cigarette breaks," Sarah later said. "I was very attracted to her. She was a very cute girl."

Sarah had strict rules where "friends," "boyfriends" and "girlfriends" fit into the scope of her life. She was outspoken about this, once saying, "A friend is somebody I like to spend my time with, share my thoughts with, hang out with." Cory Gregory, in other words. "A boyfriend," on the other hand, "or girlfriend, is someone that I'd like to get to know better, someone that I can, oh, what's the word? I don't know. 'Understand.' Someone that can understand me the same way. Someone that I would like to have a future with, maybe."

Sarah admitted later that after meeting Adrianne she saw the possibility of there being the opportunity for them to have a lesbian relationship.

"That was why," Sarah said, "we were getting to know each other first." Sarah explained that she wanted "to take it really slow" with Adrianne. Sarah had just come off that viciously hurtful breakup with a much older, adult woman who had "bruised" her feelings. She wasn't going to allow it to happen again.

What is the most you've done with a girl? Adrianne asked in one note.

A lesbian relationship was something Adrianne was giving serious consideration to. She wanted to see what it could offer. All boys at that age wanted sex, Adrianne knew. Bed you down and send you on your way. Adrianne was after more than that. She desired true love—any way she could get it. She understood another female could provide this for her, maybe more personal and deep than any boy.

Adrianne was still keeping her attachments to boys, and Sarah was doing the same thing. By this time, Sarah had her eyes on Sean McKittrick, a tall, skinny, good-looking kid with spiked black hair, who was staying out of town then, but was slated to start classes at Black Hawk after the first of the year. Sarah and Cory had made plans to pick up Sean after Christmas and drive him back to the Moline area. Sarah had always had a "thing" for Sean, she later admitted, which she hoped could be more after he moved into the area.

As each day passed, the dense and frigid December air in Illinois turned bone-chilling and arctic. Sarah Kolb felt that Adrianne Reynolds was not so much interested in her as a girlfriend, but rather was looking to be part of the crowd Sarah led. Sarah began to feel that Adrianne was trying to use her to step into her role as the group leader.

A big no-no in Sarah's book.

There was a negative aura beginning to form around them as Adrianne worked her way into Sarah's inner circle. As someone in this group explained to me later, "Adrianne was slowly trying to take Sarah's mojo from her."

At least, this was how it seemed—how those in the group, especially Sarah, interpreted Adrianne's desperate desire to be one of them.

It wasn't something that happened all at once. Or anything Adrianne set out to do intentionally, and certainly not vengefully.

"Sarah felt Adrianne was trying to take her place inside the group," said a source.

Turf. Sarah was all about protecting *her* terrain, part of which centered on Cory; whether she liked Cory (in that way) was not an issue. But as Adrianne got to know Sarah better, Adrianne and Cory became closer and started to hang around more and more.

When one looks at these two young lives in hindsight, it's clear Adrianne and Sarah shared many of the same low self-esteem issues. However, where social networking and hanging out with a group were concerned, the similarities ended. While Adrianne was tattooing her notebooks with hearts and cartoon pictures of herself and friends, fantasizing about love and lying in clover fields, dreaming of children and being married, writing poems about broken loves and the boys she liked, Sarah was scribing things along the lines of "Hate, Kill, Destroy."

Sarah's doodling was darker and self-contained, matching her tough, *Girl with the Dragon Tattoo* image— that F-the-world philosophy she and the other Juggalos lived by. Sarah was hung up on not being perfect in the eyes of society in general, and not fitting into the proper role she felt society demanded from a sixteen-year-old girl. And this was one of the areas in which she and Adrianne clashed: Sarah was being herself here, which allowed her to pick up quickly on the fact that Adrianne was trying to be someone she was not.

And this angered Sarah.

Resentment brewed.

Even hatred.

To the point where Sarah was in the process of putting Adrianne to the ultimate test to see if Adrianne was truly one of them, or just some floozy from Texas trying to fit in.

32

For Cory and Sarah, their lives outside the confines of Black Hawk Outreach, and the meager hours they worked at their part-time jobs, focused on the party house in Rock Island. This was not your typical frat house environment, a rented home run by a group of jocks or college kids having keg parties on the weekends, leaving empty pizza boxes and cigarette-filled red party cups stinking of stale beer scattered around.

This was a Juggalo house.

There was booze. Sex. And, of course, lots and lots of drugs.

"Anything we could get our hands on," Henry Orenstein (pseudonym), who also lived in the house, later told me. "Every hour of the day there was a party going on inside that house."

Not a group of kids sitting around playing PlayStation, passing a bong. This was a concerted effort to get as high as they could *whenever* they could. Even Sarah later described how there was a separate area of the house specifically set aside for getting high.

"The attic was used for doing drugs, smoking pot," Sarah admitted.

Orenstein, along with five others, including Cory (sometimes) and Nate Gaudet, stayed at the house. The main drug of choice on any given day or night was pot, but when they could get it, X (Ecstasy) was what these particular Juggalos craved most. Some cocaine moved in and out of the house, too. But it was mainly X.

"The first time we took X, it was just something to do," said one housemate. "We heard a lot about it and wanted to try it. Seemed like a good party drug. . . ."

That experiment offered an entire new world of numbness.

"Within it, we found fake happiness."

About the most Adrianne went for after she started to hang at the house was booze, if she even dabbled in that. Some said, in fact, Adrianne only drank because she felt they'd accept her more.

"We tried to get her to take X, but she wasn't down with it," said Henry.

Adrianne didn't even want to hang out upstairs in the attic, for fear of getting a "contact high" from all the pot smoke hovering in the air.

"Yeah," Sarah added, "she didn't want to be up there because she didn't do drugs. She didn't want to be around it. . . ."

Sarah was the one who brought Adrianne to the house for the first time. No one seemed to recall the exact date, but everyone agreed it was in early December, the latter part of the first week, or the beginning of the week after. Cory, attached to Sarah like a chain wallet, was with them. Sarah had planned on going over to the party house after she got out of work. She called and asked Adrianne to go along.

"Sure," Adrianne said.

"I brought her with me to hang out," Sarah recalled, "because it was an opportunity outside of school to actually get to know her better. We didn't have class together [anymore], and I wanted to get to know her better."

Walking into the living room that day, Sarah called out for everyone's attention. "Hey, hey. . . ." It was loud. Lots of talking. Music blaring. A good smog of cigarette and pot smoke hanging eye level. "Everyone . . . this is Adrianne."

Adrianne said a few words. "What's up?" She waved. Her thick Texas accent was obvious. It seemed to draw attention to her.

"Who are you?" someone asked. "Where y'all from?"

Adrianne explained.

They sat down and talked.

There was another reason why Adrianne didn't take X or anything harder than the booze and pot, Henry explained.

"Because Sarah told her *not* to."

The first time Henry Orenstein met Nate Gaudet, Nate had come out to the party house with Cory and Sarah to "kick it," Henry explained. "Nate was cool."

Nate didn't seem aggressive or angry.

"The most aggression I ever saw out of Nate," said a former friend, "was when I'd look across [the] room and watch him fuck his girlfriend. That was about the extent of the aggression I saw in Nate."

Sarah, on the other hand, wasn't someone who was all that into jumping around, displaying a high level of energy. Most in the group were mellow, laid-back.

Sarah, in particular, loved nothing more than sitting on a chair inside the living room and, listening to her music, enjoying whatever high she was on.

"Chill and smoke and drink, that was Sarah."

There was a part of Sarah Kolb all about flipping the bird to the system. She had an official army outfit (fatigues), but she had vandalized the thing as an *F-U* to the government. She put patches all over it. Covered it with Sharpie-written slurs. Graffitied it up. At this time, Sarah had bleached blond hair down to her shoulders. She wore black army boots too big for her feet, laces running up her shins. On the walls of her bedroom was a collage of photographs, some of the faces x'd out with a pen, others colored over.

Cory and Sarah's relationship was no secret inside the party house. Everyone considered them friends. Nothing more. But again, many in the house later confirmed, Sarah would use Cory's "obsession with her for her personal gain."

"With Cory, when she wasn't around," said a housemate, "he wouldn't talk about her like, 'I want to fuck her.' Cory was actually in *love* with Sarah."

And Cory was now growing jealous of Sean McKittrick, whom Sarah was talking about more and more as 2005 grew closer.

It just hurtz my heart, Cory wrote to Sarah, *when you talk about him.* He asked Sarah if she noticed how he had *always looked at the ground* when she mentioned Sean.

Cory considered Sean one of his closest friends. When Cory went to see Sean once with Sarah, Sean and Cory, according to an interview another friend later gave to police, "both attempted suicide together by hanging themselves . . . and it was Sarah who cut them down." Sarah ended up staying with them the entire night, making sure they were okay.

Then there was that stick Sarah carried in her car, a weapon everyone would soon be talking about.

"She was racist, for sure," said a QC Juggalo. "We all weren't like that, though. Especially when talking about ignorant racism. If you're just hatin' someone because of their skin color or religion, or what they believe, that's a stupid reason to hate someone. You should hate them for who they are. If I call someone nigger, it's generally because they just don't carry themselves well. They're a very ignorant person. I'll call a white person [the N-word], too. . . ."

Sarah had gone to a Catholic school, but later she talked about "not really finding anything" in what she was being taught. Nothing "solid that gave her any actual proof of what they [the Catholic establishment] were trying to tell" her "was out there."

Apparently, faith wasn't something Sarah accepted without question. One could say she was raised with a divine belief, but then, perhaps like many kids going through their teen years, society and materialism began to affect it to a point where she decided to reject it all with one broad stroke.

"There were some of us who believed that God is here and did whatever they say He did," said one Juggalo. "With Sarah, in one way she rejected Christianity, and for her family, she embraced it."

Two different people.

Both trying to please the other.

Sarah Kolb.

33

Several at the party house were upstairs in the attic smoking pot on the day when Sarah and Cory brought Adrianne over to the house that first time and introduced Adrianne to everyone downstairs.

Adrianne was out of her element in this environment. The people around her were not who she wanted to be, whether she understood that about herself or not. Yet, Adrianne was conducting herself like she had been—to borrow a Juggalo term—a social reject all her life, too.

Realizing several fellow Jugs were upstairs, partying in the attic, Cory and Sarah grabbed Adrianne and told her to come along.

No sooner had Adrianne walked into the attic than she turned around and told Sarah, "I'll meet you downstairs."

Adrianne wasn't interested in smoking dope. She had no use for it.

"Cool," Sarah said.

There were several guys up in the attic besides Cory. All of them sat around in a circle with Sarah, smoking.

As soon as Adrianne was out of earshot, Sarah turned to Kory Allison, another Jug who lived in the house, and Henry Orenstein.

"Hey," Sarah said, addressing them both, "I brought [Adrianne] here. . . . Look, she wants to party. . . . She's trying to get laid tonight. I figure I can look to you guys for that."

Cory Gregory, inhaling a hit of a joint, smiled. Nodded.

"That ain't no problem," Henry said. "Just get her back up here."

Sarah laughed. Shook her head. "Yeah."

"Our initial reaction to Adrianne being at the house that day," Henry later explained, not mincing words, "was that she wanted to fuck."

It was clear to everyone in the attic that Sarah was facilitating this for Adrianne. Sarah and Adrianne must have talked this over before arriving, and Sarah was fulfilling a desire of Adrianne's.

No one doubted this.

34

Over two hundred years before Adrianne Reynolds moved to the QC, the area was inhabited by a Native American tribe called the Sauk. Where the tribe settled later became Rock Island. At the time, the Sauk were the largest tribe in North America. One leader of the tribe, Black Hawk, was a man who, if legend has it correct, held animosity toward Americans that carried over from the Revolutionary War up to the War of 1812. Black Hawk became the only man to have a war—the Black Hawk War—named after him. This happened after he grew tired of the white man squeezing the land his ancestors had left for future tribes. Metaphorically speaking, Black Hawk's contempt for those who had impaled the societal values around him was an indication of the same disdain those Juggalos hanging out in that Rock Island party house had felt. Valid or not, it was how these kids viewed the world around them. They wanted to be left alone. Not judged by what they wore or the music they listened to. Anyone who entered the Juggalo culture, trying to be somebody they were not, was not only spitting on what the Jugs believed, but lying to them. Most of these kids could brush it off. Turn a cheek. Go on with their partying without a second thought. But Sarah Kolb was different: this sort of betrayal was personal.

In her heart, Sarah needed to know that Adrianne Reynolds was not trying to infiltrate the group, per se, and take her place. So Sarah devised that test for Adrianne—which was now, with that request she had made to Henry Orenstein and Kory Allison, under way.

They sat around inside the party house as the evening turned to night. Outside, it was cold enough to see a person's breath like smoke. Inside, the booze and drugs kept everyone warm. The chosen poison of the night was "Jack." Jack Daniel's whiskey. And, of course, lots of pot and other drugs they had on hand. For Sarah and Cory, they stuck to drinks and a gram of cocaine they snorted throughout the evening.

Adrianne was in the kitchen at one point with Cory. They talked.

In the living room, Sarah turned to Kory Allison and bumped him on the shoulder. "Go in there and talk to her. She's lookin' to hook up!"

They laughed.

Kory Allison got up and walked into the kitchen.

"Hey," Cory Gregory said to the other Kory. "What up? What up?"

Kory, with a K, nodded.

"This is Adrianne," Cory said, introducing her. Adrianne smiled her little Texas charm. Kory nodded as if he could care less.

Whatever, Kory thought at that moment. He wasn't really interested in playing one of Sarah's games, he later said.

Then as Adrianne started to talk, Kory noticed something that interested him, and he perked up.

"She had a Southern accent."

They talked; then everyone went back out into the living room.

Nate Gaudet's girlfriend, Jill Hiers, showed up at some point. Jill did not like Sarah all that much, she later told police, and thought Sarah was "creepy because she's a lesbian." Jill had no love for Cory, either, saying she believed him to be "disturbing."

"He had a lot of piercings," Jill later explained. "He is very sexual and always talked about killing."

Jill was well aware that Sarah had brought Adrianne to the house to "test" her, as Jill later put it. "Sarah wanted to see how many guys in the house she could get Adrianne to sleep with. But we all knew Adrianne was looking to hook up with Sarah. Sarah was just interested in hurting someone. She was never interested in Adrianne, because she felt that Adrianne would cheat on her with boys."

While they were sitting around, Sarah, now feeling the Jack numbing her, got up and walked over to Jill.

"Shut up!" Sarah said for no reason. "Don't talk anymore!"

Jill looked at her. "Sit down. . . ."

Sarah sat next to Jill. She said, "Hey, watch Adrianne." Adrianne was walking around the room, Jill later explained, "being the center of attention." Sarah did not like this at all. Everyone was paying more attention to Adrianne, who seemed to suck it up.

And this, Jill explained, "got Sarah *very* angry."

* * *

Later that same night, Nate Gaudet and Jill Hiers, who sometimes shared a room together at the party house, sat on Nate's bed.

Cory walked into the room.

"How 'bout we pull a train on Adrianne?" Cory said. He laughed. "She'd probably be into it." There was one instance earlier when Adrianne, someone in the group later said, walked around the room, pointed at each boy, and said, "I want to have sex with you, and with you, and with you. . . ."

This enraged Sarah.

"I'm serious," Cory told Nate.

Nate and Jill got up and left the room.

Meanwhile, Adrianne sat next to Henry Orenstein in the living room.

"I have a headache," Adrianne said, leaning on Henry's shoulder.

The pain was intense. Throbbing.

Henry had a room in the basement of the house. "Go down there," he said, "and lay down. Chill out."

Adrianne waited for about an hour, but the headache wouldn't go away.

"I'm goin' to lie down now," she said.

"Cool," Henry responded. He took it as an indication, which Sarah had made clear earlier that night in the attic when they first met Adrianne, that Adrianne was going down into the bedroom to "get herself ready." A wink-wink, in other words. An invitation for one of the guys in the house to go downstairs and have sex with her.

It was understood throughout the house that although

Sarah had brought Adrianne, and there might be some sort of a lesbian connection between the two of them, Sarah wanted to hook Adrianne up with Kory or Henry for the only purpose of seeing if Adrianne would have sex with either one, or both. Nothing more than that. Sarah later claimed that she did this only because Adrianne had made it clear to her that she wanted to "get laid."

Sarah didn't quite see the visit to the house in the same way when she later explained it in court. She called it a meet-and-greet with the gang.

"It was just to hang out, just to talk to everyone that was there," Sarah said, playing down the entire night.

Henry Orenstein realized Adrianne had been downstairs in his bedroom, trying to get rid of that headache, for about an hour. He looked at Kory. Nudged him.

"Hey . . . there's a CD downstairs in my room I want you to grab." Henry explained which CD he wanted. "On the nightstand next to my bed." He told Kory to hurry up. "Go get it now."

Kory didn't take the hint. He went up and down the stairs three times.

"Dude, I cannot find that CD," he said.

Everyone laughed.

"What the fuck! Try looking *in* the bed," Henry suggested. He smiled. Winked. "See if you see anything in the bed that interests you."

Sarah had been sitting, listening, watching this take place, everyone later agreed.

Kory went back downstairs.

"Umm, when I went back down there," Kory later said, "and noticed that she was coming up the stairs, I kind of put it together what everyone was kind of trying to do."

This time, once that basement door closed behind Kory, he did not return right away. Everyone, including Sarah Kolb, sat in the living room, laughing and getting their drunk on, knowing what was going on in the basement.

"When he went down there that last time, Adrianne was awake and . . . they took their thing from there," Henry explained.

While they were "doing it," Cory Gregory walked down the stairs to share some news with Kory.

"Your baby's mom is here, Kory."

"Shit."

Adrianne and Kory were in the middle of having intercourse, but now it was over.

Forced to finish, Adrianne came up the stairs and walked into the living room. Sarah, Cory, Henry Orenstein, and others were waiting.

After explaining how she had just had sex with Kory, Adrianne said her curfew was almost up. She had to leave.

Cory, Sarah, and Adrianne walked out of the house together.

There was very little conversation on the way home about what had taken place at the party house, according to Sarah. But Sarah wasn't happy about what had happened—Adrianne sleeping with Kory. It "upset" her, Sarah later claimed.

She never mentioned anything about a test Adrianne might have failed.

Still, everyone in the house on that night later testified that Sarah had, for one, instigated the sexual liaison between Kory and Adrianne; and two, she never showed any sign of being the least bit disturbed by it after it had taken place.

* * *

After Cory Gregory returned to the party house later that same night, after he and Sarah dropped Adrianne off, he sat with Nate Gaudet and another girl who sometimes lived at the house. They talked. Cory often blurted out bizarre things for no reason.

According to the girl who was there, "out of nowhere," Cory said, "he'd like to kill Adrianne."

He never said how or why.

Nate and the girl looked at him.

"What?" Nate asked.

"Why would you want to kill her, Cory?" the girl asked.

"Why *not*?" Cory said. "I could get away with it, and no one would know."

What could they say?

"I'd like to kill her, yeah," Cory said again.

Teresa Gregory's second husband, Cory's stepdad, owned a piece of property outside East Moline. The house had forty acres surrounding it, and at one time had been a working farm.

Continuing talking to Nate and the girl, Cory concluded, "I'd burn her body and bury her remains on my mom's farm. . . ."

35

Patricia Druckenmiller had been teaching at Black Hawk Outreach since August 2004. Sarah Kolb was one of Druckenmiller's students, who later explained how there were a few different programs the kids could take at Black Hawk. One was on the ground floor, where Druckenmiller's classroom was located. It was, more or less, a high-school completion program. There were ninth-grade through twelfth-grade classrooms and a GED program on the same floor. The upstairs classrooms were an extended variety, with older students and some bonus classes and additional GED programs.

Sarah took what was called independent study, history, and English, to be exact, from Druckenmiller. Sarah was one of the first students Druckenmiller met after going to work at Black Hawk that year.

During the first five minutes of every class, Druckenmiller made the kids open their journals and do what she called "free writing."

"There was only one rule," Druckenmiller had told her students. "You just have to keep your pencil moving, and really you shouldn't do any editing or any looking

back at it. . . . So the kids understood," she added, "that
I did *not* look at these, so they could write anything
they wanted, and, you know, it was . . . They were not
graded. . . ."

This was one way to get their young minds moving, allowing them a place where they could express who they
were, knowing that no one was going to judge them.

Druckenmiller recalled how Sarah did not have to
be pushed into completing this exercise every morning,
as did many of the other children.

"I remember not having to remind her."

At the end of the five-minute session, the journals
were placed in a stack with the students' notebooks,
wherever the kid happened to be sitting. Each student
had a "little drawer . . . assigned to him or her, and they
would put their stuff in the drawer."

Each drawer had a name tag on the front.

Keeping all of their work inside the classroom was
something many of the teachers, including Druckenmiller, mandated. If you did that, the kids could not
come in the next day and say, "I forgot my journal. . . .
I lost my textbook. . . . The dog ate it."

Rather, it was always there.

That journal, for Sarah, became more than just a way
of interpreting her feelings. It was an outlet. For her aggression. For that pent-up anxiety drumming through
her veins. For anything she wanted to vomit from her
confused mind onto the page. Every morning, Sarah
went to that paper and unleashed the demons. Only
now, as her anger for Adrianne grew to a level she perhaps could not have foreseen, Sarah turned to the journal not to talk about how much she wanted to get with
Adrianne, but how much she was beginning to despise

this new girl from Texas, who, she felt, was trying to take her place.

It didn't matter, one person from the group said, if they were hungover or not. When morning came, those who had jobs went to work, and those who had school got up and went to class.

The day following the night Adrianne had had sex with Kory Allison, she and Sarah spoke in school, according to what Sarah later told police.

Sarah said she was upset over the fact that Adrianne had slept with Kory.

Adrianne couldn't understand why. After all, she was under the impression Sarah had given her blessing.

"It will never happen again," Sarah claimed Adrianne pleaded with her that day.

"I don't want to talk to you about it," Sarah told Adrianne. Then she walked away.

Two of Sarah's friends, including Cory Gregory, then relayed a message to Sarah that Adrianne wanted to extend her apologies even more; she was truly sorry, and "she still wanted the [lesbian] relationship between them to work out."

Adrianne didn't know she had flunked a test Sarah had devised. One of the main reasons for bringing Adrianne over to the party house and exposing her to the "horndogs" who lived in the house, Sarah later told a friend, was "to see if Adrianne was really gay. Sarah was sexually attracted to Adrianne, but she needed to test her."

"Sarah hated sluts," a former friend added. "Sarah said that since Adrianne had come into the house and fucked Kory Allison, 'she's a bitch and she'll pay.'"

Sarah was back at the party house with Jill Hiers later that day after school. Sarah asked Jill to call Adrianne at home. She wanted to harass her.

Sarah leaned into the phone receiver so she could hear the conversation.

Under Sarah's direction, Jill told Adrianne she had made a huge mistake in sleeping with Kory. She should have never done it.

The call seemed to prove that they were messing with Adrianne. Teasing and taunting her. Playing some sort of a game.

Bullying.

Adrianne sounded sincere. "I made a mistake, come on. Tell her I made a mistake!"

Sarah listened and laughed.

"I will. . . ."

Sarah and Jill looked at each other. Giggled.

"It was just one little mistake and it will never happen again."

Adrianne reached out to several of Sarah's friends, telling them she was desperate for Sarah's forgiveness. But she also wanted to know why Sarah was now trying to turn everyone against her.

True. One by one, Sarah went around and started to bad-mouth Adrianne to those in the group.

Mean Girl stuff.

From that moment on, Sarah later admitted, Adrianne called her cell number repeatedly.

"Every hour on the hour."

But Sarah did not always answer.

It was as if she was torturing Adrianne for doing something Sarah herself had set up and put her stamp on. To Adrianne, she and Sarah were *not* an item. It wasn't as if she had gone out and cheated on Sarah. What the hell was the big deal?

Get over it.

The next day (now two days after Adrianne had slept with Kory), Adrianne was at the party house hanging out. She had gone over to see Henry Orenstein.

Sarah showed up and initiated an argument with Adrianne.

"Slut!" Sarah screamed at her. Adrianne was officially now on Sarah's shit list. She could do no right in Sarah's eyes.

"Why do you hate me so much?" Adrianne asked. "I thought you liked me, Sarah."

Sarah got in her face. Henry was there, watching.

"Whore!" Sarah said. Then she pulled a knife from her pocket and, after flipping the blade open, held it out in front of herself.

Adrianne looked down. "If you want to kill me," she said, "do what you must!" She started crying. Ran down into the basement.

Sarah left.

36

Several days after Adrianne had sex with Kory Allison, Sarah showed up at the Rock Island party house. By now, Cory Gregory later said, Sarah and the others—including himself—were referring to Adrianne as a "slut" and "whore." And also spreading vicious rumors about her. Yet, things were about to get much worse than name-calling for Adrianne Reynolds, who believed she could gain back Sarah's trust and friendship.

"I was just going over there to hang out," Sarah later claimed, referring to the day she showed up at the house after that night when Adrianne had had sex with Kory Allison. Sarah made it sound as though she had just happened to be in the area and decided to pop in and party a little bit with whoever was on hand at the house.

This was a lie.

Jill Hiers was there. As soon as Sarah walked in, Jill approached her. She had some "huge" news to share. From this alone, it's obvious Sarah showed up at the house because she knew what was going on.

"Adrianne's here," Jill told Sarah, "and you'll never guess where she is."

* * *

Before Adrianne had retreated to the basement with that "headache" on the night she first went to the party house, she and Henry Orenstein had sat together on the couch in the living room and talked.

"She was brought to the house, just kind of," Henry remarked later, "everybody was just walking around talking to everybody that was there. Eventually I just got to Adrianne and was talking to her for a while."

This was before Adrianne went downstairs with Kory.

Adrianne and Henry expressed a desire to see each other and hang out again in the coming days. They wanted to spend time together alone. Henry had a soft spot for Adrianne. He liked her. She was not some object to mess with and tease. Henry, who was slightly older than Cory and Sarah, undoubtedly more mature, saw Adrianne as a fragile teenager, like himself. Someone who needed a friend.

But after Adrianne retreated downstairs and had that tryst with Kory Allison and left, Henry realized he never got the chance to obtain her phone number. With Adrianne gone, he figured, *What the heck. Didn't matter.* Maybe he'd see her again, maybe not.

"I wasn't really interested in Adrianne in that way at first," Henry said. "She kind of grew on me."

Adrianne opened up to Henry earlier that night, telling him about some of the problems she'd had back home in Texas. She also spoke of her passion for singing and a career in music someday. Adrianne told Henry she loved Tony, her father, but more than that she respected him.

"She couldn't say the same thing for Joanne," Henry recalled. "Adrianne was hurt that Joanne didn't trust her."

Henry came home from work the day after that party-sex with Kory to find Nate Gaudet, Sarah, Cory, and Jill together in the living room. They were laughing. They seemed high. They had someone on the other end of the telephone line. Someone they were obviously messing around with.

It was Adrianne. They were calling her any insult they could think of.

That day, Henry soon found out, had started with Sarah showing up at the house and telling Jill she was "jealous" of Adrianne and all the attention she was getting from the group. "You call her," Sarah ordered Jill, "and talk some shit to her. I don't want that bitch over to this house anymore!"

Sarah dialed Adrianne's number and handed the phone to Jill.

Henry didn't like what he had walked in on, but he didn't say anything. He knew his place.

They were taking turns, passing the phone around, "talking shit," one of the kids later said. "Calling her [names]."

"You're a stupid bitch," Sarah said at one point. "I'm gonna beat your ass next time I see you."

"You're a liar!" Nate Gaudet shouted.

"Whore!" Cory screamed, his hands cupped on the sides of his mouth.

Then they'd all laugh out loud, sure Adrianne could hear.

Sarah and Cory viewed Adrianne as an outsider, someone who seemed "cool," but someone they didn't truly know much about. On top of that, Adrianne lived in what was a strict household compared to the rest of them. They wanted to be certain Adrianne was the person—the rabble-rouser—she had claimed to be. Sarah came up with the idea that the best way to see who she was would be to give Adrianne that little test. See if she passed.

"[Sarah] knew that if she brought Adrianne to the house," a source said, "she'd be able to test her trust, as long as Sarah didn't inform [those in the house] of her plan."

Sarah had told Adrianne that "it was cool" if Adrianne went off with one of the guys in the house and got her groove on. Some said she even encouraged Adrianne to do it. This was why Adrianne was so rattled by the name-calling and change in demeanor on everyone's part. She couldn't understand what was going on.

"She pretty much told Adrianne that everything was A-okay, but then as soon as Adrianne did it, Sarah turned around and changed her story," a source recalled.

"Slut . . . whore . . ." They continued hurling insults at Adrianne over the telephone.

"What y'all doin'?" Henry asked as he walked in on the situation.

Sarah explained.

Henry laughed along with them, he admitted. Then, after they got sick of messing with Adrianne and hung up on her, Henry said, "Hey, let me have her phone number and I'll call her, too."

Sarah jumped. "Here," she said, handing him the number. "Go ahead and call her."

More laughter.

Henry Orenstein took the number and the phone and went off into the bathroom by himself.

As soon as she picked up the line, Adrianne screamed,

thinking it was Nate, Sarah, Cory, and Jill calling her back.

"Leave me the fuck alone!"

"Yo, yo! Hold on there," Henry said. He explained himself.

"What now?" Adrianne asked. She didn't trust any of them.

"Hey, I'm not callin' to give you any shit. I'm actually callin' to see if you were serious about comin' over to hang out with me."

Adrianne went quiet. Then she stopped crying. "Sure, sure," she said.

They set up a time to meet that same week.

"Guess what Adrianne's doing?" Jill told Sarah after she walked into the party house. Jill looked toward the door heading down into the basement bedroom.

"What?" Sarah asked.

Jill pointed.

Adrianne was back, all right. In fact, Jill explained to Sarah, she was downstairs right then, having sex again—only this time with Henry Orenstein.

37

Adrianne would not have been able to go back over to the party house if Henry Orenstein had picked her up. Tony and Joanne Reynolds were somewhat onto Cory and Sarah. Adrianne had mentioned that she thought they were messing with her. Tony and Jo had seen how upset Adrianne had become over the situation. On top of that, Tony and Jo did not want boys picking Adrianne up at their East Moline home.

Adrianne had called and left Henry Orenstein a voice mail message early in the day. "Sarah turned everyone against me. . . . I don't get it! I just want to be Sarah's friend. I didn't know she didn't want me to sleep with Kory."

So Henry Orenstein had Melinda Baldwin (pseudonym), another teen who lived in the house at various times, call Adrianne.

"Yeah," Adrianne told Melinda, "please pick me up. . . . I cannot leave my house with a guy."

Melinda said she'd be right over. The plan was for Melinda to tell Jo and Tony, if they asked, that she was Sarah's sister.

Now Adrianne was back in the basement of the party house, after that phone call Henry Orenstein had set up; this time, however, she was in Henry's bed, and Sarah Kolb was upstairs with Jill Hiers, listening.

Henry, of course, being the horndog that he admittedly was, had planned all along to get Adrianne into his bed. And if one believes him, "It wasn't hard to do," he recalled. But there was more in this for Henry, he added. He liked Adrianne.

Henry Orenstein didn't think anyone else was in the house—besides Melinda Baldwin, who was upstairs in her room—while he and Adrianne were downstairs.

"We chilled," he said.

"I don't understand," Adrianne told him as they snuggled after sex, "why Sarah and them hate me so much? They said they were my friends. I don't know what I did."

For Adrianne, this was the worst part of the tension separating her from Sarah, Cory, and the others: the *not* knowing. She had no way of defending herself, sticking up for her cause, if she didn't know the problem.

Henry had no way of reading into Sarah, he said. He didn't know her that well, other than seeing her at the mall, talking to her at the house, drinking and smoking with her once in a while.

The Juggalo culture in the QC was, at one time, "pretty much open," a QC Juggalo explained to the author. "You could walk around, see somebody you didn't know, and start up a conversation. You knew they were a Juggalo and you could just start talking to them without all the frills of introductions. . . ."

Sarah was not, by definition, a Juggalette. She didn't like the rap music Juggalos listened to; but she did adhere to just about every other attribute of the culture, fitting right in.

Henry heard people walking upstairs.

"I'm goin' up there to get a cigarette," he told Adrianne. "I'll be right back."

He walked upstairs. No one was around. He went into the kitchen. Then he heard all of them in the attic above.

He went up.

"You got her down there, don't you?" Sarah asked, smiling.

"Yeah . . . ," Henry said with a bashful (if not boastful) smirk, indicating that he had slept with Adrianne. "And y'all need to leave her alone."

They busted up laughing. By now, Cory was there, too. He and Sarah were as high as they could get without falling out. Nate Gaudet was with Jill downstairs.

Henry watched as they got up and decided, he later said, "to go sit in the living room." In front of the door heading down into the basement.

They wanted to be there when Adrianne came up.

In the living room, Sarah and Cory sat together, eyes focused. Ready. Waiting. Nate and Jill came in and joined them.

Henry went back down to his basement bedroom.

"I have to use the bathroom," Adrianne said. Henry could tell she was nervous. Adrianne knew who was upstairs.

Adrianne opened the door and went straight for the bathroom. Henry came up right behind her and waited in the living room.

When she came out of the bathroom, Adrianne slipped on some newspapers spread out on the floor outside the door and fell on her butt.

The crowd in the living room erupted into laughter.

"Look at you . . . on the ground!" somebody yelled.

"They started making fun of her," one housemate re-called.

"Shut up!" Adrianne screamed. "All of you. Shut the *fuck* up!"

This brought out that different side of Sarah. She shot up from the couch and got right in Adrianne's face.

Sarah was not smiling anymore.

"You dumb bitch!" Sarah yelled. "You fucking *dumb,* stupid bitch. *You* shut up!"

"Fuck you, Sarah," Adrianne said.

The others were screaming, encouraging Sarah. Chanting. Laughing.

"Fight. Fight."

"I'm going to kill you, bitch," Sarah said through clenched teeth.

Adrianne was scared of Sarah, some claimed. "But she wasn't standing down from her that day. She stood nose to nose with Sarah."

"Why, Sarah? *Why* are you doing this to me?" Adrianne wanted to know. "I thought we were friends. Why?"

"I am going to beat your ass, bitch." Sarah refused to answer Adrianne's questions.

"Why?" Adrianne asked again.

"I am going to fucking kill you!" Sarah said.

Henry stepped in. "Come on. . . ." He grabbed Adrianne. "I'm going to get you a ride home."

"I'll kill you," Sarah kept repeating, although she didn't swing at Adrianne or attack her in any way. Sarah Kolb was, for the time being, all talk.

Adrianne wanted out of the house.

Sarah walked over to Adrianne as she left. She took

out that knife she always carried and started to open and close it, over and over. Slowly. Threateningly.

"You shouldn't fuck with me," Sarah said in a low voice a number of times as she stared at the knife.

Adrianne cried.

Jill went to console Adrianne, but Sarah put up a stiff arm, like a traffic cop. "Don't you talk to her."

Jill backed off.

Henry drove Adrianne home. All the way there, she kept asking why they all hated her so much. What had she done?

"I'll talk to them," Henry said.

Before dropping Adrianne off, up the street from her house so no one would see him, he made plans to hang out with Adrianne again.

Later, when Sarah Kolb was asked about this period during her relationship with Adrianne, she brushed it off as nothing more than a girl beginning to see the true colors of someone she had wanted to be friends with and possibly date.

Turned out, Sarah explained, she didn't like what she saw.

Sarah framed her argument with zero culpability in the fact that a group of teenagers was bullying a peer. Nor did she admit how she had set the entire situation up, for no other reason, apparently, than they were all bored with the drugs, drinking, and Juggalo life they had chosen.

Sarah said after she had left the house that first night, when Adrianne had taken off and slept with Kory Allison, she made several realizations.

"The conclusion was," Sarah said in court, "that I didn't want a future with Adrianne Reynolds."

But yet she continued to call her—or have someone else do it—and harass the girl, which she left out when talking about this period under her lawyer's questioning.

Sarah said she "had not formed a good opinion of" Adrianne after that first night. But Adrianne, even after the second time at the house (when she slept with Henry), kept calling her cell number.

"Every day," Sarah said, referring to the calls, as if to imply it was the reason why she stayed engaged in the situation.

Adrianne could not walk away from a circumstance in which a group of kids who did not like her had given her no reason why. Adrianne needed answers. Which was why she continued to call Sarah.

At school, Adrianne also continued to pass Sarah notes.

"I refused to take the notes from her," Sarah said.

This gave Sarah that power she craved. She had it over Cory Gregory, and now she knew she had it over Adrianne, too. Sarah was calling the shots. As long as Adrianne didn't know why they hated her, Sarah knew Adrianne would keep crawling back.

38

By the middle of December 2004, living life under a cloud of doubt and question, Adrianne Reynolds still couldn't figure out why her new friends were treating her so poorly.

Part of it, Cory Gregory later told NBC, was Sarah Kolb feeling threatened by Adrianne's presence in the group. Sarah struggled to maintain a position of "I'm number one." And it was clear to Sarah, Cory suggested, that Adrianne had the potential to take that role away from her. "After that first day at the party," Cory added, "they fought every single day I seen them since. Sarah would make her cry."

Adrianne, however, continued to reach out to other friends at Black Hawk Outreach and maintain relationships. She wasn't entirely broken by Sarah's taunting—either that or she never let on she was. On December 14, 2004, Adrianne passed notes with a classmate, ruminating about her dream of becoming a country singer. She saw herself working hard toward this goal. She would get over any "nerves" of being on stage, Adrianne said, *Because I want . . . I want people to like me.*

* * *

On December 15, Adrianne wrote a note to Sarah: *How come you don't talk to me?*

Two weeks later, Adrianne was telling Sarah she had been going out of her way *not* to be her friend and it was upsetting.

But again, this only gave Sarah more power to control the situation.

By the end of December, Adrianne confided in her stepmother.

"I'm scared," Adrianne told Jo.

"Scared?"

"Yeah. They're all threatening me and bad-mouthing me at school."

By this time, Sarah was talking to Adrianne again, if only sporadically, telling Adrianne, hoping to convince her, that the only way out of it all was to slit her wrists.

Commit suicide.

"It was Sarah running all of this," Jo said later. "She was the one scaring Adrianne and threatening her more than anyone else."

Even after all Sarah had done to Adrianne, Adrianne wanted to give her the benefit of being friends. She sent Sarah a note near Christmas, saying, in part: *I wanted a chance for us to start over again and to at least be friends. . . .*

In another note, Adrianne asked, *Why do you hate me so much?*

Then, *Why do you want me to die?*

Sarah responded by continuing to barrage Adrianne with name-calling and insults, and by ignoring Adrianne. Sarah and several family members were celebrating her mother's birthday at the local IHOP one night in late December. They were eating and talking when

Sarah looked down and saw that her cell phone was buzzing.

It was Adrianne.

"Give me a minute," Sarah told her dinner guests.

"What do you want?" she asked Adrianne.

Adrianne said she was hoping to talk about things. "Why are you hating on me?"

"I'll call you back. I'm busy."

Sarah never did.

39

Adrianne started to see a counselor at school in a group therapy setting. According to the counselor's notes, Adrianne—being the talkative person she had always been—shared regularly with the group and had no trouble opening up about things. Equally apparent, however, was that she did not let the group know about the trouble she was having with Sarah and the rest of the Juggalo gang.

Adrianne had a sense of where her life was headed. In her journal, she drew a picture of a cross and wrote *die* on the right-hand side of the upper arm. Underneath it, she wrote: *Death awaits you,* and signed her name.

Her birth surname was Gary. In that same notebook/journal, she dedicated a page to "Gangsta Baby," writing her name as *Adrianne Leigh Gary.* Then there was the saying she often scribbled: *Fly high or die.*

A page later, *How come you don't like me anymore?* she asked, referring, it appears, to Cory Gregory. She couldn't understand why everyone was *playing head games* with her, especially Cory. What had she ever done to him? *It hurts.*

The consummate doodler, Adrianne liked to draw pictures of crosses, roses, and hearts, with words inscribed, like tattoos. *Most guys aren't worth it,* she sketched on a page of her journal, then drew a heart with an arrow—dripping blood—through it.

Most girls aren't, either, she wrote underneath.

On another page, Adrianne wrote out a numbers game she liked to play when she was bored. The words she used in the game were "Hard Sex" and "True Love." She would determine the number of letters in the names of the people corresponding to those two-word phrases. Adrianne chose Brad Tobias and Cory Gregory. She added up the totals for each, and then multiplied those numbers to determine a percentage. That percentage of both words added together determined the compatibility of the two people. It sounded as confusing as it looked on the page, but it was something Adrianne liked to do. When she completed the game for Cory Gregory's name, Adrianne came up with 92 percent, which meant, as sex partners, Adrianne and Cory, according to the numbers, fit together perfectly.

Whatever, she wrote underneath the results.

The book was filled with the insecurities Adrianne felt. She wanted to be accepted: *Everybody ♥'s Adrianne (Pinkie),* she wrote on the top of one page.

Adrianne was insightful when writing short comments that sounded like sayings you might have heard before:

My life is my sacrifice.

Underneath that saying, she drew a pentagram with an upside-down cross inside it.

It's wonderful, but confusing, she doodled on a page, perhaps talking about her life as her friendships with Cory and Sarah were falling apart.

* * *

Adrianne wrote Sarah another letter. In all of her missives, Adrianne addressed the recipient at the top/center of the page. Giving Sarah a direct message, next to Sarah's name, Adrianne drew a devil's pitchfork heading into a heart. Sarah was her Lucifer, quite obviously, piercing those feelings of inadequacy pent up inside Adrianne. Yet, Adrianne always seemed to be willing to forgive.

Hey chick, Adrianne began, *waz up? . . . Juss chillin' in class.* She said she was hungry and tired and was wondering *how come you don't talk to me? Honestly, this weekend, I am going to have to find something to do.* But she hadn't yet figured out what to do as of yet. *Was just wondering why you haven't wrote and what not. . . . See ya, hottie! P.S. Hit me back!*

It had been almost two weeks since Cory Gregory sat on the edge of Nate Gaudet's bed and said he wanted to kill Adrianne. In her journal, Adrianne dedicated a page to Cory: *PINKIE-N-CORY,* she sketched out in the middle. ("Pinkie" was another nickname for Adrianne.) *I love Cory Gregory,* she added, *because he's respectful, cute, nice, honest, and the sweetest guy I've ever met, and I think I'm beginning to trust him.*

On that same day, during group therapy, Adrianne's counselor wrote a note detailing how Adrianne had *expressed a lot about violence . . . [and] shared with the class the experience her family has had with violence and why she thinks that happens.*

The next week, closer now to Christmas, was consumed with doubt and wonder for Adrianne. Sarah Kolb would not speak to Adrianne, who was at her wit's end over the situation. She'd reached out to Sarah time and again, and Sarah wanted nothing to do with her. Sarah failed to return her calls or write back.

Then Adrianne sat down one morning and wrote Sarah a long letter, this time laying everything out in the open. There was no way Adrianne could walk away from the relationship knowing that another person hated her guts. There was no doubt in Adrianne's mind that Sarah did, in fact, despise her in a way Adrianne had not experienced.

Adrianne opened the letter by saying how she had been talking to Henry Orenstein and he had gotten the story from Cory Gregory that Sarah had set Adrianne up that first night she went over to the party house.

The cat was out of the bag.

Adrianne called the sex she had with Kory Allison the "excuse" Sarah had invented in order to break off the friendship they had started. Adrianne was calling Sarah Kolb on her little scheme, writing:

> *If you didn't want to be my friend to begin with, you should have just said something . . . instead of being a BITCH about it and instead of leading me on. That was pretty fucked and you do fucked up shit, so you must be fucked up too. You know . . . I was still going to try to be your friend but now that I know how you are, fuck it, because you're not worth it. . . .*

Adrianne admitted in the letter that on the night she slept with Kory Allison, she did it *because I just wanted people to like me. . . .* But after doing it, she said, she understood she didn't need to sleep with a boy *to get people to like me.*

At the same time, she said, she ended up sleeping with Henry Orenstein because, well, *I liked him. . . .*

In an outpouring that must have made Sarah's blood boil, Adrianne told her straight out that people *at the house* still liked her, regardless of what Sarah had been trying to do, *because they still invite me over.* As far as Cory was concerned, Adrianne continued, *he's not your friend. . . . Me and him are ok as friends.*

Next, Adrianne made an admission. It was *a mistake,* she wrote to Sarah, *for me to have slept with [Cory] and I am not going to do it again. . . .*

The best thing Sarah could do now, Adrianne warned, *was keep your mouth shut, quit telling lies and don't be a bitch. . . . If you knew how my life has been, then you'd think twice about fucking with me again. . . . Keep my name out of your mouth.* She said Sarah should watch what she said at the house because Adrianne would find out everything. *I guess I'll either talk to you later or not. I could care less. . . .*

Adrianne lastly warned Sarah that she was *not* going to lay down and take it anymore. And if Sarah thought she was a badass and could whip Adrianne and draw a knife on her: *My brothers,* Adrianne threatened, meaning Jo's twins, *don't play.*

40

Christmastime inside the Reynolds household was a festive affair. Santa gave Adrianne what she wanted: a black, with orange-and-red flames, six-string electric guitar. There's a photo of Adrianne holding her ax on her lap. It looked comfortable in her hands. She fit that Avril Lavigne, Pink-inspired, rocker-girl-with-an-attitude image. Adrianne had a street toughness about her, along with a hard edge, both spoke to her need to express an artistic side she felt she had. Music filled part of that. Adrianne had always talked of an interest in playing the guitar, and Tony had worked hard to give the girl what she truly wanted.

Nothing appeared to be too out of whack in the household during the holiday season. The quarrel with Sarah, Cory, and the other kids at school, Tony and Jo perceived, was a problem preadult kids generally worked out on their own. If not, Adrianne would drop those friends and move on. If she sensed things were getting out of hand, Adrianne was smart enough to say something, Jo and Tony were certain. There was never a doubt in their minds that Adrianne would go to them if she believed serious trouble was brewing.

"Adrianne was just like any other sixteen-year-old girl who had been flopped around," Tony later remarked. "Adrianne never disrespected Jo (or myself), as far as saying, 'You're not my mom. . . . You're not my dad. You're not gonna tell *me* what to do.' We let her do things as long as she acted right."

And as far as Jo and Tony could tell, Adrianne was doing better.

One of Adrianne's favorite things was to head down to the YMCA with Tony whenever he went to work out. There was a teen center inside the Y Adrianne enjoyed.

"Just thinking about Adrianne at the Y and how much she loved to go there and to sing," Tony later recalled, "puts chill-bumps all on me."

Tony was one of those dads, he admitted, who profiled the kids his daughter hung around. He was quick to make judgments based on the way they dressed and spoke. Adrianne knew this (and had warned Sarah about it). So whenever she was around Tony, Adrianne watched what she said about Cory and Sarah, especially.

"The only time I ever saw Sarah," Tony recalled, "was once, when she came to the house. She had this black Goth thing going on. Face paint. Dark clothes. She never said a whole lot."

Sarah stood in the doorway the entire time.

"My dog," Tony added, "did not like that girl. That should have been a sign! My dog, a boxer, went freakin' crazy when Sarah showed up."

Tony stood there, checking Sarah out, watching his dog go nuts.

"First of all, I thought she was a guy," Tony said.

"Right off the bat. You couldn't really tell with all those baggy clothes she was wearin.' My comment has always been that Sarah, on that day, looked like a thug freak."

"This is my friend, Sarah," Adrianne said, introducing the two.

Oh boy, Tony thought, lifting his ball cap off his head, putting it back on. "O . . . kay."

"Adrianne didn't dress that way—she wore tight blue jeans and girly stuff," Tony said. He couldn't figure out why his daughter had befriended someone like this: what did Sarah offer?

"Adrianne wasn't into that Goth look." (Tony meant Juggalo; Sarah and her friends would never call themselves Goth.) "She knew better. I wouldn't allow her to dress like that."

After Sarah left, Tony turned to Adrianne. "Look, honey, I love ya. But if their pants don't fit, do not bring them into my house. Because you ain't goin' nowhere with them. I don't go for no saggy-baggy pants shit. You got me?"

Adrianne nodded. She understood.

"I remember once," Tony said, "Adrianne brought this boy over to the house. They were all in the back [of the house] playing music. There was Adrianne, three or four girls, and this one boy. The boy looked like a midget, maybe only five feet tall. They was all singing karaoke." Having some good clean fun.

Tony walked into the room. "Hey," he said, waving.

The short kid turned, "What up, dude?"

Tony looked at the ground. Took a deep breath. "Look here . . . son," he began, "I'll tell you what I am going to do. You need catch your ass up outta here, all right. If you're trying to be somebody else, you need to be *somewhere* else." Tony could tell the kid's "dude" this, "yo" that, was all an act. He was trying to be, in Tony's words, an urban-speaking white boy with his hat turned sideways and pants falling off his body. Tony was offended by this.

The boy looked over at Adrianne. "Is he serious?"

Adrianne nodded her head. "Ah . . . yeah, he is."

"You're damn right, I'm serious, boy," Tony piped up.

The kid left.

Tony never saw him again.

"It's like, when I look back and go over what Cory Gregory and Sarah Kolb said on the day Adrianne went missing," Tony said. "They said they dropped her off at McDonald's. They were asked why. 'Because Adrianne's dad didn't like us,' they both said. Well, let me tell you somethin'. That was the *only* truth dem kids done told that entire day."

On December 30, 2004, Sarah and Cory took a trip to Cedar Rapids, Iowa, to pick up Sean McKittrick, and bring him back to town.

Sean and Sarah were not, she later said, dating at this time. But she was beginning to have feelings for him.

"We had discussed a possible relationship," Sarah later said, "but it wasn't official yet."

The one thing Sarah said she was sure of at this time?

That she and Adrianne were not going to be dating. It was over. They weren't even friends. And Adrianne's persistent need for closure, Sarah added, was "becoming irritating."

41

The Juggalos hangin' at the party house planned a big New Year's Eve bash.

Lots of booze.

Lots of sex.

Lots of drugs.

One of the chief instigators of trouble on this night was Cory Gregory. He was in rare form. Cory was becoming increasingly impatient with Sarah. Every day that went by, Cory slipped further away from Sarah, perhaps beginning to accept the idea that there was no chance they'd ever be together. To Cory's great dismay, Sarah had given up on females for the moment and announced that she was exclusive with Sean McKittrick, her date for the party. Thus, the more that Cory pulled back from Sarah, the more intense and strange his behavior became. It showed how much power she had over him.

"[Cory] was the kind of person who got into your head," said one girl inside the group. "He was a nymphomaniac, for sure. But he also talked about killing people and having sex with them while they were dead." Cory, this same source concluded, "is sick—his head is all *full* of crap."

Nate Gaudet was jealous of Cory. Nate did not like it when Cory was around his girlfriend, Jill Hiers. Cory "wanted" Jill, same as he wanted some of the other girls. But only for a romp. Not so much a relationship. In that regard, Cory was exclusive to Sarah, and, it turned out, was beginning to feel Adrianne could fill that role Sarah had denied him.

"Cory would do anything for Sarah," one Juggalo said. "And I mean *kill*! Cory worshipped the ground Sarah walked on and he wanted to marry her."

During the New Year's Eve party, Nate and Jill got into a blowout. They were drunk and arguing. It started inside the bathroom. Nate was doing most of the screaming. To those outside the door listening, it sounded like Nate was on the verge of becoming violent.

Then he did.

Nate grabbed Jill by the throat.

Hearing this, Sarah kicked in the door. Dragged Nate out by his arm, pushed him to the ground, and began kicking him. Nate was too drunk to react or defend himself. He started vomiting. Stood up. Then he bounced off the walls, trying to walk away.

"You fucker," Sarah screamed, spittle spraying out of her mouth. "You leave her alone. *Never* choke a girl!"

Cory Gregory came running up. Everyone was now involved, yelling and arguing, getting in one another's faces.

Nate looked tired and depressed. He was drunk, yes. But also in a terrible state of darkness. Something was going on with the kid.

Cory grabbed him. "Shangri-La, Nate . . . ," Cory said. "Shangri-La."

"Shangri-La" is a reference to Juggalo heaven, and part of the title from Insane Clown Posse's eighth studio album, *Wraith: Shangri-La*, which was released in 2002. The cover of the disc depicts a devil-type figure without a face standing on an open book, traditional devil horns, and reptilian hands with pointed fingernails, clouds and blue sky in the background, a black bird on his shoulder. His red cape covers his head like the Grim Reaper, Mr. Death; with one hand, he is gesturing for those who wish to come to him. Among the song titles on the CD are "Walk into the Light," "Juggalo Homies," "Murder Rap," "Hell's Forecast," "The Wraith." Once again, it is a disc full of songs written by group founders Violent J and Shaggy 2 Dope that glorify death, sadistic sex, and drugs, while degrading women in every manner imaginable.

Pure filth.

Cory was down on himself tonight. After so many months of going back and forth with Sarah, she had finally come out and told him—or maybe it was the first time he actually heard and believed it—that she was never going to be with him romantically. He could fantasize all he wanted. He could hope. He could wish. He could pray. However, it was never going to be, Sarah made clear.

His life, Cory decided, was now totally worthless. He had nothing to look forward to. In making the reference to Shangri-La, Cory knew, he was sending a direct message to Nate, pointing out an option for both of them.

"Come on, Nate," Cory said, grabbing him. "Let's go upstairs."

They went into the attic.

Another friend sensed trouble and followed.

Cory had talked Nate into committing suicide with him. It was something they had discussed in the past. The way they talked about it was like one of those suicide pacts terrorists make; as if by doing the deed, there were rewards waiting for them in Shangri-La, Juggalo heaven.

They stood by the attic window. It was open.

"Come on, Nate, we're going to do this . . . ," Cory said. "Ready?"

Nate shrugged. His life was going nowhere. Fast. All he did was drink, do drugs, listen to music.

Death seemed like absolution. A safe place.

42

As Nate and Cory attempted to jump out the attic window to their deaths, that friend who had heard the chatter about suicide and followed them upstairs came up from behind and, in his words, "wrestled them to the ground."

He had saved their lives.

For the time being.

"They settled down after that."

Sarah Kolb did a lot of writing while at Black Hawk. In October 2004, she had penned a biographical essay about her life and how she viewed it up until that point. Sarah lived in Milan, Illinois, but wrote that she had been born on an American base in "Nernberg, Germany" (but probably meant "Nuremberg"). She said both her parents served in the army for a few years, which was where, she thought, she had picked up a little bit of French and German.

Juggalos all around the QC, Sarah said, were her friends.

It was her mother, Kathy Klauer, she wrote, who had raised her, and Sarah respected her for it, saying that Kathy could be *very nurturing and sweet, but when it's time to be serious, she can be a very scary woman.*

Darrin, her stepfather, was the *closest thing,* Sarah wrote, she'd felt she ever had to a *real father.*

Even though she called her stepsister a *half-blooded sister,* Sarah said, it didn't make any difference, *we still love each other the same.*

Interestingly enough, being the youngest in her family, Sarah considered herself to be a burden, yet she viewed being the runt of the litter as a blessing because she was able to watch everyone else grow, *learning from their mistakes to better* her own future.

Moving from Rock Island High School to Black Hawk, Sarah claimed, was a change she had needed in order to *get away from . . . those students [at Rock Island] who were keeping me from focusing on schoolwork.*

She planned on going to college, where she would *grasp* her *goals with a strong fist.* Sarah, clearly writing for a specific audience (the teacher), was sure about what she wanted to major in, but *concerned about getting there.* Her aim was to work in a warehouse that sold CDs so she could *talk about music all day long.*

California was where Sarah wanted to live: *better weather, more options, more people.*

It had not yet been three months since she had written that essay and here she was, consumed really, with the idea that there was another girl, whom she viewed as a slut and whore, trying to take her place inside that clique of Juggalos, where Sarah had been the focus for the past year or more. There was a narcissistic side to Sarah, which screamed out to the world that life needed to be about her, or she wanted no part of it. And anybody who came between Sarah and that spotlight would have to pay a price.

Inside the halls of Black Hawk, Sarah heard Adrianne was "getting around" even more than Sarah thought. Didn't matter that Sarah had had a hand in spreading these rumors. Some later noted that Sarah, when she first met Adrianne, saw a girl she could begin a long-term relationship with and perhaps love. "Damn, she's hot" was what Sarah said, according to a friend, on that first day she saw Adrianne enter Black Hawk. But then moments later, "I didn't mean that," she said, retracting the statement.

There was one more reason Sarah wanted nothing to do with Cory. It was something she told a friend a day after Christmas—this friend, a boy, knew what she meant.

"He's bi," Sarah told her friend. "He's got a crush on you."

This scared Sarah. She didn't want to date a bisexual male. Dating bisexual females was hard enough. Plus, Sarah considered Cory to be crazy. There were far too many demons in his head. Sarah had enough of her own to contend with. She would use Cory, sure. But that's where the relationship stood.

No more. No less.

Sex for Sarah, according to a former friend, was difficult. Not emotionally, but physically. She told a friend she would rather not have sexual intercourse with a male, because "she has a shallow vagina and it caused her pain." Another male, who claimed to have had sex with Sarah three times, said she was crazy. Very violent and aggressive.

* * *

Sean McKittrick was now dating Sarah. Sean began classes at Black Hawk after the holiday break, and he was seen often cruising the hallways with his buddy Cory Gregory. Sean had that Juggalo look to him, like Cory: baggy clothes, chain wallet, dark, withdrawn and droopy look on his face, hair shortly cropped around the ears, jarhead-like, but straight up like a jagged mountain line or rippling fire on the top, same as one of those Japanese anime characters. Sean was another one who, like Cory, listened to what Sarah said and did.

Sean and Cory passed Adrianne in the hallway.

"Whore!" Sean said.

"Slut," Cory added.

They laughed.

Adrianne stopped. This was an everyday affair now—insults being shouted from across the hallway. Outside. In class. They were ganging up on her.

Enough was enough.

"Why did you sleep with our friends?" Cory asked, walking closer to Adrianne, Sean behind him.

Cory was so different when around the others, Adrianne thought. One minute, he was calling her and talking about going out and how much Sarah was a pain in the ass and troublemaker. The next, he was calling her names.

Adrianne wouldn't answer. Instead, she later wrote in her journal, she wondered why they hated her so much for doing what they had asked her to do.

Sarah was not around. "If she was," said a friend, "Cory and Sean would sit back and let Sarah do the talking."

This said a lot about the types of kids Sarah kept in her tight circle.

Later that day, Adrianne saw a mutual friend of hers and Sarah's, Cara Sands (pseudonym).

"They still bothering you?" Cara wondered. She felt bad for Adrianne, who was beginning to bear the brunt of what was now a concerted effort to harass, degrade, and bully her. Cara had watched the entire thing play out.

"Adrianne cut her hair short and started wearing more black-colored clothes. It seemed to me that Adrianne was changing so Sarah would like her more."

"Yeah . . . Hey, I ever tell you that I'd love to get pregnant and have a child?" Adrianne told Cara.

Cara was surprised by this statement. It seemed to come out of nowhere. Adrianne, Cara later said, had been telling many of the kids in her class the same thing.

"No . . . but why would you want that, Pinkie?"

"A baby would be someone to love, without strings attached."

43

When Sarah returned to school, she put the focus back on Cory once again. Cory was beginning to withdraw more as the new year went forward. He was smoking more pot than ever. Drinking more heavily than Sarah had ever seen. But even beyond that, Sarah noted in her journal, with Sean McKittrick now attending classes at Black Hawk and trailing along with Sarah, Cory was showing contempt for—as Sarah put it—*this "me & Sean" thing*. Sarah was into Sean, perhaps content in a relationship for the first time in what seemed like a hundred years, she noted.

The following week, January 10, a Monday, Cory was missing from school. Sarah surmised he was still sleeping—probably hungover—or just had "no motivation" to show up anymore. That chronic, recurring social disease of today's youth, depression, had gotten ahold of Cory, no doubt, and would not let go. Sarah, feeling it herself, saw how miserable and morose Cory was these days; yet she didn't say anything much about it to him. At one point, Sarah resigned that she couldn't "do anything" for someone who didn't want to help himself;

and Cory dropping out or getting expelled indefinitely because of his behavior was, Sarah concluded, "his own problem."

Sean was going to be getting a job at a local car wash. This made Sarah happy. The kid would finally have some money to take her out.

Woo-hoo, she noted in excitement.

On the opposite side of the hall, in her own way, Adrianne was confronting the problems she had with Sarah. In her journal, Adrianne wrote about going to talk to Jo, her stepmother. She spoke of her willingness to face the issues with Sarah and work through them.

She's gonna give my dad a call, Adrianne wrote, meaning Jo, *and they're going to get me help and I told her what's going on with Sara and I.*

On that same day, Adrianne had a friend over to the house. Writing after the visit, she was proud of herself for not sleeping with the boy, even though he had gone and bragged about having sex with her to the kids at school the following morning:

I showed him my guitar, watched TV, ate and sang, then he left. . . . That's all that happened.

The boy had asked Adrianne to go to a party with him that night, but she turned him down, and instead left with another friend and his parents.

Adrianne entered into a penned conversation with Cory Gregory about the boy coming over to her house and what was being said around school about her that day. It seemed Adrianne could do no right. Whether she slept with a boy didn't matter anymore. The kids in school were going to say she did, anyway.

Why are you making a big deal of it? Adrianne asked

Cory. *Nothing happened! You can ask my brothers—because they were there, baby!*

Cory didn't respond.

Adrianne continued, adding, *What's your prob? Why are you hatin' on me? I thought you still liked me but you're accusing me of shit or, excuse me, thinkin' I did shit, and I didn't.*

Cory failed to respond to that statement also.

Adrianne wrote again: *What's wrong?* Beside it, she drew one of her signature sad faces, and then passed the notebook back to Cory for him to respond.

Cory wrote that Adrianne's "cross words" were pissing him off.

Imagine that! A kid whose language skills consisted of the F-word and a litany of additional vulgarities—not to mention all the sexual innuendo he talked about—was preaching to Adrianne about her use of the actual English language.

But Adrianne was smarter than that.

That's not all, she wrote back, sensing Cory was holding back. *I know it isn't. There's something else. Talk 2 me, please. Quit flippin' me off!*

Cory didn't write back. But later that night, he wrote Adrianne a letter, spelling out what was going on, and his place in it all. He addressed Adrianne as "Kid," a charming nickname he had been calling her. He explained how he had never lied to her about anything. He called himself an honest person.

Adrianne had, in the interim, called Cory on his relationship with Sarah and his role in bullying her. It seemed to Adrianne that whenever Sarah, Nate, or any of the other Jugs were around, Cory acted differently. He went with the crowd. When she was alone with him, he appeared to be her friend. Adrianne asked him which was the real Cory, and what was the purpose for the act?

Cory wrote that he wasn't involved in the rumor mill or the bullying on the level Adrianne had perceived—but he *had* gone along with that so-called test Sarah had devised back in mid-December.

Sarah wanted to see how you would be . . . , Cory wrote.

If Adrianne was wondering why Sarah did it, Cory said he had a theory. He explained that every girl he brought over to the party house (prior to Adrianne) had ended up sleeping with someone who lived there. Sarah was *picky,* Cory clarified, *when it came 2 females,* so she had to test Adrianne in order to see if she was datable. She wasn't keen on letting just any slut into the group.

Word traveling through the party house lately was that someone had passed around a sexually transmitted disease. Adrianne was infuriated by this, thinking it was another way for them to torment her, true or not.

Cory said that, as far as he knew, only Nate and Jill had it. But there was a chance, he added, that the other Kory had been infected.

Which meant there was a possibility Adrianne might have gotten it.

Cory left a postscript, clearing up something Adrianne had confused in one of her conversations with him earlier that day. Cory had said he didn't "like Sarah." Adrianne had it all wrong.

I love her, Cory spelled out.

No matter what Cory said, it was clear to Adrianne that Sarah Kolb was still pulling his strings.

Sarah had been up all night on January 12, 2005. It wasn't cocaine, X, or any other illegal substance keeping Sarah from finding some shut-eye; it was her hair.

Yes, hair.

It took seven hours, she wrote in her journal the following morning, most of the previous day, to braid her
hair. The tight cornrows had made her head burn and
throb. She couldn't sleep at all because of the pain.

As much as Sarah said she was fed up with Adrianne,
she was stringing Cory Gregory along, telling him one
thing to his face, while talking "shit" about him behind
his back. She told one friend that all Cory and Nate did
these days was drugs. They were both lazy. If they
weren't drinking or drugging, they were sleeping. She
referred to Cory as "the Jew," keeping up her bigotry-
inspired, I-hate-the-world, Nazi image. She mentioned
how Nate and Cory were buying *X . . . like crazy*. This,
mind you, *when they have rent to pay*. Cory was basically
living at the party house these days. Neither he nor
Nate had a job. The little bit of money they managed to
scrape up, *they spend on drugs*.

Two kids whose lives were going nowhere.

Sarah had zero patience for losers.

That being said, Sarah next wrote about leaving class
one day in January to go pick up a friend so they could
go buy an ounce of weed. She was excited about this.
After they scored, they were going to get high, then sit
around and roll joints until they filled a cigarette pack
with them.

Apparently, doing drugs was okay for her.

As the week of January 17 began, Sarah had Sean
McKittrick and their relationship on her mind. She
wrote about how much she liked being with Sean, but
was fighting off an ex-boyfriend who had contacted her
in a drunken rage one night and mentioned how he
wanted to get back together. The reason the ex was

pissed off turned out to be because he had seen Sarah with Sean.

At the end of this entry, Sarah noted how Cory pulled Sean aside one day and apologized to him for being in love with her. But there was nothing, Cory told Sean, he could do about his feelings. He loved Sarah. She was everything. He couldn't change that.

A friend asked Sarah if Cory would ever get over her. She said it would take some time, but ultimately he would. After all, Sarah added, *[I haven't] slept with [him] in over seven months.*

44

On January 17, 2005, Henry Orenstein got a call from Adrianne Reynolds, who sounded concerned, demanding to know what was going on at the party house.

"Hey," Adrianne said, "Sarah called me. She said everyone at the house has chlamydia." (Chlamydia is a sexually transmitted infection, common among those who sleep around. It is treatable with antibiotics.)

Adrianne was worried that maybe she had gotten it because she had slept with Henry Orenstein and Kory Allison.

"Don't worry about it," Henry assured her. "I'm clean." It was basically Nate Gaudet who got it, he explained.

"I don't believe you!" Adrianne snapped.

"Come on . . . ," Henry said.

"No, no . . . I would believe Sarah over you *any* day!"

"You can fuck off then," Henry said. "If you want to go and believe somebody who hates you, well, fuck it, go right ahead!"

Dial tone. End of the conversation.

And the friendship.

This would be the last time Henry Orenstein ever spoke to Adrianne Reynolds. She would be dead, dismembered, and buried (in two different places) within three days of this conversation.

John Beechamp worked with Adrianne at Checkers. Adrianne would approach John and complain about her hours. Checkers was not giving her enough.

"She was very cheerful, upbeat, liked to get to know people," John remembered. "She liked to make friends. Just a regular sixteen-year-old."

In many ways, Adrianne was ready to take on the world as one more curious teenager. John Beechamp had a girlfriend and three kids at home. He was twenty-six, a decade older. He saw part of himself in Adrianne: a rebellious, active teenager who needed to get past the next few years and realize adulthood was a hell of a lot simpler than those teen years, when it seemed no one understood how she felt.

John worked Saturdays; Adrianne generally didn't. He asked her one afternoon, "You want to babysit for me some Saturday?"

"Sure," Adrianne responded. She could use the extra money. But there was more to it than that. John was older. He had a family. Adrianne had always liked the idea of someone taking care of her. She didn't care that John Beechamp was already spoken for.

"Why don't we first have you come over to the house to meet my kids and girlfriend."

Adrianne agreed.

"I'll pick you up," John offered.

It was January 19, 2005. Two days before Adrianne went missing.

"Can I bring a friend?" Adrianne asked. "His name's Cory. He's a guy I like."

John didn't care for a lot of people he didn't know hanging around his house. He thought about it.

"I guess."

"Can you pick him up for me?"

"Sure," John said.

He later told police, "She had a crush on me."

Adrianne had written John Beechamp a letter disclosing her feelings. Addressing it to "babe," she opened by saying how she was well aware of the difference in age: *But listen to what I have to say, ok?*

Adrianne said how much she really liked Beechamp because he was so unlike the guys she dated. She could talk to Beechamp and relate to him in ways she couldn't with the others.

Adrianne, however, was no dummy: *I know, for you,* she wrote, *I am jail bait.* She warned him not to lead her on by *flirting* and *asking for lap dances* while at work. It wasn't *just about sex,* she made clear. *I'm fixing to be 17* soon and for the past few years *I've wanted a family and a guy who cares for me.*

She mentioned future plans. If she wasn't with a guy after she got her GED that June, she was taking off and moving back to Texas. This didn't mean settling for some loser who would ultimately cheat on her; she wanted a man. She talked about being a legal adult in eighteen months and told John Beechamp that if they were to enter into a relationship now, she had no trouble *keep[ing] a secret that long. . . .*

John later told police he tossed the letter in the garbage after reading it. He said he never flirted with Adrianne. He did, however, tell her that she looked nice, on occasion, in passing small talk, but only as a compliment. Adrianne, apparently, took the comments another way. He denied talking about having a sexual relationship with Adrianne, saying that sex was all anyone at Checkers ever talked about.

At six thirty, Wednesday night, January 19, John picked up Adrianne. Without telling her, he had begun to second-guess Adrianne's babysitting skills. Was she going to have friends come over to his house while she was babysitting? Was she going to be partying and not watching his kids?

Maybe this was a bad idea.

John then picked up Cory, as Adrianne had suggested. But instead of taking them over to his house, he drove to a friend's.

"We kind of just hung out," he recalled. "Played some PlayStation."

As far as John could tell, Cory seemed "all right, like a good guy." He was into Insane Clown Posse and that whole Juggalo movement, John could tell by the way Cory talked and dressed. But that didn't make him a bad dude. He and John talked about tattoos and ICP for a while.

"Random talk" was how John later framed the conversation.

As the night wore on, John noticed that Cory and Adrianne were kind of attached to each other. They held hands. Kissed. Laughed together. Acted like a couple.

"Hugged up on each other," John told police. "They were cuddled up next to each other and very friendly. . . ."

The night concluded without any problems. John saw a different side of Adrianne. She seemed responsible.

"Can you babysit for me this Saturday?" he asked.

Adrianne had reconvinced him throughout the night that she was the right person for the job.

"Yeah," she said. "Sure." Adrianne hopped out of the car and walked into her house.

John took off. As he drove, Cory announced, "I got my penis pierced."

What a random thing to say.

"No shit."

"Hell yeah!" Cory was proud of this achievement.

"You know Adrianne well?" John asked.

"She fucked a few of my friends," Cory said. "She wrote me a letter telling me that I'm her boyfriend."

"No kidding. . . ."

Cory said he wasn't too interested in dating Adrianne, but he said, "Yeah . . . love to fuck her."

"She told me she likes you," John shared.

"Yeah?" Cory said.

"She doesn't like that Sarah chick, though."

45

He called them his "bitches," Sarah later noted. Cory Gregory, even though she wasn't interested, would carry on, Sarah claimed, about what he liked to do to the girls he dated. One of the bitches at this stage of Cory's life was Adrianne. Cory was hanging out with Adrianne more than he was with anyone else. And Sarah Kolb did not like this. She felt slighted by it, in fact. As if Cory had gone and purposely defied her.

"*Dat* bitch is dippin' in my Kool-Aid" was how Sarah put it more than once that week Adrianne went missing. Sarah was referring to Cory and a second rumor she heard about Adrianne wanting to get with Sean—a big no-no in Sarah's rather short book of social rules.

In the eyes of his relatives, Cory Gregory had disengaged from being a normal part of the family unit seven months prior to that January. Cory was not by any means a straight-A student, polished and genteel, goal oriented and eager to take on the world as an adult. But he wasn't the trash-talking, alcohol-abusing druggie he had turned into, family members claimed, after meeting and becoming obsessed with Sarah Kolb, who seemed to have a hold on Cory that no one could explain.

Katrina Gates, Cory's half sister, the oldest of Cory's siblings, was close to her brother up until that time when he stepped away from the family and into Sarah's grasp. Katrina had moved out of the house when she was sixteen. Cory spent every other weekend with his sister, who had a daughter, Cory's niece, similar in age.

"He didn't have any time for his family anymore," Katrina said, talking about that period after Cory met Sarah. "This was strange, because he used to spend [a lot of time] at my house. He was constantly here. He babysat all of my friends' children and was just this fun-loving, outgoing boy who always had the cutest girlfriends."

There was another side of Cory that Katrina began to see emerge, however.

"I kept hearing that he was doing drugs, you know, popping pills. And Cory didn't keep it quiet." He never tried to hide what he was doing. "He'd come over my house talking stupid all the time. Saying how he smoked weed, popped some pills, did X, acid . . . whatever."

Cory's sister believed the pain Cory was trying to numb with all of this behavior was rooted in the fact that he "grew up without my mom in the house." Cory was eight when his parents divorced, an important age. This is where, psychologically speaking, Sarah fit into the mix. She filled that function as gatekeeper and authority figure for Cory, but also the feminine role, the comforter and caretaker. In Sarah, Cory found a female who could tell him what to do, when to do it, and he felt comfortable enough to accept what she said.

There were no boundary lines.

In junior high, Cory played football, had a lot of

Adrianne Reynolds was a happy child, well-liked by classmates.
(Photo courtesy of Tony Reynolds)

Eight-year-old Adrianne is all smiles in this 1996 photo.
(Photo courtesy of Tony Reynolds)

As Adrianne approached her teen years, her life at home crumbled—the only father she knew, Tony Reynolds, ended up in prison.
(Photo courtesy of Tony Reynolds)

Adrianne became her own person as she approached her sixteenth birthday in 2004. In these two photos, her personality shines. *(Photos courtesy of Tony Reynolds)*

A few weeks before Christmas 2004, Adrianne got into a spat with a girl at her school. Soon after, their relationship turned deadly. *(Photo courtesy of Tony Reynolds)*

For Christmas 2004, Adrianne was given this guitar, which would have surely accompanied her during an "American Idol" audition she had planned. *(Photo courtesy of Tony Reynolds)*

From left to right are: Josh Schatteman, Joanne Reynolds, Tony Reynolds, Justin Schatteman, and Adrianne. Adrianne's stepbrother, Justin, drove her to school on January 21, 2005—the last time she was ever seen. *(Photo courtesy of Joanne and Tony Reynolds)*

Adrianne posed for this photo at a John Deere shrine in Moline, Illinois, only weeks before she disappeared. *(Photo courtesy of Tony Reynolds)*

For the first time in perhaps her entire life, Adrianne finally felt at home while living in her father's house in East Moline, Illinois. *(Photo courtesy of Tony Reynolds)*

Adrianne met her killers at this high school, an alternative GED program at the Black Hawk College Outreach Center. *(Photo courtesy of Jo Reynolds)*

One of the girls Adrianne wanted to date when she first attended Black Hawk Outreach was Sarah Kolb, a popular "Juggalette," who had been in trouble with law enforcement. *(Photo courtesy of Rock Island County High School yearbook)*

Cory Gregory became friends with Adrianne Reynolds after Sarah Kolb, his best friend, told him it was okay. *(Photo courtesy of Teresa Gregory)*

Before becoming a Juggalo and self-proclaimed "druggie," Cory Gregory was very much into playing sports and studying. *(Photo courtesy of Teresa Gregory)*

Jo and Tony Reynolds became worried when Adrianne didn't show up for work at this Checkers Restaurant in Moline. *(Photo courtesy of Jo Reynolds)*

Cory Gregory and Sarah Kolb told law enforcement that Adrianne and Sarah had a fight inside Sarah's car in the parking lot of this Taco Bell in Moline. Adrianne was never seen alive again.
(Photos courtesy of Jo Reynolds)

This photo of Adrianne Reynolds appeared on the missing person flyers distributed around the Quad Cities. *(Photo courtesy of Tony Reynolds)*

As details began to emerge from a core group of Quad City Juggalos, Adrianne's body parts would be found in Black Hawk State Historic Site. *(Photo courtesy of Joanne Reynolds)*

Adrianne's killers chose this area, just beyond these wooden stairs, to hide her severed limbs. *(Photo courtesy of Joanne Reynolds)*

Realizing he could not escape justice, 17-year-old Cory Gregory wound up leading investigators to an area inside Black Hawk State Historic Site where he and two accomplices disposed of Adrianne's chopped-up body—this after they got high and gorged themselves on McDonald's fast food. *(Photos taken from video provided by the Rock Island County State's Attorney's Office)*

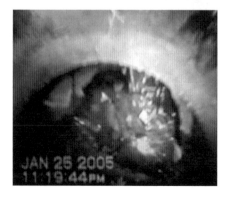

Found approximately ten feet underground and inside a manhole, Adrianne Reynolds's head and arms were recovered inside this black garbage bag. *(Photos taken from video provided by the Rock Island County State's Attorney's Office)*

The Rock Island County Jail and Sheriff's Department became the epicenter of the investigation as Cory Gregory began to talk about his role in Adrianne's murder. *(Photo courtesy of Joanne Reynolds)*

The Rock Island County Justice Center was the focal point of the litigation against the three teens charged with Adrianne's murder, dismemberment, and concealment of her remains. *(Photo courtesy of Joanne Reynolds)*

Cory Gregory ultimately led investigators to a farm in Millersburg, Illinois, where the rest of Adrianne Reynolds's dismembered body was recovered. *(Photos taken from video provided by the Rock Island County State's Attorney's Office)*

While an investigator reads Cory Gregory his Miranda rights at the second crime scene in Millersburg, Cory's lawyer (right) looks on. *(Photo taken from video provided by the Rock Island County State's Attorney's Office)*

Nathan Gaudet, one of the Juggalos Adrianne hung out with, is asked on camera by investigators if he cut up Adrianne's body into seven pieces. *(Photo taken from video provided by the Rock Island County State's Attorney's Office)*

These mug shots of Nathan Gaudet were taken after his arrest. *(Photos courtesy of the Rock Island County State's Attorney's Office)*

These mug shots show how Cory Gregory looked when he was arrested in late January 2005 for the murder of Adrianne Reynolds. *(Photos courtesy of the Rock Island County State's Attorney's Office)*

The many different faces of sixteen-year-old Sarah Kolb. This was how she looked (above) on the day of her arrest and weeks later (two photos below), after some time in prison. *(Photos courtesy of the Rock Island County State's Attorney's Office)*

Cory Gregory in his most recent mug shot. *(Photo courtesy of the Rock Island County State's Attorney's Office)*

A more mature looking Sarah Kolb after a few years behind bars. *(Photo courtesy of the Rock Island County State's Attorney's Office)*

friends, and enjoyed the innocent things kids do when they're teetering on the edge of being a teenager. It was in high school, his mother Teresa Gregory said, when Cory started to act differently.

"It was a bigger school," Teresa Gregory recalled. "So he kind of got in with a group. They don't know where they're going in life or who they are—and it's easy for a kid to fall into a group that feels the same as you do."

Teresa soon realized Cory was smoking pot.

"I'd had a lot of problems in my life when I was younger and I didn't want Cory to go down that road, so we would talk, you know. But there's going to be things kids hide from their parents. No matter how much I'd like to say he told me everything, I know that is not true."

Cory's mother said she could tout Cory's goodness all day long, and tell stories about the great things he did in his life. "But there are always going to be people who don't like him—especially in this town (the QC). There are people who love Cory to death, and there are people who are going to have bad things to say about him."

When Sarah came into the picture, Teresa said, Cory changed, not just his behavior, but his identity, and who he was on just about every level.

"If he didn't do exactly what she said," Teresa added, "she'd get mad and tell him she wasn't going to be his friend anymore."

Peer pressure. A drug in and of itself.

To illustrate how much of a pull Sarah Kolb had on her son, Teresa explained how Cory's grandfather had once given him a little truck, which Cory adored. He drove all around town in it. When Sarah heard about this and saw Cory driving, she felt that his newfound independence would eventually come between them.

"You don't need me anymore," Sarah said. Cory and Sarah had always bombed around town together in Sarah's red Prizm.

"What . . . no," Cory answered.

"Well," Teresa recalled, ". . . he parked that truck and *never* drove it again."

When Sarah went to work, she expected Cory (and Sean, too, later on when he came into the picture) to wait for her inside the mall where the cinema was located until she got off her shift.

The other major thing that truly hurt Cory, his mother said, was that Cory had introduced Sean to Sarah. Then they started dating.

Katrina Gates said her brother had told her all sorts of "stupid things" she did not want to hear. One of them was that he had feelings for other males.

"Yeah," she said, "he told me he was bisexual."

He also told his sister he "was really into gory movies."

The bloodier, the better.

Katrina began to realize how much of a hold Sarah had on Cory. He'd be at his sister's house, check the time, and say, "I gotta go. . . . Sarah's getting off work soon. I *have* to be there."

"His whole world suddenly centered around Sarah. He thrived on wanting Sarah to think so highly of him, for some reason. I don't understand why he wanted to impress her so much."

Sarah was "quiet," Katrina noticed, to the point that it "creeped me out.

"From the first time I met her, I didn't care for her. You could tell that she totally controlled Cory."

If Cory said something to his sister about where they were going, for example, and Sarah overheard, she would "glare at him," Katrina noticed, "as if to say, 'They are not supposed to know anything about us.'"

By January 19, 2005, the Wednesday before Adrianne went missing, Sarah had grown tired of Sean Mc-Kittrick. She wrote in her journal that she was *breaking up w/Sean soon.*

Sarah gave no reason or specific episode that sparked these feelings.

What had enraged Sarah into homicidal fever, however, was a letter Adrianne had written, describing how she was still friends with Cory, and that she would still be hanging out at the party house whenever she felt like it, despite a direct order from Sarah that she was not to show up there again.

At school, Sarah heard Adrianne had passed Cory a few notes. So she devised a plan to get Adrianne into her car so she could take her out to lunch—the ruse—on that Friday afternoon, January 21, 2005. Sarah wanted to confront Adrianne about everything: Adrianne's supposed crush on Sean, her relationship with Cory, and her place in the group.

Sarah's only plan on that day, she later claimed, was to beat Adrianne up; give her a good old-fashioned ass whupping for all she had done, with the hope of sending her away from the group.

In her journal, on the day Adrianne disappeared, Sarah noted her disdain for Adrianne, writing that she (Sarah) might be getting expelled for what she had been doing to cause Adrianne trouble, which only infuriated Sarah more—the idea that Adrianne had ratted her out to school authorities.

Stupid bitch needs to back off my Kool-Aid! Sarah wrote.

The flavors she was referring to on this day were Cory Gregory and Sean McKittrick. Adrianne had said how nothing Sarah did (or could do) would ever change the way she and Cory felt about each other. On top of that, Sarah had heard Cory and Adrianne were dating— that Cory had had sex with Adrianne, in fact.

Yeah, the final journal entry of Sarah's high-school life read, referencing the note Adrianne had slipped to Cory that morning, *I'll fucking kill her.*

PART III

BODY PARTS

46

The last day of Adrianne Reynolds's life, Friday, January 21, 2005, began on what appeared to be a note of reconciliation. Getting up and heading off to school, Adrianne was under the impression (soon after walking into the building) that Sarah Kolb wanted to make up and be friends again.

This was a great relief to Adrianne. She had always been willing to forgive and forget. Start anew. No, she and Sarah would probably never be lovers or best friends; but they could get along, wave to each other at parties, and hang with the same people.

Why not? Adrianne thought.

Bygones be bygones, and all that sentimental non-sense.

At ten thirty that morning, a number of kids known as the Black Hawk "weed group" were out near the student parking lot, smoking cigarettes. Beyond the pot-heads, one of the kids smoking that morning later told police, "There are two other groups—one being a 'Goth' group (meaning the Jugs), and the other being made up of males and females that are gay."

Cory and Sarah, of course, fit into both cliques.

Sarah was outside, standing next to a few girls and *three or four male subjects,* as a report of the morning noted.

"I'm going to hurt that bitch," Sarah said, looking toward the school, taking an aggressive drag from her cigarette. There was fire in her eyes. Hate in her voice. Determination.

Everyone knew who Sarah was talking about. There was excitement building in the air for a catfight.

Cory walked over. Sean McKittrick was there with another kid, who had several notes in his hand that Adrianne had written to Cory.

Sarah glanced at the notes. "Let me see those . . . ," she snapped, grabbing at them. "I want you to tear them up! Now!"

"No," the kid said, pulling the notes away.

Sean came up, grabbed the notes out of the kid's hand, tore them into pieces, and tossed the handmade confetti into the air.

The reason why Adrianne had not given Cory the notes herself—the kid who had been asked to pass them to Cory later explained—turned out because "Adrianne was afraid of Sarah." After showing up at school, that tiny bit of optimism Adrianne had when walking in that morning was quickly overshadowed by more threats and name-calling from Sarah.

The bell rang. Cory and Sarah stood in the main hallway, talking. Cory said, "Hey, did I tell you what Adrianne wanted to do the other day with me and [another guy]?"

Sarah looked at him. "What?"

"A train . . . ," Cory said, knowing the consequences, realizing how much more Sarah would hate Adrianne, and knowing how *enraged* this would make Sarah. "She wanted to run a train with me and [that guy] she is babysitting for tomorrow."

Cory was, you could say, fueling the situation between Adrianne and Sarah; promoting more trash talk about Adrianne in Sarah's presence, understanding that it would further trigger a fight between the two girls. It seemed the entire group was hankering for a brawl on this day, even pushing Sarah to make the first move.

Just before classes began after that 10:30 A.M. break, Adrianne tracked down the kid she had given the notes to.

"I need a ride," Adrianne said. She didn't say where.

"Sure," the kid offered. He had given Adrianne rides in the past.

As class started—and maybe this was part of the plan all along—the kid who was supposed to give Adrianne a ride home raised his hand and told the teacher he didn't feel good and needed to go home.

Adrianne watched her ride walk out the door.

"I really felt good," the boy later told police. "But I just didn't want to give Adrianne a ride and get involved with all that 'drama.'"

Right.

There was a groundswell of late-morning gossip flowing through the hallways: whispers of a major fight that was going to happen between Adrianne and Sarah. After first thinking she and Sarah could be friends again and resolve things without a blowup, as early afternoon approached, Adrianne understood she was going to have to face Sarah and, possibly, tangle with her. Asking that friend for a ride was Adrianne's way— one last time—of getting home without any trouble. But now she had no choice but to face Sarah.

Just after the lunch bell rang, Sarah confronted Adrianne in the hallway, forcing her sixteen-year-old rival up against a wall. Sarah was smart not to put her hands on Adrianne, but she was "in her face," several witnesses reported.

"I am going to fucking *kill* you!" Sarah said, pointing, staring into Adrianne's eyes.

Adrianne didn't move. She looked scared.

Several teachers hovered around.

Realizing she couldn't fight Adrianne inside the school without being expelled (and interrupted), Sarah allowed Adrianne off the wall.

Then, with her head down, changing her demeanor, putting on a show for the teachers, Sarah apologized.

"I'm sorry . . . I didn't mean that."

Adrianne looked at her.

Sarah stared at her foe.

"Really?" Adrianne asked.

"Yeah," Sarah said.

"Can I get a ride home?" Adrianne asked.

Cory walked up. "Yeah . . . come on, Adrianne," adding that Sean was going to be going along with them, too.

Adrianne followed Sarah and Cory out to the parking lot. Sean met them at Sarah's car.

It was just after twelve thirty, Friday afternoon, January 21, 2005, when Sarah Kolb, Adrianne Reynolds, Sean McKittrick, and Cory Gregory drove out of the Black Hawk Outreach parking lot.

"You mind if we stop at the Taco Bell in Moline," Sarah asked Adrianne, "and get some lunch before we drop you off?"

The plan (or promise) was to drop Adrianne off at her home in East Moline. Taco Bell in Moline was on the way.

"Sure," Adrianne said.

"Sarah tricked Adrianne into being her friend that day and going with them to Taco Bell," one of the kids standing in the parking lot, watching Sarah's beat-up old Prizm rattle out of sight, later said.

From what many on hand that morning later told police, the only person who didn't think Sarah was "tricking" Adrianne into this ride to Taco Bell, and then home, was Adrianne Reynolds.

47

Sarah pulled into the parking lot of Taco Bell and looked at the line for the drive-through window. Adrianne was under the impression they were going to grab a bite to eat and head to her house.

But there was a long line of cars at the drive-through, so Sarah suggested they park and go inside.

Sarah inched her car into a space close to Twenty-third Avenue. Then she shut the car off.

After taking a breath, Sarah turned and faced Adrianne. Sean and Cory were in the backseat.

"You want to run a train, I hear," Sarah said.

"What?" Adrianne asked. She could hear that familiar contempt in Sarah's voice.

"You whore. You fucking like Cory *and* Sean—don't you?"

Adrianne wasn't going to back down. She now knew what was going on.

"Yeah. I do! So *what?*"

Adrianne sat in the front seat with Sarah. Cory sat behind Sarah, Sean behind Adrianne. Sean said something, but Sarah stopped him. Then she reached over, grabbed Adrianne by the back of the head, a fist full of hair, and pulled her toward the driver's side.

"Bitch," Adrianne managed to say.

"Hey . . . hey," Sean yelled. "Stop it, Sarah. This isn't right."

"Leave us the *fuck* alone!" Sarah screamed. There were cars in the parking lot on both sides of Sarah's Prizm. The windows, however, fogged up quickly and steamed over because the heater was off and four people were breathing heavily in such a confined space.

"Don't talk to me," Sarah continued yelling at Adrianne. "Don't talk to Cory. And *don't* fucking talk to Sean!"

"Come on, Sarah, stop this shit," Sean said. He tried to break it up. "Sarah . . . ," Sean kept saying. "Stop it. . . ."

Sarah had Adrianne "by the back of the neck" at this point, Sean later said.

"If you don't fucking like it, Sean," Sarah screamed, "get out!"

Sean tried to open the door, but it was locked.

"Unlock the door, Sarah, come on," Sean said. Sarah still had Adrianne by the back of the head. "You all are going to get into trouble for this," he added, directing his comments now to Cory, too.

"Unlock the fucking door yourself!" Sarah yelled.

Sean fidgeted and got the lock open and jumped out. He was going to walk back to Cory's house, where he had been staying, but he decided to walk to school, finish the day, and then take the bus to Cory's.

Adrianne got away and grabbed Sarah by the neck, according to one account Cory Gregory first gave police, before she began choking Sarah, who was now kicking and moving wildly around, like an epileptic in a seizure.

"And then Sarah started choking [Adrianne]," Cory told police. "And they were both struggling to choke each other."

And this was where things became cloudy. Cory later told NBC that, at this point, Sarah grabbed her stick and started to whack Adrianne with it to stop any momentum Adrianne had gained. Adrianne was winning this fight.

What is clear from the documentation, however, is that the two girls struggled to gain the upper hand on each other, fighting violently and aggressively, as girls often do. They pulled back and forth on each other. Adrianne and Sarah were the same size, height, and weight. It was, if nothing else, a fair fight—that is, without Sarah grabbing her stick or Cory getting involved. Moreover, Adrianne was known to be tough—quite capable of taking care of herself. It's safe to say that by this time she all but had it with Sarah. Here Adrianne was willing to give Sarah another chance, and now Sarah had gone and lied about giving her a ride home. Her true purpose, Adrianne knew, was to confront her and fight.

Sarah let go of Adrianne's neck and backhanded her across the face. It was a good shot. Hard and heavy. Lots of power behind it.

The blow knocked Adrianne down onto the floorboard, and she ended up partly underneath the dashboard.

When she came back up, however, Adrianne thumped Sarah good across the nose with a closed fist, busting open a blood vessel.

Sarah's nose bled profusely, soaking into her shirt.

Sarah later told a friend that she'd once had surgery on her nose, and the fact that Adrianne had busted it open infuriated her. It was then that a fury she could not contain erupted inside Sarah. She had to make Adrianne pay. In her twisted mind, Sarah saw no other option now but to deliver the ultimate punishment.

As Sarah put her hands over her nose, Adrianne, one report claimed, hopped into the backseat with Cory, who wasn't doing or saying much at this stage of the fight.

"I stared out the window for the most part," Cory later said, "and smoked a cigarette."

After getting herself together, Sarah reached into the backseat, grabbed Adrianne, and then pulled her back toward the front. Adrianne kicked violently, in spasms. Her feet pounded on one of the windows, presumably the window opposite Cory's side of the car. Adrianne was now horizontally across the inside of the car: her head was facing the driver's-side backseat window, her feet facing the backseat passenger-side window.

Seeing this, Cory told police, as if he couldn't stop himself because she was there, on his lap, Cory said he grabbed hold of Adrianne's arms and pinned her down on his lap—essentially helping Sarah. He described this as an impulse, as if he had no other choice.

But, of course, Cory Gregory—if his first version of Adrianne's murder was correct—had plenty of other choices.

Sarah took Adrianne by the neck and pulled half of her body into the front seat, strangling her, holding her down, that uncontrollable wrath consuming Sarah's fragile emotions—this while Cory Gregory continued holding Adrianne's arms and feet down so she couldn't defend herself.

Adrianne was pinned.

And now struggling to breathe.

Glynn Roach Jr. worked up the road from the Taco Bell at Highland Manor, an apartment complex. Roach had been at the job about a year. Fridays were payday for Roach. He liked to treat himself to lunch.

After cashing his check, he stopped at Taco Bell.

With his lunch in hand, heading back to his car, Roach noticed a fuss of some sort going on inside a red Prizm on the south side of the parking lot, close to where he had parked his car.

"I seen a vehicle with people in it," Roach later said, "and there was a commotion in the vehicle."

Roach's first reaction to this as he walked by the car was *It looks like somebody's getting beat up*.

The vehicle was "moving back and forth like it was rocking," Roach recalled.

There was another vehicle parked between Roach's car and the one with the commotion going on inside. Roach couldn't see because the widows were fogged over. Before getting into his vehicle, however, Roach stopped, walked to the front of his vehicle, looked into the "rocking" red car two spaces over, and figured, *Ah, probably just some teenagers in there fooling around*.

A moment later, Roach started his car and drove back to work.

"And then, before—before I knew it," Cory first told police, "they quit choking each other, and Adrianne was blue."

Cory said he looked down at Adrianne after Sarah had lifted her hands from around Adrianne's neck and believed, simply by looking at Adrianne, that Sarah had strangled Adrianne to death.

"Her lips were blue and her face was blue."

Her body was limp.

"She was dead. She wasn't breathing and her entire face just turned blue."

"What the fuck . . . Sarah!" Cory observed.

Sarah freaked out, yelling, looking around, wondering if anyone had seen what happened. After all, she and Cory had just killed someone in broad daylight, during the lunch rush at a popular and busy Taco Bell. And it was clear to both now that Adrianne Reynolds, a girl Sarah had been bickering with and threatening for well over a month, was dead.

Cory jumped in the front passenger seat. Sarah pushed Adrianne's limp body into the back. It fell with a thump on the backseat floorboard.

"Sarah was scared, and I was scared, and then we—we were trying, well, we were trying to figure out what we should do. . . ."

"We'll get rid of her body," Sarah suggested.

"What? Fuck, Sarah. This is crazy. Where?"

"Aledo."

Sarah's grandfather had a farm there.

Cory lit a cigarette. They needed to think this through.

"I was scared," Cory first said, "so I helped her."

Sarah covered Adrianne's body with a black-and-tan coat. Started the car. Put the shifter in reverse. Backed out of the space. Then she drove out of the parking lot.

Cory stared out the window.

"Holy shit, Sarah. . . . You killed her."

48

Sarah headed directly for her house in Milan. When they arrived, Sarah pulled her car into the garage, quickly got out, and then shut the door behind them. Both were in a state of shock, Cory claimed, running on pure adrenaline. Cory chain-smoked cigarettes. As time passed, Sarah seemed to hold herself together, rattled more by the idea of getting caught rather than the fact they had just committed murder.

"What are we going to do?" Cory asked.

"Burn her body," Sarah suggested.

"Huh?"

"We'll get some gas and a tarp here, roll her up in it . . . and then bring her somewhere. . . ."

Cory had followed Sarah's lead up until this point, why stop now?

Sarah's stepfather, Darrin Klauer, was home. It was two o'clock, Klauer later recalled in court. Sarah and Cory walked inside the house.

"Hey . . . I parked in the garage," Sarah said to her stepdad.

Klauer didn't respond, but, "I thought," he said later, "'She doesn't usually park in the garage.'"

"I need to change," Sarah said as she walked by. She headed into her bedroom and put on a new set of clothes.

When she saw her stepfather again, after she put on a fresh pair of pants and T-shirt, Sarah said, "Cory's with me. We're going out to Aledo to wish Grandma a happy birthday."

Nonchalant. Business as usual in Sarah's skewed world.

Back in the garage, Sarah took a two-gallon plastic gas can, one of those red jobs every suburbanite has for his lawn mower. Then she grabbed a blue tarp, like the one used to cover a boat or collect leaves. Tossed them into her trunk.

Adrianne was still in the car, on the backseat floorboard, her body covered with a jacket.

"Where are we going?" Cory asked as they drove away from Sarah's house. It appeared Sarah had a plan. Or was making one up as she went along.

Sarah drove to a place called Big Island, a secluded area off Twenty-seventh Street West, in Milan. (The terrain is wooded, hilly farmland, same as around any lake. Not too many people in these parts. A few spots for fishing and hanging around. That's about it.)

She parked. "I believe," Cory said later, "it was next to a dam."

Sarah got out of the car—she had to roll the window down and reach outside to open the driver's-side door of her car, because the inside handle was broken. She walked around to the passenger side, where Cory sat. She took a quick look in every direction. Then she opened the door, pushed the seat forward after Cory stepped out, and pulled Adrianne's body out by her legs, thumping her corpse onto the cold, frozen ground.

"Help me," Sarah said, looking at Cory, again pan-ning in all directions, making sure no one was watching.

Cory and Sarah hoisted Adrianne into the trunk. (Both would later claim the other did this.)

"Where are we going now?" Cory asked.

"My grandpa's farm."

The Engles' farm was in Millersburg, a town of just under eight hundred people in Mercer County, part of the Davenport-Moline surrounding area. Sarah knew the topography of the farm well. It was a thirty-mile, forty-five-minute drive from Milan.

Perfect.

Her grandparents' farm was off the beaten path. Far away from that Taco Bell. The Engles did not even live on the farm; their residence was in a different part of town. Sarah figured she and Cory could drive onto the farm, find a secluded area away from the main road, pour some gasoline over Adrianne's body, and, like a Viking funeral, watch it burn into ash, the murder they had just committed going down in flames.

No one would ever know.

The idea that Cory later tried to sell was that the ground was too hard—frozen—to bury Adrianne, so they had to get rid of Adrianne's body by cremation. But Cory never mentioned this to police during his first interview. From what he told police, it was Sarah's plan from the get-go to torch Adrianne's body in order to cover up what they had done. Fire, after all, is one way to destroy evidence. Many first-time killers choose this path thinking it will cover up their crimes. The problem is that most crematorium ovens shoot for an optimum temperature of between 1,600 and 1,800 degrees Fahrenheit. It's not a matter of pouring some gasoline on a body and sparking a match.

That's Hollywood stuff.

Fantasy.

Sarah found a spot on her grandfather's farm, out near the edge of a wooded area and large field. There was a lake deeper into the woods, Cory later said. But this spot would do just fine.

After she parked, Sarah grabbed the blue tarp and spread it out on the ground in back of the car near the trunk. Then she reached into the trunk and, pulling with all her might, plopped Adrianne's body onto the tarp.

"Help . . . ," she said.

Cory came around and helped Sarah roll Adrianne up in the tarp.

"Come on," Sarah said.

"What?"

Sarah dragged the tarp "to this spot," Cory explained, "just [to the] right, there's like two roads, and then she took it to the lower part of the—the lower road."

Sliding Adrianne's dead body turned out to be easier than they thought; the ground was frozen solid and there was a bit of snow.

In his first account of the murder and subsequent cover-up, Cory Gregory minimized his role in the entire homicide and crimes committed afterward to the point where, reading the interview he gave to police, you'd think he was watching this from the bushes with binoculars, reporting on it. But Cory—make no mistake about it—was involved here on every level, participating in every aspect of this crime—probably much more than he later admitted. He helped Sarah in every aspect of the ordeal—and, perhaps most important, he did not do anything to stop Sarah from killing Adrianne inside her car. That is, of course, if he did not fully contribute to the murder itself from that moment after Sean McKittrick left the vehicle.

"There is no way," one law enforcement officer later told NBC, "that Sarah Kolb could have killed Adrianne Reynolds by herself."

49

The inconsistencies in Cory Gregory's version of these events began to add up as he described the murder to police in more detail. The investigators interviewing Cory had to push him continually for specifics. Ask him: *What happened next? What did you do? What did Sarah do?*

According to Cory, Sarah took the can of gasoline out of her car and poured it over the tarp containing Adrianne's body. They were deep in the woods, down in a ravine near a small stream on Sarah's grandparents' farm. (A video of the crime scene taken later, however, doesn't show an area "deep in the woods," as Cory recalled it, nor does it show a stream, frozen over or not.)

After that, Sarah took what Cory said was a "red grill lighter," one of those long-necked things with a trigger handle used to light a fireplace or gas grill, and lit the tarp. (Later, while talking about this same scene, Cory said: "I poured the gasoline on the tarp. It was a butane lighter. I used the lighter and lit it, and then Sarah and I, we just stood away. . . .")

Two different versions of one truth: burning Adrianne's body.

Regardless who lit the thing, a *poof* went up as the gasoline vapor and the fuel itself exploded.

"And then," Cory explained to police, "Sarah and I stood there, but we couldn't look. We couldn't look at it."

They stayed with Adrianne's body for about a half hour, Cory claimed, watching it burn and then sizzle out. Then they walked back to the car, which was parked away from where Adrianne's body had been torched.

Once they got back to the car, Cory explained, they sat and stared at each other without speaking.

"And we listened to music."

"I'll be right back," Sarah said after a time. She needed to check on the body. Make sure it had completely disintegrated into ash.

The fire had nearly gone out. Adrianne's body was still intact.

"Shit. . . ."

They had to do something.

"Let's go to the antique store," Sarah suggested. Inside Sarah's grandmother's antique store might be something they could use to dispose of Adrianne's body—what, exactly, Cory never mentioned.

"We need more gas," Sarah said as they rummaged through the store, looking around. It was close to four o'clock, witnesses inside the store later reported, when Cory and Sarah arrived.

Della Smoldt, Sarah's aunt, was working behind the counter. Sarah had been in the store the previous afternoon looking at a "trunk and a pair of red glasses" she seemed interested in. Smoldt said this was the first time she had ever met Cory Gregory.

"Sarah . . . how are you?" Della asked her niece.

Sarah was preoccupied. Della noticed what looked to be a "fresh scratch" on Sarah's face, she later said. She wondered what had happened. (Sarah must have washed up at home right after murdering Adrianne, because nobody later reported any dried blood on her face.)

"You okay?" she asked Sarah. "How'd you do that, honey?"

"Cory and I were wrestling around," Sarah said.

Della noticed that Cory had very short fingernails. This was a strange answer from Sarah, who seemed awfully nervous and preoccupied, Della thought. Twitchy. Out of it. Very much not herself.

Sarah's aunt went over to Mary Engle, Sarah's grandmother, who was working in another part of the store, getting ready to close the shop at 5:00 P.M. and head home. Della told Mary about the trunk and red glasses.

Mary approached Sarah.

"You want the trunk and glasses?" Mary asked her granddaughter.

Cory piped in, saying, "Sarah has acquired a recent fondness for red. . . ."

The fact that Cory had admitted to this statement says a lot about his demeanor that day. One would have to ask: *Would someone freaked out and totally shocked by a murder his friend had just committed by herself say such a thing?*

Just then, Cory and Sarah walked to the back of the store, whispered something to each other, and left.

"Sarah got more gas," Cory claimed, "and then we went back to the farm."

On the way, Sarah called one of her friends, an eighteen-year-old girl she knew. Someone old enough to buy cigarettes.

"Can you get me a pack of smokes at [the store]?" Sarah asked, "I'll meet you there."

With a fresh few gallons of gasoline and a pack of Marlboro Reds, Cory and Sarah drove back to Adrianne's body. It was close to five o'clock now, the sun had fallen from the sky, darkness settling.

Cory claimed it was Sarah who poured the additional few gallons of gasoline over Adrianne's body and lit it on fire that second time.

"We figured since we couldn't bury the body (frozen ground)," Cory told NBC, discussing this second time he and Sarah went to dispose of Adrianne's remains, "the only proper thing to do would be cremate it."

Yet, Cory never mentioned this to the police.

It was dusk now, the sky almost completely dark as molasses. As he would later explain to the police, Sarah's grandfather was out in another pasture of the farm, feeding his cows, when he noticed a car off in the distance. Brian Engle never reported seeing any flames.

Adrianne's body would not catch fire and burn into ash, as Cory and Sarah had hoped.

"What the fuck do we do now?" Cory asked, turning to Sarah for direction.

Just then, Sarah saw her grandfather coming up the road.

"Shit. . . . Come on . . . hurry."

Sarah and Cory took off, the lights on her Prizm off. Sarah drove straight to her grandparents' house.

50

After her grandfather questioned Sarah about why she had taken off with her lights out, he threw up his hands in frustration and left the room.

That was close, Sarah and Cory knew.

Sarah told Cory, "Come on, let's go."

She wished her grandmother a happy birthday and walked out of the house.

During this part of his interview, Cory Gregory said something rather interesting regarding this particular moment of the night.

"And then Sarah took *us* (emphasis added) back out there. . . ."

"Who's us?" the detective interviewing Cory asked, picking up on the odd pronoun.

"Back out to the farm," Cory answered nervously.

"Who's *us*, though?" the cop pressed.

"Uh, her grandparents' farm."

"But you said, 'Took *us*.' Who went back out to the farm?"

"Oh," Cory said, as if he suddenly figured it out, "Sarah and I . . . sorry."

As Cory went back to explaining the remainder of the night, he was more relaxed. He said after they went out there for what was the third time, Sarah poured another round of gasoline over Adrianne's body and lit it on fire. Cory didn't stand and watch this time, however, noting: "It was too hard. I couldn't. . . . It was too hard . . . because this was a person."

Adrianne Reynolds was now a *this* and a *person*.

Sarah had been on the verge of crying throughout the entire ordeal, Cory claimed. After she lit Adrianne on fire, Sarah walked over to where Cory sat and "laid her head on my shoulder."

And then—according to Cory—Sarah broke down. Cory said he cried, too, but not outwardly, like Sarah. Tears, he explained, flowed down his cheeks in silence.

They both sat, staring, while at this human being in the distance—a sixteen-year-old girl whom they both had had a friendship with, a girl Cory had had sex with and Sarah was interested in dating—burned.

Sarah got up and walked over. Cory said he stayed behind.

"And then after a while," Cory explained, "she, uh, and . . . well, she went and checked on her again. . . ."

Sarah stood over Adrianne.

"Fuck!"

The body still wouldn't burn.

"What are we going to do?" Cory asked.

"Let's go," Sarah said, motioning toward her car.

Nate Gaudet worked a shift from 11:45 A.M. to 6:00 P.M. on Friday, January 21, 2005. Nate had just gotten the job at MD Racing, a motorcycle mechanical shop in

Oregon, Illinois. By the time Sarah and Cory headed back to her house in Milan from the burn site, Nate was at his grandmother's house, getting ready for another Friday night of booze, cigarettes, drugs, and fun with his girlfriend, Jill Hiers.

Nate believed Cory and Sarah had a "closer" relationship than he and Cory did. Over the past few months, Nate had been with Cory and/or Sarah just about every day. Three weeks before Adrianne's murder, when Sean McKittrick showed up in the picture, Sean became part of this daily crew. In the days before Adrianne was murdered, Nate had moved in with his grandparents; this happened after being evicted—along with everyone else—from the party house in Rock Island for not paying the rent.

Near nine or ten that Friday night, after two failed attempts to burn Adrianne Reynolds's corpse, Cory and Sarah called on Nate for his help.

"What up?" Cory said.

"Hey . . . ," Nate replied.

"What are you doin'?" Sarah asked, grabbing the phone from Cory, explaining that she and Cory were at her house in Milan, hanging out in her room.

"I'm—I'm copping," Nate said. He was in the process of obtaining "some cocaine," Nate later admitted in court. "And can drop by after I pick it up."

"We'll be at Cory's," Sarah said.

Nate told them he would be there around eleven.

Cory, Nate, and Sarah hooked up before midnight and snorted cocaine into the wee hours of Saturday morning, January 22, 2005. According to Nate, during that entire night of partying, neither Cory nor Sarah said anything about what had happened inside Sarah's

car and the attempts they had made to destroy evidence
and get rid of Adrianne's body. In fact, Nate Gaudet's
role in what was about to become the most gruesome
homicide QC law enforcement had investigated in
decades wouldn't be set into motion until the following day.

51

Staying up most of the night to snort cocaine, smoke cigarettes and weed, trying to numb what was the reality of a horror show back at the Engle farm, Cory and Sarah fell asleep late that morning and woke up around two o'clock, Saturday afternoon.

Sarah had to work at the cinema at 3:00 P.M. So they got up and drove to Sarah's Milan house so she could get ready.

Reports were already beginning to filter into the community that Adrianne was missing. None of this deterred Sarah or Cory from their new plan. They still had a body to get rid of and evidence to destroy—if they were going to cover up their crimes.

And make no mistake what this was now about for Cory and Sarah: getting away with murder.

At some point, Sarah stopped and picked Nate Gaudet up at his grandmother's house. The idea was for her to drop Nate and Cory off at Cory's house, so they could hang out there until she got off work.

Nate sat in the backseat, behind Cory. Sarah drove.

She took a longer route, Nate later explained, not the normal, faster way.

Cory and Sarah had been looking at each other since picking Nate up. They had something they needed to share. Nate sensed it as she drove.

"Could you ever kill somebody?" Cory asked, according to Nate's recollection.

"Yeah, *could* you?" Sarah added.

"I don't know! What the fuck? . . . What are you two talking about?"

"What would you do if you ever saw a dead body?"

"What the . . . Did you guys go and kill somebody?"

There was a beat of silence.

"Yeah," Sarah said. She looked at Cory. They could trust Nate.

"What?" Nate had a feeling they were serious. "Who?"

"Adrianne."

"What? . . ."

Sarah continued, "I started hittin' that bitch with my fists and Sean got out of the car . . . and walked back to school. Then I picked up my stick and started hitting her in the face. She punched me in the nose. Then Cory held her arms back while I choked her to death."

Cory sat and said nothing, Nate later explained. He was listening, shaking his head in agreement with Sarah.

"What . . . where?" Nate asked.

"Taco Bell parking lot."

According to what Sarah said to Nate in the car as they drove, the fight had started on a different note. "She said," Nate later explained, "she asked Adrianne for a hug and I guess they started hugging, and then Sarah grabbed Adrianne by the back of her hair and said, 'Don't you ever come around Cory or Sean again.' And then she started hitting her with her fists." Sarah claimed Adrianne "broke her nose." She also told Nate that when she choked Adrianne "blood came out of her mouth. . . ."

Both of these statements were likely added to enrich the drama and "toughness" of Sarah's reputation. It is unlikely that Adrianne broke Sarah's nose, simply because the bleeding stopped rather quickly and photographs of Sarah taken in the days after do not show any injuries to Sarah's face consistent with a broken nose. Likewise, unless Cory and Sarah stabbed Adrianne, or beat her so badly with that stick that she developed internal injuries, there's not a chance Adrianne had bled from her mouth while they choked her.

More shocking than any of this, however, was what Nate said next. He claimed that after Sarah was "done choking Adrianne, Cory grabbed a belt and wrapped it around Adrianne's neck while Sarah drove. . . ."

Nate told a different version of what had happened at Big Island, implicating Cory even more. He said Sarah told him—again, with Cory in the car, nodding in agreement—that when she and Cory arrived at Big Island, Sarah parked, got out, went around to the passenger side of her vehicle, opened the door, and "Adrianne's head flopped out" of the side of the car.

This scared Sarah, Nate noted.

So she had Cory grab Adrianne's body and placed it in the trunk. (A scenario, incidentally, that makes more practical sense, seeing there was no way Sarah could handle picking up Adrianne's body by herself.)

Throughout this conversation Nate had with Sarah and Cory inside Sarah's car the day after Adrianne's murder, Cory never butted in and changed any of the facts as they were being laid out by Sarah. Rather, Nate claimed, Cory *added* to the drama.

As Sarah drove, she said to Nate, "Listen, we're going to pick you up tomorrow morning and drive out to Adrianne's body." Sarah said she had to work that day and night.

By now, they had arrived at Cory's house. Sarah let them out.

Sean McKittrick ("the mooch," Sarah called him) was at Cory's house when they showed up.

After Sarah left, at Nate's request, Jill arrived in her Ford Explorer.

They all went out that afternoon while Sarah was at work. Then Nate and Jill dropped Sean and Cory off back at Cory's house.

Cory called Nate and Jill near 10:00 P.M.: "I need a ride to the mall. . . ."

Jill and Nate picked Cory up and dropped him off.

Sarah got out of work. Cory was waiting for her.

By eleven, Sarah and Cory were back at Cory's house, where they stayed and talked for a few hours.

"I'm going home," Sarah said to Cory. "I'll call you when I get there." The implication was: *Don't do anything on your own. Wait until I give the order.*

Cory understood.

He waited.

Sarah called about a half hour later and told Cory she was home. She said they both needed to get some rest. They had a big day ahead of them on Sunday. With Nate's help, Sarah explained, they were going to finish what they had started out at the farm.

Cory called Nate at ten the next morning, January 23, 2005.

"We'll be there soon."

Nate said he'd be ready.

Just before noon, Sarah and Cory arrived at Nate's grandmother's house to pick him up and head out to Millersburg.

As Nate stepped into Sarah's car, she stopped him. "Hey, grab a saw," Sarah said.

Nate said, "What?"

Cory added, "A saw, man. Get a saw."

By now, Nate knew why he needed that saw. In his testimony, Nate explained how they had briefed him about the plan to dismember Adrianne's body and literally spread it around the state of Illinois so authorities wouldn't identify or find the body parts.

The saw was "for Adrianne Reynolds, to dispose of her body," Nate told the court.

This part of the plan was all Sarah Kolb's idea, Nate insisted.

"Hold on," Nate said to Cory and Sarah. He walked back into his grandmother's house (as Nate's grandma watched from a window), went down into the basement ("the furnace room"), and found a hacksaw that one might use to cut wood or metal. Some call it a box saw, or miter, one of those rectangular-shaped saws with fine teeth used in finishing woodworking.

Before stepping back out of the house with the saw in his backpack, Nate went into his room and put on a long, ankle-length black trench coat. He wore gloves—those black leather driving gloves with the fingertips cut off. The gloves were a Juggalo thing.

The drive out to the farm took an hour. During the ride, Cory and Sarah "restated," Nate recalled, just about everything they had the previous day, going through the plan all over again.

At the farm, Sarah pulled over and parked.

"Right there . . . ," she said, looking out the windshield, pointing.

That was the spot where Adrianne Reynolds's body lay in wait for Nate Gaudet and his hacksaw.

52

Sarah Kolb and Cory Gregory got out of Sarah's Prizm and walked into the wooded area where Adrianne's body had been burned on two previous occasions.

Dressed all in black, including a black winter wool cap, Nate Gaudet followed.

Their shoes crunched against the hard, snow-covered ground. It had actually snowed fairly heavily on Saturday, the previous day, and there was a solid covering of the white stuff, a top layer of which had hardened like two-day-old frosting on a cake.

Sarah had covered Adrianne's body that Friday night before they left. There was a ravine just beyond the path they had walked up, Nate remembered, where Adrianne's body lay, waiting.

Cory walked over to the narrow passage and removed the brush Sarah had used to cover Adrianne's charred remains.

Nate stood at the top of the ravine. He looked down at both of them removing the sticks and brush.

"Come on," one of them yelled up to Nate, who ran down the slight hill, then stood by Cory and Sarah.

264   *M. William Phelps*

They noticed "a gardening tool" Nate had with him. He found it inside Sarah's car. She had grabbed it from her house. ("It was a wooden stick with a metal claw on the end of it," Nate said. "Shovel length.")

"Shit . . . I should have grabbed her necklace . . . before I burned her," Sarah said as she looked down at Adrianne's head, still attached to her body, despite most of the skin burned away.

Nate didn't need to be asked. He knew why he was there and what to do. It was the only reason they had called him. Nate had a reputation for wading in the dark side. Some claimed he liked to maim and hurt animals, cut them up, in his younger years.

Nate bent down on one knee, took the saw in hand. The way he described what he did next sounded as if he was talking about a television show he had seen. While on bended knee, Nate said, "I started cutting her head off. . . ."

As Adrianne's necklace fell off her headless corpse and broke into pieces, Sarah reached down, picked it up and put it in her pocket.

Nate Gaudet cut Adrianne's head off, he said, "because Sarah wanted me to cut the body in pieces."

It appeared that Sarah had some sort of strange power over Nate. Note the choice of language: "the body." This is one way people who commit such savagery trivialize the act and take the human aspect out of what is heinous behavior. In using such a common choice of words—Cory and Sarah would later use the same type of references—it distances one from what he has done.

In truth, Nate didn't have to be told. After cutting Adrianne's head from her body, he moved down to

Adrianne's arms, later describing this as matter-of-factly as one could describe it: "I cut the arms off."

As Nate went from one arm to the next, Cory opened a black garbage bag they had brought with them and placed Adrianne's head inside the bag.

Sarah Kolb stood and watched all of this, Nate said, but she refused to touch any of Adrianne's body parts.

When Nate finished with Adrianne's arms, Cory walked over, picked them up, and placed them inside the same bag.

Nate moved onto Adrianne's legs. After cutting off both limbs, for reasons that he could not later explain, Nate cut Adrianne's torso in half, he said, "under the ribs."

The reason why Sarah wanted Adrianne cut into pieces was twofold: Most important, so they could hide her teeth in fear of being identified by dental records, and to place her body parts in various locations around the QC so authorities would never find her.

"If we put [her] in different places, she will be harder to find," Sarah said as Nate and Cory finished.

Cory ran up the hill, the bag containing Adrianne's head and arms slumped over his shoulder and back as though he were Santa Claus. Then he placed it inside the trunk of Sarah's car.

Nate brought the saw up and put it inside the trunk next to the bag.

Back at the site where Nate had butchered Adrianne's body, Sarah took the gardening tool she brought from home and pushed the two halves of Adrianne's torso, along with her legs, into the small gully (or "stream," they called it) running through the ravine.

The body parts sank in the mud.

Nate returned. He found a fox hole near a timber

that had fallen over and into the stream. So he forced Adrianne's legs and torso into it with the gardening tool.

Sarah brought the gardening tool back up the hill and placed it in her trunk.

When Cory explained this part of the crime to police during his first interview, he blamed it all on Sarah, never once mentioning Nate had been with them.

Cory stated that Sarah proceeded to cut the head off Adrianne's body, then the arms, an EMPD report filed on January 25, 2005, read. *Sarah then placed the head and arms in a trash bag. Sarah then cut the torso in two. The legs were already dismembers* [sic] *from the body because of the fire.* . . .

In the remainder of this particular report, Cory blamed every aspect of the crime on Sarah: from the murder to the cover-up, to the dismemberment and the hiding and burying of the body parts. It is clear from this report that he was hoping by minimizing his role in the crime, he would get off with being an accessory, and completely save Nate from any charges.

Cory Gregory lied to save himself and his friend, finally turning on the girl he had claimed all along he had loved.

When Nate returned after forcing Adrianne's torso and legs into the fox hole, a tepee-shaped structure made out of old logs and brush, he and Cory (now standing up by the car, smoking a cigarette) watched Sarah take Adrianne's necklace out of her pocket and toss it into the trunk.

"Let's eat," one of them suggested.

"McDonald's," Nate said.

Cory had a double cheeseburger. Nate ate a Big Mac.

Both later said they forgot what Sarah ordered, but she ate, too.

The job was not yet complete, however.

Inside Sarah's trunk were Adrianne's head and arms. Thus, the question remained: what were they going to do with the body parts that could identify Adrianne?

Sarah started her car.

She had an idea.

53

It had been a long day of smoking weed, dismembering and disposing body parts, which could ultimately send them all to prison for a long time, and gorging themselves on fast food. And yet there was still one important job left to be done: hide Adrianne's head and arms, the two most distinguishable parts of a human being: teeth and fingerprints.

Sarah needed gas for her vehicle. So they stopped at a pump station in Aledo and Nate pumped gas into the tank while Cory went inside to pay the cashier.

Sarah waited inside her vehicle.

For the time being, Sarah and Nate were alone outside at the pumps. What would become an important issue in the coming months, Sarah never said a word to Nate. In fact, she had every opportunity to grab Nate, pull him aside, and plead whatever case she wanted to make. But Sarah never did any of that; instead, she waited patiently and quietly.

Nate had left his bowl (a pipe for smoking weed) in his room at his grandmother's house. They needed it.

So Sarah drove to Nate's grandmother's so he could grab some more weed and the bowl.

Leaving there, Sarah suggested getting rid of Adrianne's body parts at Big Island. There was enough open area and some water. Plenty of secluded ground to choose from.

When they arrived, Sarah didn't feel comfortable; there were people fishing. Others were wandering around.

So they smoked a few bowls and took off.

"We're going to my house," Sarah said.

After parking in front, Sarah got out of the car and walked into the house.

Nate and Cory sat inside Sarah's car and smoked a cigarette.

Soon Sarah came out of her garage with a shovel.

"Black Hawk State Park," she said as she started her car. There were plenty of places inside the Black Hawk State Forest section of the site to dispose of Adrianne's head and arms: a watchtower, a bird observation area, an abandoned coal mine, picnic shelters, and plenty of thickly settled forest. According to information on its website, Black Hawk State Historic Site is a 208-acre steeply rolling tract that borders the Rock River, in Rock Island County.

Sarah knew of a spot down the main trail, which they could get to easily by parking in the yellow-lined public lot. There was a wood stairway that led to a river. She had been there before with Cory and other Juggalos. They could find a hidden location out there to get rid of the bag.

Nate, Cory, and Sarah walked through the woods for at least five minutes. It was icy and slippery, tree branches stingingly whipping them in the face as they walked.

Soon they came to a set of wooden stairs, as Sarah

later explained, which led down to a secluded area of two "dirt stairs" built into the ground.

"Here," Sarah said. "Right here."

Cory had the shovel. Nate carried the bag of Adrianne's body parts.

"Dig a hole, Cory," Sarah ordered, pointing. "Over there."

Cory walked over and put the shovel to the ground, but he had a hard time breaking through the frost barrier. It was like trying to stab a shovel through concrete.

Time for plan B.

Sarah pointed: "Try over there, then."

Nate placed the bag on the ground, walked over to Cory, grabbed the shovel out of his hands, and "walked up the hill a little bit and started digging."

The ground seemed softer over there, for some reason. Nate was able to plow right through the first few inches of earth as though the ground had thawed. As he did this, the shovel hit something, making a *ding*.

Concrete?

"A manhole cover," Nate said. A cement lid.

Perfect.

"Help me out, Cory."

Cory walked over. He and Nate hoisted the lid off the manhole.

The hole was about "twelve feet deep," Nate estimated later. He was wrong. Based on the videotape taken by the police, the hole is about eight to ten feet deep. There were rocks and concrete cinder blocks strewn about the bottom of the hole. It was a concrete pipe, actually, probably part of the park's rainwater flushing system, or a sewer drain, either active or abandoned. The hole went straight down, and then another pipe crisscrossed through it at the bottom in a T formation.

Cory ran over, picked up the bag of body parts, and dropped it inside the drainage ditch.

They stood over the hole and looked down at the bag.

Was this a good idea? Sooner or later, some workman would have to go down into the hole. Looking from the top of the hole down at the bag—with Adrianne's head pressed tightly against one corner of the plastic—they could actually make out her facial features. It looked as if a piece of black latex had been stretched over a skull.

Unconcerned someone might stumble upon this gruesome bag of body parts, they left.

When all three got back to Sarah's car, they sat and smoked a cigarette.

Cory began to fear the worst. Adrianne's name was already popping up in the news. People were out looking for her. Flyers were being hung up all around the QC. Cory became uncharacteristically quiet.

Sarah took a deep drag from her Marlboro.

"Don't worry about it," Sarah told them both. "Everyone will think she's a runaway."

54

There was a parking lot directly across the street from Cory Gregory's house. After completing the final task of Adrianne's murder and cover-up, Sarah Kolb drove to Cory's neighborhood and parked there.

Cory got out. "I'll talk to you later," he said.

Something was happening with Cory. He was turning whiter shades of pale. He had started to shake. He walked with his head down, hands in his pockets, eyes darting from side to side.

Sarah didn't know what to think.

Nate went to get out of the car, but Sarah put a hand on his shoulder, stopping him.

"What?" Nate asked.

"Take the saw (from the trunk) and put it in your book bag."

Nate Gaudet did what he was told. Then he followed Cory into the house.

Sarah drove off. She had to go to work.

* * *

Cory called his sister Katrina Gates. He hadn't been stopping over Katrina's as often as he had in the past. But he wanted to talk.

"How are you?" Katrina asked.

"Oh, the police are following me around. They think I know about a girl who went missing."

This was true. By Sunday night, the police had a good bead on Cory and Sarah, and they believed both knew more than they were saying. Either that or they had something to do with Adrianne's disappearance themselves.

"Who cares what they say, Cory!" Katrina said. Katrina was under the impression, after Cory explained, that Adrianne had taken off with her boyfriend, and Cory and Sarah were covering for her. "Don't *worry* about it."

"But why are the police following me around?" Cory asked. He couldn't leave it there. His conscience, some said later, was beginning to get the best of him.

Katrina could hear the panic in her brother's voice. He sounded scared.

"Cory, who really cares? The cops are just doing their damn job. . . . This is *no* big deal."

"I'll be over," Cory said.

During the first interview he gave to the police—during which he said he had no involvement in the actual murder of Adrianne Reynolds—Cory Gregory was asked why he went with Sarah Kolb and helped her cover up this gruesome, violent crime.

"Because I love Sarah," Cory said. "And I was scared because I was in the car with Sarah and I thought . . .

I thought, since I was there with her in the car when it happened, that I was *automatically* in trouble for it. . . ."

This *love* Cory espoused for a girl who had specifically told him she would *never* love him back in the way he had hoped would soon be put to the ultimate test.

55

On Monday morning, January 24, 2005, Cory Gregory's family began to notice a change in the boy. Cory had always been a quiet, reclusive teen, known more as a "druggie Juggalo" inside what was a tight circle of friends. He was acting very out of character on this particular morning.

Cory and Sarah left school early on Monday morning. It's safe to say that neither could concentrate on schoolwork. Sarah reiterated to Cory at some point that morning that the cops had been calling her all weekend, asking questions about Adrianne and what many in school had reported to police was a fight that had taken place between Sarah and Adrianne the previous Friday inside Sarah's Prizm. Sarah was confident, however, that she had given the police the right answers.

Sarah told Cory to stop fretting. Adrianne's disappearance was being viewed as that of a runaway. There was nothing to worry about. Sure, the murder and cover-up had not gone as planned or expected, but they would soon be in the clear. Nobody, moreover, was going to find Adrianne's body.

Stay cool, man. Keep your head.

Cory's gut spoke to him all day. When three people know about a murder . . . uh . . . there is *plenty* to be concerned about. Sooner or later, one of the three will crack. Successful murderers commit heinous acts by themselves and tell no one. It is one of the reasons why serial and professional contract killers can commit murder for decades without being caught.

Walking out of school, Cory and Sarah ran into a classmate.

"I cannot talk right now . . . ," Sarah said. She wouldn't look at her friend.

"What's wrong?" the student pressed.

"Can't talk," Cory added.

"We got into something bad," Sarah admitted through the open driver's-side window of her Prizm before taking off, out of the school parking lot.

Sarah dropped Cory off at his sister Katrina's, and took off without saying anything that was ever documented.

"He was pure white," Katrina Gates recalled, seeing Cory that early afternoon. "A funny white color."

Cory was acting fidgety, too. Looking down at the ground. Not talking. Shaking. Pacing inside his sister's house.

"What's wrong with you, Cory?" Katrina asked.

"Oh, I just don't feel good."

"No, Cory, I know you too well." Cory didn't want to eat. He said he wasn't sleeping.

They talked for a while.

"I gotta tell you something," Cory confided to his sister.

"Wait!" Katrina said, stopping him. "I know you all too well, Cory. Whatever it is you want to tell me, I think it's best you go to Dad." Katrina wasn't equipped, she said later, to handle anything Cory was prepared to confess. She honestly believed Cory was going to say he had helped Adrianne run away and had been hiding her out.

"Just by the way you are right now," Katrina told him, "I know you . . . Cory. . . ."

"Okay."

"Cory, I need to say this," Katrina said before he left her house, putting a hypothetical situation to Cory in motion. "If there was one person in the world who knew where [your niece] was hiding out, and they wouldn't tell *me*, how would that make all of us feel?"

Cory was close to his niece. Katrina wanted Cory to put himself in the position of Adrianne's family and think about things from that perspective.

Hands in his pockets, head pointed toward the floor, Cory stared at the carpet.

"What do you mean?" Cory asked.

"Well, Cor, if she ran away or something happened to her, is it fair to me to spend the rest of my life trying to figure out what happened?"

Perspective was the picture Katrina wanted to paint for her little brother. A common New Age way to artic-ulate this, of which Dr. Wayne Dyer once said, is: *If you change the way you look at things, the things you look at will change.* Katrina was saying, *Smarten up, kid, and tell the girl's parents where she's hiding out.*

Katrina later said she wasn't thinking that Adrianne was dead; she believed Cory and Sarah had driven Adri-anne out of town and helped her run away; and that they were now two scared kids who didn't want to admit they were involved.

Cory broke down. Started crying. Sat on the couch.

The tears, Katrina recalled, came upon him and would not stop.

"Take me home . . . ," Cory said. "I need to talk to Dad."

Cory arrived at home and Sarah called. Now, though, Sarah had a different outlook. She said something that spooked Cory.

Sarah said her parents had hired her an attorney.

What had Sarah told them?

Cory went numb. He called a friend for a ride to his mother's workplace.

He walked into Teresa Gregory's office with his head hung low, hands in his pockets, his skin gray like concrete.

"What's going on, Cory?" Teresa asked. She knew right away something was up. She had never seen him like this.

Cory looked up at a video camera in the corner of the office ceiling. "Is everything being recorded?"

"Come on," Teresa said. "Let's go outside and talk."

"The girls got into a fight," Cory explained. He lit a cigarette. Took a deep pull. Blew it out in relief. Then he talked about how Adrianne and Sarah fought inside Sarah's car on the previous Friday, how Adrianne was now missing, and the fact that the cops were calling and asking him and Sarah questions.

"Listen, Cory, if you guys know where this girl is, you had *better* tell someone. Her parents are likely worried."

There was a pause.

"Is she at the party house in Rock Island?" Teresa wondered. She knew about the house and its sordid past.

"No. We don't even have the house anymore. Those guys got kicked out."

"Where is she, Cory?"

"I don't know. We dropped her off. . . ."

"Cory, *what's* going on here?"

Cory paused. "Sarah and her parents are going to see a lawyer."

That put a pit in Teresa's stomach.

"*What* is going on, Cory? Why in the heck is she going to see a lawyer?"

Teresa's son now paced in front of her. His head was bowed down again. He spoke softly, as though people were listening. At times, he looked in all directions as though someone was watching them.

Pure paranoia.

Teresa knew at this point something was drastically wrong—something beyond a runaway child. She could feel it. Teresa had been a mother many times over, and there was no mistaking that maternal instinct, screaming at her to ask more questions and find out the truth.

But Cory would not say anything.

"If you guys haven't done anything wrong, you have nothing to worry about," Teresa said.

Teresa had a doctor's appointment that afternoon. Cory left his mother's workplace without saying much else. But after her doctor's appointment, Teresa stopped at the Moline Police Department. She asked a cop at the desk what was going on with this missing child who was in the news.

He said Adrianne's case was an East Moline PD investigation. They at the Moline PD had nothing to do with it.

So Teresa left there and started driving toward the EMPD. Along the way, Cory phoned her and said he needed a ride from a friend's house. He was stranded there alone and wanted to go home.

Cory was at Sarah's. She and her parents had taken off somewhere.

Teresa went to get him.

Inside the car, on the way back to Cory's house, Teresa pressed her son again, demanding to know what in the world was going on. Now was not the time to hide anything. Teresa told her son she needed to know, so she could help him.

Cory would not tell her. Instead, "I spoke to Dad. He said I need to go see a lawyer."

"Okay . . . ," Teresa answered, rolling her eyes, her heart ready to burst out of her chest.

When they got to Cory's house, Teresa and Bert Gregory called a lawyer.

"We didn't even know *why* we were calling a lawyer for him," Teresa said later. "We didn't know what he was so scared of."

Cory still wasn't talking.

They found a juvenile attorney out of the Yellow Pages and took Cory to see him, not knowing why.

The lawyer came out of the room after speaking privately with Cory and said, "I don't handle this sort of thing."

Teresa and Bert looked at each other.

"You'll need to call a defense attorney," the lawyer explained.

A chill shot through Teresa. The juvenile attorney gave them a name. They took Cory to see the guy right away.

After Cory and the lawyer talked, the lawyer came out and said, "What does he need me for?"

Bert and Teresa were confused.

"They're going to question him about this missing

girl," Teresa said. "Cory's nervous. Can you just be there for his rights?"

The attorney said sure.

The next morning, Tuesday, January 25, Teresa called the attorney. She was at work. She wanted to know that everything was okay with her son.

"Everything seems fine," the lawyer said. "They (the police) are just questioning all the kids. . . . There's nothing to worry about."

56

Bert Gregory came home late Tuesday afternoon to find his son wearing a path in the carpet. The look on Cory's face spoke loud and clear: he was expressionless; his skin tone white as paper; there were dark circles under his eyes. He had a surreal look about him, like a vampire. He was shaking. Sweating. Chain-smoking. Bert could not ever recall seeing his boy in such a state of fear and panic. Even on the previous afternoon, when they met with the attorneys. No. This was a different Cory Gregory. Whatever he wasn't talking about was growing inside him like a virus, a cancer, eating away at any sanity the kid had left.

Funny, what guilt can do.

"What's wrong?" Bert asked. Cory had stayed at his mother's house the previous night. By this time, Cory's parents had told him that he was not to return to school until the matter was resolved, and he was *not* to speak with Sarah.

Cory looked up at his dad.

Tears.

"Cory . . . *what's* wrong?" Bert asked again.

He kept repeating this question.

Cory cried. His entire body shook. "I need to go talk to the police with my lawyer," Cory said softly.

"Come on, Cory. What's going on here?" Bert pressed.

Then Bert started to cry. He hugged his son.

Cory would not say anything more. So Bert called Teresa. He asked her to come to the house, and see if she could get Cory to open up about what was troubling him—why, in fact, he needed to speak with the police.

Teresa Gregory had seen her son on the previous Thursday (the day before Adrianne's murder). Cory had stopped by Teresa's work then. He was alone. Teresa, who knew the attachment Cory had with Sarah, asked where Sarah was and why she wasn't with him.

Cory shrugged. "She's mad at me, Mom."

Teresa asked why.

"'Cause I went out with somebody she don't like."

Teresa was puzzled. She asked who her son was talking about.

"Just a girl from school."

"Look, Cory," Teresa said, "Sarah's *not* your girlfriend. You can go out with any girl you want."

"Yeah, that's what I told her."

"Who was it that you went out with?"

"Adrianne," Cory said, and he explained who she was and a bit about what was going on between Adrianne and Sarah.

This was the first time Teresa Gregory had ever heard Adrianne's name.

Teresa had not seen her son on that Friday, when he was with Sarah murdering Adrianne. This was strange,

Teresa thought as the day came and went. Cory had always stopped by her work on Fridays. "That's payday," Teresa recalled. "He always wanted money. They all hit me up for money! Come on, if I didn't see one of my kids on Fridays, I saw all four of them."

It wasn't until Saturday, January 22, that Teresa saw Cory next.

"Did you see what's going on?" Cory said to his mother that Saturday. "The news is reporting about that missing East Moline girl. . . ."

Teresa said no, she had not heard anything about it. "What's up, Cory?" She felt her son was trying to tell her something.

"Oh, she went to school with us," Cory said. "Yeah, and . . . we all went out to lunch yesterday (Friday). Then Sarah and I skipped the rest of the day at school and went out to her grandmother's for her grandma's birthday."

Teresa wondered why her son was telling her these things. Teresa asked him why he had skipped school.

"Oh, um . . . Sarah . . . ," Cory said, stumbling through his words. "Sarah, uh, she wanted to go see her grandmother. Her cell phone wouldn't work out there, and um . . . when we got back, there was messages from Adrianne's parents asking if we knew where Adrianne was, because they thought she ran away."

Teresa wasn't stupid. "Do you *know* where Adrianne is, Cory?"

"No, no . . . we dropped her off at home—well, a block from her house."

On Sunday, Cory called his mother. "The cops keep calling me, Mom."

"They are going to do an investigation, Cory. Do you *know* where the girl is at?"

"No," Cory answered.

The police never called Teresa Gregory.

Like his ex-wife, Bert Gregory also was under the impression that Cory's breakdown on Tuesday evening, January 25, was related to what had been going on with Adrianne: the fact that Tony Reynolds had been over to the house looking for Adrianne the previous Friday; and, on the same night, Cory had said something to Bert about Sarah and Adrianne getting into a fight inside Sarah's car. Add to that the behavior Cory had displayed over the past two days, the lawyers, talk of going to see the police, and Bert Gregory and his ex-wife knew this was a very serious situation.

This was not some runaway kid Cory and his friends were hiding out.

"Did something happen to Adrianne inside that car?" Bert Gregory asked his son. There was a certain gravity in Bert's inflection. He knew.

Cory nodded his head, indicating yes. He turned toward his mother. "Mom, I'm so sorry. I'm *so,* so sorry."

Teresa's heart fluttered, she later remarked. She and Bert knew their lives would never be the same.

"Did the girl get hurt in the car?" Bert asked.

Yes, Cory motioned, moving his head up and down, tears coming on.

"Did she get hurt bad, Cory?"

"Really, really a lot," Cory answered.

"Cory, is she dead?"

Cory could tell that his dad wanted an answer.

He looked at his parents. Nodded yes one more time.

"Well," Bert wanted to know, "where's she at?"

Cory could not speak.

Bert Gregory called Katrina Gates, Cory's half sister. "You need to get over here. . . . It's all bad," he said. Bert was crying.

"What's going on, Dad?" Katrina asked.

"The girl . . . that girl . . . she's not alive anymore!" Bert said.

Katrina could hear the pain, fear, guilt, not to mention frustration and confusion in her father's voice. *How could these kids do this?*

"He was just freaking out," Katrina recalled.

Katrina didn't remember driving from her house across town to her dad's so she could be with her family. But Cory was there when she arrived.

"My dad was devastated and, like, on the floor bawling."

"How could your brother get involved in something like this?" Bert kept saying out loud.

Cory was trembling like a junkie deprived of his poison. Sitting. Rocking back and forth. Then standing. Pacing. Staring at nothing.

"How? . . ." Bert repeated.

As late afternoon wound down, Cory lay in bed with his father. Katrina was nearby, kneeling on the floor. Cory and his dad were just staring at the wall, the ceiling, lost in thought. No one said anything.

Then Cory spoke: "Dad, I should have listened to you. You always told me . . . 'It only takes one second to ruin your life.' And now I've done ruined mine. I am going to prison for a long time."

PART IV

"I DIDN'T MEAN TO KILL HER"

57

At 11:09 P.M. on January 25, 2005, Cory Gregory stood in the parking lot of Black Hawk State Historic Site and stared down at the hood of the police car in front of him. Cory had his coat zipped all the way up, hands in his pockets, his shaved head exposed to the cold air. The officers with him, ISP agent Mike Scheckel and EMPD detective Brian Foltz, were part of a team, including several other investigators and a state police dog, all of whom were prepared to head into the dark and frigid night to uncover Adrianne Reynolds's head and arms. Cory had sat at the EMPD station house and given investigators a narrative of what had transpired over the course of the past several days, minimizing his participation in the murder as much as he could manage. As of now, investigators had no idea Nate Gaudet was involved—better yet how.

There were times during that interview when things weren't adding up for investigators, and they called Cory out on his answers. After all, the investigation had yielded scores of interviews with Black Hawk Outreach students, Juggalos and Jugalettes (especially), on top of several other friends and family associated with Sarah Kolb and Cory Gregory. The cops knew a hell of a lot more than Cory was giving them credit for with his slipshod responses and passive involvement.

". . . You got two people in front of you fighting," one investigator asked Cory quite pointedly during the interview, talking about that moment inside Sarah's car when she and Adrianne started arguing, "and you don't do *anything* to break up the fight?"

"No" was all Cory said.

"Nothing?"

"No."

"Basically, you're told that after it happened, this is going to happen. 'We're going to go out and do this. We're going to go out and do that.'" It was important during this type of interview, when law enforcement was in the information-gathering mode, not to reveal anything they had uncovered before they locked a suspect down to a statement. In lying, Cory was digging himself a hole, falling deeper away from potential negotiations with the district attorney (DA) in the future. "And you didn't have *any* input whatsoever? You didn't help out with *anything* at all?"

"No."

"Nothing?"

"No."

"But you just went along for the ride?"

"Yes."

Cory told police next that he didn't even watch the fight—rather, he sat and "smoked a cigarette and looked out the window" while Sarah and Adrianne fought like cats.

The investigators interviewing him knew this was all lies.

"Basically, during the altercation in the car, you said you weren't looking. Did you maybe hear a thud, like something hitting? You know, you can hear like a punch? Anything like that?"

"I heard," Cory said, but then he hesitated, stalling, thinking, ". . . I heard them hit the sunroof."

"What hit the sunroof?"

"Uh, I don't know. That's . . . that was about the time when they were . . . they got halfway in between the seats."

"Was either of them asking you to help?"

"Both of them were."

"They were both asking for help?"

"Yes."

"And you didn't do anything?"

"No."

"So what happens when we, uh, recover the body parts and we find out that, um, Adrianne's got a gash on her head? How do we explain that?"

"I don't know."

"Okay," the investigator said, frustrated, ". . . I am having a hard time believing that *one* young lady choked another young lady out. You observed the body. Was there *any* injury on her face or on her head?"

"Her mouth was bleeding."

"That's it? There was no injuries on her head or any-place else?"

"Not to my knowledge."

There was a break in the interview. The investigators knew Cory was stonewalling.

"What I need to know," one of the investigators asked, "is what *really* happened in the front seat of that car?"

"I know," Cory said. "I'm having trouble recalling everything right off the bat." Cory's transparency was obvious to these lawmen, who were trying to say, in not so many words, that the more evasive Cory Gregory became, the lesser his chances were to catch a break on the back end of this ordeal.

Fess up or fall hard.

"Because I have a funny feeling that when we do recover the body parts, we're going to find injuries that cannot be explained by what you told us happened. And then, well, right away, that, you know, that throws a little *kink* into the whole situation. So we need to know everything that happened, and we need to know the whole truth."

"I understand."

"Okay, so we need to know what happened," the investigator repeated, adding, ". . . because what you're making [it] sound like, you know, just, it just happened, there's a lot more to that, isn't there?"

Cory looked at the investigators. Took a breath. "Well . . ."

Cory scanned the paper outlining his Miranda rights that sat on the hood of the cruiser as they stood outside on the night of January 25, 2005, inside the parking lot of the Black Hawk State Historic Site. After briefly reading through his rights, Cory signed off before leading the team down into the woods to find Adrianne Reynolds's body parts.

"Cameraman, lead the way," Detective Brian Foltz said as they started past a NO MOTORIZED VEHICLES sign, stepping onto the path leading down into a deeply settled wooded area of the park. The ground, frozen and covered with snow was crusty and brittle under their feet—that is, until they hit those wooden stairs and clip-clopped down, one person at a time.

"Get some flashlights," a cop yelled.

The walk toward the manhole containing Adrianne's head and arms was slippery. The cop holding the video camera, focusing the point of view of the film over Cory's shoulder, had a hard time keeping it steady, giving the entire video an eerie *Blair Witch* feel. The shot stayed mainly on Cory as he led the way, hands in the pockets of his down jacket, his collar stretched over his mouth, a strange *I'm screwed* gaze in his eyes and implicit in his demeanor.

"I think if we go down that other trail there," one of the cops said as they struggled to get a foothold while slipping down a steep slope, "there's a better, easier way."

"Are we here?" another cop asked. Cory, ahead of the group by several steps, had stopped at the bottom of the hill and looked around.

The place seemed familiar.

"I think it's way down at the bottom," someone said, meaning the manhole.

At one point, the cameraman almost fell, the camera bouncing all over the place.

"Whoa," someone said loudly.

Careful. . . .

Cory looked around, trying to locate the exact parcel of land.

It was 11:16 P.M. when they stopped.

"Seems we got a spot right here," someone said.

Cory pointed.

This wasn't it.

They continued down an even steeper slope. It was

muddy, icy, dark. Tree branches slapped them in the face as they walked.

A minute later, Cory spied a set of timbers on the ground laid out in a square-shaped pattern, one side missing.

He pointed to the ground nearby and walked off to an area without speaking.

"This is it?" a cop said, looking at Cory.

Cory nodded.

"Are you sure?"

Cory looked down at the spot and nodded his head again.

How could he forget?

Everyone backed away. The cop holding the dog, a German shepherd, let him go. The canine bolted directly for the area and put its nose to the ground.

A German shepherd's sense of smell is ten times more sensitive than a human being's. That may not sound like much. But consider the numbers: the shepherd has 200 million olfactory cells (think of these as tiny odor-smelling sensors or antennae), as compared to 20 million in a human being. Thus, a shepherd is far more equipped to find a corpse buried ten feet belowground. Still, what is called by scientists the "bouquet of death," or the unique aroma of a dead person concealed in a particular area, is something that still baffles researchers who study cadaver dogs and their sense of smell.[2]

---

[2]Some of the information in this paragraph and the quote following it is from an article, "The CSI death dogs: Sniffing out the truth behind the crime-scene canines," by Laura Spinney, Wednesday, May 28, 2008, *The Independent*.

Two of the by-products of decomposition, reporter Laura Spinney wrote in 2008, *putrescine and cadaverine, have been bottled and are commercially available as dog training aids. But they are also present in all decaying organic material, and in human saliva.*

No matter how he did it, after he was unleashed, the police dog searching for Adrianne's remains took about thirty seconds to find the exact spot over which that bag of Adrianne's head and arms lay ten feet underneath. The worked-up canine circled a small area for a few moments. Then, with his tail wagging like a sprung car antenna, tongue flopped out, snout to the ground, he focused on one spot about the size of a garbage can lid—this before lying down on his belly, looking up at his master, waiting for further instruction.

The master said something.

The dog dug into the ground with his front paws.

The master tossed a bone over the dog's shoulder, which sent him on his way. Another cop walked over to the hot spot with a shovel.

With one poke into the ground, there was that *ding* of concrete just below the surface.

The dog had been spot-on—literally.

One officer dug for under thirty seconds, exposed the manhole cover, lifted it up, and then hoisted the weighty lid to the side as if it were a bundle of newspapers.

The cameraman walked over and caught the moment on tape as they shined their flashlights down into the hole.

And there it was: the garbage bag.

"How far down we lookin' at?" someone asked.

"Oh, ten feet," said a cop.

There was some chatter between them for a few beats regarding how the bag sat at the bottom of the hole and how dangerous it might be to just jump in and retrieve it. The hole could cave in on them.

Speaking in a descriptive tone, one of the cops spoke into the camera's microphone, describing the scene, "We have a black bag, looks like something protruding from the side. . . ."

Another cop interrupted, adding, "Yeah . . . looks like there could be a head right there." He shined his flashlight on the corner of the garbage bag. "Looks like a skull."

The cameraman zoomed in on the corner of the bag.

"Right there at the top."

"We're going to need a ladder."

58

The next morning, January 26, Cory Gregory was at home. The Rock Island County State's Attorney's Office (RICSAO), responsible for prosecuting the case, allowed Cory to stay at his parents' house while investigators were in the process of recovering Adrianne's body parts.

Cory was talking and helping. He was not going anywhere.

Katrina Gates was at the house that morning with the family. Cops from the EMPD and the ISP were on their way over to pick up Cory so he could lead them out to Sarah's grandparents' farm. As Cory waited, Katrina took a jacket off the coatrack in the house and went to put it over her brother's back. He looked cold. He would need something to wear while out at the Engle place.

Cory jerked away suddenly.

"He about hit the floor and passed out," Katrina recalled. "I mean, he turned ghost white. I had never seen a person turn this shade of white like that before."

Because of a jacket?

"What is your problem?" Katrina asked.

"Get that coat away from me—*get it away from me!*"

"Why, Cory? What's wrong with you?"

"That coat was on Adrianne!" Cory snapped. "How did it get here? It was in Sarah's trunk. . . ." (The same black-and-tan coat that Sarah had placed over Adrianne inside her car after they murdered her.)

"I believe Sarah was setting him up to take the entire fall," Katrina recalled. "I mean, how could that coat have gotten into our house?"

Katrina started to shake. Gooseflesh appeared on her arms.

"What am I supposed to do with this coat?" she asked.

Bert Gregory stepped in. "That has to go to the lawyer. It's evidence."

EMPD detective Brian Foltz looked into the camera and stated his name. He had a clipboard and pen in his hand. Cory had a terribly ashen color about his face that contrasted sharply with the black coat he wore as he stood alongside lawyer Dennis DePorter.

Investigators had picked up Cory at his father's house. By 10:30 A.M., they were out at the Engle farm in Millersburg, Illinois, where there was no shortage of law enforcement men and women waiting.

Cory listened to Foltz "re-Mirandize" him. The seventeen-year-old Juggalo had noticeable dark circles under his eyes, a chatter of his lower jaw due to the bone-cold temps and nerves, his face all but hidden inside the pointed covering of a black hoodie. De-Porter wore a black do-rag over his head, glasses, and, in all due respect, looked more like a biker than a lawyer watching over Cory's rights. Cory had told cops he could help them find the remainder of Adrianne's body parts and show them where the events he had described in his first interview had taken place.

Once again, Cory led the way. They were walking in what must have seemed like a remote section of the farm to Cory and Sarah at night (and truly was to anyone unfamiliar with it), but during the daytime seemed directly off the well-worn path of a dirt road running through the farm.

As they came upon a tepee-type structure of sticks and long branches of wood stripped of bark, the cameraman located and filmed a "burned area," as he called it, on the ground near a small tree. Just beyond that was a larger area of burned wood and scraps of a blue papery material on the ground.

"There's a piece of the tarp there," the cameraman observed, focusing the camera closely on top of it.

In front of an area of burned ground, where small pieces of the tarp Sarah and Cory had used to wrap up Adrianne's body, was that tepee-shaped structure, which was actually a beaver or fox hole over a small, mostly dried-up stream, where Nate and Sarah had placed the remainder of Adrianne's body.

It was 10:54 A.M. when the cameraman zoomed in through the stacked sticks and logs. There was something inside the structure.

One of the investigators got down on bended knees and shined a flashlight into the mesh of branches and tree limbs. Other cops walked over and pulled off the limbs.

By eleven thirty, an investigator, on all fours, leaned down into the hole below the branches and limbs as a colleague held him back by his belt.

"I gotcha . . . ," he said.

Half his body was inside the hole, the other half outside.

"Oh, man," the cop said, "I gotta lose some weight."

There were laughs among them. This was how cops dealt with situations where they knew that what they were going to recover would never leave their minds. They would face the images on this day forever embedded in their brains. Joking around was one way to cope with the inevitable horror in front of them.

By noon, they had recovered half of Adrianne's burned and charred torso from the hole, along with the other half, and one of her legs. They laid the body parts out on what looked to be a dark blue body bag unzipped and spread open. It was a strangely sad and peculiar staged scene of what looked to be props from a Hollywood movie set. Adrianne's right leg, its foot and toes entirely intact and clearly distinguishable, was the most chilling, recognizable body part of the lot. Here was this teen's leg and foot, dismembered at about the middle of the thigh, sitting next to two chunks of blackened flesh, with very little skin left—all that was left, besides a severed head and arms, of a young life.

As the cameraman zoomed in and out, focusing for a period of time on each individual body part, a horrific understanding arose from the images juxtaposed against other parts that seemed entirely foreign. It was clear, for example, exactly where Nate Gaudet—a name cops had not yet heard as being connected to this case—had sawed off the bone on Adrianne's torso/hip. This video, with all of its low-tech, grainy, shocking imagery, depicted the horror these kids had perpetrated. When a jury had the chance to view the video, it was going to be all over for Sarah and Cory.

* * *

With Adrianne's body recovered and Cory in custody (still talking), it was time to bring in Sarah Kolb.

Over a twenty-four-hour period, the investigation had yielded several new developments. The EMPD had obtained a search warrant for Sarah Kolb's car and had found *1 strand of hair from the passenger side* and *1 piece of fabric from the front passenger side seat—[along with a] possible blood stain.* Investigators had spoken to twelve more witnesses who knew Sarah from Black Hawk Outreach, each giving cops one more piece to fit into a puzzle that was beginning to form the clear picture of an arrest warrant with Sarah's name on the top.

Investigators had interviewed Brian Engle, Sarah's grandfather, for a second time, on January 26, 2005.

"I spoke to Sarah," he said. The conversation had taken place earlier on that same day.

"And? . . ."

Brian didn't seem as though he wanted to talk. He said begrudgingly, "Well, she told me she is going to 'take care of it' all." She was crying, he added. It appeared Sarah was in the process of coming forward and speaking about her role in the tragedy. "She and her mom are looking for a new attorney." The first attorney they had spoken to did not want to take the case.

"Can you tell us anything else, Mr. Engle?"

The guy knew more. Cops were certain of it.

"Look," he said, "I don't want my daughter to hate me. Whatever Sarah has to say will come from Sarah. She is meeting with a new attorney soon and will be going to the police station. You'll know soon enough."

"Has she ever told you anything about this?"

"No. Never. She has never said anything incriminating. And even if she did," the farmer added, "I would not tell you guys."

"It's vitally important for you to continue to cooperate with us. As the head of your household," the investigator said meaningfully, trying to twist the grandfather's arm a bit, "you should not be putting yourself in jeopardy by withholding evidence or information. Whatever Sarah did should rest on *her* shoulders."

Brian thought about the cop's quasi-threatening statement.

"I'll call you if anything new comes up."

59

Jill Hiers took a call from Pat Corbin, Nate Gaudet's grandmother, several days after Adrianne disappeared, she explained to the ISP, when two troopers interviewed her on January 26, 2005.

"Nate's mother was also on the call," Jill told police.

Both Nate's grandmother and mother, Jill told police, told her during that phone call that "Sarah killed that girl."

Jill explained how odd Nate had been acting and how he was wearing that trench coat on January 23, the day she picked him up at his grandmother's house. In not so many words, Jill tried to ask the women during the call if perhaps Nate was also involved in Adrianne's murder.

They didn't want to hear anything about it.

Jill told the women she was calling Nate at work and asking him point-blank what the hell was going on.

The call ended.

Nate had an eerie ringtone. He looked down at his cell, that strange music playing, and saw that it was Jill calling him.

"What?"

"Tell me what happened," Jill stated.

"Sarah did it!" Nate said. "Cory didn't."

"How . . . what . . . You have to tell the police what you know."

"Sarah killed Adrianne. She was mad and jealous of her. Adrianne had a thing for Cory and Sean."

"What happened?"

"Sarah reached into the backseat and began choking Adrianne by the neck . . . and then . . . well, then Cory finished her off with a belt."

Nate went on to say Sarah and Cory were the only two in the car when this occurred. He told Jill that Sean had exited the vehicle and walked back to school by then. Sean McKittrick was not involved.

Jill couldn't believe what Nate was telling her.

"Sarah carried her out of the car," Nate continued, "put her in the trunk, and then took her out and burned her."

Jill had a feeling there was more. She implored Nate to keep talking.

"Last Sunday," Nate explained, "Sarah and Cory called me to see if I wanted to go paintballing with them. They told me to bring a saw to cut some wood for targets. They were playing mind games with me. When we arrived to where we were supposed to be playing paintball, I saw something covered in a tarp. Cory and Sarah kept asking me, 'Do you believe we could kill someone? Do you think you could kill someone?'"

"Nate . . . ," Jill said. "You *have* to go to the police."

"There's more. Sarah asked me, 'Do you think we have a body under there? Do you believe us if we told you there was a dead body under there?' Then I saw the most horrifying thing I have ever seen in my life. They removed the tarp and no one spoke. She was burned! We lit her on fire again."

As they stood watching the fire sizzle out, Nate explained to Jill, "I asked them, 'Is this why you wanted me to bring the saw?' And they just kept telling me to 'do it, do it, do it.'"

Nate did not need to be told; he knew what Sarah and Cory meant by "do it."

Cut Adrianne into pieces.

"Why did you do this, Nate?" Jill asked. She was appalled. Scared. Worried. Confused. Her boyfriend, she had just realized, had dismembered another human being.

"They told me to" was all Nate could say.

By the end of the conversation, Nate told Jill that "Cory and Sarah had planned the whole thing at school" on the morning of the murder.

Premeditation all the way.

On the afternoon of January 26, Sarah Kolb was arrested and charged with Adrianne Reynolds's murder.

Then Sean McKittrick was hauled in. Booked. And questioned.

The local media went into a frenzied state. Reports buzzed that four teens had been arrested for murdering and dismembering a peer.

Detective Brian Foltz took a call late that afternoon from Tom Kolb, Sarah's father—that is, Sheriff's Deputy Tom Kolb. The guy was a law enforcement officer in Idaho. He said his ex-wife, Sarah's mother, had called to tell him what was going on. It was the first he had heard his daughter was in custody and under arrest.

"Why has my daughter been arrested?" Deputy Kolb wanted to know.

Foltz explained the murder charges. "I cannot discuss any details of the case, however."

Tom Kolb left his phone number.

ISP case agent Mike Scheckel stopped by Nate Gaudet's place of work and approached the gawky, skinny Juggalo as the sun set that same night. The state police acted on a tip from one of Nate's family members, who found "a bloody saw" in the basement of her house.

Nate looked nervous, twitchy. Ready to crack.

"I need to talk to you, Nate."

"Yeah."

"Your mother and grandmother asked me to come and get you, take you back to your grandmother's house so I can interview you."

Nate dropped his shoulders, looked toward the ground. ("I knew I was going to jail," he later said when describing this moment.)

"You know why I need to speak with you, Nate?" Scheckel asked.

"Yes, I do," Nate answered.

Nate wore that dark-colored, wool winter cap and a black T-shirt. He sat slouched deep into the cushion of his grandmother's couch in the living room; old-school walnut paneling comprised the backdrop. Nate had his hands folded in front of him. He stared into the camera as though he was getting ready to talk about himself for a singles video.

Yet the look on Nate's face told another story. This kid was scared shitless. A boy in a man's world. The jig was up.

Nate knew it.

For the first several minutes of the interview (with two investigators who did not know Sarah and Cory's names until Nate told them), Nate Gaudet talked about how he met Sarah through Cory and how they started to hang out together. He said he did not know Adrianne well and had only been enrolled at Black Hawk four days when she disappeared.

"Who strangled [Adrianne Reynolds]?" was the question of the hour. Did Nate know who—Cory, Sarah, or both—carried out the murder? This was the central focus for cops. They had two different versions of what had happened.

"Sarah strangled her," Nate said.

"How did she strangle her?"

"With her hands."

"She use anything else?"

"On the way, they put a belt around her neck."

"Who put the belt around her neck?"

"Cory."

"What did that belt look like?"

"Black, with holes in it."

"Did you see the belt?"

"Yup."

"Where was it?"

"In [Sarah's] car."

"Okay, what happened next?"

"Me and Cory," Nate said, using his hands to explain, pointing down at his palm at times, gesturing and waving his hands in the air at others, "chopped up the body."

"Chopped it up? With what?"

"A saw."

"Did you 'chop' it, or did you 'saw' it?"

"Sawed the bone," Nate remarked with a patronizing

tone, as if to say, *Come on, dude, how does one chop a bone with a saw?*

"What parts of the body did you saw?"

"The head and the arms."

"What parts of the body did Cory saw?"

"The legs."

Nate answered several questions about Sarah and Cory and the day he spent with them. He gave all the names of those inside the party house who knew Sarah and Cory. Then one of the investigators asked, "When did you cut the body up?"

"Saturday," Nate said. As he turned his head and the investigator asked him to be more specific about times and what had happened, a loud wail came from the background. It was a woman's cry, presumably Nate's mother or grandmother, who, for the first time, had learned what Nate had done. As Nate described in more graphic detail the time and place of the dismemberment, the woman continued to weep in animated, loud tones. Listening to this, one gets a sense of how many people this gruesome crime was in the midst of affecting—a ripple effect that would continue to grow as the days, months, and years passed.

"So you cut the body up on Saturday," the detective said over a tremendous moan, with the woman now adding between sobs, "Oh, my God. . . . Oh, my God. . . . No . . . no. . . . Oh, my God."

The investigators wanted to know why Sarah chose to bury Adrianne's head and arms in the park.

"I don't know."

"Why'd you decide to help them?"

Nate did not hesitate to answer this question: "'Cause they're my friends. . . ."

It was, in the scope of what these kids had done, a

cold response drowned out by a wailing woman, crying hysterically, while chanting loudly, "Oh, my God. . . . Oh, my God. . . . No, no. . . ." Police officers had just asked a seventeen-year-old boy why he dismembered a teen peer he barely knew with a hacksaw, and the only answer he could come up with was "'Cause they're my friends."

60

It was thirteen degrees on the morning of January 27, 2005, when Dr. Jessica Bowman got into her car and drove to work. The sun shined bright on this day, but the air was bitterly crisp and cold, the high for the day predicted to be no more than twenty-six degrees.

There were two red body bags wrapped in white sheets waiting in the cooler inside Bowman's autopsy suite—both contained the remains of Adrianne Reynolds. The autopsy of Adrianne's body parts was performed at the Memorial Medical Center in Springfield, Illinois, a three-hour drive south of the QC. Bowman began the autopsy at 10:30 A.M. Beyond her normal duties of logging an official report for the state, the pathologist was in search of a cause of death, which would give law enforcement the advantage when continuing to talk to Cory, Sarah, Sean, and now Nate Gaudet. If they knew *how* Adrianne was murdered, that information could help in determining *who* committed the crime.

Bowman, with medical licenses in five different states,

was able to cut open and explore the inside of Adrianne's lungs, where she uncovered no sign of "soot in the airways."

This was important.

It proved Adrianne was dead when they torched her remains.

The doctor found many other significant factors as the morning progressed, including *minor hemorrhage within the scalp and a laceration over the left eyebrow without associated hemorrhage; no lethal blunt force, sharp force, or gunshot wound injury identified; evidence of dismemberment of the body* after [author's emphasis] *initial thermal injury due to lack of thermal injury of the deep neck tissue and both cut surfaces of the upper arms.*

Of course, no one had said it, but there was always the underlying possibility (not to mention concern) that, despite what Cory and Nate had told police, Adrianne had been dismembered while she was still alive, or shortly after her death, then set on fire. There were even rumors floating around the QC that Adrianne was alive and breathing when Cory and Sarah took her out of the trunk, so they beat her to death with a shovel.

The evidence seemed to show that none of this could be true. This one piece of evidence told the doctor that Adrianne was not alive when her body was cut up.

It was small, but when Adrianne's family found out, they would be comforted by this news.

In what would make Tony Reynolds proud—if there was a silver lining under any of this horror—was that the toxicology report came back negative: Adrianne was clean. No drugs. No booze. The tox screen checked for every possible drug the teen could have ingested: amphetamines, antidepressants, barbiturates, benzodiazepines, cannabinoids (THC), cocaine, lidocaine, methadone, opiates, and several others.

Bowman concluded that the cause of Adrianne's death was *undetermined*. She found *no evidence of lethal blunt force, sharp force or gunshot injury*, but noted there was *limited examination due to severe charring and dismemberment*. Probably most important to the investigation, thus far, was the fact that Dr. Bowman could not exclude several causes of death, including *asphyxia due to strangulation either manual or with a ligature, compressional asphyxia, smothering, or a combination of compression and smothering (burking)*.

There was little skin intact on Adrianne's body parts that Bowman could find. Furthermore, for some reason, Adrianne's neck has been cut in half, and her anterior lower neck was found to be absent.

Why?

The doctor felt the leftover tissue was in keeping with carnivore activity—an animal of some sort had eaten part of Adrianne's neck.

There was no way for the doctor to find out if Adrianne had been sexually assaulted—beyond submitting a rape kit including swabs taken of her internal sexual organs, because her *vaginal and anal orifices cannot be visualized due to the severe thermal injury*. If she couldn't get a good look at Adrianne's vagina and anus, there was no way for the doctor to test for any trauma.

The doctor found some skin on Adrianne's right hand; she uncovered a metal ring band on Adrianne's right first finger, wide and red, the word "hottie" printed on it.

Dr. Bowman discovered a violent injury, which would have been made by a fairly hard blow above Adrianne's left eyebrow and another behind her left ear. The skin had been separated, each injury about *4.5 cm in maximal length;* the skin break about *5.2 cm* long. There were *patchy areas of hemorrhage . . . noted on the scalp, but the underlying skull and brain show[ed] no trauma.*

Someone had struck a blow to Adrianne's head with an object of some sort, but there was not enough force behind it to penetrate and/or bruise her skull.

The person who struck Adrianne was weak.

Adrianne's organs were mostly intact, except for her kidneys, which Nate Gaudet had cut in half when he dismembered her torso. Many of her remaining organs had been cooked, essentially, and were of no use to the doctor's examination. Adrianne's thymus, a *lymphoid organ situated in the center of the upper chest just behind the sternum,* was missing, once again due to *carnivore activity.* None of Adrianne's bones showed breakage or trauma, except, obviously, where Nate had cut them in half.

Cory Gregory was charged with two counts of first-degree murder and one count of "concealment of a homicidal death." His bond set at a million dollars.

Cory would not be sleeping at his father's house any longer.

The headline on top of the fold that day told a confused community mourning Adrianne's untimely, shocking death, in the largest font a newspaper generally used, exactly what had happened to the sixteen-year-old: MISSING TEEN DISMEMBERED. The sub headline was more shocking: *Search has grisly end; classmate, 16, arrested.*

The photos accompanying the headline were of Sarah, handcuffed, wearing a white turtleneck, baggy blue jeans, a sobering look of despair on her pale white face. She was being led from one building to another by sheriff's deputies. Although Sarah was sixteen, she would be turning seventeen on April 23 of that year. For now, she would be held as a juvenile. But she would be transferred to an adult facility—and charged as an adult—in a matter of months.

To the left of that photo was the familiar picture of Adrianne with her bob cut, a smaller headline underneath Adrianne's unforgettable smile, a caption spelling out the person she was: *Adrianne "cared about everything."*

Sarah, who had been booked on first-degree murder charges, was being held on a $1 million bond at the Mary Davis Home, a detention center. She was the only suspect named publicly, thus far. "Other suspects" were involved in the crime, accompanying articles in the newspaper promised, but were being left "unnamed" at this time. The reason, many in the know assumed, was that Sean McKittrick, Nate Gaudet, and Cory Gregory were talking to police. And there were still questions left to be answered regarding who would be charged with which crimes.

Cory was in Rock Island County Jail, talking not only to the police, but his cellies—digging himself a deeper hole. The jail staff had been told to "keep an eye" on Cory as the early-evening TV news came on at five o'clock the night after Sarah was arrested. Why they did this was never discussed in the report detailing what happened next, but it's safe to conclude that, for prosecutors and cops, they were still not on board with the idea that Cory was an innocent bystander and Sarah acted alone. It was that one comment a few witnesses had shared with police.

The belt.

Authorities knew Cory had lied about Nate's role—he had never mentioned Nate's name to the police. Rock Island County state's attorney (SA) Jeff Terronez, taking charge of the case, wanted to get a feel for Cory's reaction to Sarah's rather public arrest. See what he said about his interview with police and the arrest of the girl he had proclaimed his undying love for.

Corrections officer (CO) Erin Taylor was at her guard station inside the jail when she called into Cory's cell via intercom to ask Cory to clean up. When Taylor hit the intercom button, opening up a direct line between the two of them, before she spoke, Taylor overheard a conversation Cory had with his cellmate.

"Do you know that Reynolds girl?" Cory asked.

"Nope."

"Yeah, well, I killed her."

His cellie said nothing.

"Hey, Gregory," Taylor said over the intercom, "you want to clean your cell?"

"Yeah," Cory answered.

Cory was in a holding cell later on that same night when he opened his mouth again. It seemed he couldn't shut up about what had happened. Or maybe Cory was trying to put a reputation for himself in play within the limits of prison culture? Cory was a small boy in a large man's world. He was going to be spending a long time inside the system; he had better set himself up now as someone to fear.

Or pay later.

Cory talked about how the girl "he was with," a prisoner in his holding cell later told police, strangled another girl. Then, still not mentioning Nate (and now outright defending him), Cory said Sarah cut up Adrianne's body.

"I was there," he told the guy, "but I had *nothing* to do with the murder."

He told another cellmate Sarah had killed Adrianne, but he panicked. After realizing Adrianne was dead, Cory said, he and Sarah froze Adrianne's body (outside in the cold weather) for two days after the murder, then cut her up.

"There was not a lot of blood," Cory added, "due to the body being frozen."

More newspaper reports were published late the following afternoon: SECOND TEEN CHARGED IN REYNOLDS SLAYING. Cory Gregory was now part of what was becoming a high-profile murder case inside the QC. One of the articles explained how "other suspects" could be arrested in the days to follow.

Meanwhile, Sean McKittrick's father called the EMPD. He said his son had some things to say about the murder and he wanted to bring him in to talk it through.

McKittrick, with his dad, gave the ISP a videotaped interview, explaining every piece of the murder puzzle Sean knew, sparing no detail.

Then the floodgates—helped by the local news coverage—opened for investigators: witnesses, one after the other, came forward.

Jo and Tony Reynolds were overwhelmed. The idea

that Adrianne had been cut into pieces—and all of these kids talking to the cops had known something about the crime—was too much for them to bear.

"It was devastating," Jo said later. "When the police came at two in the morning [that Wednesday night], all they told us was 'We found Adrianne's body in a park.' The next day, we listened to the police conference on television and that's when we found out her body was dismembered."

The police had "dashed"—Jo's word—over to Tony and Jo's East Moline house on Thursday to tell them Adrianne's corpse had been burned, and that a few of her body parts were still missing, but they had recovered most of her torso, a leg, her head, and arms. They suggested (again, according to Jo and Tony) that after the autopsy, the best thing to do was to have Adrianne cremated. Much of her body had been badly burned. It seemed like the only proper thing left to do.

Complete the process Sarah and Cory had started.

"I'm not sure how I really feel about cremation," Jo explained, "but it seemed to be the only answer."

This sparked a riff between Tony Reynolds and Carolyn Franco, Adrianne's birth mother. Carolyn wanted Adrianne's body shipped back to Texas, but Tony wasn't about to let his only child leave his side again. Tony felt if he let Adrianne's body go, he had nothing to bury, so they proposed to Carolyn that they split Adrianne's ashes and have her buried in both places.

"Carolyn really wasn't for it," Jo remembered, "but agreed."

Adrianne's ashes would be buried in Moline next to Tony's younger sister.

"We ultimately had a private burial," Jo explained.

"We bought Adrianne a pretty pink cremation box. It had a pink rose on it. The burial was just our close family and a few close friends."

Within a few days, however, remembering Adrianne Reynolds would be a public affair, and would include, incredibly, several unexpected—and unlikely—mourners.

PART V

PINKIE'S TIME

61

Rock Island County SA Jeff Terronez was thirty-four years old when Adrianne Reynolds's murder was brought to his attention. Terronez's office was in charge of making sure those responsible were charged and prosecuted to the full extent—the QC community would expect nothing less.

Terronez had been on the job eight weeks when this gruesome case of teen-on-teen violence took top priority for him. In the moments after Adrianne's remains had been recovered from Black Hawk State Historic Site, and Terronez was informed, the SA later told *Quad-City Times* reporter Barb Ickes, he went home "in the wee hours" of that night and, carefully and quietly, opened the door to his daughter's bedroom, where he stood for a moment and watched her sleep. Then he "pulled [her] out of bed" and "rocked her in the rocking chair."

Considering the depravity of the crimes, it's safe to say Jeff Terronez wasn't the only father in the QC appreciating his daughter a little more during those days. The case had been tough on all of those in law enforcement who were involved. This type of murder, with young people involved, pulled at the heartstrings; many of the cops investigating the case had kids the same age, and they could not help but consider the what-if questions associated with staring an evil of this magnitude in the face.

Even with all of the sorrow and wonder floating about the QC over Adrianne's murder, Tony Reynolds still had his detractors.

"Where was this guy all of her life?" asked one QC resident close to the case. "For sixteen years, this guy did nothing for his kid. Then she's murdered, and he's all over the news and in the papers getting his 'fifteen minutes.'"

The newspapers were calling Adrianne's homicide "the biggest" murder case to hit the county in over a decade, and perhaps it was; but Terronez, not yet a polished public official who could rattle off sound bites on the cuff, had little to say about the case he was building against Adrianne's murderers.

One of the problems Terronez faced was figuring out who actually killed Adrianne, while looking at the fight inside Sarah's car that had erupted between the two teens. Sarah wasn't talking. Cory was telling different stories—some of what he had to say just did not add up.

Still, quite surprisingly, the way Terronez framed his case publicly, observers would think it was a slam dunk: "The evidence . . . will show that during that lunch period, in the Taco Bell parking lot, Sarah Kolb began an attack on Adrianne Reynolds . . . [and] Adrianne Reynolds was murdered."

By whom, exactly, Terronez wasn't saying at this

early stage. His team was still in the process of collecting evidence.

Part of the case, in the form of a report Terronez had received, centered on one of the crime scenes: Sarah's red 1991 Geo Prizm. ISP crime scene investigation (CSI) techs John Hatfield and Thomas Merchie had taken over a request by the EMPD to go through Sarah's car, millimeter by millimeter, and see what they could come up with. The inside of the Prizm had a story to tell, a story that could then be matched up against what Cory Gregory was saying.

The Prizm inspection took place inside the East Moline City Maintenance building on Tenth Street. EMPD detective Jeff Ramsey was there waiting for the two CSI techs; he filled both men in on what they had thus far.

Mud was uncovered inside the trunk of Sarah's car, an area of the vehicle that smelled potently of gasoline. The interior of the car was filthy: clothing, books, fast-food containers, food wrappers, and personal items scattered all over the floorboards. Searching through this mess, Hatfield sprayed luminol on the seats, carpet, floorboards, dashboard, and windows; then he took a "forensic light" and ran it over the same areas to see what he could find.

The search yielded very little blood or trace evidence—only that one swath of carpet, which was reported earlier.

Terronez got his hands on a report regarding the contents of the black garbage bag found at Black Hawk State Historic Site, which had been looked at under close forensic examination in the lab. Investigators were confident that they found many different things that could ultimately help Jeff Terronez and the state's attorney's office. Yet, the most incredible piece of evidence to come out of that bag was Adrianne's body parts themselves, along with the way in which they had been uncovered.

Surreal did not begin to describe how gruesome this part of the investigation became. *Examining the contents of the bag,* a report filed by the ISP indicated, *revealed the victim's severed head and two severed arms, with hands attached to the arms. The skin of the victim appeared to have been burned. A melted blue, plastic-like material was observed on the remains. A red ring on the victim's right index finger and several earrings in the victim's ears were also observed. A small chain-like bracelet was observed on the victim's right wrist.*

Terronez had to realize that once a jury got a chance to hear this evidence, with nothing else added to it, the appalling reality alone was going to be hard for them not to feel for the family and convict Adrianne's murderer or murderers. The key was to build a circumstantial case around the results of this horrifying crime and the forensic and pathological evidence. The idea was to lead jurors in the direction of the horrendous events by building up the blocks of the relationship among Cory, Sarah, and Adrianne.

A major part of the court case was proving that the ringleader and true motivator behind Adrianne's murder was Sarah Kolb. Still, Terronez needed Cory Gregory to convict Sarah; and, conversely, Sarah to convict Cory.

Or did he?

The RICSAO had Nate Gaudet, who was in no position to bargain. Nate's testimony would prove pivotal and, probably, the most important in terms of the after-the-fact argument. But the real mystery was the relationship between Cory and Sarah. How would those two respond to each other in court?

As the investigation continued into the weekend of January 30, 2005, a key piece of evidence emerged. It was the work of a concerned citizen, a guy whose daughter had told him something he thought might have the potential to solve the case.

Bill Hodges (pseudonym) called the EMPD and explained that his daughter had handed him a composition book. "A female friend of hers at school," Hodges said, "gave her the book and told her to get rid of it."

Hodges met with a cop inside the parking lot of a local McDonald's. It was 1:40 P.M. when Hodges stepped into the cop's cruiser and explained that his daughter had just called him. "She was very upset" because she had Sarah Kolb's notebook/journal from school, which another girl, Jennifer Fox (pseudonym), had placed in her book bag and told her to get rid of immediately. Hodges's daughter was afraid she was somehow now involved.

She wasn't, of course, but the EMPD needed that notebook. The cop asked if Hodges knew the contents.

"My daughter asked the girl what was in the book," Hodges said. "[Jennifer] replied, 'It's Sarah's diary, and it says things in it bad about Sarah killing Adrianne.' My daughter told me that this girl wanted her to destroy the book." There was even some indication, Hodges added, that kids at school had made threats against his daughter, saying that if she didn't do what she was told, she would end up like Adrianne.

"Where is the book?"

"I have it . . . and I didn't understand the significance of the book until I read it myself."

According to a police report detailing this tip, Jennifer "approached" Hodges's daughter on January 31 and asked her if she had destroyed the book.

"No," Hodges's daughter told Jennifer. "I gave it to my father."

Jennifer "Jenn" Fox, a classmate of Sarah's, had a slightly different story to tell. Sarah had given Jennifer rides home from school on occasion, with Sean McKittrick and Cory Gregory tagging along.

"Honestly," Jenn said later, "Sarah was so nice. I couldn't even believe what happened. She was the sweetest girl ever! This thing blindsided me. I didn't believe it until she was [later prosecuted]."

One of the reasons why Sarah had insisted on giving Jenn rides was because Sarah told Jenn it was "too dangerous" for her "to walk home from school" by herself. It's also safe to say that Sarah might have been trying to get with Jenn.

Still, there was some genuine friendship and concern there on Sarah's part, Jenn insisted.

"She knew that I liked girls," Jenn said, "but I don't think that was ever the issue here with us. She never pressed anything toward me that way. She never hit on me, or anything."

Sarah hated that Jenn rode the bus home; but, more interesting, Sarah equally hated that the guy Jenn was with would, in her words, "make her" ride the bus. Sarah, it is clear, had this strange love-hate feeling where guys were concerned: she didn't think many guys valued the affections of a female, and she did everything in her power to see that she took care of the girls she liked, either romantically or on a friendship level.

Sarah was always quiet about her family history in front of Jenn. The reputation Sarah had, according to Jenn, was that of a tough girl. Jenn described inside the school was not a lot different than how others spoke about it: the school was made up of "misfits," she said. "You had your little groups—the Mexican group, who spoke Spanish in class all the time. Then you have the blacks. Then you had the freaky kids, those Juggalos, and then there were a few of us who didn't fit in anywhere.

"Very segregated," Jenn commented. "You messed with one, you messed with all of them."

When Jenn heard about Sarah's arrest, she thought of the journals they were asked to write in every morning and figured the journal would hurt her friend. She didn't take the notebook to cause trouble, but more out of her loyalty to Sarah and belief in her innocence. Jenn knew where Sarah's journal was all the time, because Sarah was always asking her to put it away.

"So I went in there, took it out, looked at it, and realized it said something about how Adrianne was messing with Cory and that was her 'Kool-Aid,' and that she shouldn't be messing with him and that she was going to kill her for it."

But after reading it, Jenn took it a different way. Sarah was pissed off, she thought, that this girl wanted to "get with" Cory. How many kids in school say "I'll kill you" or "I'll kill her," and so on, every day?

"I didn't take it as though she was going to 'kill her.' I believed Sarah was going to beat her up."

As Jenn was reading the journal, a friend looking over her shoulder said, "You should rip that page out!"

"I ain't ripping out nuttin'," Jenn remarked.

"Take it home then. . . ."

I'll take it home, Jenn thought, *and if they ask for it, I'll give it to them.*

After police spoke to Hodges, three detectives knocked on Jenn's door.

"We heard you have a journal," one of them said.

"Ah, like, yeah."

They wanted to come in.

"And proceeded to ask me a zillion questions about Sarah and if I was there [when Adrianne was killed]. They wanted to know why I wasn't at school that day [Adrianne was murdered]."

Jenn told them she wasn't at school because she didn't feel like going.

"One of the detectives had been [talking to me] weeks before about some other stuff."

They kept, Jenn insisted, "trying to drill me, and I didn't know anything."

Jenn did not even know Adrianne. "And Sarah," she said, "never talked about her to me."

The detectives explained that the RICSAO would be in touch. Jenn would have to testify if Sarah's and Cory's cases went to trial.

62

Joanne Reynolds did not want to go, but Tony insisted. Anything, Tony felt, but sit around the house and ask himself why, stare out the windows and wonder, think about what he did wrong, see Adrianne's face and feel her presence anywhere he turned inside the house.

So they piled into Tony's vehicle and headed out.

It was Saturday night, January 29, now a week and a day after Adrianne's murder. There was a candlelight vigil inside Black Hawk State Historic Site, close to the spot where Adrianne's head and arms were recovered. It was, of course, slated to be a moment of reflection. Emotions in the QC were raw. Teens didn't know how to feel. Members of this otherwise calm farming community in Middle America had committed a ghastly act of evil, and people were trying to figure how this could have happened and why. It wasn't as though some random killer had stumbled into the QC, picked Adrianne, and took her life. She was murdered by her peers. Shocking. Alarming. Sure. But more than any of that, the murder was a brutal reality check, letting the community know that times had changed, innocence was gone.

Among the approximately one hundred mourners standing, holding photos of Adrianne, were about fifty members of the Quad City Juggalos. The local newspapers reported that Adrianne—along with Cory and Sarah—were "members" of the group, but Adrianne was certainly no Juggalette. The vigil, in fact, had been organized by the local Juggalos, specifically a twenty-five-year-old guy who, the newspaper reported, "never knew Ms. Reynolds." The man told reporters that although he had never met Adrianne, he considered her "family" because she was a Juggalette.

Tony and Jo believed the Juggalos were "supportive" during their time of mourning. They respected that some of them were reaching out to extend a hand of love. They were saying, with this vigil, that they were sorry. This wasn't a crime perpetrated by what Juggalos represented. It was important to them to get that sentiment across to Jo, Tony, and the media.

Jo and Tony walked out into the snow-covered area where everyone was gathered. As she stood in silence, Jo looked on the ground and found "some burned-up papers," and not knowing all the facts of the case, she believed that on the spot where she and Tony now stood mourning Adrianne was the actual crime scene where Adrianne's body was burned.

Jo felt sick.

"This was all like a puzzle," Jo recalled, talking about those early days when police weren't telling them much. "We found out a little at a time."

Jo and Tony had received a letter from an unnamed Juggalo who wanted to say how sorry he was about what had happened. He said he liked Adrianne, had dated her, and cared about her as a person. The Juggalo wrote that Adrianne was a *sweet girl who did not deserve any of this*. He said he wished he *could have been more of a friend to her,* apologized for her death, said he was praying for her family, and knew Adrianne *was in heaven with the other angels*.

The letter was signed *anon*.

"Who sent us the letter?" Jo asked as she and Tony stood among the crowd of mourners, candles burning.

No one answered at first.

"I did," said a teen, who stepped forward out of the crowd.

It was Henry Orenstein.

"Thank you for your letter," Jo said.

"I am a Juggalo," Henry said. "But I never wanted Adrianne to die. I liked her a lot."

Everyone had white candles. Tony and Jo held pink candles in honor of Adrianne's favorite color.

The QC Juggalos opined to the *Dispatch* newspaper that "they joined the group [became Juggalos] because they didn't fit in anywhere else."

There they stood at the vigil, wearing Insane Clown Posse T-shirts and hockey and football jerseys, very few of whom donned greasepaint on this night, staring down at an excess of candles on the ground, which burned a bright orange glow in their faces. The self-pronounced spokesperson for the Juggalos made an interesting point in speaking to *Dispatch* reporter Kristina Gleeson, explaining that in high school there were groups of kids, the jocks, geeks, preppies, druggies, etc., but those "left over" were the Juggalos.

Part of the idea in having the vigil, the Juggalo spokesperson told Gleeson, was to let those kids in the community know that if "they hear someone say they're going to hurt someone else, they need to tell an outsider."

It was a gesture across the aisle, a way for this group to say: *Don't judge us* all *by the actions of a few.*

Some of the Juggalos at the vigil insisted that Insane Clown Posse's songs inspired them to put their salvation in God, citing an Insane Clown Posse lyric that spoke of God's calling as a "carnival" and that "all Juggalos" needed to "find Him."

In all fairness to reality, however, it would be hard to bookend this type of argument around a band whose core "artistic" function (if you'll allow me the gross use of the term in accordance with ICP) as "artists"—again, using *this* term very loosely—is to pen songs about killing and maiming and drinking and sex. One need only to Google the lyrics for a song called "Cotton Candy" to be schooled in the idea that no matter what the Juggalo movement says about Insane Clown Posse's integrity as songwriters, it becomes clear that God is as far removed from this band's set of inherent values as is any moral fiber whatsoever.

At the end of the vigil, mourners stuck their candles in the snow like on top of a birthday cake and left the park in silence.

Not long after Tony and Jo got home, several Juggalos showed up at the house.

One of them stepped forward and handed Jo and Tony a frozen pink heart that had formed in the snow by accident as the candles melted.

"We want you to have it."

Close to four hundred people turned out for a memorial service that Adrianne's family held at the Esterdahl

Mortuary on Sunday, January 30. The Reverend Gregory Moore, speaking to the crowd that sat dazed and stunned by this tragedy, wondering how the hell they had wound up sitting and mourning the death of a sixteen-year-old girl—for what seemed like no reason anybody could explain—referred to Adrianne's killers as "undeniable evil." The pastor said that none of what had happened could "ever be explained," "forgotten," or "made right."

There was no explanation. No why. No purpose. No justifiable motive. It didn't matter what the perpetrators would say in the coming days and weeks after they had time to consider their behavior. They were predators. Teens who had set their sights on a girl, decided to make her life as miserable as they could, then killed, burned, and dismembered her. What could come out of such a display of horror?

And there was, according to a source who spoke to me under the guise of complete anonymity, an indication that this inexcusable, evil crime (along with many others committed by that group inside the Rock Island party house) was committed under the pretext that these teens thought going into the situation that if they committed the murder before their eighteenth birthdays, they would get off with slaps on the wrist and be charged as juveniles.

The reverend made an indelible point when he told the crowd that what had happened to Adrianne happened "outside of God's creation." There was no other way to frame this. It was a crime no human being with a sense of right and wrong, or an intrinsic understanding of life being the precious gift it is, could have committed. The people responsible for this were empty inside, the reverend suggested. They were despicable. They were the Devil working his evil ways.

Adrianne's guitar—that tangible, subtle symbol of her dreams—stood in the mortuary, alongside flowers and wreaths and photos.

Friends and family stood and talked about Adrianne's smile.

They spoke of how family members walked on the park grounds where Adrianne's body parts were found so they "could feel her presence."

They talked about the fact that Adrianne would always be watching over them.

How she had "blessed their lives," whether she knew it or not.

How they yearned for one more day with her.

The ceremony, fittingly, ended with a version of "Amazing Grace," the tune Adrianne had belted out so many times inside her room practicing for *American Idol.*

Tony and Jo did not speak. They weren't able to, Jo later explained. "It was a long day. I think we greeted people for two hours before services started, and it took people forty-five minutes in line to reach us. It was like people came out from my past. My best friend from fifth grade sent flowers. . . ." An old boss showed up. Neighborhood kids Jo hadn't seen for years attended. There was even a trial witness there. Turned out the guy had gone to grade school with Tony, and he wanted to pay his respects.

"The local florist," Jo concluded, "had donated all the flowers—and it was amazing how many flowers were there. We had two wreaths made from the dried flowers, and they still hang in Adrianne's room today (six years later)."

63

As each day passed, Sarah and Cory got stronger, emotionally. Cory was beginning to show signs of getting his head together, now having time to regroup and think about the future. Sarah was not talking. She was going to fight her way until the end. Cory didn't indicate a desire to say much more than he had already, but the feeling was, sooner or later, Cory could be broken.

After the interview with police at his grandmother's house, Nate Gaudet had been released, knowing, of course, the hatchet was going to fall on his freedom any day. The time came at 4:30 P.M., January 31, 2005. Nate was picked up at his grandparents' house, taken to the Rock Island County Sheriff's Office (RICSO), and then turned over—because of his age, sixteen—to the Rock Island County Juvenile Probation system, where he was booked as being "delinquent" because he was on probation for a previous unnamed crime. The new charges, however, were a bit more serious than any crime Nate could have committed in the past. He was charged with "acting in concert with others, with the knowledge that Adrianne Reynolds had died, by dismembering the body of Adrianne Reynolds and concealing some of the remains. . . ."

Nate Gaudet was on his way to juvenile hall.

Cory Gregory and Sean McKittrick had agreed to take lie detector tests, both of which were conducted back on January 26. The results of these tests came in late in the day on January 31.

In Cory's case, the test was built around the idea that Cory, during his first interview, had told police that all he did was help Sarah move Adrianne's body, "but did nothing else to help conceal or dispose of the body."

Cory was obviously lying. The cops knew this, and they had several reports to the contrary. So they asked Cory during his lie detector test, "Prior to going to Taco Bell, did you plan, or have knowledge, that Adrianne was going to be harmed in any way?"

"No," Cory answered.

"On January 21, 2005, while in the parking lot at Taco Bell, did you actively participate in any way in killing Adrianne?"

"No," Cory answered.

"Besides on Big Island after Adrianne's death, did you help move her body at any other time?"

"No."

"Did you participate in any way in sawing up Adrianne's body?"

"No."

The results of the report confirmed what police had believed all along. In the opinion of the examiner, based on polygraph recordings, Cory Gregory was "not telling the truth. . . ."

The questions posed to Sean were a bit different.

"On January 21, 2005, did you see Sarah Kolb and Adrianne Reynolds physically fighting in her car at Taco Bell?"

"No," Sean answered.

To this question, the examiner believed Sean was lying.

"Do you know what happened to Adrianne Reynolds?"

"No," Sean said.

"Did Sarah and Cory plan to harm Adrianne?"

"Yes," Sean answered.

To those last two questions, the examiner indicated Sean's responses were "erratic and inconsistent" to the point of which the polygraphist could not tell if he was telling the truth.

64

The first hearing surrounding Adrianne's murder took place on Tuesday, February 1, 2005. The fulcrum and mainstay of the state's cases were Cory and Sarah, of course, both of whom were in court to hear the charges officially filed, enter pleas—both ultimately pleaded not guilty—and find out if the cases merited enough evidence to go to trial.

This was the first time many of the gruesome details were made public. One of the more revealing pieces of testimony came when one of the investigators explained to the court that Nate Gaudet's grandmother actually had found the bloody miter saw that her grandson had used to dismember Adrianne. It was in the basement of her house. She called police. They quickly took off to grab Nate at his job and bring him back to the house for that now all-important videotaped interview he gave. From there, the public learned for the first time that Nate had told police he overheard Cory and Sarah talking about killing Adrianne *two* days before she was murdered.

Bombshell.

Steve Hanna, Cory's attorney, who took over for DePorter, made a good point when he asked the investigator if the state had any *trace* evidence linking his client to the murder. People could say what they wanted about Cory Gregory, but where was the *evidence* tying him to these crimes?

"No," the investigator answered, explaining that the ISP was still waiting for results from several forensic tests. The case was only two weeks old.

In the end, Judge James Teros issued an "order of the court" for police to obtain hair, blood, and fingerprint samples from Cory and Sarah.

Sarah's jury trial was set for April 4, 2005 (same as Cory's).

Things were moving at warp speed, apparently.

Over the next few weeks, affidavits and search warrants were unsealed and the public began to hear the minutiae behind the crimes. The state compiled its list of witnesses and informed both defense teams representing Cory and Sarah that it was unlikely the state's attorney was going to be interested in sitting down and cutting deals.

The fact of the matter was, however, the state was waiting for Cory and Sarah to fall on his or her sword and, begging for a plea, enter into an agreement to become a state's witness against the other. It was, truly, one of the only ways the state's attorney's office was going to be able to prove first-degree murder charges.

Cory Gregory was still telling people he loved Sarah and would do anything to protect her. Most knew, however, that his mind would change once Cory got a true taste of what life behind bars inside a state prison was like. The Illinois Department of Corrections (IDOC) had seven maximum-security prisons, some of which held on to reputations for being one step away from hell on earth. The men inside these places did not play on a field inhabited by children; these were tough men—men who could take a kid like Cory and turn him out quickly.

Near the end of February, the state took the death penalty off the table. It was a long shot, by and large, anyway. Juries were not known to send kids to death row, to begin with. Add to that the lack of any concrete forensic or trace evidence, and SA Jeff Terronez and company were going to be lucky to get convictions, let alone twelve votes for execution.

Back on February 4, the ISP submitted a list of some thirty-two items for testing to the Morton Forensic Science Laboratory. That list had given several clues as to the case the state was in the process of building against Sarah and Cory, the results of those tests not boding too well for either defendant. There was blood found in Sarah's room at her house, on her clothes, on the saw used to cut Adrianne up, and hair and DNA samples on the stick discovered in Sarah's car. Item number 26 was a "black leather belt," which looked to be the weapon used to strangle Adrianne, at least according to several witnesses who had spoken to Cory. Number 32, handed over to the state police by Steve Hanna, Cory's attorney, was the winter coat that had freaked Cory out back at his house.

Cory and Sarah, in light of this new evidence, were in trouble.

Then the results of Nate Gaudet's polygraph came in, and somewhat confused things. For example, Nate answered "Did Sarah Kolb tell you that she choked Adrianne Reynolds?" with a resounding "yes." And the question "Did Cory Gregory and Sarah Kolb tell you that

Cory Gregory held Adrianne Reynolds's arms so Sarah could choke her?" with an additional unimpeded "yes."

This scenario, of course, made the most sense. There was no way Sarah Kolb could have killed Adrianne by strangulation alone. Sarah just wasn't strong enough— and there was plenty of evidence indicating Adrianne was a hell of a lot tougher than Sarah. It was Cory himself, moreover, who put that strangulation theory out there.

Yet, all that being said, a new problem within this dynamic emerged. The polygraphist indicated Nate's test showed the boy was "not telling the truth," but that the test couldn't be trusted because Nate had been in psychiatric treatment within the past ninety days, making one wonder why they had even tested him.

What few people knew was that Nate had been treated for bipolar disorder his entire life. He was on meds at the time of the murder.

The final question on the test was "Are you the only person that sawed apart Adrianne Reynolds's body?" This yielded a "yes" response from Nate, which the examiner indicated he could not render an opinion on because of Nate's "lack of emotional response."

The most chilling aspect of this was the idea that Nate Gaudet sat and admitted to sawing up a human being but had absolutely no emotional reaction to it whatsoever.

Flat. Numb. Hollow.

A shell.

If nothing else, the polygraph showed how desensitized Nate was to the real world.

Which made one wonder: was Nate Gaudet a clinical sociopath?

* * *

Investigators dug up some interesting evidence as they spread out and spoke to several of Sarah Kolb's classmates at Black Hawk. Everything Sarah had written or talked about had now taken on a new context. Sarah's scribbling and her doodling were no longer just the pastimes of some strange girl jotting down her thoughts at random. In looking at some of what she had written (with the idea that no one was ever going to see it), investigators had to scratch their heads and wonder how deep Sarah was touched by whatever demon seed had been planted inside her. On an English syllabus handout, Sarah covered the facsimile with incomplete sentences (ironic in and of itself) and various words that were on her mind at the time, as well as arbitrary thoughts speaking to how dark the world inside Sarah's head was on any given day. The paper was not dated, but it must have been written within the past six or seven months.

Starting at the top, Sarah apologized, repeatedly, writing she was *fucking sorry* for any number of things, including an unnamed person whom she viewed as *always being right* and Sarah *always [being] wrong*. She said she wanted to *die*. She wasn't *good enough*. Sarah felt *ugly*. She called herself a failure. She wanted to *slice the years* (whatever that meant) and make all the pictures in her head disappear. There was *no way out*. She considered herself to be *nothing special*. She called her life "hellacious." She said she was lonely, and when she felt that way, everyone in her life was walking away from her, as opposed to consoling and loving her unconditionally. She wrote the word "masterpiece" above the word "mutilation."

And so there was Sarah Kolb writing these types of

random thoughts on one end of the hallway; while at the same time, Adrianne Reynolds was writing things along the lines of *Love and hate is just a game. / Played by a bunch of people / Who just want to get laid.* On top of *In agony I'm screaming, crystal tears of blood pouring down me, with a jagged blade in my hand, I'm engraving diagonal lines. . . .* (Perhaps this was Adrianne's artistic way of dealing with the cutting she identified as being a release from the emotional pain she endured.)

The remainder of the poem / song lyrics, whichever it was, went on to encompass a horror vibe that included the narrator drinking blood, driving stakes through Adrianne's heart, *realizing you can never begin again.*

In another short rambling, Adrianne wrote of always trying *to be perfect, but nothing was with it. I don't believe it makes me real, I thought it'd be easy, but no one believes me.*

One has to look at this—these two girls, both of whom are trying to figure out what their subconscious and conscious minds were telling them—and see the similarities between the writings: both pens scream for attention and a desperate need to fit in somewhere. Anywhere. This while maintaining an identity in a school where most of the students had none. Both Sarah and Adrianne had been blessed with looks, friends, and intelligence. Both were smart enough to express themselves through their art (namely, music, drawing, and writing). They had no trouble sitting down and putting their thoughts on paper.

Yet, for some reason, their personalities clashed, and Sarah believed the only way to get back at Adrianne for what Sarah felt Adrianne had done (that betrayal of trust inside what was a core group of friends) was violence. Sarah's way of handling life's difficulties was to make a fist. When someone upset her, she attacked. Whereas Adrianne, when someone wounded her fragile spirit, worked at trying to get that person to love her or, at the least, like her again. It was that thought of someone not liking her that bothered Adrianne more than anything else.

65

Trials are prone to delays. Thus was the case for Sarah and Cory. On April 23, 2005, Sarah's seventeenth birthday, Sarah was told she was being moved from the juvenile detention center she was being held at to the Rock Island County Jail, an adult facility, but not until she finished the school year. Sarah's trial was scheduled for August 8; Cory's set to begin a day later. Attorneys for both sides, however, were still not sold on the notion that those dates were going to work. It was too soon. Everyone had a right to a fair and speedy trial, but both sides needed time to prepare.

Jo and Tony Reynolds wanted justice. If they had to wait a few extra months, so be it. That May, something interesting happened. Jo Reynolds sent Sarah's mother, Kathryn Klauer, an e-mail with the subject line **Adrianne**.

Tony and Jo felt the need to reach out. Tell Kathryn how bad they felt. Jo—more than Tony—wanted Sarah's mother to know that there was pain all around, and that she understood how both families felt it.

When Kathryn opened the e-mail, Jo said, she wanted Kathryn to know how sorry Jo and Tony were, and how bad they felt for Sarah's family. Jo said she and Tony didn't blame them for anything, adding how she was praying for both families to have the strength to get through what was going to be trying times ahead with the trials and media frenzy.

Jo also stated the fact that—no matter how hard she tried—she could not get the thoughts of what had happened to Adrianne out of her mind. Ending the brief e-mail, Jo wanted Kathryn to know she didn't hate her and didn't want harsh words to come between them.

Jo Reynolds sent her e-mail at 2:54 P.M. on May 24.

An hour and a half later, Kathryn Klauer responded.

She said she didn't hate Jo and Tony, either. She would love to meet and have lunch and talk things through someday. Would Jo be interested?

Then came a few suggestions, which told Jo and Tony where Sarah and her case were undoubtedly headed. Kathryn called Cory Gregory a "monster." She stated that he killed Adrianne, and she mentioned that Cory had threatened to kill Sarah, too. Kathryn added, in all caps, that she hated Cory. She finished the e-mail with, **Adrianne was a beautiful girl.**

Two hours later, Jo wrote back. She said she wouldn't mind meeting sometime. Now was not going to work, however. She and Tony were having more bad days than good. All it took was a glance at Adrianne's picture and the tears came. Sitting across from Kathryn now would be too much. The reason Jo had written to begin with was simply to say that she and Tony did not blame Kathryn or Sarah's family for what Cory *and* Sarah had done.

Take care, Jo signed off, hoping that would be the end of it.

Just under two hours later, that familiar chime went

off on Jo's computer, and in came a long e-mail from Kathryn that told Jo and Tony many more things about Sarah's defense. It was going to be hard, Jo now felt after reading the e-mail, to reach a hand across the aisle.

Kathryn opened with words any mother in her position might be inclined to say, talking about how there was nothing but memories around her home and how quiet the house was these days without Sarah's laughter and smile. The woman missed her daughter. It was disheartening to think Sarah could be locked up for the rest of her life. Kathryn said all she did lately was cry. Then she mentioned something about having evidence that would prove how easily it would have been for Kathryn to be in Jo's shoes—meaning, surprisingly to Jo, that Sarah could have been murdered.

As she read, Jo wondered what in the world Kathryn was talking about.

Sarah, murdered?

Further on, Kathryn explained that the true monster was Cory. He might have killed both their daughters, Kathryn insisted, on that day, but something stopped him.

Huh?

Kathryn said how Sarah had told her she was frightened of Cory killing her and then heading over to Sarah's house to kill Kathryn.

Sarah Kolb was casting quite the tale of woe out into the water here—and, apparently, she had her mother hook, line, and sinker.

Sarah had told Kathryn that Cory knew how to get inside Sarah's house without a key. He also knew Kathryn wore hearing aids and would have trouble hearing an intruder break into the house because Sarah had told Cory that Kathryn took the hearing devices out before she went to sleep every night. She said

Cory could have killed her while she was sleeping. Sarah's stepfather was at work on most nights until two or three in the morning. Cory knew that also.

Oh, my goodness, Jo thought. *What is this?*

But there was more.

Kathryn explained next how Sarah had become terrified of Cory. She mentioned how the driver's-side door to Sarah's Prizm did not open from the inside, and once Sarah was in her car, she was at Cory Gregory's mercy.

She had no idea why Cory had killed Adrianne, and even Sarah, Kathryn added, could not come up with an explanation. Kathryn was certain Cory planned the murder and also planned to make Sarah his scapegoat. This was the main—and only—reason, Kathryn had surmised in her heart, that Cory had allowed Sarah to live.

So he could set Sarah up for the murder of Adrianne Reynolds.

Kathryn called Cory a sick person. She said her family would never forget Adrianne. It was so sad that Cory had killed her—and on Sarah's grandmother's birthday, to boot! How dare he maim that special day for the family.

Before concluding, Kathryn said she and Sarah were planning on planting flowers in Kathryn's yard at some point. They chose the colors—red, white, and pink— for a reason. The white flowers would symbolize Sarah's innocence. That had to be first and foremost. The pinks, of course, were for Adrianne and her memory. And the red would symbolize the innocent blood that Cory unjustly spilled.

Jo shook her head while reading.

Nowhere in that final e-mail of the day between

the two women was there any mention of Sarah taking responsibility for her role in Adrianne's death. To Jo and Tony, the idea that Sarah Kolb was an innocent bystander was a slap in the face to the memory of their dead sixteen-year-old daughter.

Who in the hell was Sarah Kolb kidding with her lies?

66

Cory Gregory was climbing the walls inside his prison cell as the month of June came to pass. He and Sarah had been incarcerated now for four months and some change. Cory was on suicide watch, according to a report filed by a corrections officer in early June. When this same CO checked on Cory during the day of June 3, 2005, she found him "acting a little strange." He was "pacing back and forth in his cell . . . talking to himself."

This behavior was out of Cory's normal routine, the CO said. The boy usually slept and read.

Not much else.

After reporting her concerns, the CO was advised to keep a close eye on Cory.

Nothing came of it.

A few days later, Cory was working out with a fellow inmate inside the gym. They started talking about Cory's case.

"Sarah," Cory said, "began hitting Adrianne with the stick."

"No shit," the inmate responded. Cory had already

explained who the two girls were. Their background. "What'd you do, man?"

"Adrianne done hit Sarah in the nose—bloodied it bad. Sarah was losing the fight."

"What did *you* do, Cory?"

"Sarah asked me to help."

The inmate stopped what he was doing, "And? . . ."

"I grabbed that bitch by the neck and began choking her! I pulled her into the backseat with me and choked her until she was blue."

"Shit, man. . . ."

"Yeah, then my friend Steve (Cory was *still* protecting Nate), he came out to the farm, where we tried burning her body—and Steve cut her up."

"Did you cut her, too?"

"No, no, man. I held her body parts down while Steve cut her up."

Cory was in his cell on June 15, pacing again. This time, however, he had stripped himself naked. The CO monitoring his behavior found this to be odd because "in all my dealings with him, [Cory] has never exposed himself."

"You okay in there?" the CO asked.

"Yeah!" Cory snapped . . . pacing.

A while later, the CO went back, found Cory doing the same thing, and asked him again if he was all right.

"Yeah! Why?"

"You're doin' a lot of pacing, Gregory. It's not like you."

"Well, you're just probably used to me sleeping all day, aren't you?"

The CO noticed Cory's wrists; both had long, "horizontal scars."

"That happen lately or before you came in here, Gregory?"

Cory looked down at the scars. "They're old."

As the August trial dates for both defendants neared, Sarah's attorney motioned for a continuance and the judge allowed it, setting a new trial date for Sarah on Halloween, October 31, 2005. This would be the final delay, the judge promised.

The state, on the other hand, had made an oral motion on July 20, 2005, to continue Cory's case until Sarah's concluded. They were still lining up witnesses and investigating, and there was also an indication on Cory's part that he might be willing to plead out his case.

The state was interested in hearing what he had to say.

Cory's new trial date was set for November 7, 2005.

The judge set a plea date in Sarah's case for October 24, seven days before her trial was slated to begin. That would allow Sarah to consider the facts of the case, the evidence building against her, and give her some time to think about her future. If she wanted to accept a guilty plea and cut a deal, that was the day to do it.

Meanwhile, Sarah was having a hard time adjusting to life inside an adult prison population that was seemingly putting her to the test.

On August 8, 2005, near 9:30 P.M., a CO inside the Rock Island County Jail noticed Sarah sitting on her bunk, her head hung down, shoulders drooped, tears rolling off her cheeks. She was "visibly upset," the CO later explained.

"You okay, Kolb?"

Sarah shook her head. No, she wasn't.

"What's up? What's going on?"

Sarah looked over toward a neighboring inmate's cell and motioned with a head nod that she didn't want to say anything out loud.

"You need to speak to me about anything, Kolb, in private?"

Sarah nodded. Yes, she did.

"Get dressed. I'm going to finish my bed check and then come back for you."

The CO spoke to the nurse on call and asked her to hang around. Inmate Sarah Kolb was being brought in for a little powwow. The CO wanted the nurse there.

Sarah was then walked down into the medical unit, where she could speak to the CO and nurse in private.

"What's up, Kolb?" the CO asked. "I'm concerned about you."

Sarah didn't look so good.

"[Tisha] (pseudonym) is severely tormenting me . . . calling me a murderer and calling people on the phone during my hour and talking about me loud enough to taunt me."

Sarah, it appeared, was getting a taste of her own bullying. How ironic that she didn't much like it.

"What else, Kolb?"

"Well, [she] threatened me. She said, 'I'll take care of this during a visit someday, or in the hall on the way to a visit.' This is very disturbing to me." Sarah started to cry again. "I think she's even been inside my cell, reading some of my papers associated with my case."

"How so?"

"I came back from an attorney visit one day last week

and found my cell open—[she] was out [in the corridor] cleaning."

"Doesn't mean anything. . . ."

"No, but [she] asked me questions later on that day about my case that only someone who read that stuff would know."

"So what?"

The report of the conversation indicated that Sarah claimed that Tisha *later . . . mentioned a codename and something about a purse or a bag,* and the only other people who knew about those items were her attorney and Cory Gregory. Sarah was greatly concerned about this.

"I keep notes in my cell and these notes," Sarah explained to the nurse and CO, "contain information on my case that could prove to be incriminating for me."

Inmates were always looking for material to barter. If they found out something about a major case going to trial, they could use it to chip away at their own time. Was Tisha trading info about Sarah for time off her own sentence?

"What are you worried about, Kolb?"

"[She] threatened to go to the state's attorney with the information. I need you to move her away from me. I cannot take it anymore! I don't know what I am going to do."

"Are you suicidal, Kolb?" the CO asked.

"No. I would never hurt myself."

"Okay."

"But under this type of pressure and anger," Sarah warned, "I might do something to hurt someone else. This is why I should never be put in a cell block with other girls."

"I don't think there's much we can do for you, Kolb, but I will speak with the shift commander."

The CO checked. Tisha was not going to be moved from the block, but she was placed in a cell at the end of the corridor, away from Sarah, so they would not be neighbors any longer.

The two were listed as enemies, the report concluded, *and a note was posted . . . to keep the two separate at all times.*

This would not be the end of it, however. And Sarah wasn't telling the entire truth of the matter.

67

A mental-health evaluation was ordered on Sarah Kolb after that little problem she had with Tisha. There was, after all, another side to this story—namely, Tisha's.

That "code name" Sarah had mentioned to the CO and nurse was chosen by Cory and Sarah as a mission title for killing Adrianne, and the "purse" or "bag" was actually a backpack only Cory and Sarah knew the whereabouts of. What was in the backpack was anybody's guess.

The nurse who evaluated Sarah pulled her aside a day after Sarah had reported Tisha. Confronting Sarah, the nurse said, "You told her, didn't you?" The nurse was referring to what Sarah and Tisha, who were close friends at one time, had discussed when they used to hang around together.

Sarah looked defeated. She stared at the nurse, whispered, "Yes. This is why I am so scared."

Tisha was running around telling everyone that Sarah had admitted murdering Adrianne, and Tisha was planning on going to the state's attorney with the info.

Continuing, Sarah said, "Tisha and I were a lot alike six months ago. I did not appreciate what I had. I wanted the best car, the best clothes. I was always jealous because I thought other people had more than I had. I was so jealous that I wanted what everyone else had."

A day later, two COs and the nurse caught up with Sarah and spoke with her again. Tisha was still taunting her, Sarah said. It was beginning to break her down. She was on the verge of losing it.

"You don't know what that's like," Sarah explained. "Being called a murderer . . . is something that I am going to have to live with for the rest of my life, and I don't need anybody throwing it in my face constantly. I am going to hurt somebody else! That's what I do. I have a temper."

They brought Tisha in later that same day.

"This all stems from an argument we had over cleaning," Tisha insisted. "I used to be close with Sarah. Sarah confided in me. Yeah, she told me *everything*. She's scared now? Hell, she should have been scared when she was telling me her whole story."

The girls were finally split up. Tisha ultimately met with investigators.

Nate Gaudet had given cops a second interview in March. Enough time had elapsed by then for Nate to come to terms—in some sense—with what he had done. The memories were still fresh enough in Nate's mind for investigators to double-check and figure out if he was telling the truth. By now, it was clear to Nate that he was going to be spending some time in prison, but not anywhere near the amount his cohorts faced.

"Sarah," Nate explained, ". . . started punching Adrianne in the face, and then Adrianne broke Sarah's nose, so Sarah had Cory hold Adrianne's arms while Sarah choked her to death . . . and beat her with a wooden stick."

Nate further explained how Adrianne's corpse "started to stink," so they put her in the trunk and drove out to Big Island, eventually ending up at Sarah's grandfather's farm.

There was no question that when Cory and Sarah picked Nate up that weekend at his grandmother's house, they asked him to go back into the house and grab a saw, and Nate knew *exactly* what that saw was going to be used for. He did not have to be persuaded or threatened, he claimed.

Premeditation once again became evident. Investigators asked Nate an important question: if Adrianne and Sarah did not like each other, as everyone had been suggesting, and were not getting along at the time of Adrianne's murder, how did Sarah get Adrianne to agree to get into the car on that day?

Nate said Cory helped out with that. Cory convinced Adrianne she should go to Taco Bell with him for lunch, and that he would make things cool with Sarah.

"Why was [Sarah] acting [as if she was Adrianne's friend]?"

"Just to do what they did."

"And what do you mean by that?"

"Uh, so Sarah could get her in the car so they could bring her to Taco Bell and kill her," Nate said.

"How do you know that?"

"'Cause they told me!"

Later on, during the same interview, investigators asked Nate, "What, if any other involvement, did Cory Gregory have in this homicide?"

"Cory took the belt and put it around Adrianne's neck while they drove to Big Island to put the body in the trunk."

SA Jeff Terronez sat in on the interview. The SA was preparing his cases. Nate Gaudet was obviously going to be one of the SA's main witnesses. Terronez was worried about those lie detector test questions Nate had failed to answer truthfully.

"You understand," Terronez asked Nate as the interview wound down, "I cannot put you on the witness stand and have you testify to something that is not true?"

"Yes."

"You have to tell the truth."

"Yes."

"If you don't tell the truth, I can prosecute you for lying on the witness stand under oath—you understand that?"

"Yes."

"And that's completely different and separate from what you're facing right now."

"Yeah."

"You would get separate time and everything else if you're lying on the witness stand under oath—you understand that?"

"Yes."

Terronez carried on, asking Nate several more times

if he understood the ramifications of lying on the witness stand.

Nate didn't back down; he kept telling the SA he understood.

Thus, for the SA, there was not much else he could do besides prepare for trial against Sarah Kolb, who was, as the summer of 2005 came to an end, showing no signs of wanting to cut a deal and testify against her counterpart, Cory Gregory.

68

According to legend, Halloween is the day marking the end of the harvest season and the beginning of what are long, dark, cold winter days juxtaposed against all of the bone-chilling, frigid nights ahead. An old Celtic tradition says that the first day of November is the time of year best associated with death. Therefore, in one sense, Halloween could be considered a celebration. A time to don one's best costume and scare away those ghouls, ghosts, and goblins that might bring the end of life the following morning.

For Sarah Kolb, sitting and facing her fate inside Rock Island County Circuit Court on October 31, 2005, the Honorable James Teros presiding, jury selection on this day concluded with eight jurors being chosen.

First thing the following morning, November 1, four additional jurors—and three alternates—were selected, and all were sworn in.

The *People of the State of Illinois* v. *Sarah Kolb* was under way.

SA Jeff Terronez had announced he was not going to be calling Sarah's mother, Kathryn Klauer. All the SA would admit to reporters regarding the decision was that he had certain reasons for scratching Klauer. Yet, the main witness everyone was talking about—a man not on Terronez's list—was Cory Gregory. Why wasn't Cory going to testify on behalf of the reputed love of his life? He was there, inside the car. Cory had witnessed the murder. He could give jurors a play-by-play of what had happened.

"Cory had a constitutional right not to testify" was all Terronez would tell the author later (through a third party).

Terronez wore a brown suit over a white shirt, red tie. He carried his files and a few charts into the Justice Center courtroom on the morning of November 2 in one of those white (with blue lettering) PROPERTY OF THE U.S. POSTAL SERVICE containers. In his rather brief and not well-planned opening statement, the SA explained how Sarah Kolb met, befriended, and then murdered Adrianne Reynolds. Sarah, dressed in black slacks, a white turtleneck under a gray sweater, sat quietly, listening, looking over her shoulder every once in a while to sneak a peek at family members there to support her. One of those, her mother, Kathryn Klauer, was photographed walking into the courthouse holding a photo of a young Sarah, her blond hair hanging over a broad smile, an obvious happy child with a zeal for life.

As he addressed the jury, it was amazing to listen to how much SA Terronez left *out* of his opening argument, along with the few details he included. By the end of his first breath, Terronez said, "Adrianne's fatal mistake in judgment was that she tried to befriend the defendant, Sarah Kolb."

It was showboating (but true), and sounded more like a teaser for an episode of *Dateline* or *48 Hours*. Not the product of a polished state's attorney. The pressure was definitely on Terronez; this was his first major jury trial since being elected.

Terronez laid out his case by describing that ride to Taco Bell that Sarah, Sean, Cory, and Adrianne took on Friday, January 21, 2005. Oddly, he gave jurors a brief layout of the parking lot, promising maps and charts.

"You will hear that Sarah Kolb, together with Cory Gregory, committed first-degree murder in two counts and committed a count of concealment of a homicidal death," Terronez said.

After this, he launched into a short argument about how Sarah had driven Adrianne's body out to the Engle farm and tried to get rid of it by fire. Terronez kept saying "they," meaning Cory and Sarah, but it was Sarah giving the orders on this day, an important detail Terronez failed to make.

Nate's role came up next.

"Nathan Gaudet will testify in this case, ladies and gentlemen, and he will tell you about a car ride . . . and Nathan Gaudet will tell you about a physical attack that took place in Sarah Kolb's car at the hands of Sarah Kolb, together with Cory Gregory."

And yet Nate was not there; his testimony regarding this would be third-party hearsay. It was Sean McKittrick who would describe this scene. Sean was there. Inside the car.

Sparing no graphic detail, Terronez described the way in which Nate dismembered Adrianne's body while his friends watched and guided him.

The SA mentioned Black Hawk State Historic Site.

He talked motive on Sarah's part—but he didn't mention what it was.

And, quite surprising, simply because he *did* have

the evidence to prove this part of his case, Terronez said, "I *don't* expect you to hear evidence of a premeditated plot."

Why ring *that* bell?

Perhaps hoping to talk his way into a guilty verdict, Terronez then spelled out the jury's "job" when they ultimately took the case back into the jury room—a direction a more experienced prosecutor at this level would have been expected to give during his closing. Terronez, though, reiterated what the judge had said already that morning, calling jurors "fact finders," saying how the jury's main purpose was to take the facts and apply them to the law.

And then he was done.

Not even ten minutes into it.

Appointed defense attorney David Hoffman had a reputation as being a tough no-holds-barred competitor inside a courtroom, not to mention an advocate for going after what he believed to be injustice. The well-dressed, experienced attorney, with fluffy white hair and a cotton white mustache, stood and, after addressing jurors, went right into the problems he had seen with Terronez's case.

"I found it interesting . . . that the state does not claim that there is evidence that Sarah actually killed Adrianne Reynolds."

Whispers and murmurs followed that statement.

"And secondly," Hoffman continued in his scratchy smoker's voice, "the issue of no premeditated plot?"

Hoffman was essentially saying something many in the room had likely pondered: With no evidence and no premeditation (*without* Cory Gregory), how in the heck was SA Terronez going to prove Sarah Kolb murdered Adrianne? Where was the state's magic hat and white rabbit?

Hoffman next did a smart thing, something experience had taught him long ago. He hit on a note that he would continue going back to throughout the trial.

"What I want you to pay is *very* close attention to . . . [the] very heavy continuous press coverage . . . where on the news, in the papers, everywhere, people are talking with each other. And there are things that are being recorded, sometimes attributed to certain people and sometimes not. So I want you to pay close attention to separating rumor, innuendo, opinion, and what purports to be news from what people actually *know* and what is actually *fact.*"

Hoffman was at the top of his game.

"I ask you to remember that you are dealing with teenagers," Hoffman said a while later. "Miss Kolb is here on trial as an *adult.*"

These were the same issues a state's attorney generally addressed during his opening, with the hopes of heading off any arguments before they were allowed to fester.

Hoffman asked the jury to "pay close attention to what their relationships are, a lot of people will use the term 'friends' and I think one of the things you need to do is separate out as to who is actually whose friend. . . ."

He then spoke of how SA Terronez had haphazardly used the word "they" throughout his opening.

"I want you to pay close attention to what is actually attributed to a specific person, who did or said what. Not the 'they.' It is easy to say 'they' all went somewhere. Well, who did what, where?"

Hoffman pointed out the fact that every time Nate

Gaudet talked to police about the case, he changed his story.

"It was different. . . . So pay close attention to Mr. Gaudet. I don't know what he is going to say, but we have records of what he said in the past, so we can compare them."

For the next ten minutes, Hoffman focused on the evidence—that is, the bludgeoning stick, the blood, the carpet in Sarah's car, the "graphic evidence" of Adrianne's skull. He encouraged the jury not to be taken in by what a *witness says* about the evidence, but only what DNA *analysis* of the items proves.

Good points. All of them.

In the end, Hoffman told the jury to listen carefully to the "charges," what they were, and how they applied to his client. He asked the men and women of the jury to "separate in your minds . . . what happens that causes Adrianne's death from what happens to her remains afterward, because that is the part that is going to be most graphically offensive to you."

Jeff Terronez objected to this.

The judge said opening arguments were not intended to be closings.

It was the perfect segue for David Hoffman to conclude on what turned out to be an extremely powerful note: "I've said enough to you. You are going to hear the evidence, and you already know what Mr. Terronez and I say is *not* evidence. So we will start now."

SA Jeff Terronez's first few witnesses set up the feud between Sarah and Adrianne. Classmates of both girls talked about how Adrianne slept with Sarah's friend at the party house that night in December, and then turned around and flung it in Sarah's face, which upset Sarah.

One of the girls told jurors that Adrianne, who could be extremely rancorous herself, told Sarah in school some days after the party night in December 2004, "I met two of your friends, and I fucked them both!"

Then East Moline police officer Kevin Johnson took the stand and talked about how, on the day after Adrianne disappeared, he spoke with Sarah by phone. She was talkative and seemed more than willing to describe the relationship between herself, Adrianne, and Cory. There was even one part of the conversation, Johnson noted, when Sarah became concerned about Adrianne.

"She said," Johnson testified, "that Adrianne said she was in love with Cory, and that she said [to her], 'I don't know how you can be in love with him, you barely know him.' And then she told—Sarah told Adrianne that—that Sarah likes Cory, Cory likes Sarah, but Cory doesn't like Adrianne."

It came across as the soap opera Sarah had made it out to be.

"Did she say what conversation took place next? . . ." Terronez asked.

"Um, she told—she told Adrianne that she hated her and that she was a slut and she spreads like Jiffy."

"That she spreads like *what*?"

"Like Jiffy."

"Did she make any reference to what 'spreading like Jiffy' meant?"

"No, she didn't. She had talked about how promiscuous Adrianne was with other guys, having sex with other guys."

Johnson answered a few more questions about the

phone call with Sarah. Terronez played the recording, and then Hoffman passed on asking the cop any questions.

Next up for Terronez was Sergeant Timothy Steines, a cop with the Rock Island Police Department. Steines had been brought into the case on January 25, 2005, by a request from the ISP and EMPD. He immediately dispatched half his unit, he said, to aid in the investigation. Steines was on the stand to verify that he brought along a team of officers to the Black Hawk State Historic Site on the night Cory Gregory led everyone down into that ravine where Adrianne's head and arms were hidden in the manhole.

In a moment of reflection, the gallery realized why that ninety-pound steel manhole cover (they had seen it in the video) had been so easy for Steines to lift off and toss aside like a Frisbee. Steines was a six-foot three-inch, 235-pound monster of a man.

"Did you ever observe the contents inside that bag?" Terronez asked, encouraging the cop to describe what they had found inside the manhole.

"I did."

"And what did you observe inside that bag?"

"There was a head and two arms."

"And in what condition?"

"Badly burned and . . . in pieces."

"They were severed?"

"Yes."

Hoffman had only three or four questions for Steines, which were centered on the officer's size and how many of his men—"around ten"—he brought out to the park on the night Cory Gregory led them to Adrianne's head and arms.

* * *

Because of witnesses Tim Steines and ISP crime scene investigators John Hatfield and Thomas Merchie, SA Terronez was able to introduce the two videotapes recorded that night and the next morning as investigators recovered Adrianne's body parts from the park and Sarah's grandparents' farm. If nothing else, the tapes proved that Cory had shown police where Adrianne's body parts were hidden. And Hatfield, talking about his inspection of Sarah's car, was able to explain that the trunk smelled of gasoline, the accelerant Cory had told the police he and Sarah had used to burn Adrianne's remains, adding further credence to Cory's statements.

69

The following day, November 3, began with the technical side of Terronez's case. It seemed the SA was following a playbook written by those prosecutors before him. On the previous day, Terronez had set up the relationship between Adrianne and Sarah; then he progressed into the search for Adrianne's remains, how Sarah became involved, and ended the day with videotape images of Adrianne's charred body parts. This morning, by calling Dr. Jessica Bowman, the pathologist who had inspected what was left of Adrianne's corpse, Terronez was going to give the jury the results of the murder the state claimed Sarah Kolb and Cory Gregory had committed.

Bowman would also inject the trial with its first bit of shock and awe.

Assistant State's Attorney (ASA) Peter N. Ishibashi questioned the doctor, who quickly rattled off her long list of credentials.

Ishibashi then asked Dr. Bowman to explain—of all

things!—what an autopsy was in respect to finding out how a human being had died.

It seemed a bit unnecessary.

From there, Bowman talked her way through examining Adrianne's body parts, slowly detailing every graphic cut, char, muscle tissue size and weight, along with the condition of Adrianne's scalp, leg, arms, head, and torso.

After saying that she could not give the jury an "exact cause of death," Bowman surprised some in the room when she said she had come to a "different diagnosis . . . based upon what I saw. And the differential diagnosis includes strangulation, either manual or with a ligature, compressional asphyxia, and that would be when somebody would sit on the body, preventing the chest wall from moving up and air from getting into the lungs."

The doctor was saying Adrianne was, in effect, smothered to death.

Bowman next talked about "blunt-force trauma," admitting that there was "no evidence of lethal blunt-force trauma."

ASA Ishibashi had the doctor explain the term "asphyxia."

Then, several questions later, he asked Dr. Bowman if there was a way to tell if Adrianne was alive when Cory and Sarah lit her on fire.

"There was no evidence to suggest she was alive at the time of burning."

Smartly, Ishibashi ended there. The worst thing a prosecutorial team can do is keep one of its experts on the stand, talking technical terms nobody really cared much about. The plan should be put a specialist up there, get her to give the money sound bites, and then quickly get her off the stand. Any more than that and the team is belaboring the technical facts of its case, which juries, by and large, do not want to hear.

David Hoffman went right for an opening he had apparently felt the state left him, asking Dr. Bowman if she had noticed any "missing teeth" on Adrianne's skull.

"No missing teeth," the doctor testified.

Thus, if Sarah had beaten Adrianne with her broom handle stick, as witnesses would soon testify, why were her teeth intact?

Then Hoffman was able to get the doctor to admit that strangulation generally involved a "choke hold," and not necessarily smothering, and that it would, in fact, be "easier" to choke someone to death rather than smother.

"It would be much more likely with a choke hold," Bowman agreed.

"I have nothing further," Hoffman concluded.

The media had watched and photographed him walking into the Justice Center. He looked scared and ghost white; his dark black hair was cut respectfully short.

SA Jeff Terronez called Sean McKittrick. The Juggalo was obviously nervous; he walked in with a fidgety way about him, and it was clear Sean did not want to be there. Sauntering by Sarah Kolb's table in front of the bench, Sarah's former boyfriend didn't take his eyes off the floor.

He sat in the witness chair.

Sarah stared at Sean as the bailiff adjusted the microphone to his height.

The former boyfriend of the accused was now eighteen years old. Sean had a way about him: congenial, yet hard. Court viewers got the feeling that the kid had been through a lot in his short life and would rather forget about it and move on.

He pointed Sarah out for the jury. She wore a long-sleeved, buttoned-up shirt, and held steady a look of despair and disdain on her ashen face.

Sarah was a fighter. That much was clear in her manner.

As he spoke about how he met Cory and Sarah, Sean McKittrick seemed to drift off. He was hard to hear.

The lawyers and the judge told him to speak up.

Within a few minutes, Sean walked jurors into the party house and introduced them to Nate Gaudet and several other Juggalos who hung out at the house. Then the SA had him talk about the relationship between Adrianne and Sarah. Sean had a backseat view of the tumultuous period between Adrianne and Sarah. He had witnessed Sarah's hate for Adrianne through Sarah's point of view, beginning at the first of the year, when Sarah and Cory picked up Sean in Cedar Rapids and brought him back to the QC. As far as his relationship with Sarah, Sean McKittrick said, he saw it slipping "at a down slope" by the time Adrianne was murdered, "and I noticed that it was not going to last, so that time (January 21, 2005), I would say it was over."

Terronez had Sean explain the setup at school. Class times. When the students had breaks. Where Sean and his crew hung out.

Sarah's name kept popping up as the leader, the one person they all went to for rides and advice.

Quite surprising, Sean said Sarah had never spoken to him about Adrianne, which made one consider the question: if Adrianne was so much the focal point of Sarah's wrath, why wasn't she discussing the girl with her boyfriend, arguably her closest confidant?

Sean categorized the relationship Cory and Sarah had as "odd."

After a few more questions about Cory and Sarah's relationship, Terronez had Sean get into the reason why he was there: Taco Bell.

First Sean jumped down off the stand and talked jurors through several maps and photographs of the Taco Bell parking lot that Terronez had set up.

Sean said when Sarah grabbed Adrianne by the hair, his "attention" was piqued.

"How did she have hold of her hair, sir?" Terronez wanted to know.

"By the back of her head."

It was clear the attack was unprovoked. Adrianne had never said anything, nor had she hit Sarah before Sarah grabbed her by the back of the head and warned her to stay away from Sean and Cory.

And that was about the extent of Sean's role in all of this. When Sarah failed to heed his call to stop bullying Adrianne, Sean bailed out of the car and went back to school.

Terronez asked Sean several questions about times and when he had spoken to Sarah and Cory, but Sean didn't have much information to share. Sarah, he said, wouldn't speak to him. The prosecutor did not ask Sean anything about the relationship he had with Sarah, or if kids in school were talking about the animosity between Sarah and Adrianne.

* * *

Throughout the remainder of the day, Jeff Terronez and company brought in Brad Tobias, Henry Orenstein, Melinda Baldwin, Kory Allison, and several other students/friends of Sarah's. Each provided a different take on the relationship Cory had with Sarah, along with the tenuous relationship Sarah had with Adrianne, and how the two collided like electrons after Sarah set Adrianne up with that social "test" at the party house.

The jury got it: Sarah was pissed that Adrianne had failed.

And it was obvious Adrianne would not let it go without an explanation.

November 4, 2005, gave the jury several witnesses whose testimony centered on Sarah Kolb's building hatred toward Adrianne Reynolds and the fact that she wrote about it in her journal. By the end of this day, jurors understood that Sarah might have told several of her coworkers and friends she knocked Adrianne's teeth out during a fight, but, according to what the pathologist had testified to, the evidence failed to back it up.

It was obvious that Sarah Kolb was a liar—but was she the one who instigated and carried out this vicious murder? That was the question here, one that SA Jeff Terronez had not quite proven.

The court took a break for the weekend.

Back on November 7, a clear Monday, the sky so blue and cloudless it looked like water, the testimony bolstered Sarah Kolb's case more than the state's. Darrin Klauer, Sarah's stepfather, talked about how he had observed an obsessive relationship between Cory and Sarah, with Cory routinely complaining about having other people around Sarah, many of whom he had to "contend" with at times. It was a strong argument for a case of revenge on Cory's part.

The only true piece of incriminating evidence SA Jeff Terronez could get out of Darrin Klauer—and it wasn't much—was the fact that he found it "odd" when Sarah parked her car in the garage on the night Adrianne was murdered and again the day after.

After a few more witnesses, who also described the bizarre behavior on the part of Cory Gregory and Sarah Kolb following Adrianne Reynolds's disappearance, Mary Engle was called to the stand.

Sarah's grandmother looked terrified of speaking against her granddaughter.

Once again, in what seemed to be a big buildup to nothing, as if the witness was going to drop the proverbial bombshell and blow the case against Sarah wide open for everyone to see, Mary Engle didn't have much to add.

Her testimony sort of went like this: "Was it dark out when [Cory and Sarah] left [the antique store]?"

"It was dark out before I left Aledo. It was January. It was—there was a storm coming in."

"So you specifically remember a storm coming in?"

"There was a sleet storm coming in, yes."

Inconsequential evidence, essentially, that, in the grand scheme of this case, meant little.

Then Jeff Terronez moved on to a pack of cigarettes that Sarah and Cory were looking for, which they could not find, and ended his direct examination of Sarah's grandmother.

The state had made a case for it being odd that Sarah Kolb was out at the Engle farm that weekend. David Hoffman keyed on this point for a brief moment, asking Mary how often she saw her granddaughter.

"Whenever they were in town," Mary said, meaning Kathryn Klauer and Sarah, "to go to the doctor or whatever, they usually stopped. Just every now and then, Kathy would come down, just periodically. There was no set schedule. Any given day, I could be babysitting for some of the other grandkids."

Seeing the opportunity, Hoffman asked Mary Engle if she ever saw Sarah with Cory before that day inside the antique store.

"No."

On redirect, Jeff Terronez asked Mary Engle a strange question, one that seemed to help Hoffman's case more than his own: "Just so I'm clear on this," Terronez said. "To your knowledge, Sarah Kolb had a specific plan to be out in Aledo the afternoon of January twenty-first?"

"Yes, she did."

It was to say happy birthday to her grandmother with a birthday cake.

Lunch came. The judge adjourned until 1:00 P.M.

* * *

As far as trials go, this one did not have the drama or intensity of a *Perry Mason* episode. Nor had it yet given jurors that *CSI*-inspired forensic evidence of supercomputers, high-tech gadgetry, or groundbreaking testimony from experts weighing their responses while chewing on the earpiece end of their glasses. There was no yelling. No screaming at witnesses. No testimony that sent newspapermen out into the hallways calling their editors in a frenzy.

Still, an astute trial watcher would be able to see what was happening here: that the dynamic in this courtroom had shifted. A story was being told, however subtle. A tale of teen drama, entrenched in the common everydayness of ordinary life for a bunch of dropouts and druggies who decided to give life one more crack before giving up completely.

Brian Engle, Sarah's grandfather, testified after the lunch break.

Engle had a farmer's well-mannered way about his posture and attitude. He was a guy who certainly didn't mince his words. He'd tell people how he felt, regardless of what they wanted to hear.

He told the jury that his farm was 160 acres. It was remote. "There's a blacktop road on the one side [going in] and a gravel road on the back [going out]."

Engle then explained how he had spotted that car on Friday, January 21, 2005, in a pasture and chased it away, only to find out later it was Sarah and her friend, Cory.

With that, SA Jeff Terronez had placed both Cory Gregory and Sarah Kolb on the farm on the night Adrianne was murdered.

Engle also claimed to have never seen Cory before that night.

When David Hoffman was given his chance at Sarah's grandfather, he said he didn't have anything to ask the man.

The final witness of the day was John Engle, Sarah's second cousin, who testified to finding a pack of Marlboro Reds out on the farm near two sets of footprints in the snow.

70

Wry questions fired randomly at witnesses don't win murder cases. Ostensibly unimportant questions, however, become necessary in order to either get a witness to feel comfortable, or to act as a hand-holding mechanism to walk a witness down a road of dropping that one statement that can—with any luck—take a case over the top.

On Tuesday, November 8, 2005, SA Jeff Terronez called his most important witness to date, Nathan Gaudet, who had pleaded guilty in February 2005 to "concealing a homicide." After Nate finished testifying, he was going to be shipped straight back to the detention center holding him until his sentencing, which would come after the litigation against Cory and Sarah had concluded.

Nate could put Sarah at the murder scenes and give the jury his best recollection of the conversations he'd had with both assailants. It was Nate, after all, to whom Cory Gregory and Sarah Kolb had admitted to murdering Adrianne.

With his hair buzz cut, UFC short, wearing a blue

T-shirt, a look of contempt on his face, sixteen-year-old Nate sat and looked toward the wall, staring into the pale nothingness that had become his life.

The boy who cut Adrianne into pieces spoke softly. He was almost afraid to answer the questions—certain, of course, that each answer would ultimately (at least from where Jeff Terronez stood) tighten the noose around Sarah's neck and, at the same time, make himself out to be the monster those in the QC had judged him to be.

In the months following Nate's arrest, his family had been threatened. Called names. Spat on. Given dirty looks at fuel pumps and the supermarket. They had tried to come to terms with what Nate had done. And they felt the impact of a community, by and large, that hated this kid, who he was, and those who had reared him.

"I think that what Nate Gaudet did," one person closely connected to the case later told me, "was worse than what Cory and Sarah did."

Nate did not want to be known as the snitch of the case. But what could he do? He had a lifetime ahead. If he could get out of this with a light sentence, maybe— just maybe—Nate Gaudet could get a second chance.

Terronez had Nate explain how Sarah and Cory brought Adrianne around to the party house.

"She," Nate said, meaning Sarah, "was putting Adrianne through a test to see if she would be loyal to her in a dating relationship."

Nate discussed his drug use. How he, Sarah, and Cory ended up together on that Saturday, January 22, 2005. It was during a car ride that afternoon, Nate explained to jurors, when Cory and Sarah talked about "killing somebody." Could Nate himself, they asked, ever digest the possibility they had actually done it? When Nate said no way, and showed signs of disbelief, Cory and Sarah decided to show Nate their handiwork.

Nate had a hard time speaking up. The grimmer the subject matter, the softer his voice got. It was clear he wanted no part of going back to that day that changed his life.

For the next ten minutes, Nate went into what Sarah and Cory had told him about how they had killed Adrianne. According to Nate's version, Cory and Sarah were equally responsible for Adrianne's murder.

Then Nate talked about taking the saw from his grandmother's house.

He said it was Sarah who ordered him to get the saw and cut up Adrianne.

He said he knew why he was "grabbing the saw" when he left the car that day and went down into his grandparents' basement.

"Whose idea was it to dispose of Adrianne's body?" Terronez asked.

"Sarah Kolb's."

After Nate told the jury he drove out to the farm with Sarah and Cory, he spoke—in brief, but very stunning and powerful sentences—of what he did next as though he was talking about helping a friend paint her house or wash a car. He had detached himself from what he was saying, totally uninvolved on an emotional level.

"I cut the arms off."

The key word there being "the," as opposed to "her" or "Adrianne." In saying "the," Nate was taking the person out of it, whether he realized it or not.

". . . I cut one off at a time, and Cory grabbed a

black garbage bag and picked up the head"—again, "the"—"and arms with the garbage bag and put them in the bag."

"Where else did you cut?"

"I . . . both of the legs and torso."

"The," again.

"You cut the torso?"

"Yes, sir."

"Where at?"

"Under the ribs."

"And you were successful in terms of cutting the torso?"

"Yes, sir."

"And you cut the legs, you said?"

"Yes, sir."

"Was that the extent of the cutting that you did, sir?"

"Yes, sir."

Nate told jurors how Sarah stood and watched throughout this horror show.

"Did Sarah touch any of the body parts, sir?"

"No."

Nate confirmed that the main reason why they cut Adrianne's head and arms off was to hide those body parts so dental and fingerprint records wouldn't be found in the same spot as the torso and legs. It was the only way to accomplish this task, he suggested.

Terronez asked Nate what they did after they chopped Adrianne into pieces and began to plot how they were going to get rid of the body parts.

"We drove to McDonald's in Aledo."

"You drove to McDonald's in Aledo?" Terronez repeated.

"Yes, sir."

"What purpose? . . ."

"To eat."

"Were you hungry at that point?" The prosecutor seemed to harp on this for no apparent reason other than its shock value.

"Yes, sir," Nate said, looking away.

A few questions later, after discussing the necklace Sarah took from Adrianne, Terronez went back to: "Did everybody eat at McDonald's?"

"Yes, sir."

It wasn't long after that when SA Jeff Terronez passed Nate Gaudet to David Hoffman.

After a ten-minute break, David Hoffman went right into his problem with Nate Gaudet's testimony. He began by asking the teenage Juggalo about the videotaped interview he granted police on January 26, 2005, in relation to his testimony before a grand jury and two additional interviews with police. Hoffman had a problem with the synchronization of all three.

Or the lack thereof, rather.

First, though, Hoffman asked Nate about his drug-using habits during the same time frame—that Saturday and Sunday, January 22 and 23—when he was with Cory Gregory and Sarah Kolb, and the following week, while he was being questioned by police.

"Were you on drugs at the time?"

"Yes, sir."

"Were you on Ecstasy?"

"Yes, sir."

"Were you using marijuana?"

"Yes, sir."

"Did you, in fact, use it on Saturday *and* Sunday?"

"Yes, sir."

"Did you use cocaine Saturday?"

"Yes, sir."

"In fact, Mr. Gaudet, did you see things that weren't there and hear things that weren't said?"

"Not really on that day. I was just . . . Sometimes I will see shadows or something like that when I'm coming down off Ecstasy."

Hoffman asked Nate to explain several comments he had made to police, some of which he had since rescinded and denied.

"Did you tell the police that you had no idea why you were going out [to the farm] with them that day? You thought [you were all] going out for some paintball exercise?"

"Yes, sir."

"First you ever heard about this killing was on Sunday. Isn't that what you told them?"

"Yes, sir."

"Was that just a lie?"

"Yes, sir."

"And why were you lying to them?"

"So I wouldn't be caught."

This type of back-and-forth went on for an hour or more. Nate admitted he lied to the police on several occasions to serve his own needs. Jurors had to consider that this boy was on three different drugs—two of which greatly affect the mind—and he had lied to police. What good was his testimony, taking all of this into account? Hoffman was suggesting. How reliable a witness was a drug-using liar? Could Nate's testimony—the idea that the murder was Sarah's idea from the get-go—truly be trusted as tangible enough to put a young girl away for no fewer than fifty years?

Finally David Hoffman, clearly frustrated by Nate's tepid responses, said to the boy, "I guess it is a small point, but you say this drive around took place between noon and two o'clock, or noon and three. [But] the last time you testified (in front of the grand jury), it was four. You've read your testimony from the last time and you know that's wrong, right? So you changed it?"

"I didn't see the part in the testimony. I skimmed through it a little bit."

"Okay, you changed it, didn't you?"

"Yes, sir, because—"

But Hoffman wouldn't let him finish. "And it is because you *knew* she (Sarah) was at work from three to ten?"

"I thought she went to work at four."

"I have no further questions."

Jeff Terronez did his best to clean up what little integrity Nate Gaudet might have had; but in the end, the boy had lied and David Hoffman was able to get him to admit it.

Concluding the seventh full day of the trial, Jeff Terronez called several important witnesses, a few of whom gave the jury a reason—albeit small—to find Sarah Kolb guilty.

Pat Corbin, Nate's grandmother, tearfully testified about finding the saw that Nate said he had used to cut up Adrianne's corpse. Pat told jurors that after finding out Adrianne went missing, putting a few things Nate had done over the course of that weekend together in her mind, she had a "gut feeling" to take a stroll down into the basement, where she knew Nate had been earlier that day.

And bingo—there was that bloody saw.

Sarah Kolb's older sister testified about how she had helped Sarah "hide a shovel and gardening tool," along with Adrianne's necklace, shortly after the murder.

A coworker at Showcase Cinemas in Davenport, Iowa, where Sarah worked, claimed Sarah offered to sell him her Prizm for $300 the day *after* the murder, but Sarah's mother told her she could not get rid of the car.

All of this was circumstantial evidence, but evidence—nonetheless—that at least pointed toward Sarah's guilt.

Two more witnesses concluded the day. Both offered little in advancing the state's case.

On November 9, 2005, SA Jeff Terronez called the last three witnesses of his case, bringing the total somewhere near fifty.

First up was EMPD officer Josh Allen, who called Sarah Kolb on the day Adrianne Reynolds was reported as missing.

Terronez played the tape of the phone call, on which Sarah had set up that McDonald's story that she stuck to all weekend.

The next two witnesses were females Sarah had met at the juvenile detention center she had been housed in after her arrest. Both admitted Sarah said Adrianne had died inside Sarah's Prizm.

And that was the end of the SA's case.

* * *

Reporters caught up with David Hoffman outside the courtroom as he smoked a cigarette. They asked him if his client was going to take the stand.

Hoffman said he didn't know.

The truth of the matter was, if Sarah Kolb was going to point a guilty finger at her coconspirator, Cory Gregory, she was going to have to do that from the witness stand herself.

71

Germane to the argument of whether Sarah Kolb murdered Adrianne Reynolds by herself was who you chose to believe. The only way, Sarah knew, she could get her story across to the jury—*and maybe reach one* (which was all it took)—was to tell it herself.

Which was exactly what she did.

On the morning of November 10, 2005, after SA Jeff Terronez rested the state's case, and David Hoffman began his defense with four witnesses—none of whom added anything to Sarah's innocence—the judge took a lunch break.

Shortly after one o'clock, Sarah stood from the defense table in front of the judge's bench as David Hoffman motioned that his next witness was the defendant herself.

Sarah's auburn and black hair was now down to her bony shoulders. She wore a black shirt and sat in the witness chair with a steely look of *how dare you accuse me!* penetrating from her engaging blue eyes.

The word the media overused in terms of Sarah's demeanor on the stand was "emotionless." That stone of a woman, who had been the ringleader of a small group she ran with back in high school, was determined to tell the jury exactly *why* and *by whom* Adrianne Reynolds had been murdered. Sarah had a plan. No doubt about it. She was prepared to talk through what had happened inside her car on that day, but maybe more important to her case, what had led up to that moment in her Prizm when she and Adrianne got into an argument that quickly turned violent.

Sarah was seventeen, a child in the court of public opinion, an adult in the eyes of the law. David Hoffman had her talk about how she met Adrianne. The two girls shared some likes, Sarah said—specifically, Sarah was attracted to Adrianne sexually and they were both interested in dating each other.

"Did you ever have sex with Adrianne Reynolds?"

"No, I did not," Sarah admitted.

Sarah went into how Adrianne had sought out one of her "friends"—Kory Allison—at the party house and had sex with him. She mentioned nothing about setting her up with a test. The way Sarah framed it, one would think Adrianne walked into the house and set her sights on Kory.

"Okay, at that time, did it make you angry?" Hoffman asked, giving his client the opportunity to tell the jury that it really didn't matter whom Adrianne had sex with. All it did was show Sarah the type of person Adrianne was, which was somebody Sarah did not want to be around.

"I wasn't angry. I was upset."

Adrianne had violated one of the core values that Sarah had proclaimed to be at the heart of any of the friendships she had: loyalty.

Sarah said she saw Adrianne as a slut. In fact, the

more she learned about Adrianne's promiscuity, Sarah added, the more she realized she did not want to date or even hang out with her.

But Adrianne persisted. She needed to know why Sarah didn't want to be her friend. Sarah said Adrianne called her five to ten times per day, badgering her about why the friendship had ended. She kept asking Sarah why she was so pissed off at her. There was one day, Sarah testified, when Adrianne had one of her step-brothers call Sarah and leave a nasty voice mail.

"Were the telephone calls irritating?"

"Yes, very."

Sarah talked about dating Cory for one week in May 2004, when they first met, before Adrianne even came into the picture. Sarah had to break it off, though.

"Why?" Hoffman asked.

"Because [Cory] intended to want something I didn't want. He wanted to have sex with me, and I didn't want to have sex with him."

Sarah said that she frankly wasn't attracted to Cory "in that way." They were more like buddies.

"Did you care who he had sex with?"

"No."

This line of questioning opened up an onslaught of Cory Gregory bashing. Sarah said Cory often talked about his sexual exploits and it "grossed [her] out." She didn't appreciate how he referred to his "dates" as "bitches." It was degrading to females, some of whom Sarah had found attractive and interesting. Sarah stuck up for the underdog, especially if there was something in it for her emotionally.

Sarah said Cory often lied to her. And that "friends don't lie. . . . They're not supposed to, anyway."

One of the lies that Cory often told, Sarah soon

found out, was that he had not started to hang around with Adrianne. He lied to Sarah about his relationship with Adrianne, she said, because he thought she'd be upset that he was becoming involved with someone she didn't like.

To that, Sarah said she was not angry or upset that Cory was hanging out with Adrianne, but she was mad because he had lied to her about it.

"There was no reason," Sarah added, for her to be mad about Cory and Adrianne getting together. "I mean, if he had just said, you know, 'I'm going to go,' you know—excuse me—'get a piece of ass from Adrianne,' I would have said, 'Okay.' But the fact that he actually *lied* to me about it, that's what bothered me."

Sarah talked about how Sean McKittrick became integrated into her tight-knit group of friends, and that she began to realize that Sean was a "mooch," a slacker among slackers, who didn't want to do anything with his life. Yet, before any of that happened, Sarah got word from a mutual friend that Adrianne was running around telling people she was going steal Sean away from Sarah as revenge.

". . . Did [Brad Tobias] tell you anything about Adrianne's interest in your boyfriend, Sean McKittrick?"

"Yes."

"What did he tell you?"

"He said Adrianne was going to supposedly try to get Sean to break up with me to date her."

"Okay. Did that make you angry?"

"That made me *very* angry."

"Okay. So at that point you were angry with Adrianne Reynolds."

"I was pissed!"

"And why?"

"Because he was my *boyfriend*. She could have had anybody she wanted, but she had to be messing with *my* boyfriend."

That Kool-Aid Sarah Kolb was talking about. Many had presumed she was referring to Cory Gregory when she wrote in her journal about Adrianne Reynolds "dipping" into her Kool-Aid.

This was the reason, Sarah explained, why she had written that note in her journal. The feeling she espoused to the jury—which was probably true—was how many teenagers out in the world on any given day say, "I'll kill you!" It's a euphemism for being pissed off at one's peers.

Sarah testified about meeting Adrianne for a smoke outside on the morning of January 21, 2005. They talked. She claimed Adrianne confided in her that she didn't have any girlfriends and all that the guys she knew wanted to do was use her for sex. She pleaded with Sarah for a renewed friendship. Sarah felt for Adrianne, she said. So she invited her to lunch at Taco Bell—and Adrianne accepted.

On the way to Taco Bell, according to Sarah's version, she asked Adrianne several times if she was okay, if everything was cool between them.

Adrianne said she was feeling better about the relationship.

They had made up.

As Sarah parked, she and Adrianne talked. Sarah asked Adrianne if what the others had been saying about her liking Sean was true.

"I think he's hot—I like him," Adrianne said.

"She really had a smug look on her face, like she thought it was funny, like she was kind of trying to make me mad," Sarah told jurors, describing the conversation.

This statement didn't make much sense in the context of the day. Sarah herself had just finished telling jurors how Adrianne was crying and begging, essentially, for them to be friends again. Why would Adrianne take a complete turn and say something she knew would make Sarah mad? On top of that, Sean and Cory did not report Sarah and Adrianne having this conversation.

Sarah said the comment "freaked" her out. So she snapped at Adrianne, lashing out verbally, "Stay the fuck away from me! Stay the fuck away from Sean! And stay the fuck away from Cory!"

"Were you angry?" Hoffman asked.

"*Very* angry."

Sarah admitted that she grabbed Adrianne by the hair. When she did that, Adrianne "curled up into a fetal position." She cried. As tears streamed down Adrianne's cheeks, Sarah explained, Sarah "felt small" and "let her go."

She said Adrianne never struck her.

They talked some more, Sarah testified. Sean had left the car by this point. Cory was still in the backseat, not saying anything.

Then Adrianne began talking about Cory and an older guy—the man Adrianne worked with at Checkers, whom she was going to babysit for that weekend—who were both pressuring her to have sex with them that previous Wednesday. This was when, Sarah claimed,

Cory reached around from the backseat and grabbed Adrianne by the neck.

If Sarah was to be believed, Cory lost all sense of himself.

He snapped.

"He put his arms around the seat," Sarah told jurors, ". . . and he was just kind of grabbing onto her, holding her."

David Hoffman asked where Cory Gregory had grabbed Adrianne Reynolds.

"Just like this"—Sarah showed jurors what she meant—"kind of around the neck."

As Adrianne tried to get out of the car, Sarah said, Cory yanked her into the backseat.

Sarah said she yelled at Cory: "What the fuck are you doing?"

She was startled by Cory's outburst and rage; he was choking Adrianne.

Next, Sarah said, she turned around in her seat and looked at the two of them. They were struggling. Fighting for position. Adrianne was kicking and trying to get her breath.

"When I looked in the back, he had that stick that everyone is talking about up against her throat and she was, she had her hands . . . trying to push away from it. And I started yelling at him and screaming, 'Knock it off,' and 'Quit it,' and little things like that, because I didn't think, you know, I didn't think he was going to kill her. I just thought that he was trying to beat her up or something. So I said, 'Knock it off! Quit it!' . . ."

Hoffman asked Sarah to talk about what Cory was saying while he was allegedly choking Adrianne to death with the stick.

"He was telling me, you know, that this has to happen, and that she is not one of us, and that she is trying to separate us, and she wants to make [me] hate [him], and she, you know, she just doesn't belong here, and it's better off this way."

Sarah claimed she told Cory—while he was supposedly choking Adrianne to death with the stick—that she was going to call the police if he didn't stop.

"What did he do?" Hoffman pressed.

"He hit me."

"Where?"

"In my face."

And so, according to Sarah, this was how she got that bloody nose.

From Cory's hand.

Sarah said she watched as Adrianne Reynolds took her last breath. She said she saw Adrianne "releasing air from her body."

Dying, in other words. Sarah Kolb was looking into her backseat at Adrianne Reynolds as she gasped for one final breath.

"'She's dead . . . ,'" Cory kept saying, Sarah explained, "in a matter-of-fact tone."

Sarah said she didn't think what had happened was real. It was all like a dream.

"I was in shock. . . . He just killed somebody in my backseat."

There was some discussion at that point if, in fact, Adrianne was actually dead, or passed out.

So Cory, Sarah explained, said, "Well, if that's what you think, I'll take care of it!"

This was when he grabbed the belt—"I don't know

from where"—and he "wrapped it around her neck . . . and fastened it . . . like a noose."

Cory covered Adrianne up with a coat and stepped out of the car.

Sitting in the front seat a moment later, Cory turned to Sarah and, after grabbing the belt and holding on to it, said, "'Drive,'" she claimed.

When Cory got out of the car near her house in Milan, Sarah said, she phoned her sister for advice. But her sister did not answer the call.

Cory returned after walking into Sarah's garage to check if anyone was there.

"Keep driving," he said. "Your stepfather is still home."

From here, Sarah maintained, heading off to Big Island was Cory Gregory's idea, as was putting Adrianne in the trunk.

Sarah was obeying Cory because, she said, she was scared of him.

"I just saw him kill somebody."

Sarah then headed out to the Engle farm. Once again, under Cory's direction, she said.

From this point forward, Sarah maintained, Cory Gregory told her what to do and when to do it. She was dismayed by the sight of Adrianne Reynolds's glossy eyes staring at them as they went about the business of dragging her corpse from the trunk to an area of the farm where they then began trying to burn her body. The pronoun Sarah used most during this portion of her testimony became obvious.

He wrapped her in the blue tarp.

He tried to burn her.

He said not to tell anyone.

He. He. He.

Sarah Kolb portrayed herself as a scared, insubstantial teen who had just witnessed a murder and was now involved in the cover-up with a stronger, controlling boy. None of these events had she willingly participated in.

72

Sarah Kolb told jurors as she continued on the afternoon of November 10, 2005, that Cory Gregory threatened her.

"His exact words were, 'If you tell anybody, if you do anything, I will fucking kill you. I will fucking kill your mom. I will fucking kill your dad. I will fucking kill your sister. I will fucking kill [your nephew]. . . . I will fucking kill your cats.'"

Sarah had named one of her cats Psycho.

The problem with Sarah's version was that none of the testimony by other witnesses backed her up. Sarah had had several chances to turn Cory in, call someone, go to the police station, fold into her mother's arms and plead for help.

She never did any of that.

This idea that Cory Gregory was going to murder everyone in her family (and her cats) was absurd. Cory Gregory, if one went back and looked at his behavior after this murder (some of which was caught on videotape), was in no position to hurt anyone. The kid was devastated and destroyed. He could not eat, sleep, speak, or even stand up for long periods of time. Much less take out an entire family.

In any event, Sarah continued to spin her tale of woe. She was so afraid of Cory, in fact, that she stayed at his house that night Adrianne Reynolds was murdered. Her reason for this, Sarah Kolb claimed: "Because he told me I had to."

The following day, Saturday, Sarah went to work. She didn't tell anyone at work that some lunatic had killed a girl inside her car and was threatening to kill her and her family. Instead, she told coworkers—well, actually, she bragged about—how she had smashed Adrianne in the face and busted a few of her teeth, which was a lie.

Sarah admitted that Cory had told Nate Gaudet after they had picked him up that day how *she* had strangled Adrianne, but she was, of course, too afraid of Cory to correct him or butt into the conversation he was having with Nate as she drove.

If she wanted the jury to believe her erroneous, concocted story, Sarah needed to explain the McDonald's connection. So she blamed that on Cory, too. But she involved Sean McKittrick, saying, "[Cory] told Sean that Adrianne and I had got in a fight and that she hit me and I hit her back, that she broke my nose and that we made up and dropped her off at McDonald's."

Cory told Sarah she needed to stick to this story. Or—you guessed it—she and her family were as good as dead.

As Sunday came, and Sarah was back at home, she believed she was too deeply involved by then to go back and explain to anyone that Cory had killed Adrianne. Plus, she added, she was still in fear of Cory sneaking into her house and killing everyone.

Regarding the dismemberment of Adrianne's body,

Sarah claimed she watched it from the top of a hill, looking down, and that Cory had threatened Nate, telling him he was involved to the point of no turning back.

Nate, of course, did not agree with this.

Sarah took things a step further with regard to Nate and Cory cutting up Adrianne's body into pieces. She claimed Nate and Cory, while they were completing this incredibly horrific act, cracked jokes.

"It grossed me out," Sarah said. She meant this literally. The jokes were so "disgusting" that she became physically ill while they were laughing at what was the most awful thing she had ever witnessed in her sixteen years.

Throughout midafternoon, Sarah proceeded to tell jurors that she never spoke to anyone about the case besides Nate and Cory. She never talked to her coworkers about anything.

Apparently, all those people who testified were making up things.

The problem with this argument was that unless Sarah had said something to her coworkers that weekend, there was no way any of them could have known the facts they brought forth. It was absurd to believe Sarah did not talk about the fight she had had with Adrianne.

She said she never told any of her cellmates about the case. It never came up, in fact.

They, too, like all the others, were liars.

In the end, Sarah was "shocked" by Adrianne's death, she said.

"How do you feel about women being hit?" Hoffman asked.

"It's not right."

"Is this a special thing to you?"

"Yes!"

After David Hoffman looked down at his notes, checking to see if he had asked his client everything he needed, he turned Sarah over to SA Jeff Terronez.

If one was to believe Sarah Kolb's direct testimony, a person would have to draw the conclusion that she wasn't complicit in anything that had happened to Adrianne Reynolds on the day she was murdered.

73

If Jeff Terronez was ever going to prove to the voters who put him in office that he was the right man for the job, this was the prosecutor's chance. There is a certain white-glove touch and polished manner that prosecutors need to adhere to when questioning a murder defendant. This, seasoned prosecutors say, comes with experience. An attorney doesn't want to try to drop the hammer on every single lie he believes the defendant has told. Instead, he picks his most powerful arguments and keys on these, without, of course, running the risk of passing up a golden opportunity to prove to jurors that they are being taken for a ride by an unremitting liar.

Terronez began with Nate Gaudet. He asked Sarah Kolb, who seemed oddly cool, calm, and collected, several questions about Nate driving around with her and Cory Gregory on the day they dismembered Adrianne's dead body. Terronez wanted to know if Nate was "correct" in testifying about what had happened on that day.

Sarah answered yes to just about every question

Terronez posed. It got to the point where some in the gallery wondered where Terronez was heading with so many questions to which Sarah repeatedly said yes.

What the state's attorney tried to do, it soon became clear, was ask Sarah if every one of the witnesses he had put on the stand had effectively lied about what she had told each one of them, or her behavior during that weekend. The SA's suggestion in asking Sarah all of these questions related to previous testimony was designed to point out, without saying it, that in order for Sarah Kolb to be telling the truth, all material witnesses the state had put on before her had lied or perjured themselves.

This was laughable. There was not a chance. Two people who don't know each other—any fool knows—cannot tell the same lie.

It is impossible.

Terronez brought out the fact that Sarah had even spoken to the police twice that weekend. During those calls, one of which the jury had heard, Sarah sounded fine. She never mentioned how scared she was of being Cory's next victim.

And then there was that little problem of Sarah lying to the police when she didn't have to.

". . . So all of these people that have testified that you told them that you either struck or strangled Adrianne Reynolds," Terronez stated at the conclusion of his long list of facetious questions, "they are *all* incorrect? Is that your testimony?"

Sarah didn't bat an eye. She leaned in: "They were *all* incorrect."

A few questions later, Terronez, in a patronizing tone, said, "Everybody is out to get you, aren't they, Miss Kolb?"

"That's not what I said. . . ."

For the next five minutes, Terronez went through the same list of questions again, asking Sarah if each witness was correct or incorrect.

The SA had made his point. It was time to move on. Emotion cannot play a role in a good, well-thought-out direct examination.

Terronez seemed to get on track and chipped away at Sarah's argument of being held hostage by Cory Gregory that weekend. He asked Sarah how tall Cory was and how much he weighed.

She said she had no idea, sassily snapping: "You would have to ask him!"

Terronez asked Sarah if she knew of any weapons her grandfather kept inside his house, where she and Cory had ended up that night after being chased off the farm by the same man.

Again, in an irritable inflection, Sarah Kolb said, "I don't live there."

Terronez wanted to know why Sarah never ran to her car and took off as Cory was lighting Adrianne on fire. Sarah had the keys. She could have left Cory out there to fend for himself. Drove home (or to the police station). Warned everyone in her household that a madman had killed Adrianne and was coming for them next.

"Because I just watched him kill somebody, and I was afraid to run," she answered. "I was afraid to do *anything* other than listen to him and do what he told me to do."

Terronez had Sarah tell the jury how much time she spent alone that weekend. In doing so, she made the point that she had every opportunity to go to the police, but she was too afraid.

"Were you scared?" Terronez asked.

"Yes, I was scared."

"So under those circumstances, ma'am, when you were scared, you came up with a story that wasn't quite truthful, correct?"

"Correct."

"You're here in front of this jury. In a matter of days, they're going to be deciding whether you're guilty or not guilty of first-degree murder. You heard a lot of testimony in this evidence. You've heard what people have had to say to this jury. Are you scared now?"

"Yes, I am. Is there a reason why I shouldn't be?"

The judge intervened. "You don't answer a question with asking a question, Miss Kolb."

Sarah cracked a smile. Then: "It's the truth," she said.

"I am *not* going to instruct you again!" the judge warned.

Jeff Terronez and Sarah Kolb went back and forth for a time, heatedly discussing certain aspects of the case. Sarah was determined not to give Terronez an inch. She disagreed with him—as he did with her—on just about everything. It became tiresome. The facts of the case had spoken. Terronez had done a respectable job in that regard. But now, he was trying to force a square peg into a round hole—and it wasn't budging. If his goal was to get Sarah to make an admission, or catch her lying, *good luck.*

"You grabbed hold of her, didn't you?" Terronez asked Sarah.

"Yes, I did."

"Told her to stay away from all of you?"

"Yes, I did."

"Then Cory took it upon himself to do what he did?"

"You'd have to ask him."

"You were there, ma'am. I am asking you."

"Okay, yes."

"Without any instruction, without any input from you?"

"Yes."

"Even though all of these witnesses said that you had reason to hate her, you were just a bystander?"

"Yes."

"Even though all these witnesses testified that you took part in it, you were a bystander?"

"Yes."

"You said that *Cory* punched you in the nose and caused it to bleed in the car?"

"That's correct."

"And that you had to get a napkin and try to stop the bleeding."

"Yes."

Where was SA Jeff Terronez going? The gallery was waiting for a punch line that never seemed to come. In fact, after a few more questions, Terronez switched subjects entirely, asking Sarah about the dynamics of the relationship she had with Cory Gregory and how angry she was that Cory and Adrianne had entered into a friendship.

Sarah would not agree.

Then Terronez asked Sarah how she felt about Adrianne Reynolds having sex with Henry Orenstein and Kory Allison.

For what seemed like the umpteenth time, Sarah said she was "upset."

So Terronez asked if Adrianne had called her a slut.

No.

Had Adrianne hit her?

No.

Had Cory held Adrianne's arms down while Sarah choked her.

No.

"So when Nate Gaudet says you told him all those things—he is incorrect?"

"Yes, he is."

Terronez's big moment came when he asked Sarah to read the final journal entry she had made. She had written about being expelled *for spreading the fucking Jiff* and calling Adrianne a *stupid bitch* and telling her to *back off my Kool-Aid*. Sarah had no choice but to finish reading the entry, telling jurors how she would *fucking kill her.*

"That was written the day she died, correct?"

"Yes, it was."

"So when all these people say that on the same day you told them you would kill her, or that you *wanted* to kill her, or that you were *going* to kill her, they're *all* incorrect?"

"Yes," Sarah repeated. "They're all incorrect."

"But you cannot deny that assertion from January twenty-first in your journal entry, correct?"

"Correct."

"I have no further questions, Your Honor."

David Hoffman stood and asked Sarah Kolb several questions on redirect that, in the scope of things, didn't amount to squat. It felt as if Hoffman was fulfilling a duty rather than truly getting to something that could help Sarah.

All told, Sarah's testimony did not go that bad. She stayed her ground. Never broke. And sounded as though she believed herself. The arguing she did back and forth with Jeff Terronez was more a reflection on the state's attorney.

On recross, Terronez seemed to backpedal somewhat.

"Miss Kolb, prior to January twenty-first, Adrianne Reynolds had made you angry?"

"Yes, she did."

"She made you angry again in the car when she talked about Sean?"

"Yes, she did."

"She gave you a smug look and you felt insulted?"

"Yes, I did."

"And you did nothing about it?"

"I grabbed her by the hair."

"And that was [the] extent of it?"

"I . . . uh . . . yelled at her."

"Nothing more physical?"

"No."

"Cory took over from there?"

"After Sean got out of the car, after I had let go of her, yes."

"No further questions. . . ."

74

Court was closed on Friday, November 11, 2005, for Veterans Day, and the subsequent weekend, but everyone reconvened on Monday, November 14. Before David Hoffman rested his case, the state called a rebuttal witness.

Cory Gregory's neighbor.

The girl had testified on the previous Thursday, after Sarah Kolb had concluded her direct and cross. Cory's neighbor claimed that on the night Adrianne Reynolds was murdered, she saw Sarah and Cory together.

"Sarah was sitting on Cory's lap," Laura Lamar told jurors, "and [she] had her arm around him."

A brilliant move on SA Jeff Terronez's part.

Even more damaging to Sarah's testimony was that Lamar explained how Cory was "really quiet. . . ." Whereas Sarah appeared bubbly, definitely not "nervous," or "on edge."

This was hardly the behavior of a girl who was scared to death that the boy who had just killed someone was going to kill her and her family.

Sarah was back on the stand that Monday, November

14, refuting Laura Lamar's testimony, saying Laura was drunk, seeing things. It never happened the way she had framed it and, Sarah's attorney seemed to presume with his questioning, Miss Lamar had perhaps mixed up her days and thought she saw Cory and Sarah on *Friday* night, when it was actually Thursday.

During his final rebuttal, SA Terronez contested Sarah's drunken neighbor claim, saying that in order to believe Sarah Kolb, one would have to agree that every witness lied. Terronez jokingly mentioned something about a gathering that was going to be held at a local club in Sarah's honor: "The let's-all-get-together-and-frame-Sarah-Kolb party."

Some found this funny; others thought it to be over-the-top.

In any event, both attorneys gave closing arguments, which turned out to be uneventful and unmoving. The idea in closing out a case is to wrap it up nicely in a bow, giving jurors several reasons to take a definite side. Neither lawyer was able to do this convincingly. There was much backpedaling and *don't believe this, believe that* sort of rhetoric, words that sounded more condescending and pleading than anything that might remotely sway jurors one way or the other.

Judge James Teros gave the jury its long list of instructions on Tuesday, November 15, first thing in the morning, and the jury hit the carpet soon after to begin deliberating.

They spent the entire day discussing the case.

By 4:32 P.M., one hour and twenty-eight minutes before the close of deliberations for the day, the first sign of trouble for the state came in the form of a question. Jurors said they were having "trouble" defining the term "intent."

Judge Teros provided the legal definition. Intent is pretty straightforward. Any legal dictionary will give various forms of the same meaning: *The determination or resolve to do a certain thing, or the state of mind with which something is done.*[3]

The fact that the jury was asking was not a good sign for Jeff Terronez. It meant the jury was considering the fact that Sarah might have been involved, but in a lesser degree. Gerald and Kathleen Hill, coauthors of some twenty-five books, including *The People's Law Dictionary, Real Life Dictionary of the Law,* and *Encyclopedia of Federal Agencies and Commissions,* astutely define "intent" in terms any layperson can understand, calling it the *mental desire and will to act in a particular way, including wishing not to participate. Intent is a crucial element in determining if certain acts were criminal.*

Still, all of this seemed a waste of time. The jury did not have the option to find Sarah Kolb guilty of a lesser charge. In Terronez's words to the press later that day, jurors faced an "all or nothing" verdict when making a decision. Where the term intent came into play, some speculated, was in the description of the two counts of first-degree murder with which Sarah had been charged. One charge was written to include the notion that Sarah Kolb "intended to kill" Adrianne Reynolds; while the additional charge stated that Sarah's actions on that day inside her car corresponded with a "strong probability of death."

---

[3]http://www.lectlaw.com/def/i053.htm

Things got even worse for Terronez on Wednesday, November 16, when the jury came in and asked the judge what "presumption of innocence" meant.

The words seemed simplistic and self-explanatory; yet when broken down into what they meant in actual terms of the law, things got a bit fuzzy. Basically, the presumption of innocence, again, according to Gerald and Kathleen Hill, *requires the prosecution to prove its case against the defendant beyond a reasonable doubt.*

In asking about this, was the jury saying the state did not accomplish that task?

It seemed so.

The jury ordered lunch after the judge read the definition.

At 3:40 P.M., with a total of sixteen hours of deliberations in the books, Judge James Teros did something no judge wanted to do.

Declare a mistrial.

The jury was unable to come to a verdict based on the charges.

Tony and Jo Reynolds, who had stayed fairly quiet throughout the trial, erupted into tears. Jo was wearing a T-shirt with Adrianne's photo; Tony was dressed in a leather jacket over button-up shirt and tie. On the front steps, outside the court, they held a photo of Adrianne. Tony looked beaten, his eyes and cheeks swelled from tears, his face sagging.

Tony's only response, which he repeated over and over as he walked away, was "I can't believe it! I just cannot believe this. . . ."

Turned out there was one guy, Mark Hurty, the foreman, who couldn't vote guilty.

Hurty told the press that although he firmly believed Sarah was *not* innocent, the state did *not* prove its case.

"I have nothing but sympathy for the family of Adrianne Reynolds," Hurty told reporters. "My heart breaks for them."

What upset many was that Hurty had told the media he did not "have a clear understanding" of the judge's instructions.

Although Sarah Kolb wasn't a free woman, a hurdle heading toward that destination had been cleared.

SA Terronez would have to go back to the drawing board now and do it all over again.

"Jeff did not want to speculate about the reason for the hung jury," someone in Terronez's office told me when I asked Terronez for a comment regarding the mistrial.

"I thought Jeff Terronez did a good job," Jo Reynolds said, speaking for her and Tony. "He explained a lot of things to us. The day we found out, Jeff and his assistant came to our house and explained how victims of violence would help with funeral expenses and other expenses we had. I used to show up at Jeff's office when I felt a meltdown coming, and he would take me in his office and I would cry and he would pump me up again until my next meltdown. Jeff was very caring to our needs. We felt [the SA's office] did a good job. The evidence was there. It was just one [juror who] wouldn't commit."

The court scheduled Sarah Kolb's retrial for February 2006 during a special hearing in late November, a week after the QC had had time to consider what had happened. The community was outraged by the mistrial and couldn't understand how the jury had failed to reach a verdict. Talk radio got busy discussing the case. Message boards on local Internet chat rooms lit up with vile and vulgar posts directed toward the juror and Sarah. Those who loved Adrianne were left in a fog of discontent, shaking their heads, wondering what in the name of justice had gone wrong.

One juror spoke out to a local paper about holdout Mark Hurty, saying Hurty was the only one on the jury not to agree with a guilty verdict. Near *chaos ensued,* *Times Dispatch* reporter Brian Krans wrote, *as 11 people tried to change the foreman's mind. . . .*

That one juror who spoke out said that by the time a mistrial had been declared, she had "had it" with the entire process *and* Mark Hurty.

"If we could have fired him, we would have," juror Jeanette Roman told the newspaper.

75

Cory Gregory came out swinging on November 28, 2005. The talk around the QC was that the prosecution needed Cory to win its second try against Sarah Kolb. Well, Cory was now prepared to start talking—if only a little—as Christmas, 2005 approached. The first thing he did was grant Chris Minor, a reporter for WQAD News Channel 8, an interview on camera. During that interview, Cory proceeded to say, with his attorney present, that he had lied about his role in the murder of Adrianne Reynolds, but he was now ready to come clean.

Cory was pissed that Sarah had thrown him under a bus. He wanted to set the record straight and make it clear that Sarah had "made the entire story up" while on the witness stand.

He did not kill Adrianne. He had no reason to.

This was true. Cory did not have a motive other than he had told friends before the murder that he wanted to know what it felt like to kill someone.

The former Juggalo was eighteen, living in prison. He still had that street cockiness and punk attitude. Cory wanted the public to know that he was no killer.

He might have helped Sarah, he told television news reporter Chris Minor, but he did not instigate or carry out a plan to attack and murder Adrianne. That was Sarah's doing. *She* started the fight. *She* grabbed Adrianne by the neck. *She* choked Adrianne until she was blue. And *she* ordered him to burn Adrianne's body, before coming up with the idea to have Nate Gaudet cut her into pieces.

Cory spoke like someone who knew Sarah. He told Minor that Sarah had always had an "image problem." She was obsessed with the notion of being the "perfect person." Cory also knew firsthand that Sarah lied to people all the time—and here she was lying once again, this time to save her own skin.

Cory pointed out a fact that Jeff Terronez had failed to spell out clearly during the trial: that in one of her own letters to Sarah, Adrianne had asked Sarah why she hated her so much. This proved, in Adrianne's own words, that Sarah had told Adrianne to her face that she despised her, something Sarah had denied on the witness stand. The word Sarah kept using in place of hate was "upset." She was upset with Adrianne. Not angry. Or odious. But disappointed and troubled that their relationship hadn't worked out.

Steve Hanna, Cory's lawyer, would not allow his client to go into specifics with Chris Minor, pending the outcome of Cory's forthcoming trial. But Cory wanted to state emphatically, for the record, that Adrianne's murder was a "fight . . . [that] went too far."

He showed remorse and empathy during the interview for the first time, saying he was seeing horrifying images of the murder and cover-up as they played over in his mind. But Cory seemed to be less than truthful with Minor, saying that he had "no idea" the fight Sarah had in the car with Adrianne would erupt into violence and murder. This statement went against the information several interviews with witnesses not used during Sarah's trial had reported. These were fellow students and Juggalos and friends of Cory's and Sarah's who spoke about Cory planning the murder with Sarah, and he and Sarah talking about it days before.

Hanna minimized Cory's role in the murder by telling Chris Minor that his client just happened to be "in the wrong place at the wrong time."

After explaining to Minor how he had "cried several times" since Adrianne Reynolds's death, Cory said he couldn't wait for his day in court so he could tell the world exactly what had happened inside Sarah's car. He was looking forward to sharing the truth about Adrianne's murder and Sarah's role in it.

Looking at this, one couldn't help but think it was just another blasé round of that same *he said/she said* nonsense that Cory Gregory and Sarah Kolb had been talking since their arrests.

76

Sarah's attorneys filed a change of venue motion in early January 2006. What was interesting about the motion became how her new attorney, public defender Baron Heintz, worded a section regarding the media's coverage and public response to Sarah's case. The lawyer had a solid argument. Heintz focused on twenty-five thousand references to Sarah's case on the Internet he had uncovered, which indicated that Sarah Kolb could likely not get a fair trial in the QC. In fact, Heintz smartly pointed out, some of those people who had posted on message boards anonymously said they would go to the extraordinary length of lying to the judge during jury selection in order to obtain a seat on the jury for the sole purpose of convicting Sarah.

Steve Hanna saw an opportunity, and, a day later, he, too, said he would be filing a change of venue motion under the same circumstances for his client.

On Wednesday, January 4, 2006, despite the exorbitant costs argued by Jeff Terronez of transporting nearly fifty witnesses out of the county, Judge James Teros issued his ruling. Teros granted the motion and allowed the change of venue, which could take the case from Moline to Chicago, Peoria, Rockford, or Dixon.

A major win for Sarah. A fresh set of eyes and ears would get her case. If she had gotten to one juror previously, there was nothing stopping her from getting to another.

Judge Teros sent the trial an hour and a half, almost one hundred miles, northeast of Rock Island County, to Dixon, Lee County. His hope was that the mileage between the two counties would make the media's impact transparent. Sure, some in Dixon had heard about the case, but the talk there was not centered on it as much as it had been in Rock Island, where Sarah Kolb was still hitting the front page, above the fold, not to mention headlining all the local TV newscasts.

77

The second round in the *State of Illinois* v. *Sarah Kolb* began much in the same fashion as the first: the same dull opening arguments; the same list of witnesses, testifying about the same things they had months before; the same gallery reactions to testimony that teetered on the verge of pointing a finger directly at Sarah, but never managed to get completely there.

SA Jeff Terronez went about prosecuting Sarah in the exact same way, building his case on the relationship Sarah Kolb and Adrianne Reynolds had; the bitter feud that erupted between them after Adrianne slept with two of Sarah's friends; and the idea that Sarah became incensed when Adrianne started to dip into Sarah's Kool-Aid. Once again, Terronez did not offer a smoking gun. He never brought in any of those character witnesses to describe how Sarah reacted to disappointment throughout her life, or people Sarah had gotten into fights with in the past. He relied on Sarah's journal and the testimony of former friends who said Sarah had had it in for Adrianne.

On February 21, 2006, a second jury was given the

case. The only difference that would soon prove to be momentous was that Sarah had decided *not* to testify this time around. Even more shocking was that she and her lawyers chose not to put on *any* witnesses and offer *no* evidence.

By late afternoon on the first day of deliberations, the jury had asked two questions relating to the law, both of which were quickly answered by Judge Teros.

The following day, the jury—this time made up of seven men and five women—continued deliberations until 1:30 P.M., shortly after an announcement came indicating they had reached a verdict.

Judge James Teros brought everyone into the Lee County courtroom and summoned his jury. Fixing himself in his chair, the heavyset judge spoke: "I've been informed that the jury has reached a verdict. I understand that for many of you this will be a very emotional moment. Please . . . I ask that you be calm and that you be collected."

The jury was escorted into the courtroom.

"Ladies and gentlemen of the jury," Teros said, staring at the group, many of whom would not look up, "I understand you've reached a verdict."

"We have, Your Honor," the foreman, a young-looking, dark-haired man, unafraid to face the judge and Sarah Kolb, said.

"Would you please give [the verdicts] to the court so they can be published."

The bailiff walked over and took the paper in his hand. He then handed it to Judge Teros, who, without much fanfare, in his deep voice, said, *"We, the jury, find the defendant guilty of murder in the first degree. Count one. We, the jury, find the defendant guilty,"* the judge looked up for a brief moment, *"of murder in the first degree. Count two. We, the jury,"* he continued, *"find the defendant* guilty *of concealment of a homicidal death."*

Sarah Kolb was found guilty on all three counts.

The outcome for her could not have been worse.

The newspaper back home in the QC ran a one-word banner headline with Sarah's mug shot on the right side of the page: GUILTY.

There would be no celebration on Sarah's part tonight. The jury had spoken clearly, sending Sarah Kolb—and, more important, Adrianne Reynolds and her family—a direct message.

When Sarah returned to the Rock Island County Jail that evening, she didn't run into her cell, curl up in a ball to start crying, as perhaps some might have assumed. Instead, Sarah Kolb put in a request for a haircut—a rather bizarre style that spoke, in some strange way, to the people of Illinois who were now calling her a murderer. There's no doubt Sarah was making a point when she sat down in the barber's chair and had the prison stylist shave her entire head into a buzz cut, with the exception of two long, inch-thick strands (bangs) of black hair that hung from the top of her forehead down past her lips, like two walrus fangs. It looked almost as if Sarah had grown a mustache that started at the top of her head and sloped down around her mouth on each side. Was this her way of poking fun at that photograph used during Adrianne Reynolds's disappearance, the same one that the missing person flyer made famous, which depicted Adrianne with the same bangs hanging down in front of her face?

According to Sarah, she shaved her head to let a good friend of hers know that she was okay with the guilty verdict. She was a survivor. Years before, when this same friend's mother developed cancer and had lost all her hair, Sarah reportedly shaved her head in solidarity with her friend and her friend's mother.

Regardless of why she did it, what became clear was that Sarah Kolb was still making front-page, above-the-fold headlines, only now the story was about her new look, and the threat from Mercer County prosecutors, where Adrianne's remains were found on the Engle farm, who were considering filing additional charges against Sarah for dismembering Adrianne in their county. Mutilating a body was a felony that could garner the convicted murderer an additional six to thirty years on top of what Sarah was going to receive for the murder.

78

Teresa Gregory stood behind her son on April 27, 2006, a seasonably cool Thursday afternoon in the QC, as a subdued and subtly defiant Cory Gregory pleaded guilty for his role in the murder and dismemberment of Adrianne Reynolds. Cory must have weighed his options after seeing what had happened to Sarah Kolb, who some were saying could get upward of almost one hundred years with the additional charges, and reconsidered taking a plea deal, as opposed to rolling the dice at trial. Why the state would deal with Cory *after* Sarah was convicted perplexed many, but Cory was offered a chance at one day feeling the sun shine on his back a free man—and he grabbed it.

Under the plea agreement, Cory was going to receive a sentence of between twenty and forty years, which would allow him to walk out of prison at some point. Part of the deal, a request Tony Reynolds had made to Jeff Terronez, included Cory having to face the family of the girl he had helped murder and cut into pieces.

It would be a few more months before Cory Gregory was sentenced.

Tony and Jo went into the prison to visit with Cory after he pleaded. Jeff Terronez had told Tony he would ask for the meeting between Adrianne's family and one of her killers, but he "thought it would never happen," Jo recalled.

Tony wanted to look in the eyes of the person who had killed his daughter. The questions, for which maybe there were no answers, that Tony and Jo wanted to ask were "What was so bad that you had to kill her? Why couldn't you both just walk away?"

"We wanted to know the truth about what happened," Jo said.

Cory sat staring at the floor as Jo and Tony stood on the opposite side of the glass separating them.

"I did nothing but watch," Cory finally said, meaning he did not initiate Adrianne's murder.

"You're a liar!" Jo snapped.

"Why lie?" Tony asked. "If you didn't do anything, why would you plead out to forty years in prison?"

"Okay . . . okay," Cory said, according to Jo, "I put the belt around her neck. I held the belt."

Tony brought a photograph of his daughter. As Cory tried to explain his way out of it, Tony slammed the picture against the glass between them.

"Look at her!" Adrianne's father said.

Cory gazed at the photo for a brief moment and quickly dropped his head.

Jo and Tony walked out.

They received a letter shortly after visiting with Cory, who was now apparently interested in confronting his behavior and facing his victim's family. In that short missive, Cory explained how, when Jo and Tony had gone to see him, he didn't have the nerve to look at them in the eyes and talk about what had happened. He mentioned how he wished every day that he could take back what had happened. He said he was truly sorry. He knew that what he did was an unforgivable act on his part, but he wanted the Reynolds family as a whole to know how sorry he was for committing the "act."

Lastly Cory wrote that if he could give his life to bring Adrianne *back, I would in a second.*

Cory Gregory was sentenced in early July to forty-five years, the maximum penalty he could have received. During the proceeding, Cory looked at Jo and Tony Reynolds. He said, "Tony, Joanne, and the rest of the Reynolds family, I am truly sorry. Truly, I am. If I could someway give my life to bring Adrianne back, I would do it."

Cory turned to his father, Bert, and his mother, Teresa, and apologized for putting them through the ordeal of their lives.

Teresa stood behind her son, tears falling down her cheeks.

"I cried because I never wanted my son to have to grow up in prison," Teresa said later. "He was so young and had so much life ahead of him to grow and mature and experience the many wonderful things that life can be. I cried because he had thrown that chance away."

Cory faced Judge Walter Braud.

"All I can say and ask of the court is," Cory said, his voice firm and unwavering, the orange jumper he wore reminding the packed gallery that they were staring at an admitted murderer, "to show me some kind of mercy."

Judge Braud took a deep breath. "Well, it's too little, too late, Mr. Gregory."

* * *

During the summer of 2006, an announcement came that Nate Gaudet, after pleading guilty to one count of "concealing a homicidal death," had been sentenced "up to five years" and was serving his time at the Illinois Youth Center in Harrisburg, Illinois.

Nate was punished as a juvenile in exchange for his testimony against Sarah Kolb. The way he was sentenced would, theoretically, give Nate the chance at parole before his twentieth birthday. But nobody believed that would ever happen, considering what Nate had done.

"I was appalled," Tony Reynolds said. "That boy cut up my little girl and got away with it."

About six weeks after he pleaded guilty, Cory Gregory had a change of heart. Sarah Kolb's sentencing hearing was coming up. Now, as the first week of August fell on the QC, Cory decided he wanted to take back his guilty plea and take his case to jury trial.

His lawyer filed the appropriate motion. In it, Cory's lawyer said it was the sentencing that changed his client's mind—that forty-five years, which could have been in the neighborhood of twenty, was inconsistent *with the defendant's history of peace and tranquility.*

Further into the motion, Cory stated that because he had been poorly educated and had very little "command" over the English language, he did not fully understand that his conduct resulted in first-degree murder charges. He also said he felt threatened to take the deal—that if he didn't, he was staring down the barrel of much more time. He said he believed if he gave investigators a confession and told the SA's office what had happened, he was trading that information for a lighter sentence, under the impression that forty-five years was the cap.

Cory called the judge's sentence *excessive and inappropriate.*

A local reporter called Jo Reynolds at work and asked her for a comment. Had Jo and Tony heard that Cory wanted to take his case to trial and take back his original plea?

"What?"

The reporter explained.

"That son of a bitch. He held the belt!"

The end of August came and Sarah Kolb was in Judge James Teros's court once again to receive her sentence. This was Sarah's chance to plead for herself and ask the judge to take into consideration all that had gone on (or wrong) in her life.

Sarah put on witnesses and spoke to the court by way of a prepared statement. At one point, she read, *"I was so good at not feeling that I felt no feeling as [Adrianne] died."* This after comparing her situation in life to Adrianne Reynolds's, making the claim that neither she nor Adrianne was wanted by many of the adults around them throughout their lives.

"If I really could have one wish," Sarah said, *"it would be to change the mistakes I've made. . . . Nobody else seemed to care,"* Sarah added, her voice cracking, *"what I was doing. I think it rubbed off on me. I know I could've done more to stop what happened."*

During the testimony portion of the hearing, Sarah's defense presented three witnesses, the most powerful being Sarah's sister, whom Sarah looked up to. Sarah's sibling told the court Sarah was "an abused child who was punished inappropriately."

No details were given.

Tony Reynolds took the witness stand and spoke for his daughter. In tears, Tony said, "Adrianne came into this world kicking and crying. She left the same way."

Dressed in blue jeans and a dark hooded sweatshirt, Sarah sat at the table in front of Tony and cried as he explained what his daughter meant to him.

Then the judge spoke.

Teros wasn't buying any of Sarah's nonsense. He talked of his disbelief that Sarah had been abused. She had provided no evidence of the fact other than crocodile tears and hollow words. He also said, which shocked some in the room, that Sarah possessed a "dark side" and he was convinced that she was capable of "killing again if she became angry." He classified Adrianne's murder as a deed done by two teenagers "for nothing," adding at one point, "*But* for you, Miss Kolb, this murder doesn't occur," being sure to point out then how he thought Cory Gregory was just as responsible. Either teen, Teros made clear, could have stopped this senseless act of violence.

Sarah shed more tears as Teros handed down a sentence of fifty-three years: broken down, the judge gave her forty-eight years for committing the homicide, along with an additional five for concealing it. The max he could have given the Milan teen was sixty for the murder alone.

After the sentencing, Jeff Terronez was outside

giving reporters one more grab for the nightly news, saying the case, in its entirety, was "replete with evil."

SA Terronez then pointed out something he felt had been missing from the proceeding, telling everyone that he was "not surprised" to hear Sarah offer no apology to the Reynolds family for killing their child.

Judge Walter Braud allowed Cory Gregory his day in court—but not in the form of a full-fledged trial. That motion Cory had filed deserved a hearing. Here was Cory's chance to plead his case.

Cory took to the witness stand as Judge Braud listened. The teen said his "mind was clouded by drugs, alcohol, and depression" during that time when he "allowed" his attorneys to "convince him to plead guilty."

This opened up the opportunity for Cory to bring the court into what he classified as his tortured life of drug and alcohol abuse. Cory said he started drinking alcohol at the ripe age of fourteen, and he graduated to "a half gallon of whiskey or vodka every weekend" by the time November 2004 through January 2005 came.

Further along, Cory stated that after he started "smoking marijuana in 2003," at the peak of his use, he claimed to have gone through a "half ounce a day." Ecstasy was something he and friends used on "a weekly basis." Cocaine was a drug he had tried, he said, about "twenty to twenty-five times" from the age of fourteen until his arrest.

When asked about the plea deal itself, Cory responded, "I didn't feel like I had much of an option, really. I just assumed my lawyers were looking out for me."

The blame game.

In truth, Cory sounded like a gambler who had

purchased the wrong lottery numbers and was now complaining to the state that he should have looked at his tickets before leaving the window.

Rock Island County Circuit judge Walter Braud had a look of *are you done now?* on his face after Cory finished testifying on his own behalf.

SA Jeff Terronez put on a good argument, focusing on the fact that Cory had plenty of sobriety time in jail before making his plea. There were no drugs or booze clouding his mind—just plain old-fashioned reluctance.

Braud called Cory's testimony and motion to withdraw his plea "buyer's remorse," adding quite sharply, "At this sale, you can't take it back!"

The motion was denied.

Jo cried out facetiously as Cory was escorted out of the courtroom, saying, "Boo-hoo. Boo-hoo."

Teresa Gregory shouted from her seat over Jo's words, "Love you, buddy."

Tony Reynolds put it all into perspective later when asked about all the posttrial nonsense, saying, "It really doesn't make any difference what they do. Adrianne is still not coming home."

79

Tony liked to take a three-mile jog every morning. The run kept the aging trucker in shape. Made him feel good—as good as good would get, that is—throughout his day. Since the months after Adrianne's death, Tony had wanted to purchase a special vanity license plate from the DMV: LIL BIT. It was a way of putting a reminder of Adrianne on his truck that he would see every day.

After calling the DMV and asking about the tag, he was told it had been taken, and there wasn't any version of LIL BIT available to him at this point.

Tony's heart sank. This one thing. So much had happened. He felt guilty in so many different ways. He just wanted to honor his daughter.

After the legalities surrounding Adrianne's murder concluded—there would be appeals, but they would take time—Tony got back into the swing of his routine, which included that morning run.

He usually took off somewhere near 4:30 or 5:00 A.M. He liked the quiet and dark tranquillity of early morning when no one was around.

One morning, after stretching in the driveway and taking off down the street, Tony came around a corner near his house and stopped abruptly in his tracks.

There it was.

LIL BIT.

Right in front of him.

Sitting on the ground near his house, the same vanity license plate that Tony had wanted to purchase.

Bizarre coincidence?

"That was Adrianne," Tony said later, his voice scratchy with emotion, "telling me she was okay."

Adrianne Reynolds hadn't dated the poem, but the underlying message she wanted to convey was unmistakably prophetic—an eerie portend of her life. Adrianne felt an end was near. She knew, in some strange way, her time on the planet was limited.

She titled the poem "Welcome to My Life."

Although she didn't date it, it was not hard to tell that Adrianne wrote this near the time of her death, when those around her—the people she believed to be friends—had turned their backs on her and she couldn't understand why.

> *A painful life to be broken,*
> *but will never be.*
> *I scream in agony for someone*
> *to be there for me.*
> *Is there a reply?*
> *No!*
> *Wanting to unleash the demon*
> *inside just won't work for anyone*
> *but me.*
> *I cry, but no one hears me,*

which makes me burn inside.
I feel and keep reaching, far,
but there is nothing.
Nothing but blackness and
raging death.
Awaiting me is the fire
of screaming agony.
There I find "myself" screaming also,
but is someone there to hear me?
No!
I'm ignored by my dark Angel because he
has forgotten and left me screaming
in the burning pits of hell!!!

If there was one thing about Adrianne Reynolds no one could deny, it was how closely in touch this young girl was with her feelings. Adrianne wanted nothing more than to be loved. Doodling one day at work, Adrianne sketched the opposite side of her shattered life's coin on a guest check, one of those light-green-and-white pads greasy spoon waitresses use to take orders. She titled it "My Perfect Life." It was her way of dreaming out loud. There was darkness, sure, but light, too. Adrianne could see it off in the distance.

And she wanted it.

On the top of the green ticket, she wrote the name of the guy she dreamt about, a kid back in Texas she had fallen in love with and, presumably, lost her virginity to. This was the man she saw herself having children with someday.

Her dream car was a Benz.

Her favorite color was red. (Not pink, as so many had said.)

Her job? Singer.

Kids' names: Michael David, Erica May, Kiara Rachelle.

Adrianne wanted three kids. That was it.

As for money, *Doesn't matter,* she wrote, *as long as we're not poor.*

She saw herself living in a house or a mansion.

But that didn't matter, either.

As long as I have my family and the one I love.

EPILOGUE

This case was one I truly wished did not have to be written. This murder, more than some of the others I have covered, seemed senseless and tragic in so many ways. They all do, of course. But this case had a particular heartbreaking quietness about it that grew on me as I entered each stage of Adrianne Reynolds's life, and stayed with me every day I worked on it. I kept a photo of Adrianne close by. I wish I had known her.

The path of Adrianne's life was predictable in its aftermath. Her killers were despicable and heartless. Sarah Kolb refused to allow others to infringe upon her "Kool-Aid" (whatever the flavor of the moment was), and it angered the teen to the point of murder. Cory Gregory, on the other hand, not only showed how cold and careless he was for not stopping the fight in Sarah's car, which escalated into murder, but also by participating in it. What made Cory much more selfish and heartless, in my professional opinion, was the fact that he befriended Adrianne in those days before her murder. It seemed to me, if I didn't know better, that Cory and

Sarah had talked about Cory befriending Adrianne so they could, at the very least, get her into Sarah's car and beat her up—if not carry out a premeditated plan to kill her.

And for what?

Jealousy?

Revenge?

I don't buy it.

The outrage the Reynolds family felt continued long after Cory Gregory and Sarah Kolb were sentenced. Nate Gaudet was being denied parole by the board year after year. Yet, in November 2008, on his twentieth birthday, Nate was released.

The boy who had carved Adrianne Reynolds into seven pieces and stuffed himself at McDonald's afterward had served two and a half years of an "up to five-year" sentence. I was told Nate went into therapy while in prison, but he was quickly told he didn't need it.

How can this happen in our American justice system?

Nate was driven to an undisclosed location in another part of the country (I heard) far away from the QC. This decision was based on the anger—and threats—from the community Nate and his family received. Many people believed Nate was more evil than his two "homies," as one blogger put it after Nate was released. Another blogger encouraged Juggalos in the QC to find Nate upon his release and give him a beat-down.

Tony Reynolds, who had sat in front of the parole board to argue against Nate's early release, said if Nate had planned to apologize, he could stuff it. Tony did not want to hear any words of empathy from the boy.

I reached out to Nate and his parents, who—through

a third party—said they were considering talking to me. In a brief missive, I told them:

> *I don't think your entire story has been told, especially by the one person who knows it best. I was hoping I could count on interviewing you. . . . I would allow you to tell your story without censorship or constraints. Allow you (and perhaps family members and friends) to talk directly to my readers and show them who you truly are. I am sure that what you admitted to in court does not define or reflect who you are as a human being, or your life as a whole.*

I never heard from Nate or his mother. His father, Andrew Gaudet, called about five months after I sent that letter. We talked for close to two hours. There is a pain in Andrew's voice I'm convinced will be there for the rest of his life. The man seemed at a loss for words as we started talking. He had a hard time understanding and comprehending why and how this had happened. Nate had called his father about a year after his release from prison.

"Hey, Dad. . . ."

"Son."

"I'm doing all right."

Nate would not say where he was or where he planned to live. He had a job. He was building a new life.

I got the impression from talking to Andrew Gaudet that he and his son had had a good relationship, until divorce came in between them when Nate was thirteen.

This one moment in Nate's life—however gruesome and horrific—certainly was not something anyone in his family saw coming. There are reasons why teenagers drink and drug (which Nate was actively involved in daily), namely, to forget about their lives and the pain. I wanted you—the reader—to hear from Nate himself why he did this, which was the reason I wrote to him. In speaking with Nate's dad, however, it's clear to me that Nate himself is not certain what happened and why.

"While he was in jail during that first month," Andrew told me, "Nate had this look and sense about him that he was going to walk out of jail any day. He didn't grasp the situation."

Nate did tell his father that Cory Gregory and Sarah Kolb threatened his life if he did not participate. Nate told a Juggalo friend the same thing.

I could find no other corroborating evidence of this, however. In fact, all of the evidence I found indicated to me that Nate Gaudet willingly and willfully dismembered Adrianne Reynolds simply because his friends had asked him.

I wrote to Sarah Kolb, who sent me back a scathing letter tainted with that same anger she had shown others throughout her life.

Sarah said she did not appreciate me intruding on *what semblance of a life* she has at this point. Nor did she like the idea of me reaching out to her stepfather (which I did via Facebook) or any other family member. (Sarah's stepfather and mother are no longer together. Darrin Klauer was clear regarding not wanting any part of being interviewed.)

From that point on, Sarah seemed to brag about her story being of interest to other authors before me, letting me know that her life was *not a fucking story* or a *thriller*. She indicated that she had *stayed out of the media* since her story broke because she didn't *want to talk about it*.

That falls in line with who Sarah was before her arrest: the consummate denier. Unwilling to face the nightmare that has become her life, or the horrors that she has caused other families.

In her familiar condescending tone, Sarah encouraged me to write to Cory Gregory and ask him about his role in the case. She said she was *sure he'd be willing to talk about it*. (She gave me his address and prisoner identification number, just in case I didn't have it.)

She said if I was lucky enough to find Nate (I sensed a sarcastic laugh there, as if she knew where he was), then I should speak with him, too.

Unlike what she didn't do for the Reynolds family, Sarah apologized to me for, in her words, *being belligerent*. This entire episode was a *touchy subject* for her, she admitted.

Go figure. Sarah took the life of a sixteen-year-old girl, and talking about it (confronting it) had not made her feel so fuzzy inside.

She wished me luck with my *novels*, clearly not understanding that my books are nonfiction.

And that was it.

It is my belief she'll talk openly about this someday in the years to come. Sarah is still immature. She is still locked in that fantasy that what happened was somebody else's fault. That she was cajoled, tricked, and set up by a friend.

The problem is, the evidence in her case does not support that argument.

It took Cory Gregory months to get back to me. He had been "in seg" much of the time and was unable to write, I was told by his mother. In his letter, Cory asked me to call the prison and speak to the legal department so someone from that office could set up a phone call between us. Cory said he would *hear me out* and, if he liked what I had to say, he would talk to me. But *no promises.*

Phone calls between inmates and journalists don't work like that. I explained to Teresa Gregory that her son would have to put me on his call list and phone me collect. I would gladly accept any calls from Cory Gregory. I gave Cory a deadline, as I am under tight deadlines myself.

As I handed in the manuscript, I had not heard from Cory.

I asked Teresa Gregory for a final word about her son. Teresa has been beaten down by this tragedy. You can hear it in her voice. There's a pain that will never go away. I often talk about the ripple effect of one murder—this case proves that theory.

Teresa's astute and perceptive answer was: *If I was to say anything about this as a final word it would have to be a warning to parents and teenagers to understand that life can change in the blink of an eye. That one wrong decision can and will change your life path forever. Teenagers are very impulsive and have not had enough life experience to understand that the way they feel and think at the moment is not always going to be the way they feel or think. Depression, drugs and the longing to fit in to the point of having the willingness to do anything for a "friend" are warning signs we as parents so often miss. Please, parents, talk seriously to your teens, find out what they think and how they feel.*

Good advice.

Teresa went on to say thanks *for allowing me to say a few words about my son. I love Cory and I always will. We are not a horrible family and Cory is not a horrible person at heart, even though what they did was horrific.*

Both Sarah Kolb and Cory Gregory appealed their cases.

Both appeals were denied.

Tony Reynolds wanted me to publish one of the poems he wrote for Adrianne. I think it explains a lot. I have not edited this poem:

> *Roses are red, violets are blue.*
> *I'm sorry Adrianne, I wasn't always there for you.*
> *Your life was never easy,*
> *And a lot of it was very sad.*
> *But after you came up here,*
> *I just wanted to be your dad.*
> *I wanted you to smile,*
> *I wanted you to have fun.*
> *I wanted you to know you were my only one.*
> *I know before you left this world, you knew I loved you.*
> *And I know you loved me too!*
> *You touched everyone's life while you were here,*
> *In their hearts you'll always be near.*
> *Uncle Mike fixed your string,*

But it broke again!
I got the message,
I won't mess with it again.
Except to look at it now and then.
You're singing with the angels now.
I see you in the front row.
Doing your best, stealing the show.
God had a plan for you,
and singing with him was it,
You keep singing girl,
Don't you ever quit.
Cause your Adrianne Leigh.
The one I call Little Bit!
Love you, Daddy

The Reynolds family has a website: http://www.caring bridge.org/il/adrianne/index.htm. You can go there and read additional poems, write to the family, sign the guestbook, peruse more photos of Adrianne, and read anecdotes about her life. I cannot vouch for the accuracy of anything on the site; I did not use it as a source for this book.

THANKS

I need to express my gratitude to those Juggalos and former friends of Cory's, Sarah's, and Nate's for trusting me and agreeing to interviews. Your insight into this obscure and misunderstood culture was something I valued immensely as I wrote this book, not to mention your courage for admitting your own faults and talking about the lives you led. I stripped the Juggalo movement bare in this book. I did not want to come across like Tipper Gore, circa 1985, stepping up on her soapbox in front of Congress, pooh-poohing music lyrics as evil, influential, and degrading. But come on, anyone who reads the lyrics to an ICP tune (and many of the other bands associated with Psychopathic Records) with an open mind cannot honestly deny the vulgarity and violence, not to mention disrespect and disregard for females. This sort of shock rap, or horror rap, is not confined to ICP and Psychopathic Records, of course, but I found it to be at a level of disgrace unlike anything I have come across. If I have offended fans of the band, well, I'll own that.

Anybody who knows me understands that I am grateful for their help and support when writing a book. It takes a group of professionals to publish a successful book; my literary posse is populated with smart and hardworking people, many of whom continue to support my career and work hard for me behind the scenes.

I want to thank everyone at Beyond International for supporting me throughout the years by asking me to participate in the "Deadly Women" series. Andrew Farrell, Geoff Fitzpatrick, Therese Hegarty, Elizabeth Kaydos, and everyone else at Beyond with whom I have worked over the years have been respectful and gracious. These are top-notch people working in a tough television landscape.

Certified forensic examiner and founder of STALK, Inc., serial killer expert profiler John Kelly has been a true gentleman and longtime friend; and whether he realizes it, John's insight helps me in more ways than I could ever put into words.

The most important part of what I do is the reader. I need all of you to know that I am entirely grateful and humbled by the fact that you keep coming back, book after book. I truly respect your opinions, read every letter and e-mail (even though I cannot answer every one personally), and write these books for you.

Many, many thanks.

Of course, I would not have written this book without the support of Joanne and Tony Reynolds, and I appreciate the trust they put in me to write about Adrianne's life. I hope I kept my promise of answering some questions they had about this case.

Court reporters Candace Zaagman and Francine Morgensen were gracious and helpful. I appreciate how quickly they were able to turn around my orders for transcripts.

Rebecca Bernard was my only hope inside the RICSAO, a public office that needs to be schooled in what public documents truly are and why the public deserves *unobstructed* access to them. Rebecca Bernard (my savior there!) came through with thousands of pages of documents no other reporter had reviewed. Those documents, as they always do, changed this book.

Jeff Terronez refused to speak with me and did not return one of my calls or requests for interviews. He did, however, grant NBC interviews when he sat down with *Dateline*.

Teresa Gregory was open with me, and I greatly appreciate her honesty.

My family is always there: Matty, Jordon, April, and Regina. My friends too: Mark and Ann Gionet; Josh, Mike and Olivia; Wendy and Dan; Katie and Alex Tarbox; Jean Valvo; everyone at St. Luke's; and those great people who surround my life. I appreciate all of you for allowing me to talk so much about what I do.

Kensington Publishing Corp.—Laurie Parkin, the Zacharius family, in particular, and my editors, Michaela Hamilton and Richard Ember, along with Doug Mendini, and every other employee who works on my books—has been there with me for well over ten years now, supporting me and always trying to figure out how to reach more readers. I am both indebted and grateful for having such a great team of publishing people in my corner.

Lastly Peter Miller, my business manager, has been a constant in my life and career. I am blessed to have him working for me. PMA Literary and Film Management, Inc., anchors Adrienne Rosado and Natalie

Horbach-evsky have been equally important and helpful to me throughout the years. Without their love of books and tenacity to get things done, I would be lost.

Thanks, ladies!

Enjoy this exclusive preview of M. William Phelps's
next exciting true-crime release!

NEVER SEE THEM AGAIN

Four bloodied bodies . . . a dark secret.

M. William Phelps

Coming in March in hardcover
from Kensington Books

Turn the page for a preview

PROLOGUE

It was just after six o'clock on the evening of July 18, 2003. Eighteen-year-old Brittney Vikko (pseudonym) had been calling Tiffany Rowell, her BFF since middle school, for the past ninety minutes. Something was wrong, Brittney knew. She could sense it. She kept dialing Tiffany's number, but she wasn't getting a response.

Brittney had spoken to Tiffany's boyfriend, Marcus Precella, earlier that day, after Marcus had answered Tiffany's cell phone, saying, "She's in the bathroom." It was close to four o'clock then.

"I'll call back," Brittney said.

Thirty minutes later, Brittney began phoning.

But no one—not even Marcus—picked up.

"I was in the area, so I drove over to Tiffany's house," Brittney recalled. Brittney's boyfriend, her nephew, and her boyfriend's cousin went with her.

Brittney drove. They stopped at a McDonald's after leaving an appointment Brittney had downtown, at 4:10 P.M. A few minutes after six o'clock, Brittney pulled into Tiffany Rowell's driveway in the stylish suburban neighborhood of Millbridge Drive, Clear Lake City, Texas. She noticed immediately that Marcus and Tiffany's vehicles were there. Tiffany's truck was parked in front of the house, its back wheel up on top of the curb. Marcus's car was parked next to the garage in the driveway.

Brittney pulled in behind Marcus's vehicle.

Odd, she considered, looking at both vehicles. *They must be here. . . .*

Brittney got out and rang the doorbell.

No answer.

She rang it again.

Nothing.

She knocked. Then she tried to look through a nearby window with both her hands cupped over the sides of her eyes to block the light.

But again, not a peep out of anyone inside.

Brittney kept banging, harder and louder, eventually forcing the door to creak open.

Brittney's boyfriend and the others watched from inside Brittney's vehicle as she carefully—and slowly—walked into the house.

"Tiff? . . . You here?"

Something seemed peculiar about the situation. It was eerily quiet inside the house, a steely, metallic smell in the air.

The door left unlocked and open? Both cars in the driveway and no one around? This was so unlike Tiffany.

Where was everyone?

There was a short foyer Brittney had to walk through before she entered the living room.

She took five steps and found herself standing, staring at a scene that, at first, didn't register.

Then, as Brittney's boyfriend got out of her vehicle,

he saw Brittney come running like hell back out the same door she had just walked through.

Brittney Vikko was screaming, a look of terror on her face.

"Call the cops!"

Out of breath, approaching her boyfriend, who was now looking toward the house, "Call . . . the . . . cops!" Brittney yelled again. She was hysterical.

So her boyfriend walked up to the doorway and approached the inside of the house.

Then he came barreling out the door, screaming.

Brittney was on the ground by then, yelling, crying, smashing her fists into the grass. Her boyfriend noticed a neighbor across the street talking on his cell phone.

He ran toward the guy. "Call the police! Call the police!"

The man dialed 911.

"There was blood everywhere," Brittney's boyfriend later said, describing what he had seen inside Tiffany Rowell's house.

1

It happens when your life is static. Nothing is happening. Just out of high school, you're still running on teen angst. To think about college seems overwhelming. Your parents are getting on you. Life is not something you want to think about right now. You want to go with the flow. Take the summer and *discern*. And yet, that's when a good dose of reality—in all of its ugliness—grabs hold and shakes you.

When you're least expecting it.

In the second largest city in the south central portion of the United States, the atmosphere was volatile on this day. The three *H*'s were present: hazy, hot, humid—a fourth counting the city of Houston, the largest in Texas, fourth in the country. The dew point was near seventy-five. "Oppressive," they call stickiness in those numbers, about as high as it can get without rain. In addition to the stuffy air, it was almost ninety degrees. The kind of day when a "severe storm," the talking heads on the Weather Channel like to get excited about, could roll in at any time, darken the skies as if it were night, turn on the torrential downpours, kick up damaging winds, and drop hail the size of Ping-Pong balls.

Ah, yes, summertime in the Bay Area of Greater Houston. Sunny out one minute, and the next you're running for the nearest storm shelter.

As the skies decided what to do, yellow POLICE LINE DO NOT CROSS tape fenced off Tiffany Rowell's house from the road and swelling crowd. Strands of the familiar crime scene ribbon fluttered in mild gusts of wind, slapping and whipping, making a noise of a playing card flapping in a child's bicycle spokes. Lights of blue and red flashed against the sides of the house, pulsating a warning to the residents of this exclusive community just outside Houston, where some say "the city's wealthiest and best educated" lived, that something horrific had happened inside the one-story contemporary. Brittney Vikko running out the door screaming, neighbors heading inside to have a look, only added to talk circulating around the block that evil had reared its nasty face in an otherwise quiet residential district.

Clueing everyone else in were all the cops roaming around. The coroners' vans parked along the street. The detectives huddled together, talking things over: pointing, measuring, comparing notes. Flashbulbs inside the house made lightning strikes in the dusk. Whatever was beyond the slightly ajar front door into Tiffany Rowell's house was surely going to be big news in the coming hours and days. Anybody standing, staring, wandering about the scene, was well aware of this. Still, this neighborhood in Clear Lake City, Texas, "a pretty peaceful area," according to one resident, was used to the sort of high-profile crime—especially murders—the discovery inside the Rowell house was going to reveal. Who could forget that homely-looking woman who wore those large-framed glasses, a dazed look of nothingness in her eyes, Andrea Yates? While her husband was at his NASA engineering job nearby one afternoon in June 2001, Andrea chased their five kids through the house and, one by one, held each one underwater in the family's bathtub. Then she calmly called police and reported how she'd just killed them. And what about the infamous astronaut, Lisa Nowak, who, in February 2007, donned an adult diaper and drove from Clear Lake City to Florida—some nine hundred miles—to confront her romantic rival at the airport, the tools of a sinister plot to do her opponent harm later found inside Nowak's vehicle. And lest we forget the dentist's wife, Clara Harris, who would run her cheating husband down with her Mercedes-Benz after catching him with his receptionist, whom Harris had gotten into a hair-pulling catfight with only moments before the homicide.

Those notorious crimes, on top of all the murder and rape and violence that *doesn't* make headlines and "breaking news" reports, all happened here, within the city limits of this plush Houston suburb, just around the corner from this quiet neighborhood, where all the attention was being thrust. In fact, inside the Rowell house, some were already saying, was a tragedy of proportions that would dwarf anything Nowak, Yates, or Harris had done: if not for the severity and violence connected with the crime, the point that, among the four dead bodies the cops were stepping over, taking photos of and studying, not one of the victims had reached the age of twenty-two, and three of them were teenagers.

* * *

Neighbors, reporters, and bystanders gathered on the opposite side of the crime scene tape as cops did their best to hold back the crowd.

Some cried openly, their hands over their mouths.

Oh, my God. . . .

Others asked questions, shook their heads, wondered what was happening. After all, this was Brook Forest, a "master-planned community." Panning 180 degrees, street level, you'd find well-groomed lawns (green as Play-Doh), edged sidewalks, expensive cars, boats on trailers propped up by cinder blocks waiting for the weekend, kids playing in the streets. Brook Forest certainly isn't the typical place where violence is a recurring theme. Not to mention, it was just after seven o'clock on a Friday evening, the scent of barbeque still wafting in the air, and the murders had occurred, by the best guesstimates available, somewhere between 3:14 and 3:30 P.M.

That was the middle of the day, for crying out loud. A mass murder had taken place, and no one had seen or heard anything?

It seemed so unimaginable.

Investigators were talking to Brittney Vikko, getting her version. But she had walked in *after* the fact. As far as the neighbors standing around could see, nobody had noticed anything suspicious in the neighborhood or at the Rowell house all day long. The Rowell place was located on Millbridge Drive, a cul-de-sac in a cookie-cutter farm full of them, a neighborhood sandwiched between the Lyndon B. Johnson Space Center and Ellington Air Force Base, Galveston Bay a ten-minute drive east, Clear Lake just to the south, ultimately spilling into the Gulf of Mexico. This is suburban bliss, likely created in a civics lab somewhere, maybe by a former NASA

engineer (the region is full of them) or some city plan-
ner driven to construct middle-class perfection; but
certainly not a haven for a crime on this scale.

"I walked inside and saw Tiffany and a guy on the
couch," Brittney Vikko told police, "and another girl on
the floor in front of the television. At first, I thought
they had been partying too much—and then I saw all
the blood."

With the sight of carnage in front of her, Brittney
Vikko bolted out the door and screamed for her boy-
friend to call the police. Neighbors, cops, fire trucks,
EMTs, started to arrive shortly thereafter.

Consoling the community best he could, Houston
Police Department (HPD) homicide investigator Phil
Yochum released a statement, hoping to calm things: *"I
think it happened very quickly; but it was very, very violent.
It looks like some type of confrontation happened at the front
door, then moved into the living room."*

There had been no sign of forced entry—that familiar set of words cops use when they don't have a
damn clue as to what the hell went on. A news release
gave the concerned and worried community a bit
more detail, but was still vague: *The bodies of four people
were discovered . . . two males, two females . . . shot multiple
times, and two of the victims had sustained blunt trauma to
the head.*

The last part of the release was an understatement—
two of the victims had been beaten savagely. And the
blood. My goodness. From one end of the living room
to the other. Two of the victims were found on the
couch, facing the television. Looked like neither had
moved in reaction to what had happened. One of them

had a bullet hole—execution style—straight through the center of his forehead. Looked like some powder burns on the side of his head, ringed around another hole, which meant someone put the barrel of a weapon up to his skin and pulled the trigger.

As patrol officers did their best to hold back the swelling mob, a woman pulled up, parked her car sharply with a shriek of rubber, jumped out, and limboed underneath the crime scene tape as if ducking under a wooden farm fence.

Police stopped her before she could get close to the front door.

"Tell me that it's *not* the Rowell house," she said. "Tell me . . . please tell me it's not the Rowell house. Please!"

The police officers looked at each other.

Of course, it was.

The woman doubled over. Fell to the ground, then began sobbing in loud bursts of guttural pain. An officer went over and helped her up, eventually walking her off toward a private area of the yard, out of sight and earshot of the crowd.

Earlier that day, George Koloroutis had taken off on his Harley from his home a few miles away from this Brook Forest neighborhood in Friendswood. George was in a meeting at work. It was around 3:30 P.M. when he got this "sinking feeling" in his gut—*Something's wrong*. George wasn't a believer in the paranormal or ESP, but this sudden rotten sensation nagged at him.

"Something was out of order," George recalled. "My perfect little family unit was in a funky state. My girl is somewhere where I don't want her to be." He was talking about Rachael Koloroutis; she had been staying at the Rowell house with her best friend, Tiffany. George believed Rachael belonged at home.

With his oldest daughter, Rachael's sister, off to college, but home for the summer, the disunity in the family unit started to get to George and he left work early, around four thirty. When he walked in the door at his home in Friendswood, George asked his oldest daughter, Belinda (pseudonym), if she wanted to head out for a ride on the bike to grab a bite to eat. George wanted to talk to Belinda about Rachael, who had been out of the house for a little over a month, ever since graduating high school. George thought Belinda could offer some insight. He didn't like the path Rachael was on. He figured talking to Belinda, whom Rachael looked up to and had been as close as sisters could be with most of their lives, would help.

The ride, the food, and the talk turned out to be overly emotional. George dropped Belinda back at home and took off alone on his Harley—"I was not feeling good . . . this whole Rachael thing"—and decided to go out and find Rachael and talk to her. He ended up not being able to locate Tiffany Rowell's house and, instead, found a bar, ordered a few beers, sat and listened to the band.

Consequently, George couldn't hear his cell phone going off as details of what had happened at Tiffany Rowell's house hit the airwaves and people started calling him.

"I'm glad I didn't hear it," George said, looking back, "because the messages on my cell phone were horrifying."

George finished his cooling-off period at the bar and headed home. As he pulled into his driveway, he noticed that his wife's car was gone.

Odd.

His oldest daughter then came running out of the house, a look of fear on her face.

Even stranger.

"What's wrong? . . ." George asked, dismounting his bike, taking off his helmet.

"Dad . . . Dad!" Belinda screamed. Her face was white, George realized. "There's four teenagers dead at Tiffany Rowell's house! They know that two of them are Tiffany and this guy Marcus."

George's stomach tightened. His heart raced.

Rachael!

George went into the house, grabbed his youngest child—a daughter, eight—and told Belinda to get into the car. They were heading over to Tiffany's house.

After George had dropped Belinda at home earlier in that evening, before heading out to the bar, he had tried to find Tiffany Rowell's house so he could go speak with Rachael. He drove into the Brook Forest neighborhood, but couldn't find Millbridge Drive. He'd only been there one other time and it was at night. Giving up on his search, George had headed to the bar.

But now they were driving toward Tiffany's under Belinda's direction, Belinda explaining what she had heard on the news about four teens found dead.

George was in a panic. He pulled up. Saw all the vehicles. The police tape. The cops. A group of people milling about. He told Belinda to sit tight behind the yellow police tape inside the car. Wait with her sister for her mother.

Meanwhile, George crossed the police line and started for the door heading into Tiffany's house.

A large cop stopped him before he could walk in.

"My name is George Koloroutis. You can't stop me, man, please," George pleaded. "I think my little girl might be in there."

Tears.

George was a big dude, with some serious bulk, and perhaps out of his mind by this point. All he could think of was Rachael in there needing his help.

George had always been the protector in the family—the man who took care of everything. Suddenly he felt helpless and weak as gum.

"Mr. Koloroutis, please," the cop said as calm as he could manage. "Please don't make me have to stop you from going into that house. I don't want to have to do that." There was something in the cop's voice that told George he wasn't kidding; he would do what he had to do to stop him. "If I have to do this, Mr. Koloroutis, other guys are going to run over here. We're going to have to hold you down. Cuff you. And it's going to be a miserable experience. Please, just *don't* go in there."

George looked at him. "I understand. I just need to know if that's my daughter."

By now, there were close to fifty people gathered. George fell back into the crowd. His wife, Ann, showed up. They decided to have someone take his youngest daughter and bring her to a neighbor's.

Then they stood and waited.

Rachael Koloroutis, just eighteen years old, was indeed lying dead on the floor inside that house, her body riddled with bullets, a good portion of her skull bashed in. What George or anybody else standing there—including all the detectives and patrol cops and crime scene techs—didn't know then was that the answers to this mystery would take years of old-fashioned gumshoe police work, a lot of it by George Koloroutis himself. It was going to be thirty-six months—almost to the day—before a suspect worth considering was brought in. It was going to turn into a case that would take investigators through nearly a dozen states, halfway across the country, and involve one of the most intense and puzzling murder investigations the HPD had ever probed. And when all was said and done, wouldn't you know, the murderer had been right under everyone's nose the entire time, within reach— the least likely suspect imaginable.

MORE SHOCKING TRUE CRIME
FROM PINNACLE